THE

ODYSSEY

OF A

MANCHURIAN

Also by the author

Baba: A Return to China upon My Father's Shoulders

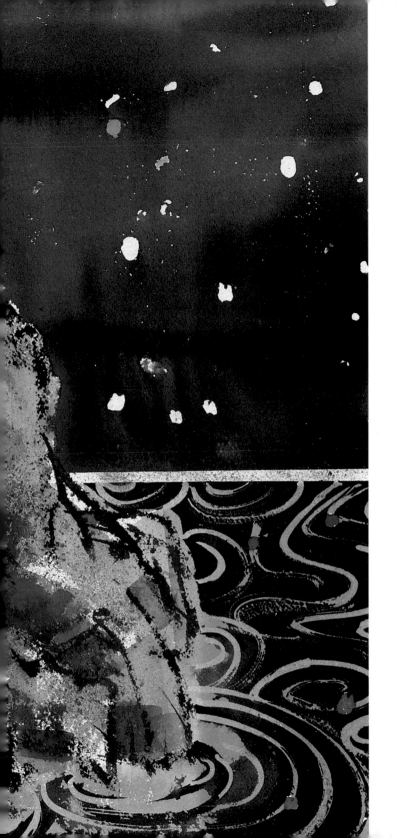

THE
ODYSSEY
OF A
MANCHURIAN

BELLE YANG

HARCOURT BRACE & COMPANY

New York   San Diego   London

Requests for permission to make copies of any part of the work
should be mailed to: Permissions Department, Harcourt Brace & Company,
6277 Sea Harbor Drive, Orlando, Florida 32887-6777.

Library of Congress Cataloging-in-Publication Data
Yang, Belle.
The odyssey of a Manchurian/Belle Yang.
p.   cm.
ISBN 0-15-100175-8
I. Title.
PS3575.A53038   1996
813'.54—dc20   95-53111

The text was set in Granjon.

Designed by Lisa Peters and Lori J. McThomas
Calligraphy by Joseph Yang
Printed in Mexico
First edition
A B C D E

For Laning Yang,

my mother, my Buddha

ACKNOWLEDGMENTS

To all of you who have helped to steer this boat of mine down the ten thousand gorges—

Sandra and Bram Dijkstra, Rubin Pfeffer, Drenka Willen, Yoji Yamaguchi, Dori Weintraub, Chris Vaccari, Deborah Warren, Vaughn Andrews, Lori McThomas Buley, David Hough, Rita Holm, Kathryn Miller, Debra Ginsberg, Sally Kim, Steve Malk, Patti Compton, Steve and Nancy Hauk, Richard Gadd, Judie Telfer, and Sally Lilley—

may there always be protective spirits to guide you in your respective journeys.

CONTENTS

CONTENTS

The Chinese believe knowledge lies in the stomach. A well-read man is said to have "plenty of ink in his belly." To anticipate a man's every thought is to be a "bug in his belly."

It is the deep memory of the stomach that leads Baba ("Father" in Chinese) to reminisce about the *hamatumi*, or "the toad spitting honey"—a small round sesame cake stuffed with red bean jam—and about the *jianbing*—a pancake wrapped around a stick of deep-fried dough. Baba swallows hard and his Adam's apple bobs when he recalls these and other treats sold on the streets of Northern China. When I press him just a little harder, a stream of stories tangentially connected to the savories flows forth.

In taking his recollections and re-creating the landscape of his youth through pen and brush, I have come to know the child in my father. To see him—a man in his sixties—twiddle his thumbs and hum tunes as he stares up into the April sky is to look upon the carefree round face of a child of ten on a spring morning when the ice has melted from the Western Marsh. To understand my parent is to make sense of the past, see it linked to my own belly like an umbilical cord, even as I see the future emanate from my own breath.

The weight of the past has converged upon me like a slow river, and it is a wonder to me that Baba is a creature of so strong a memory as to have borne it these many years alone. It is a miracle that he managed to find his way out of the maze of war, cherishing myriad tales of disappeared lives in his heart. It is a trick of the stars that I, the daughter of Joseph Yang, would find my way back to him, separated for years by the gulf of our inclinations. It is by the grace of Heaven that we arrived in America in a time of peace, our rice bowls daily filled, for who can possibly tell stories when the belly is so empty that it cannot remember?

Carmel, California
August 1995

THE

ODYSSEY

OF A

MANCHURIAN

1947. AN EVENING in May. There had been rumors of fearsome things at work in the world outside; now their fingers had crept into the garden itself. My father stood in the courtyard and listened. In happier days he would have heard new leaves unfolding, tendrils spiraling up the trellis, the breathing of soon-to-awaken cicadas in the soil beneath his feet, punctuated by the chatter and squeals of children. Now there was only graveyard quiet. Most of the tenant families in the houses circling the prosperous House of Yang upon Western Marsh, in Xinmin City, had disappeared, seemingly leached into the very soil. Only the quavering flames of a few makeshift oil lamps could be seen in the windows across the courtyard, telling of stragglers, huddled in the clouded light, bullied into crouches by the sudden eruption of artillery.

As Baba entered the kitchen, he half expected to see his mother and aunts at their usual dinnertime bustle; but he knew better: the House of Yang had been toppled like a worm-eaten old pine in a storm, and the birds had all scattered. In the recent weeks, he had escorted family members to the greater safety of Shenyang, the capital of their province, Liaoning.

The city was heavily garrisoned by Nationalist soldiers, who could be cruel and venal, but at least these men of the Central Government, unlike the Communists in the surrounding countryside who called themselves the Eighth Route Army, did not murder men to wrest away land and property. To Shenyang the majority of the clan had gone, seeking refuge from the civil war in Manchuria that followed the Japanese surrender in the summer of 1945.

In the kitchen was the solitary figure of his sister-in-law, no longer the plump young bride of a year ago, the rose of her complexion now faded. She hunched over the stove, slapping five cornmeal pancakes in a ring inside the big wok: three for supper and two for Baba's journey.

At the dinner table, Third Sister-in-Law dropped big tears—columns of tears breaking away from her square face like phrases crumbling off old pages. Baba and Third Brother did not look at her. They fingered their limp pancakes halfheartedly, tearing chunks out in silence.

"Who'd have thought it would all end like this: four noisy generations under one roof and now only rooms swept by ghosts," said Sister-in-Law and sighed. "Look at all the cobwebs," she said, pointing to the corners of the ceiling. "A house knows it's been abandoned, and it tells the spiders to all come runnin' and spin their webs.

"Number Four will go away tomorrow; that leaves just you and me." She studied her husband's simple face as if she were seeing him for the very first time. No, the couple would not follow Baba south: the prospect was much too frightening. Home was still the best place to be, however shabby it had become.

All the upright villagers and townsmen they had ever known had made an art of staying put, rarely straying beyond the threshold of the familiar. If circumstances forced them to venture out for a few days, they consulted the Imperial Almanac for a propitious hour to travel, lest any evil befall them on the road. At home, all the days are blessed; away from home, each hour is cursed, so the adage went.

Except for mystics and artists, travel did not stir the hearts and imaginations of the Chinese. The art of hovering around the hearth—where the Kitchen God could keep watch, where the pair of Door Gods at the front entrance and the single one at the rear stood guard against demons, where the spirits of the ancestors surrounded people and blessed their days—this art

of staying-at-home had been perfected by the folk of the Middle Kingdom down through the ages.

The three washed down their pancakes with soup—a few pieces of last year's spotty dried cabbage boiled in water. Luckily, a crock of fermented bean paste remained for them to share; the Nationalist troops quartered on their property, mostly men from the South, had eaten just about everything else—the pigs, chickens, ducks, geese, the sorghum and wheat in the granaries—but they had kept away from this briny mash that, in their opinion, tasted unpleasantly of Northern soil.

What will these two do? Baba wondered, as he listened to the melancholy sound of Third Brother, two years his senior, slurping soup.

My father's third brother was born in the Year of the Tiger, but he was no tiger.

When he was three, Nainai, my grandmother, gave him a pipe custom made for tots. (As a toddler, Nainai herself had been fitted with a pipe by doting parents who wanted to spoil their youngest child.) The pipe pacified an already quiet, docile child. The little one sat cross-legged upon the *kang* in meditative silence, huddled over the bronze fire pan, his dimpled hands artfully working the bowl of the pipe in the charcoal to light the tobacco. When he smoked, his demeanor was entirely that of a gaffer in his seventieth winter.

But in the second year of Third Brother's tobacco habit, a cough began vexing his throat which grew nastier as autumn deepened into winter. Nainai sought the herbal doctor, but his syrup of honey, almond oil, snakeguard, menthol, ginger, and loquat could not dampen the pain in Third Brother's throat, harsh as salt rubbed into a wound.

On the fifteenth day of Eleventh Moon, Nainai made her way to Granddaddy Temple and sought the help of Old Man Hack, a minor deity who occupied one end of the long altar in honor of the pantheon of gods. Old Man Hack sat two feet high, and his wrinkled face assumed an exquisite agony, the prelude to a roof-rattling cough. Nainai hung a necklace of four salted turnips about the long, extended neck of the god, and burned incense in the bronze urn set before him. The wooden statue, black with the years and smoke, had already been similarly festooned by pilgrims who had arrived earlier in the morning.

A necklace of salted turnips was not an of-fering; it was not a bribe for a cure. Rather, it embodied the pesky cough itself. Nainai, in hanging the vegetables about the god's neck, wished to transfer the burden of her son's trouble onto someone else. Old Man Hack had been sent from Heaven to bear all of mankind's plague of coughs.

What was the fate of the salted turnips? In the evening, the monks living at the temple came out and nibbled them for supper.

Shortly after Nainai's visit to the temple, Third Brother's ailment was borne away. It seemed Old Man Hack had done his job—though taking the pipe from the child may have had something to do with the cure.

It was evident at an early age that the boy would grown up *lao shi*, honest in speech, honest in deed. He was ploddingly decent and slow to anger. It was also not hard to prophesy that he would fall prey to bullies. When he began first grade, he would often come home in tears. "Little so-and-so punched me in the back of the head when I was walking home," he would bleat to Nainai. But there was no wooden deity upon whose neck his mother could hang this sort of trouble. Yet when Baba joined him at school two years later, Third Brother would gain an ardent champion, a feisty bantam cock raised on hot peppers to defend the honor of the House of Yang.

"After school, we'll clobber that kid who's been picking on you. We'll make him see flowers in Heaven," Baba would tell his brother. "You grab him when I corner him. Two against one—he's dead!" But when the battle was joined, Third Brother stood with his arms hanging limply at his side and studied the skirmish at a safe distance. This so infuriated Baba that, when the pair returned home, he gave his brother two swift kicks in the shins. "Why're you so spineless! Why'd you back out on me like you did when I fought the cousins for you? Why can't you ever stand up for yourself!" he shouted. Tears of frustration squeezed out of Baba's eyes.

The two boys ended up in the same class one year, for Third Brother was a drab student and had to repeat second and fourth grades.

One will often notice an odd cast in the eyes of ducks and geese: they cock their heads and hold a faraway gaze, as if straining to hear fading music. Third Brother had a similar look as he grew older. Folk often asked, "Is that Number Three a bit hard of hearing? What's he listening for?" But Third Brother's ears were perfectly healthy. "If he's not going deaf, then what's he tossing about in his head? Aiya, that one lives in his own world."

Third Brother did not join the other children in games or go on outings into the countryside. He stuck close to home, for he liked to watch the hired hands at the House of Yang rebuild a crumbling wall or shore up a foundation. When allowed to help, he methodically handed the laborers the required bricks, one at a time. Baba, who knew how to read his brother's face, could tell he was experiencing sublime joy.

It was Baba whom the grown-ups sent out into the world as messenger, not Third Brother. They could count on Number Four to memorize the long missives and invitations accurately and recite them with flair; they could trust that he would speed along on his short little legs and return promptly; they knew he would neither be bullied along the way nor return home with clothes torn by dogs. Baba was astute enough to press open the gate just a crack and, at the sound of barking, cry out, "Ooh! House of Zhang! Call off your dogs!"

Third Brother, however, would likely barge in and meet with fangs, and if he were fortunate enough to escape the dogs, he was certain to stand before Master Zhang and stammer, "My grandfather said to tell you—my grandfather said to say—ah, ah, I forgot...."

Third Brother graduated from elementary school at the age of fourteen. It was the end of his career as a student. He refused further education and stayed home, where he was happiest.

In spring, when corn was planted in the South Garden in nice neat rows, crows came to tug on the tiny shoots to get at the three or four kernels buried in the soil. Uncle Yu and Uncle Zhao, the hired hands, could not waste time on guard duty for a mere two mu of corn, but Third Brother was eager for the work. Although he was a poor student and displayed no musical or artistic abilities, his hands were surprisingly clever at devising useful objects. He fashioned a scarecrow from hay and rags. He rigged up an alarm bell using an empty kerosene tin, which he yanked on with a rope as he squatted in the shade of an ancient sycamore, cool and comfortable. *Dang-dang-dang-dang!* sounded the alarm when the crows, crying *gua! gua! gua!* came to feast. The realm of the garden and the sky above, racing with clouds that resembled mules and cows and pigs, provided Third Brother with boundless entertainment.

A visiting kinsman from Zhangwu said to Nainai, "Number Three is already so big and tall and still sitting at home playing games with crows? It is a shame!

"Now I know a fellow in our township who runs a soy sauce and vinegar distillery. His ancestors hail from Shanxi, and as you know, all the master soy sauce and vinegar makers come from that province. Why don't I take that Number Three of yours home with me, and make him an apprentice to this fellow? The House of Yang's got plenty of land to spare; in a couple of years, he'll be able to start up his own business right here in Xinmin."

The kinsman made the offer of a career to Third Brother: "Hey, boy, you'll like it at the distillery. It smells good there; makes you think you're eatin' fried bean sauce over noodles all day long. And best of all, they've got an even bigger garden for you to run around in." The boy had no idea what apprenticeship entailed. He scratched his scalp, pondered for a few moments, and wordlessly nodded in agreement. He liked the idea of a bigger garden to play in. Nainai prepared his gear and his bedroll, and off he went in the back of the cow wagon for the two-days' journey to Zhangwu.

Apprenticeship was hard work; not a moment

for idle play, the entire day strung with chores. Third Brother was instructed to rise before dawn to sweep the grounds; he was even expected to empty the proprietor's chamber pot. But the young man did not perform any of these duties. He sat in his room and he blubbered. *Wu-wu-wu*, he cried far into the night, disturbing even the mice that came out of the walls to nibble.

His tears were not for fear of work. At home he would rise at cockcrow to let out the ducks and chickens from their pens. No, he was not crying because he was lazy; he had just never been so far away from home.

"This can't go on. It's been three days. We can't let this child from the House of Yang cry himself to pieces," said the proprietor. The geniality had drained from his face and all that was left was a bewildered look.

"Hey, ain't that the wagon that belongs to what's-his-name from Zhangwu? Hey, ain't that Number Three ridin' in back of it?" shouted the hired hands at the House of Yang two days later. "Back so soon? Must have been a quick study, eh?" they quipped.

Once Third Brother threw down his belongings in his old familiar room, the world looked friendly again. His tears had barely dried before he was silently and joyously reestablishing himself in the South Garden, inhaling deeply the fragrance of a spring day.

Hence there was no more talk of sending him away to learn a trade, but since he was such a "cabbage head," according to Nainai, there was talk of finding him a wife who could look after him.

When he was eighteen, a peasant girl his own age from the village of Second Terrace, some thirty li north of Xinmin, became his bride.

How perceptive the matchmaker must be, Baba thought. These two were meant for each other, tied together at birth with destiny's red string. Like Third Brother, Baba's newest sister-in-law did not take part in family activities unless pressed to do so. When Baba told jokes, she would stand to the side and cock her head, with that faraway look of the ducks and the geese in her eyes. Whenever she understood a jest, the corners of her mouth would lift into a slow smile. When teased, she would blush violently. On a rare occasion, when confident that she had understood the talk, she would offer a country adage or two.

Third Brother and his wife have only a few days of food left, if that much. They will soon be resorting to thumping the table with their fists and catching the sesame seeds that leap out of the cracks.... At least they have no little ones to feed, Baba said to himself. He finished the last morsel of pancake.

The three remaining members of the House of Yang went to bed early; oil for the lamp could not be wasted on talk.

For the first night in many weeks, Baba slept soundly. He was resolved to go away; no more wavering like a small flame in the wind. The wars, the interminable wars, had left only crumbs, not enough to fill the belly of a sparrow; how could they possibly fill the belly of one whose limbs were still growing so furiously? There were no more reasons to stay. He had done everything in his power for his family. He had borne a burden far heavier than his elders could have expected from a youth of eighteen.

I'm the number four son ... I'm of too little significance to be missed, Baba believed. Had Yeye, my grandfather, taken time from his meditations, his all-engrossing striving for enlightenment, to show some interest in the education of this earnest, sensitive, prideful son, then my father's entire life course would not have met

with its momentous consequences. I am certain he would have remained in Manchuria.

Yeye's indifference to his fourth son's education was Baba's greatest disappointment and hurt. The *qi*—the life force—that coursed through his young soul did not heal wounds quickly. He was no lighthearted boy. He possessed the keenest memory for both kindnesses received as well as injuries. He could forgive, but he would never forget. Yet he was not one to brood; his successes were his revenge.

Baba was buoyed by the hope that perhaps in the South he would be able to attend university. If he had the money, he would have flown to Beiping or Nanjing—land held securely in the hands of the Central Government—as many of his friends and classmates had already done, fleeing with the faculties of various Manchurian universities. But as it was, he would not even have been able to pay for a train ticket, had the lines been open.

So he would set forth on foot in the morning. His few books and clothes were secured in a bag devised from a square of cloth.

In the muted light of dawn, he stepped across the threshold of the front door. It was the first of the countless steps in this dangerous business of leaving home.

As he approached the South Gate, he turned and looked back. His sister-in-law stood weeping, a silent pulsation of anguish running through her body, her forehead pressed against a panel of the front door as she tried to hide her tears.

The tears were mostly for herself. Number Four had been the one with the ideas. Number Four the wit. Number Four could be willful and feisty, cross when he could not have his way, but in their hour of need, he had been the one to assist the too-old and the too-frail with an almost maternal gentleness and selflessness. She had never seen this side of him before. Once he was gone, she would have to muster strength enough for herself and her sweet, simple husband, a man who fared better with mules, horses, and cows than with humans. Yes, Number Four was leaving. To each his own road, his own labors and sorrows.

She leaned against the door panel, unaware that her forehead was touching the face of a Door God armed with his many swords, bows, and arrows, and dressed in a coat of mail made from dragon scales. The god's fierce stare was said to cause the stars in the heavens to tremble. The poster had faded and tattered. It had been several winters since they had celebrated Spring Festival, the Chinese New Year, with the changing of the woodblock prints.

"O dear Gods, if you still possess the magic, please keep these two from danger," Baba said to himself. He tore his eyes away. The windows, their latticework stripped for firewood by soldiers quartered on their property, stared lidlessly, vacantly into his back.

Third Brother, hanging his shaggy head like a doleful donkey, walked a few paces behind Baba. The only stirrings about town were the ghostly figures of armed Nationalist soldiers.

"Remember what I've told you: take Sister-in-Law to Second Terrace. Your in-laws there in the countryside will surely be able to spare you some food," Baba said to him. "Listen closely—do not follow the family into Shenyang. It may be heavily garrisoned against the Communists, but you're not made for the city and you won't be able to get around. You won't survive."

The brothers arrived at the Western Checkpoint.

Once the generators had been forcibly removed by the Russians, who had appeared in Manchuria immediately after the Japanese surrender to plunder what was left, the electric fence that ringed the entire city to fend off bandits was made useless, and soon the wires and posts themselves were removed by the occupying Nationalists and by the townsfolk themselves for their own purposes. Now a deep trench replaced the fence, and this angry gash in the earth abided in the attempt to fend off the Communists. Only through the four existing checkpoints, marked by tall concrete pillboxes, could people enter or leave Xinmin.

"Who are you! Where're you going!" brayed a guard startled from the wilderness of daydreams. In these turbid days, folk who remained in Xinmin did not dare travel to the countryside, for it was easy to leave the city but difficult to reenter, now that food was in short supply.

"I'm a student." Baba presented the card that was his school ID. "I'm headed for Jinzhou," he said with purpose in his voice, but he had only snatched upon the name of the first large city to the south.

The soldier motioned him on.

Third Brother's back was shaking as he sobbed, but he made no sound. Baba could not bear to look at him. He walked through the break in the wire and heard the swift closure of a phantom gate. Though he had often traveled this way, the very air now tasted strange. There was a vacant and dreary hush, the silence that follows the last clang of the cymbals and the final whine of the trumpets.

After walking a stretch beyond the checkpoint, Baba drew himself up to his full height and looked back. The stubborn, motionless speck that was his brother stood framed by concrete posts.

My father was walking out into the world. My third uncle was staying home. This had always been the rule.

As Baba signaled with a wave for his brother to go home, he felt as if he were looking upon a quickly receding shore. How could my father have known that in the moment of walking across the border, fate, which had at birth shaped their lives differently, would exaggerate the contrasts even more—so much so that a stranger in the future would never be able to guess that he and Third Brother had been born to the same man and woman.

When he gave one last look back, his brother was gone.

Where are Shilin and Big Eyes? Baba wondered as he turned, once again, to face the road. Are they still in Xinmin? How are their families doing? At school they called us boys the Three

Musketeers. And what about Lily? I did not say good-bye to her, either.

Each weekday morning, from the direction of the marketplace, Shilin, tall and lanky, and Big Eyes, seeming even rounder and squatter in contrast to his companion, would push open the small door nested in the big door of the North Gate, which when fully swung open would allow the entry of horse carts. They had come to fetch Baba for the walk to school. Shilin and Big Eyes, both from modest families, liked to visit the ten mu of the North Garden at the House of Yang with its pavilion, and its temple, mysterious within the forest of flowering "pearl plums," built in honor of the eerie family mascot Great-Grandfather Fox. Their young souls were overwhelmed by the lavish display of the seasons, the blooming things riotous in the spring and summer. In the fall, when grapes festooned the arbor, the grounds would double as a tennis court once the eggplants, peppers, and cucumbers were harvested.

Lily would come, too, for Baba's youngest aunt, who was a mere one year his senior. Baba loved to tease the girl, drawing attention to himself by kicking a rock out of her path or point-

ing out something on the ground that might startle or amuse her.

The children were all in the seventh grade, a raucous gang of five that did not find its way to school directly. The five of them attended the academy run by Western missionaries; the girls and boys studied in separate buildings.

"Do you like Lily?" Youngest Aunt asked him one day, wearing a face so earnest it made him squirm.

Baba was silent.

"If you like her, I'll tell her your feelings. Then you two can become sweethearts."

Her words frightened him. "Please don't tell her," he pleaded. "I do like her very much. But if you tell her, it'll make everything strange between us." Although he and Youngest Aunt were good friends, Baba clearly understood their inviolable positions in the family; he always showed her the degree of respect expected of a nephew for a paternal aunt.

Many an afternoon, Lily would come to the House of Yang to do homework with Youngest Aunt; if the hour was late, the Patriarch would ask Baba and Youngest Aunt to escort the girl home. Just as often, Youngest Aunt would need to be ushered home from the House of Huang,

where she played with Lily. The streetside section of Lily's home served as a clinic, where her father and mother practiced a hybrid of Western and traditional Chinese medicine.

"Eh, who is this little, round-headed child? He's rather comely. What number is he?" Lily's mother asked Youngest Aunt one day. Her jacket was warmly fragrant with herbs.

"That's Zuwu. He's my eldest brother's number four son."

"Ah, is he? Number Four," she said, turning to Baba with a waggish smile upon her plump face, "I caught you as you tumbled out into this world. The same with your mother's next one —a girl, and a most difficult birth. We almost lost that one!"

Baba did not know what to say to her as the mother continued to banter and tease.

"Don't be shy with me, Boy; why, when you arrived in this world, you came bare-bottomed, and I was the first one to bathe you and to dress you up and make you decent."

Lily was the only child of the doctor and the midwife. She was nearly a head taller than Baba and as skinny and wan as a bean sprout. Baba did not stop to consider whether her face was pretty or not beneath the regulation bobbed hairstyle of a female student, shaped like half a watermelon rind. Certainly there was nothing odd or disproportionate about her features. All he knew was that she was a girl, the only girl he spent any amount of time with outside of those in his family, and he rather liked being around her. She had nice manners, and she was calm and good-natured, counter to the talk among the men that Manchurian girls were prone to be spoiled, bossy, and cross.

In June of 1945, the friends graduated from high school. By winter, the war between the Communists and Nationalists had spread to Manchuria. Baba had no news of Shilin and Big Eyes—or of Lily.

One day, during a lull in the fighting, when the Nationalists seemed to have gained the upper hand in Xinmin, Youngest Aunt rushed into his room. Her chest heaving, she blurted, "You're still very fond of Lily, aren't you? You know, a matchmaker was here today to see the Patriarch. Rich Old Dong, the official, wants to marry his daughter into our family. He wants you for son-in-law. You've never even met her. It's a bad idea! What if you don't like her? I wouldn't agree to it if I were you." She narrowed her eyes. She did not say more, but Baba

knew of her scheme to see him married to her best friend one day.

When Shenyang seemed securely under Nationalist control, Baba began to attend the Number One Polytechnic. Every Saturday afternoon, he would make his way home by train, a journey over two hours long. One weekend, to his surprise and delight, he spied Lily, her lips pressed tightly together, among the crowd at Shenyang Station. They had not seen each other in more than a year.

"I'm at the Women's College here," she said. Her flushed face fluttered with a graceful yet pensive smile. There was still a trace of down above her lips.

The lines for tickets were long and unruly; at seventeen Lily wore the splendor of her youth quietly and nobly, and disliked the jostling. Baba braved the line and bought their tickets. He fought for a seat once they were on board and insisted that she take it. When there was room next to her, he sat down. Thrown against her by the crowd, he allowed his forearm to linger against hers. When he closed his eyes, all his senses were rapturously aware of blood coursing against blood beneath mere layers of skin. He was fascinated by her hands resting upon her lap, the blue of the veins. He inhaled her cool fragrance, full of secrets. Unlike the women at the House of Yang, who held no mystery for him, she fired his curiosity.

In the ensuing weeks, they often came upon each other at the station. Although there had been no agreement to rendezvous, the meetings occurred too frequently to have been by mere chance. On the train ride home, they traded news of family and talked about Youngest Aunt and her new position as a schoolmistress.

One Saturday, as Baba walked Lily home from Xinmin Station, the girl fixed her eyes on him and said, "Can you come inside for a bit?"

"Why?" asked Baba.

"No reason. Just come and sit for a while." She hesitated and continued, "Well . . . my mother wants to take a look at you."

"Why should your mother take a look at me? She's seen me before. I'm not so interesting to look at. No, it's late, I'd better get home."

"Oh, but you must come inside. Mama simply wants to see you," she said, tucking strands of her glossy hair behind one ear.

"For no other reason?"

"No other reason."

The matter was not as simple as Lily had suggested. No sooner had he greeted Mrs. Huang than he heard hurried footsteps from the hall, and the tall figure of Dr. Huang, Lily's father, appeared in the living room with words of welcome and inquiries after the Patriarch's health. The man polished his wire-rimmed spectacles with a handkerchief.

"I hear you are in the sciences. My girl here is not so clever, so she's taken up literature," he said with a short laugh. Baba noticed the resemblance between the man and his daughter in their gentle eyes. The father's were brimming with anxiety that a smile could not hide.

Lily's mother did not tease Baba as she had once done; silently, respectfully, and with moist eyes, she scrutinized Baba's healthy face—no trace of whiskers, a full sensuous mouth, straight nose, dark brows, and eyes glittering with confidence.

She studies me closer than I care for, he thought. I prefer her old manner, her quick tongue, sharper than a knife.

The father spoke of the war, his hands clasping and unclasping upon folded knees. He talked about the sabotaged railways, the derailed cars. He said he hoped Baba would look after his daughter on her way to and from school in Shenyang. "Yang Laojun, your grandfather, is an old friend of mine," Lily's father repeated several times. "I've known him for many, many years."

But who doesn't know the Patriarch of the House of Yang upon Western Marsh in these parts? No one carries himself as elegantly as he does; no one comes close to being as handsome, Baba thought, chest swelling with pride in his grandfather.

On Monday morning, Baba came for Lily, arriving at her house before dawn, when lamplight was necessary to tunnel into the darkness. He shivered from the damp and cold and stuck his hands deeper into his pockets. He abhorred rising early, and normally went to great lengths to avoid it.

"I hate school," Lily said once out of her parents' earshot. The tip of her nose was red from the cold. "That's why I wanted to wait till this morning before going back. I don't like to study, but my father makes me." She tossed her hair.

Baba carried little as usual, just a small sack with two clean shirts Third Sister-in-Law had laundered for him, but Lily limped along beside him with an enormous black canvas bag slung over one shoulder, holding in the other hand a sack filled with parcels of all sizes.

"Why should you girls carry so much," he said to her, annoyance in his voice. "You say you don't like to study, so it can't be books in here." He relieved her of her black canvas bag.

"Hey, this is even heavier than it looks."

"It's the jar of pickled vegetables Mother makes for me each week. There's only steamed sorghum in the dining room, little of anything else. I hate the food. I've been losing weight."

Baba's height had surpassed Lily's, and he now stood a full head taller.

"You're so spoiled. We don't have it any better over at our school, but I've got a huge appetite," said Baba. "Let's take a look at the goodies." Baba felt inside the bag and pulled out a jar made from opaque white glass used by Lily's father at the clinic to hold medicine. He pried open the lid and inhaled deeply. "Mmm, that sure smells good. Must taste terribly good," he said, making a greedy face.

"If you like it, go ahead and take it," said the young woman without blinking.

"But what about you?"

"It's all the same. I get to eat very little of it anyway. The other girls help me gobble it up in a day or two: many of them can't go home

—home's too far away, in another county. Go ahead, you take it, Yang Zuwu. I just won't have any this week."

"I was only fooling, Lily. I don't want to snatch food away from a skinny thing like you. I'm a mean, tough old pig in the wilds—*oink! oink!*—I'll eat anything tossed to me," Baba said, thumping his chest. "I don't need your precious pickled vegetables."

The fighting on the Manchurian plains intensified. The Nationalists in the cities and towns felt the noose tighten around their necks as the Communists seized the surrounding countryside, cutting communication lines and choking off food supplies.

The train ran even more infrequently between Xinmin and Shenyang. On one occasion, the two stations up the line from Xinmin, Gaotaishan—High Terrace Mountain—and Masanjiazi—the Three Houses of the Ma Clan—were simultaneously attacked in the night by guerrillas. Their objective was not to take over the two stations but to distract the Nationalist soldiers so that tracks between the two stations could be destroyed. As usual, the lines were patched up in two days' time.

Baba took a train bound for Shenyang. As it passed through Gaotaishan on the freshly repaired line, he began seeing distinct footpaths in the snow radiating from both sides of the track like herringbones, leading to sleepy hamlets consisting of a handful of houses, ringed by leafless poplars.

To clear such a distinct path in the deep snow, there must have been a least four or five people tramping along in a line, Baba thought. Those phantom Eighth Routers came three nights ago and sawed off the telephone poles running alongside the railroad track. Looks like they've been cut at waist level . . . and these must have also been the points at which the tracks had been pulled up, carried off, and buried some distance away. After they'd accomplished their mischief, the men returned home by the same paths.

For Baba, the patterns of the guerrillas' footprints were maneuvers as plain to see as a diagram of ballroom dance steps. The paths in the snow would lead avengers easily to the culprits' very thresholds, but the Nationalists were too scared to venture out from their eroding strongholds in the cities and towns.

Thin threads of smoke curled lazily out of the chimneys in the hamlets. The guerrillas must be snoring under their quilts on their toasty kangs now that it's daylight, thought Baba. They are like mice, storing up energy for their nightly visits. The jittery cats, on the other hand, can never close their eyes!

When the train reached Masanjiazi, further up the line, Baba saw more than a dozen corpses sprawled in the trackside ditches, partially buried in snow. These were bodies of the peasant guerrillas killed by Nationalists defending the station.

Lily's father wouldn't make her go to school under these conditions. I'm certain of it, thought Baba. A good excuse for her not to attend. She must be safe at home.

It was also useless for Baba to try to catch a few days of classes in Shenyang each time the tracks were repaired after the rounds of sabotage. He was traveling on the rare train to the capital in order to reunite family members and arrange housing for them. When he returned to Xinmin, he used every scrap of his wit and courage to find food for the women and children remaining at home. He had neither time nor heart to look in upon the Huangs. He would not set eyes upon Lily again.

Baba turned and faced a stillness that spread into the horizon under an arid, blue sky. The lavender shadow of one stray cloud raced up and down the dunes and dissolved. A narrow lane lay before him, threading through the mounds of yellow sand deposited by the River Liu, which flowed in from Mongolia. Willows, the foliage already grown thick, lined the way and crowned the dunes like stubbles of chin whiskers. Flashes of silver in the distance told of ponds dotting the land.

"So I am now within the district controlled by the Eighth Route Army," Baba said, "but where are they? There's not a soul on the road." Tales of Communist atrocities, told by relatives who had fled the executions in the countryside, shuffled in his head like a deck of cards as he picked his way down the road.

By midday he had reached the meandering river, rippling gold, mumbling a vague soliloquy. It ran shallow but wide. He removed his shoes, rolled up his trousers above his big knobby knees, and began to wade across. The coarse sand felt good massaging the arches of his feet and between his toes.

From the rim of the distant bank he saw a figure emerge, silhouetted against the sky like a black finger. The person also waded into the water and glided ever so slowly toward him. The only sound was the gentle slurp of the water as Baba's legs disturbed the surface and his anxious heart fluttered.

As the person neared, he recognized the sallow young man with big ears. An old classmate. There was also a look of recognition on the other's face, the squinting eyes emitting a cold light. They slipped past each other in a silence loaded with suspicion.

I wonder if he's a scout. And if so, for which side? He carries no bags . . . doesn't seem to be headed for anywhere in particular; he loiters, pretending to stare into the water. Looks just like a heron searching for dinner in its own shadow.

Baba reached the opposite bank, quickly clambered up the slope, and skittered down the other side, losing sight of the river.

Ahead of him, the road continued to slither in and out of the dunes and willows. He could see remnants of the old roadbed before the latest flood had given it a new course.

Silence wrapped in deeper silence. Where were the birds? No erratic flight of swallows crazed by the onslaught of spring. Had there been birdsong, the notes would have struck his ears as loud as gongs.

Not a soul ahead of him.

When he had traveled several *li* from the river, he glanced back up the road and saw two figures following at a distance, one of whom shouldered two baskets on a pole. Baba slowed his steps.

"I wish they would hurry up and catch up with me—would be good to have company." But even as he said this, a feeling of dread swept over him. "What if they mean to do me harm?" His heart seesawed between loneliness and distrust. He alternately slowed and quickened his pace. And as he did so, he sensed the pair behind him slow when he slowed, and quicken their steps when he hurried forth.

The road, roughly paralleling the sabotaged railway, was clean of cow patties or horse dung. In peacetime, horses clopped by and cow wagons groaned leisurely, but now no one dared to display his treasured beasts—that is, those the Nationalist soldiers had not already absconded with and yoked to the war.

He had been on the road for several hours, yet his nerves remained as raw and taut as the strings of an *erhu,* certain that danger was all around him.

The road now led him into a dark section, shadowed by thick willows that spilled over from both sides, forming a sullen tunnel.

"Guo lai! Guo lai!" came a voice like

firecrackers that pulled him to a stop, sharp and short. "Come here! Come here!"

The tender willow leaves shuddered, and from the greenery appeared a man whose face was bluish with unshaven stubble; his great bulbous eyes, like those of a goldfish, were frozen in a stare. The man waved a gun and motioned for Baba to enter the copse.

Baba's heart flapped like a fish on land. When he looked back up the road, another figure, lean and lanky, also waving a gun, emerged from the thicket. There must be more of them up ahead, lying in wait, he thought. There was no escaping: he had been snared like a rabbit.

Baba followed the orders that twisted out of the man's thin lips. He left the road and allowed himself to be swallowed up by the willows, shot with shafts of milky green light, the color of jade. Cobwebs became entangled in his eyelashes and the trees hooked their fingers into his clothes. The earth emitted cool vapors.

"Keep going!" ordered Pop-Eyes from behind.

As the willows thinned out, he saw many footprints in the sandy soil. Beyond a small hillock, a group of people—men, women, and children—slumped upon the ground in a pitiful pile, prisoners all. Their spirits seemed to have wilted like cabbages in the sun. They paid Baba little attention as he approached, each person's eyes fixed to a spot on the ground.

Baba guessed them to be recent immigrants to Manchuria—those who still had relatives living in Shandong or Hebei and could call these south-lying provinces home. It was likely many had traded their scant property in Manchuria for a handful of silver coins, perhaps a gold ring or two, in their hurried flight from war.

Six men in peasant dress stood guard over the prisoners. They spoke in anxious undertones and broken phrases. It seemed to Baba that they had been arguing.

"All men must bow down to us and honor us with gifts of money and precious things," said a hunched little man, wearing a smirk on his otherwise dingy, rustic face; though nervous, he clearly enjoyed his power to terrorize. "We are the greatest warriors under Heaven; we are not afraid of either the Eighth Routers or Nationalists."

In the midst of civil war, the redbeards—for these men surely were bandits—preyed on quarry deemed too small by the two contending forces, in some cases betraying the men and women of the very hamlets and villages that had hired them as protectors.

"Who are you? What have you got for us?" Pop-Eyes said to Baba.

"I'm only a student. I haven't any money." The man studied Baba's downy face, the skimpy cloth sack slung across his back and nodded, as if to say, "You certainly are a puny catch."

"Then get on over there by yourself, away from the others," the man said with impatience, indicating the direction with a rude thrust of his chin. He drew his pistol. "Sit yourself down and don't let out as much as a peep."

Soon two more unlucky travelers were shoved into the clearing like sacks of sorghum, their homely faces moist and pale with fear. These were the fellows Baba had seen following in the distance. Their bodies were searched and silver was gleaned from the tiny cloth purses hidden under their shirts. Baba did not know how much farther these men had to travel. It would take at least another week to reach Jinzhou. The fellows would have to beg all the way there.

"All right, you bastards, turn around and lie down with your noses to the ground," Pop-Eyes said through his ragged yellow teeth. "If we hear a sound or see any of you move, we'll drill you with 'black dates!'"

It was best to oblige: no one wanted bullets planted in their backsides.

As Baba pressed to the ground, he heard the quick succession of many footsteps in the sand, the swishing of bodies plunging through the willows, the whinnying of horses, then felt the thud of hooves. After that, there was such an awful hush, he thought he could hear the sun creeping across the sky.

At last, after what seemed like an eternity of minutes—choked by the silence, chilled by the rustle of the wind—he tentatively lifted his head.

"They're gone," he said. One by one, folk scrambled to their feet and dusted off their clothes and cursed.

"They'll get theirs soon enough," an old granddad said and spat on the ground. "When the Eighth Routers or the government soldiers get a hold of those sons of turtles, they'll finish off every last one of them.

"They think they can avoid these black days. They're just the same as us—just fishes swimming along at the bottom of the pan. Once the fire's lit up from beneath, they'll go belly-up on top just the same as the rest of us."

Some were silent, preoccupied with arranging their belongings in the riffled bags and baskets. The gold or silver now gone—perhaps their entire life's savings—they had little to cheer them down the road. Their faces reflected the anguish in their hearts.

Baba did not wait for the others. Hunger and thirst racked him. He walked ahead, squishing mud underfoot, and made his way to one of the ponds that dotted the roadside. The reeds along the bank were shooting up amidst last year's bent and brown growth, for the peasants who harvested them to sell as kindling had not come with their sickles when ice capped the ponds.

Baba brushed aside the duckweed floating on the surface. He stopped and listened to the profound uncertainty that reigned on a spring day.

"Those who have guns will always bully those who don't," he said to himself. "Life seems as savage and senseless as dogs who fight over a pig's bladder, thinking it is meat. They chew and they chew, but they cannot swallow the darn thing.

"What dangers lie in wait for me? What will tomorrow bring?"

It is just as well that men cannot foresee the future, cannot envision the years necessary to scrabble out of those deep, dank holes into which they tumble, or foresee the mountains that will suddenly sprout at their feet once they have regained the wind and sunshine. Had my father stood at the Western Checkpoint and witnessed the possibilities unrolling beyond the horizon, his knees would have buckled, his heart would have heaved. He would not have had the courage to step into the unfamiliar landscape. He would have shuffled home with my third uncle.

Baba cupped his hands to drink. The water dribbled down his dusty neck and wet his shirt. There was no point in pondering the future. For the moment, all that mattered was that the water, tinged with the fragrance of reeds, tasted good, and the pancakes, salted by his sister-in-law's tears, tasted like home.

THE SUN PEERED at the solitary traveler before sliding down the rim of the plain. A blast of chill wind pressed against my father's back, urging him on, while the grass whistled *xiuxi, xiuxi, xiuxi*—rest, take a rest, sleep. Then the air was still and silent and it seemed all the critters—snakes and squirrels, hares, and sparrows—had nestled down in their nice dry holes.

Must have traveled at least seventy *li* on this first day, but I haven't been detained by soldiers of the Eighth Route Army—I'm not even sure if I've really seen a Communist, Baba thought. I know they're around. It is too quiet. No dogs barking. They always kill the dogs first . . . like they killed my Labrador, Big Black. Howling dogs give away their movements in the night.

"Hai, to be within a circle of familiar faces, to eat a hot meal, and to close my eyes," Baba said and sighed as he stumbled on in the waning light.

What has become of our kinfolk in the neighboring towns and villages? he wondered. The face that loomed before him—faint eyebrows framing kind eyes, freckles on high cheekbones—was that of Mother Cao, who lived in Baiqipu, to the southwest.

Mother Cao was a country girl with little education when she married Master Cao, a learned man of talent. During the waning days of the Qing dynasty, when her husband was honored with an imperial post at the southern extreme of the Middle Kingdom, she remained behind in the town of Baiqipu—Garrison of the White Banner—to take care of the home.

Upon settling in the South, Master Cao took up a concubine whose relatives fattened up their own pockets through their ties to him. Years later, when he lost his post, the woman refused to follow him on his return to his native Manchuria. But there was Mother Cao, his faithful wife, waiting for him. Her heart remained as true as the needle of a compass. A son and a daughter were born to them.

The Cao family was respected in Baiqipu; the history of an imperial appointment decorated their name and caught the attention of folk like a gleaming gold tooth. When the son married and a baby was born, the family numbered six. The House of Cao rang with laughter, and peace reigned in their hearts.

In the year the beautiful and learned

daughter from the House of Cao married his eldest brother, Baba began venturing to Baiqipu during holidays to visit his new kinfolk, whose spacious house was filled with blue-and-white porcelain and curios of the Qing and Ming dynasties.

Mother Cao was a benevolent soul with Buddha's placid demeanor. In her house, never once did sorghum touch a guest's lips. She served him costly white rice, or noodles and chive pancakes made from bleached flour.

"Mother Cao, I'm just a kid. You needn't feed me so well," Baba would say.

"Aiya, dearie, you're from a large family. I know what that's like—eating steamed sorghum all the time. It's rare you come for a visit. It's a nice change for you to eat white rice for two or three days," she would reply, her smile radiating like sunrise.

Master Cao was no less generous a host. His most prominent features were his square jaw and large, soulful eyes. He was a talented calligrapher who told wonderful "palm-of-the-hand-stories"—anecdotes. But Master Cao, unfortunately, had one terrible vice: having been steeped in the ways of officialdom, he had not been able to resist the lure of opium.

"Child, never let this stuff spoil you," the man would say by way of apology when Baba found him veiled in its sweet haze. Baba liked the fragrance and breathed deeply. "It is evil and will consume you and everything you care for." The hush that followed was a silent sigh, an admission from Master Cao that he was helpless in its grasp.

When his habit drained the family coffer dangerously low, he went to work for the Japanese as the director of the opium station in his hometown. The new position, needless to say, was convenient for his own consumption. There at the station the addicts came to be registered and buy their weekly ration, squares of opium tar wrapped in wax paper.

Because he officiated in the traffic of a product that did great harm to others, it was prophesied that his family would come to a bad end. Folk clicked their tongues and whispered, "Father Heaven has eyes and will bring retribution."

When the Japanese surrendered, the supply of opium was disrupted, and Master Cao began injecting morphine, available on the black market. Soon after, the House of Yang received news of his death. His addiction had coiled about his soul and had squeezed the last breath of life out of him.

Within a few months of his death, the Communists surrounded Baiqipu. One evening, his son, ever the curious one, was drawn into the heart of town by the sound of battle. He soon came running home, crying to family and visiting neighbors, "The Communists have broken through the Nationalists' defense! The guns are coming this way! Lie flat on the kang, all of you!"

He had no sooner flung himself facedown on a bamboo pallet than a projectile broke through a papered window and rolled underneath him.

"Aiya!" those in the room heard him scream, a cry more hair-raising than the *huwoolong!* of the grenade. They saw his shadowy form rush for the front door before crumpling to the floor. When they turned him over, they saw that he had no face.

The daughter-in-law went mad at the sight, and after she returned to her mother's house to be looked after, only two helpless souls remained in the House of Cao: one old woman and her little grandson, but even this child soon took sick and died.

Mother Cao is living all alone, thought Baba as he dragged himself down the road. The night was fast coming on. I'll stop in Baiqipu tomorrow, see how she's faring. It would be heartless of me not to look in on her. She treated me as well as, if not better than, her own children.

But tonight Baba would call on the family of the two Jin brothers. The village of Sitaizi—Four Terraces—was a detour in his southward journey, but warm memories of a long friendship steered his heart that way. There was some distance to cover before he would reach the House of Jin. He had thought he would be among kinfolk before dark, but his legs had grown heavy and his progress achingly slow. He could feel the bite of blisters, which were forming on his feet.

What's become of them since the Japanese surrendered? he wondered. The brothers were often mistaken for each other; there was nothing particularly outstanding in their features to draw men's notice: just simple, country faces produced from a common utilitarian mold.

When asked about the past season's harvest, the elder knocked the ashes from his long pipe and said in a slow, gentle voice, "*Bu cuo, bu cuo.* Not bad. Can't say it's been bad." The younger responded with a wide grin to reveal a notched front tooth, the result of many years of cracking stony watermelon seeds.

In prosperous, peaceful times, the Yangs and the Jins frequently exchanged visits and stayed in one another's homes, though how the families were related was a matter so convoluted that no longer did anyone attempt to unravel the tie. So distant a kinship that eighty poles, attached end to end, would miss hitting, folk were wont to say.

Each Spring Festival, the two brothers arrived at the House of Yang, bearing a gift of white rice which they had cultivated on their own land. Some five years ago, they even brought along one of two gigantic black roosters that Baba had seen on a visit to their home and had taken a great fancy to. "They are most beautiful! What a handsome addition to any flock!" he exclaimed to the brothers.

At the House of Yang, the big black bird emerged from its cage with a heroic strut. The creature nearly came up to thirteen-year-old Baba's waist and was more than twice the size of the Yangs' own pair of roosters, which had been lording it over the hens in the barn.

Not surprisingly, these diminutive males were soon given no peace. The newcomer ran after them with its great glossy wings held back—like an authority with his arms folded behind him—but it ran swiftly, silently, staring them down with a look of deadly determination. The smaller roosters soon grew shy of courting the hens, and skulked about in the dark recesses of the barn, casting rueful looks.

"That bird will probably go after the young ones next and will peck out the eyes of the toddlers," the grown-ups said, giving Baba cross looks. "It's all your fault for bringing this calamity about."

But what to do? They could not insult the Jins and return their generous gift, nor could they be so heartless as to put the handsome rooster in a pot and eat it. The alternative was to cook their own roosters, but this was too drastic a measure: the Yangs were a proud clan and could not possibly admit defeat by sacrificing one of their own, even if it were a mere bird.

At the end of two weeks, the family had lined up in full support of their meek roosters, and the demonic intruder was put back in its cage and escorted out to the faraway hamlet of Erlinsuo, lying in the direction of Inner Mongolia. It joined the flock at the house of Baba's maternal grandmother, and how it fared out there no one dared ask, lest it be returned.

On Baba's subsequent visits to the Jins in Sitaizi, he was warned by his family to confine his praises within the walls of his own belly.

The stars were thick about a pale crescent moon that hung from the branches of the trees, and dew had alighted upon Baba's shoulders when he arrived in Sitaizi. The way was familiar and he had no trouble finding the house even in the night. It was a modest abode of five rooms for a small family.

But where are the doors? he wondered when he arrived at their gate. He sensed a barrenness, a void. His footsteps crunched too loudly in his ears. He entered the front garden and walked up to the house, where the light from an oil lamp stretched feebly out the open door. A dark figure emerged, with sloping shoulders, large ears, and hair closely cropped.

"Second Brother," Baba said.

"Number Four! Is it you? Why did you come here? Did anyone in the village see you?" From these pinched and pallid words, Baba knew it was wrong for him to have come.

"I saw no one," he replied. The man quickly pulled him inside by the elbow.

The family had just finished supper, and women put away the bowls in silence. Another man came forward. Baba could not clearly make out the face, but he sensed that it was masked by fear and alarm.

"Number Four, why have you come to our home?" said the man in a hoarse bass. It was the elder Jin. The emphasis was on the word "our," as if the gods had brought down a plague upon them without provocation.

Baba briefly told the brothers of the dissolution of the House of Yang.

"We've had it bad here, too," said the elder brother. His eyes grew smaller and folded into crescents. "Landowners have been denounced and beaten and everything taken from them. We have a couple hundred *mu* of land and are not considered a poor family . . . we are expecting them to come for us soon. . . .

"Things are not as in the old days: now we have to report visitors to the village headquarters," the man continued. He sat silent, thinking, the conflict of emotions boiling in the furrows of his brows like a storm cloud. Baba anticipated the man's next move with trepidation. He wiped his clammy hands on his trousers.

"Well . . . if you leave early tomorrow morning—before dawn—I guess no one will know the difference," the man said after a prolonged silence. Baba let out an audible sigh of relief and nodded.

"Have you eaten?" the elder brother asked. He glanced furtively at the window.

Baba shook his head.

"Ah, of course, I know you haven't," the man said, scolding himself for his reluctant hospitality; he was struggling between an embrace of friendship and his instinct for survival.

"Do you have any leftovers?" said Baba.

"Yes, there's still some in the wok," replied the younger brother. "We cannot light the stove again: the smell of smoke will make the neighbors suspicious."

Baba felt a chill even down to his toes after eating the cheerless meal; anxious eyes stared down at him with each mouthful. The cold sorghum and pickled cabbage remained a hard, grinding knot in his stomach.

"I know how tired you must be, Number Four," said the younger Jin as soon as Baba had set down his bowl. "You can stay in the back room where we keep the tools. There's a kang covered with rush mats in there for you to sleep on.

"Let's put an end to the talk; it's not wise to talk. We've got to put out the lamps."

Baba had no opportunity to ask about the family, whether the younger brother's son was still studying in Shenyang; whether their old parents were still alive. Baba could not account for all the individuals; in their own home, the Jins dodged the frail light like thieving mice.

He was shown into the back room.

"Sleep with your feet toward the edge of the kang," the younger brother said, patting the spot where one's head would normally rest. "If there's trouble, I'll tug on your feet. In this position, you can jump off more quickly."

Baba did not take off his shoes.

What an idiot I was to come here! I've only brought them more trouble, he thought as he lay down, hugging his cloth sack. But he was too tired for prolonged self-reproach.

It seemed to him he had no sooner closed his eyes than he felt a terrifying tug on his feet. He grabbed his bundle and lunged off the kang, ready to speed out the back door and hurl himself into the night.

"It's all right. It's all right," whispered the younger brother. "It is almost dawn."

Baba was wide awake now. He realized he had been asleep for many hours. His body, especially his legs, sore from his travels, was stabbed by pain from his sudden leap off the kang.

From the restless, rustling sounds coming from the other parts of the house, he guessed that no one in the family had rested. Throughout the night, they must have been listening with terror for noises outside, hearing the talk of enemies in the sighing of the leaves and grasses.

"Number Four, it is unlucky we meet in these years of trouble. It breaks my heart that we've had to let you hole up like this," the man murmured.

"Don't feel bad on my account, Second Brother. When I return this way . . . ah, when things get better—as I am sure they will—I'll come see the family again."

The man led him out to the back garden, which was surrounded by a high wall. Baba was shivering, not so much from the cold as from an uneasiness.

The man seemed to hold his breath as he opened the creaking gate. He stuck out his head to inspect the road. There was no movement in either direction.

The sun had not yet made its appearance, but the sky to the east was already a silvery gray, like the belly of a fish.

The man whispered explicit directions to Baiqipu, where Mother Cao lived in isolation. "She'll be able to put you up for the night," he said.

Baba made sure not to go that way.

THE SUN WAS stealing toward the range called Yiwulu Shan—The Witch Doctor's Portal. In the limpid light, the rocks encrusting the hooded peaks shone like pieces of agate. My father had been on the road for nearly a week, and having left behind the land of the yellow sand, he was now traveling through an unfamiliar region of black, fertile soil where all about him the deep green fields of soybeans were painted a burnished red by the westering sun.

Baba squinted. Ahead of him in the distance, in the knee-high soybeans, he saw what seemed to be a line of children, armed with spears taller than themselves, scurrying toward the main road upon which he was traveling. They loitered once they reached the road.

Baba grew wary; he slowed his steps. These little ones with their sharp weapons are waiting for me, he thought.

"Stand where you are!" shrill small boys ordered as he approached, aiming their thicket of gleaming spears at his chest. Tassels as red as blood danced where the blades met the wooden shafts.

There were so many of them, runny-nosed, with nubby shaven heads and dark eyes glinting with mischief. They were in such constant motion, it was difficult to count their number. Baba guessed there were nearly two dozen boys. He stood several heads taller than the tallest among them.

"What's your business!" they demanded.

"I am a traveler."

"We know you're a traveler! Do you think we cannot see that?" said an older boy, wrinkling his pug nose.

Baba stifled laughter. "Tell me, what's the name of this region?"

"Hey, you're in our country! We do the asking! And you haven't answered our question: What's your business!" The child stamped his feet.

"No business. I am a student."

"Oh, a student, eh? A person who learns books. The boss says we're not to allow your sort to pass." And turning to the others, he said, "We must take him to the village and have him spill the beans to the boss."

"*Zou, zou, zou!* Walk, walk, walk!" the children broke into a chant as they boiled like a school of small fishes all around him. "You'll have to confess in the village!" They jabbed him with their spears.

"Wah! Take it easy with those things!" cried Baba. The children struck him repeatedly in the calves with the wooden shafts.

When I was small, we used to love to play tricks on the grown-ups, Baba remembered. We'd scare the passersby along South Street just outside the House of Yang with pretend weapons, not these very real blades prodding my rear and the small of my back.

When he was four years old, he loved to climb the wall at the House of Yang to peer at the children of the tenants who were making a racket on the street. If a grown-up sauntered by, the children mimicked the call of a trumpet, *"Deer-dee, deer-dee!"* and sang, "You rotten nasty thing! Blow the trumpet, pound the drum! Send you off to the killing ground. PIANG! goes the gun." At the word "PIANG!" each child snapped a large folded triangle of paper, which created a wonderfully violent sound. The noise sent them giggling and hooting in a paroxysm of glee.

When the startled adult whirled and scowled, the tiny devils would scuttle, run for their lives.

The elders at the House of Yang disap-proved of their own children playing with the ragamuffins outside, but Baba and his cousins looked on with envy. "Come out! Come out 'n' play!" the derelicts would call, nodding and motioning with their arms to the prisoners who poked their heads over the wall like a string of brown sparrows.

Once Baba was sure the elders weren't watching, he would press open the gate and join the antics. The older boys helped him fold his snapping paper gun. What delicious fun it was to make trouble for the big people.

"Zou, zou, zou!" the children shouted. Baba did not know whether to laugh or cry. I meet up with soldiers of the Eighth Route Army at last, he thought. These tikes aren't playing the foolish little games I played as a kid. These, with their sharp spears, are in deadly earnest. They do not run away. The world is turned upside down: now the big people are frightened of the little ones.

Ha! If it weren't for the local bosses who back them up, I wouldn't mind flinging a few of these kittens into the soybean field by the scruffs of their necks.

He was not so much unnerved by these bite-sized demons as he was annoyed: the sun was setting, and he had hoped to travel farther before nightfall.

Two boys scampered ahead to alert the village of a captive. Another two, marching in front of him, led the way with their spears resting upon their small, proud shoulders. The others continued to bristle around him like ants carrying a grasshopper back to their anthill.

In this manner the children swept Baba into their village in a cloud of dust and into a vacant courtyard wherein a mud house stood, shriveled and solitary. Many pairs of little hands shoved him inside.

The room was gloomy and sharp with the smell of mildew. In line with the door was a long table, at which five men plied abacus beads, dipping their brushes in ink and making entries in ledgers. A large man with the meaty shoulders of a bear sat at the head of the table, wearing an olive green uniform.

No one said a word to Baba. Occasionally, one of the men in the plain dress of peasants would lift his eyes from his task and give him a cursory inspection, his eyes assuming the darting, anxious look of subordinates. A severe silence prevailed, a self-conscious sobriety.

Who am I supposed to "confess" to? Baba wondered. When he turned around to see if the children would give any indication, he found that every last one of them had vanished without a trace.

Baba stood motionless as a post and waited. The soles of his swollen feet burned. His mouth was dry and cottony with anxiety. It was some time before he heard himself addressed by a husky voice.

"Gan shenme de? What do you do?" the man in the olive uniform said, leaning back a little in his chair. One side of his face seemed higher than the other, and he had buck teeth, made all the more prominent by the shortness of his chin. He was not a Manchurian; his drawl revealed him to be a native of Hebei Province, to the south.

"I'm a student."

"Where're you headed?" The man's torpid eyes returned to his paperwork.

"To Jinzhou to see relatives." Baba knew that the moment called for a lie of a short, innocuous nature; the long-winded truth would only invite a further string of questions.

"Got a road pass on you?" The man barely glanced up at him.

"No."

"Why not?"

"I've come from a district under Chiang Kai-shek," Baba replied.

"Which Chiang district?"

"Shenyang."

"Let's see your papers."

Baba gave his student ID. The man set it aside, dusted his sleeves, and resumed his writing.

Like a mendicant before the magistrate, Baba was forced to wait. His calves throbbed. He shifted his weight from leg to leg. His stomach wrenched. He felt faint, and the cold sweat of hunger beaded upon his brow. Only the snapping of the abacus beads could be heard.

"You've come from territory of sinister rule. Our district here, however, shines in the light," the man went on. He spoke slowly, as if savoring each precious phrase.

If his mind had not been tinkered with, he would be a simple, hardworking peasant, thought Baba. His words are without a breath of humanity.

"In a short time, your relatives in Jinzhou will come under our leadership. Save yourself the walk. Wherever you go, we will go. We will liberate all of China, then we will go on to de-liver the world. . . . It is best you stay with us and make your contribution to the People."

Baba was anxious to resume his journey. His chest rankled with loathing and fear, but he tried to prevent his thoughts and emotions from floating to the surface. He studied the speaker's face, the small eyes and dark pitted skin, swollen with the thrill of his power. What does he intend to do with me? I can't show weakness. A willingness to compromise will bring only more trouble, Baba repeatedly warned himself. It was a lesson that had been seared into his soul.

Soon after the Japanese surrender, friends in a theater company, knowing of Baba's flair with a brush, recruited him to paint posters announcing their new play. The company traveled to the countryside to perform a drama about life under the Japanese rule.

At the village headquarters, where the company was hosted, their dinner of steamed sorghum and cabbage soup was suddenly disrupted by a queer, half-human noise.

"Aba! Aba! Aba!" came the jarring cries of a beggar, a middle-aged man with shaven head, in soiled, threadbare clothes; his bent dark figure was framed by the open door. *"Aba! Aba!"* he persisted in his eerie nonsense, all the while

pointing at his gaping mouth. In his other hand, he grasped an empty rice bowl, the pottery chipped around the rim. He stared at the diners with steady, intelligent eyes.

"Go away! Beat it! There's nothing for you to eat here!" Gao, the leader of the company, rose from the table, his sallow, scowling face blemished by a scattering of pockmarks. A gaunt figure, he waved his long arms and strode forth on his generous legs to chase away the beggar. The unwanted visitor slipped out of sight.

"Very strange . . . the mute are almost always deaf. They can't hear, so they can't learn the sounds of speech," said Gao, staring out the open door. "Now this beggar couldn't talk, but he sure seemed to be able to hear. I could've sworn by his expression, he understood my command."

And just as dinner drew to an end with a ringing of bowls and the clatter of chopsticks, the beggar returned. *"Aba! Aba!"* the man babbled with great urgency.

"Ai, something's mighty peculiar," said Gao, frowning. He approached the man and commanded, "Open your mouth!" The beggar obeyed like a child.

"His tongue and throat, they look normal. No damage. . . ." It was upon further inspection that Gao noticed the belt the man wore beneath his jacket. Instead of the black sash that peasants commonly wear, he saw a belt braided from long strips of purple, blue, and white cloth.

Gao slowly returned to the table and whispered, "Get the police over here, quick! This guy could be an informer for the Eighth Routers. The belt must be some sort of identification."

When the police arrived, they wrenched back the beggar's arms, sending his alms bowl crashing to the ground, where it split cleanly in two. The fellow did not resist. He was handcuffed and taken away, the cry of *"Aba! Aba!"* fading into the warm autumn evening, churring with the songs of crickets.

Baba was troubled. This Gao is no ordinary man—he has so much sway over the police, he thought, rubbing the sweat from his nose. Few people own guns these days; I saw a big black revolver under his shirt.

In three days, as the company prepared to travel forth to another village, the police approached Gao and said, "Hey, that beggar's been moldering in the cell. Hasn't been fed. What do you want us to do with him?"

"Gao, give him supper and let the fellow go.

What's the point of mistreating a poor peasant?" someone said.

"Well, let's pay him a visit," replied Gao. To see a smile at this moment upon the face of a man who rarely smiled was almost macabre.

They arrived at the jailhouse, a primitive affair in back of a mud building. Inside, opposite the windows, were three wooden cages built high upon a kang. The place stank of human waste. The beggar, its sole inmate, who had been squatting in the center cell, began pacing and yammering at the sight of visitors.

A moment later, a bowl of rosy steamed sorghum, topped with a few pieces of pickled vegetables, was carried in on a tray by a policeman.

"Aba! Aba! Aba!" The beggar cried louder at the sight of food, shaking the bars of the cage.

Gao, breaking away from a tête-à-tête with the police, walked toward the cage, swinging his long arms. His thin mouth was pressed tightly, like a scar on a melon.

"We know you are able to speak. You're lying to us," he said. "You're a spy of the Eighth Route! No use pretending you aren't. Confess!"

"I thought we came here to feed him and set him free," Baba blurted.

"If you don't talk, if you don't cooperate, you're going to rot here. We'll leave you here forever. You think this nice little supper is for you? No, you won't have it. We're going to let you starve here . . . unless you talk." To judge from Gao's cruel, flinty eyes, his threat was genuine.

The shadow of a struggle passed over the prisoner's face. He blinked nervously. Even his body expressed intense agitation and doubt. Tears gleamed in his eyes. Baba felt profound pity for the man.

"Talk!" Gao commanded.

"Aba! Aba! Aba! . . ." and then suddenly, "Only give me food and then I'll talk . . . I am starving," came the distinct, unmistakable words like one long sob.

For a moment, everyone was struck dumb. Gao raised an eyebrow; Baba saw that he was as astonished as anyone else in the room.

The prisoner devoured the food, making loud smacking noises all the while. Once he had licked the bowl clean with his tongue like a mongrel, he heaved a great sigh and said in a smothered voice, "I'm a native of faraway Stone Mountain. Been working the land all my life until I was recruited here to see about the movement of government soldiers . . . was working with two others . . . one disguised as a traveling herbal doctor, the other as a peasant, wandering the villages, sharpening knives and scissors for housewives...."

"Oh, Heaven above! A cat will play with the mouse—even allow it to run a few paces—before the kill," Baba said to himself. He felt sick to his stomach.

"The prisoner will be executed. Spies are all executed. Why would the authorities make an exception in the case of this poor soul? It is obvious this fellow, so easily starved into confession, is no professional. He's probably had minimal training. This peasant has been used by the Eighth Routers.

"If he hadn't talked, if the fellow could've resisted the lure of food two minutes more—just two miserable minutes longer—Gao would probably have ordered the police to let him go.

"I should never have joined up with this company; I should never have come here to be a pawn of the Nationalists...."

Baba could not sleep that night.

"A bowl of sorghum, the simpleton could not resist the lure of a bowl of sorghum. For one bowl of sorghum he has condemned himself and the others...."

"Speak up! Are you willing to stay on with us in service of the People?" a voice rapped against his reveries, loud and sharp. Baba had lost the thread of the monologue. The man's small, close eyes suddenly gleamed like a snake's; they were staring straight into Baba's for the very first time since he had been driven here by the troop of belligerent children. A fly-blown window, revealing a sky the color of wine, framed the man's bulky form.

"I'm not a spy. I've nothing to hide," Baba said to himself to bolster his resolve. "I only wish to leave this infernal cottage and steer myself south, away from territory under the Eighth Route Army. I only want to leave. Whatever this fellow will do to me, I must not buckle under."

Baba took a breath and struggled for an answer. As he tried to summon his wits to cough up a suitable reply, two women entered the room, empty rice bowls stacked tall in their hands.

Murmurs of delight swirled in the air, and the four men in peasant dress began pushing aside their ledgers. There followed a great commotion, the scraping of furniture on the floor, benches and stools scooted back.

"Hai, you need a rest. It's enough, it's enough. He's but a boy. Let him go. It's been quite a day. It's suppertime already," a woman said, heaving a long, deep sigh. Baba's heart leaped.

His interrogator was stubbornly silent and rubbed his short chin.

Another woman, wearing a blue-and-white apron, sailed in, carrying a steaming crock in both hands. "*Chi-ba! Chi-ba!* Eat! Time to eat! Don't delay and let the food grow cold," she said. The fragrance of sorghum permeated the entire room.

"*Hao, hao.* Yes, yes," joyous voices cried in concert.

"Well...all right, I guess you can go...." The man eyed the crock of sorghum with undisguised longing. With a barely discernible nod at Baba, he dismissed him.

"But I need my ID back."

The fellow picked up the document, gave it a long hard look as if still reluctant to let loose his prey. Then he tossed it disdainfully back onto the table, deliberately sending it to land out of Baba's reach. Baba leaned and stretched across the table and snatched it up.

"We're sorry to see you leave the light to walk back into the darkness" were the last words Baba heard as he sped out the door.

The sky was a deep purple. The ragged peaks of The Witch Doctor's Portal reared higher and higher as the sky dimmed to black. There was an astringent snap to the night air.

Ji-ji-ji-ji-ji! A bird was startled in the bean field as Baba, stumbling, felt his way along a furrow. He was steered by the hope for a bowl of sorghum somewhere down the road.

"GRANDFATHER, CAN YOU tell me the way to a monastery?" Baba asked an old man in the street whose good-natured face was like a dried persimmon with its wealth of wrinkles.

"Why the monastery, my young friend?" replied the gaffer.

"I'm a refugee from up north. I need a place to rest." Baba's throat was so parched it was painful for him to speak. The shoulder upon which he had slung his sack ached.

Jeeps and military trucks raced about, drowning their talk, assailing them with clouds of dust and grit that filled their eyes and mouths.

"There is one at the northwestern end of town. The abbot is known to be generous. His temple is small, but his voice carries much weight here in Xingcheng." The old man pointed out the way with his gnarled staff.

Baba had been on the road for more than a fortnight. On each foot were blisters in varying stages of growth and eruption. He limped along, hobbled by pain, adjusting the weight of his body to accommodate his complaining feet.

His days and nights had been uneasy: he did not have the road pass necessary for travel through Communist territory. Fearful of detention, he had stayed away from the towns and villages and had sought shelter late at night with peasants in the mud huts situated in the outskirts. The peasants would have provided Baba food and shelter without recompense, but were quite happy to take his old shirts or trousers when proffered. Long before sunrise he was up and tramping the road again.

Baba had entered Nationalist-controlled Xingcheng with difficulty, subject to a long interrogation at the checkpoint; he was reluctantly allowed to enter, for food was in short supply in the city. Now, within the embrace of its ancient walls, he hoped for a few days to rest and mend.

There were many monasteries here, but the old man had given him directions to a small temple that was known to be especially kind to wayfarers. It was built in an old section of town where the sun, filtering through the web of ancient cypresses, played upon the flagstones like golden pebbles awash in a stream. Baba passed under stone archways built to celebrate pious sons and daughters—legacies of a more gracious time. He found the entrance to the monastery and entered.

The courtyard had been newly swept and sprinkled with water from a watering can to keep down the dust. Whoever did the job is a serene person, thought Baba, for the marks of wetness along the path are even and have a nice serpentine pattern. A coolness descended upon him such as when one comes to the edge of a very deep lake; peace settled upon his heart. Stone stairs as white as jade led into the temple hall.

Inside, enveloped by the soft mist of incense, redolent of a southern forest, men and women kneeled before bronze Buddhas, their prayers welling from their souls and spilling forth from their devout lips to lap upon the shore of wakefulness.

The pilgrims brought offerings of food, which they carefully placed upon the altars. On adjoining tables, long slips of bamboo held in bamboo vessels told one's fortune for a few coppers. Benches, ornately carved, lacquered red and detailed in gold, lined the walls and invited the faithful for a rest. As the gaffer had told him, the temple was small—but therein lay its enchantment. Baba could see that no love or cost had been spared in its construction.

He sat in the deep shadows of an altar and watched, but nowhere did he see a monk. There was a layman in his fifties, back slightly bowed, with a tranquil yet resolute face, wandering from altar to altar, dusting off incense ash. Perhaps he was the one who sprinkled the water along the path in the pretty pattern, Baba thought.

The brief rest upon the bench made it even more painful for him to walk again. He staggered over to the man and asked, "May I see the abbot?"

The man stared at him. It was no wonder: Baba had not washed in days. His hair was matted with grease and dirt, and his face was mottled with a brown film.

"What for?" The man cocked his head, trying to discover what sort of person Baba was.

"I'm a student on my way south. I'm looking for a place to rest for a few days—just too tired to walk any farther."

"You wait here. I'll see what I can do." The stooped figure disappeared into the eastern apartment, one of a pair of "ear chambers," rooms attached to either end of the temple hall like ears on one's head. He soon returned.

"The Master says he would like to see you," the man said, smiling a little.

Baba picked up his bundle and followed the man into the apartment, a clean, book-filled room that reflected the uncluttered, steady thinking of its occupant.

A stream of sunlight, entering from a northern window, fell upon the upturned hands of an old monk who sat cross-legged on the southern kang. His head was as smooth and round as a gourd; he was robed in gray and wearing spotless gray cloth stockings. His handsome, unlined face shimmered with light thrown from a source the eyes could not define.

Years later, my father would recall the impression made upon him in those first fragile moments: "It was as if I had come upon a stone carving endowed with life . . . as if his spirit had been inward-looking for ages, folded like the heart of a great mountain. And suddenly, he was casting his gaze upon me with that same slow, steady regard that he had shown himself."

Baba nodded to the abbot, who extended his arm, motioning for him to take a seat. The old monk looked keenly upon his face for a long time—deep, solemn, penetrating eyes shot with a warm, clear light. He spoke in a voice old and still: "Brother Zhang tells me you are from Shenyang. Where are you headed?"

"Shanhaiguan. Eventually, I'd like to get to Beiping, though I do not know if the lines remain open."

"Tell me, what have you seen on your journey?" asked the old man.

"There is much fighting to the north. Shenyang, Jinzhou are the only large cities still under Nationalist control—also my county of Xinmin—but all other territories are lost to the Eighth Route Army. The Central Government troops are afraid to come out; they squat in those besieged cities, waiting and waiting for relief."

"And what of the temples?" asked the abbot.

"Outside the hamlets and villages, I saw that the tiny Tudi temples, ruled by the neighborhood god and his wife, had been destroyed—not just desecrated, but leveled. Just small piles of incense dust, here and there. The same is true for the larger temples that honor the city gods; I could only make out what remained of their foundations. The Eighth Routers, they hold nothing sacred. They have no religion."

The old man's face remained as placid as ever. No surprise registered there. By the slight lowering of his eyelids, he signaled that he had understood Baba's words.

"But, Abbot, I cannot claim to know about the temples inside the villages and towns. Maybe they're still intact," said Baba, trying to soften his report.

"Perhaps with Buddha's protection, this temple will be saved," said the old man gently.

Baba did not reply. His stomach made a loud noise.

"The room on the western side of the hall is where Brother Zhang lives. You may stay with him. I do not wish to prolong your weariness with talk; I know that you are in great need of food and rest."

The western "ear chamber" was also neat and orderly. Zhang, sitting on the edge of the kang with his hands resting on his knees, seemed to have been waiting for him. The bedding had already been laid out for Baba.

"It is almost June; the evenings are mild. You won't be needing a heavy quilt," he said. His tranquil countenance expressed neither cheer nor melancholy.

"Master Zhang, do you have a washbasin I can borrow?" asked Baba, scratching his head with both hands. Flakes of dirt showered down.

In the shade of the plum and pear trees in the back garden, he drew water from the well and doused his head. The water freed his face of dust, freed his mind of gritty thoughts. He removed his shoes. Gently, he peeled off the strips of cloth that he had been using as bandages for his blistered feet. He scrubbed the cloths clean and laid them out upon a woodpile to dry. He cooled his feet in a basin of water.

Brother Zhang saw the bloody blisters clustered together like red willow gall. He was now certain that the young man had indeed walked a great distance; whatever suspicions he had that Baba was an Eighth Router spy were now erased from his mind. The man did not report the arrival of a guest, as the Xingcheng police required.

Zhang gave Baba a needle and thread to break the blisters, showing him how to heat the needle in the flame of an oil lamp: singeing the skin with the hot needle helped to keep the punctures open, allowing the water to flow unimpeded. There was an almost maternal gentleness to the old bachelor. He helped Baba dip the thread in oil so that its passage across his raw, inflamed flesh would be less painful.

Baba sighed with happiness as he put his feet up on the kang.

Supper was a special treat for him: they ate *mantou* made from fine white flour that had been brought to the temple as offerings. Baba munched the steamed bread rolls with his eyes closed in ecstasy; he devoured each of them in two or three bites. War raged in the countryside, and food had become scarce, but the devout continued to proffer their best at the altars to Buddha.

That night Baba tumbled into sleep as soon as his head touched the kang. He did not rise until the sun, high above the monastery wall, nudged him out of his dreams.

During the day, Baba trailed Brother Zhang and helped him with the chores: he watered the garden, dusted the altars, swept the courtyard, and sprinkled water in curious patterns along the paths. His feet troubled him still, but the pain was now less acute.

Often he would stop in his work, sit on a bench in the temple, and idly watch the comings and goings of the pilgrims. He was very attentive as to what delicious morsels they had brought for the Buddhas. The sound of their prayers soothed him.

He saw little of the old abbot that day.

On the second night, long past midnight, the gentle ringing of a brass bell, sounding like drops of water breaking the surface of a pond, rippled into Baba's dreams and awakened him. This was followed by the crisp tapping of a "wooden fish"—a hollow, nut-shaped instrument—that accompanied the abbot's chanting. The moon that peeped into the room through the window dusted the floor like frost.

Occasionally, in the great distance beyond the city, Baba heard the nightly exchange of gunfire between the Nationalists and Communists. But trouble seemed incapable of reaching him here. The peace that enveloped him was not of this world.

I've arrived at an oasis, he thought as he lay on the kang, lulled by the music of the temple. He hoped the moment balanced in harmony would last forever and was afraid to move lest the magic be broken.

I have never imagined anything so delicious in this world, was his last thought as he dipped back into dreams.

In the morning, Baba felt a great reluctance to leave, but he was sufficiently rested and did not want to overstay his welcome.

"It's time for me to continue on my journey," he told Zhang.

"The Master would like to see you," the man replied. Resting one elbow on the handle of his broom, he looked thoughtfully at Baba.

The abbot was meditating, smiling inwardly like a slumbering child.

"Thank you for all the kindness you've shown me. Now I must get back on the road," Baba said, breaking the silence of the room.

The abbot slowly opened his eyes and spoke: "Child, I can see that in your previous incarnations, your heart has been close to Buddha. With a little more knowledge and preparation you will make even greater strides.

"Rest a while longer. We are not short of food. After the midday meal, return here to my chamber. I will impart to you some useful knowledge."

"Stay as long as you wish," the old man continued after an interval of silence. "There is still fighting ahead of you on the road. Can you not hear the bellowing of cannons in the distance near Baimiaozi—the town of the White Temple? Passage south will be difficult."

Baba returned to Brother Zhang's apartment to tell the happy news of his stay. After taking the midday meal with the man, he cleansed his face and hands by the well and returned to see the abbot.

"Can you sit cross-legged on the kang?" the abbot asked, tapping his own knees.

Baba shook his head. "No, I'm afraid my limbs have never been supple enough for that position, Master." Baba remained in his chair.

The abbot lit a stick of incense, settling the room into a deeper level of peace.

"I am now well over sixty—I've lived beyond *yijiazi*, a full cycle allotted by Heaven and Earth," the old man began.

"When I was your age, I attended university in Beiping. Afterwards, I went overseas to study in France. When I returned, I was given a highly coveted position in the warlord government, but there was too much ugliness that came with power; I came to know the worst in men . . . my position became increasingly distasteful to me.

"Then, one day, in a moment of solitude, I awakened to a different kind of knowledge. With renewed strength, I took my leave of 'the world of the red dust'—the world of desires. I found solace here in Xingcheng, and here I built this temple from the alms I collected from the rich and the poor."

He traced his fingers upon the words in the volume that lay open before him. "This is from the 'Diamond Sutra,'" he said, and turning his body slightly toward Baba, he explained the passage: "In the universe, all that is visible is a dream, a bubble, a shadow, lightning, morning dew. If one lives one's life with unclouded eyes, sees the world of appearances as transitory, one will transcend pain, the pain of restless longing and discontent; only then will one be released from the endless cycles of suffering...." He lifted his eyes to look upon Baba's face, but they were reaching far deeper.

"Child, there is nothing for you out there. I can teach you all that you need to know. It is not necessary to step outside to understand the world; the farther one goes, the less one knows."

And then the old man folded his hands and closed his eyes. Baba left him to his meditation.

He passed that evening as before with Brother Zhang, and as on the previous night, he was softly awakened by the clear ring of a bell stretching into the darkness.

I know the abbot wishes me to stay on—to study under him, he lay thinking. Ah, how easily I could remain.... If this were only peacetime.... But I have seen the desecration even of the harmless little rustic temples, and I fear there is no possibility for this place to stand.

The old abbot believes too much in the power of the Nationalist troops; the Central Government presence is felt strongly within this city, but it's only a matter of time until they are defeated.

It's just as what I read as a child in *The Romance of the Three Kingdoms*: if an army is sur-rounded by the enemy, has no food, no means to pay its men, and no prospect of a rescuing army from outside, then it is doomed.... Just as Shenyang and Jinzhou are doomed.

The old abbot—it's hard for him to see beyond this temple, tucked away in the untrafficked part of the city, lying low where the wind and rain seem unable to lash against it. He is lulled into a false sense of security.

I have certainly fallen under the spell of this place. Here all fears have been lifted from me. My burdens are not forgotten: they simply do not weigh on the present. Even physical pain seems remote; it is remarkable the way the sores and blisters on my feet have healed. How strong I feel. Everything seems precious here, every word, every meal, every moment....

On the following morning, he gathered his belongings and prepared to go. Zhang handed him a package of *mantou* for his journey. Baba thanked him and entered the abbot's chamber to say good-bye.

"Master, I have rested and have recovered my strength. I am grateful to you for all that you have done for me."

The abbot turned toward him and, lifting his flowing sleeves, he said, "Be careful. The town of the White Temple is still unclean. It is best for you to walk the extra distance and skirt the conflict. Do not venture into the fighting.

"Have you food for your journey?" the old man asked. Baba realized it was the abbot who had instructed Brother Zhang to give him the package of food.

"You were meant to walk in the path of the light," continued the abbot. "Before you venture forth, burn incense and ask Lord Buddha for guidance and protection." The old man's eyes, filled with ages of memory, watched Baba intently, perhaps reminded of his own youth.

Baba entered the temple. He waited for others in the hall to finish their prayers. He lit three sticks of incense from the flame of a candle. Holding the incense sticks with both hands, he raised them high above his head in homage and then set them lightly, one by one, in the sand contained in the urn. He knelt before Buddha and kowtowed three times. He prayed—his heart heavy with hope, heavy with doubt.

"I do not know if Buddha exists, but I do know that goodness exists in men like the abbot," he said to himself.

He rose to leave. Upon reaching the white stone stairs that led outside—outside to the alley, then the succession of wide streets, and ultimately, to the dusty, boundless highway he was to travel—Baba, on impulse, wheeled around and called out, "Old Master, take good care! One day, when I return to Xingcheng, I will come see you again!"

His voice echoed in the emptiness.

There came no reply.

FROM THE TEMPLE at Xingcheng, Baba pushed south into a land of rolling hills, coming upon mute villages tucked away in the long spring grass. He was, once again, adrift in the hush of Communist territory. To the north, the jagged Witch Doctor's Portal Range beckoned like fingers for his return.

In a handful of days, he came to Shanhaiguan, where the Great Wall wades into the sea. He tasted salt in the air, saw the sunlight streaming down from the clouds in a gold curtain over the water. He took leave of Manchuria, entering the land clasped within the arms of the Great Wall, stepping into China proper—civilized China protected against marauding nomads. (The successive waves of invaders, each in turn, had been absorbed by the Chinese; the hoofbeats of their small steeds resounded across only the pages of history.)

So, too, had Baba reentered a pocket of Nationalist territory. The Nationalists were the government, but their military controlled only the cities, while the countryside was the domain of the will-o'-the-wisp Communist guerrillas.

A train ran south from Shanhaiguan; it stopped frequently to check the tracks, fearful of Communist sabotage. It was a daylong journey to Tianjin.

As Baba waited at Tianjin Station for a train to Beiping, voices rang out like shots. The cackle of bowls and the spill of chopsticks spun him around on his heels. Pancakes were strewn on the ground like lily pads. Three men—two brandishing crutches, a third wielding a cane—had overturned a vendor's stall, their eyes ablaze upon their sallow, hungry faces. The red crosses embroidered upon the breasts of their rumpled gray uniforms identified them as disabled veterans. In their anger, these legless and armless moved about with surprising agility to thrash the sound-bodied.

"I have four mouths to feed at home. I make little enough as it is," the hapless vendor whimpered, his arms thrust out before him, and his head tucked low to ward off blows.

"We lost our limbs for China!" came a thunderclap of a cry. "We were ready to lose our lives for the likes of you! But now fine folk stroll by, averting their eyes. No one cares. No, the government does nothing. They only humor us with movie tickets and free rides on the trolleys!" The man's empty right sleeve, which had been tucked into the waist of his trousers, had come loose and flapped at his side.

"I lost this leg so you could keep struttin' round on yours," said another man, prodding the vendor in the chest with his crutch. "I say we eat for free!"

Military police patrolling the city hastened away: wounded veterans were known to travel in spiteful mobs, ravaging shops that demanded payment for goods and injuring those who had come in between to break up the fight.

Baba's heart sank and came to nest in his stomach. "I've walked nearly a month to flee the fighting," he said to himself, "but now that I have reached Huabei—this land stretching between the Great Wall and the Yellow River—I see that there is no peace here, either."

China, seemingly homogeneous to the foreigner, is a vast land of small communities, each fiercely jealous of its own ways. As a Manchurian south of the Great Wall, Baba was a stranger. The Tianjin accent he heard all around him recalled the torments of childhood. His family had fled the Japanese to Tianjin in 1934; with his distinctly Manchurian accent, he had been ostracized by his classmates and bullied even by the schoolmasters.

They called my three brothers and me "bumpkins from beyond the Wall," Baba remembered. They mocked us, but at the same time they were envious, because Manchuria, a fertile land, filled the rice bowls of her natives most generously.

At last his train departed. It tiptoed northwest from Tianjin, picking its way through uncertain territory, and pulled to a stop in Beiping late in the afternoon when the shadows were long and deep. The air tasted familiar to him. His family had moved to this ancient capital in the autumn of 1937, nearly ten years before, when Tianjin, in her turn, had fallen to the Japanese, who were hungry for more territory.

Graciousness, humor, artistry, refinement, and, above all, love of peace characterized old Beiping, even as a series of warlords swept into the walled city after the collapse of the Qing dynasty—Yuan Shikai, Duan Qirui, Wu Peifu, and Zhang Zuolin—mere mortals scheming to become the Son of Heaven.

The temperament of the city, to a large degree, had seeped under Baba's skin during his family's years of residence here, for a child's spirit is fashioned by the wind that blows and the water that flows through the landscape.

―――――――――

The family lived on a quiet, imperturbable *hutong*, or lane. Unlike the port city of Tianjin, modernized under the influence of the Europeans, the Beiping boulevards and long, maze-like *hutong* retained their unflustered charm, rural in their effect. Rarely did households open up their gates to allow passersby a peep into private lives. Each family kept to itself behind tall walls, behind the fastidiously maintained gate with its pair of stone lions, standing guard to either side, the door lacquered a righteous red and adorned with fancy brass knockers—a fresh and pretty face for all to see, but the quality of the heart was anyone's guess.

On his way to school each morning, Baba passed along a length of tumbled-down wall which used to surround the "Jujube Forest," a courtyard populated by its namesake trees (its fruit tasting like dates), but also graced by persimmons and walnuts. Next he would come upon the Courtyard of the Luo Clan. Like that of the family who owned the previous property, the Luo family fortune was in sharp decline, and the family rented out rooms, so the big House of Luo had become a hive of small households. Passersby wandered into the garden at will, the rigid sense of privacy having crumbled away with the wall. Baba stepped in through a gap. It was a shortcut he loved to take, for beneath the spreading branches of a grandfather elm, snack vendors peddled their temptations.

It was customary for Beiping schoolchildren to eat out rather than have breakfast at home; with the four coppers from his mother now warming in his pockets, he made a studious choice.

In winter, his favorite food was sweet potato, burning hot, roasted in an oven fashioned from an old oil drum that had been walled with clay. "Which one do you want, young 'un?" asked the vendor, stamping his feet in the snow. Then, lifting the lid, the man warmed a hand over the opening. Baba stretched for a look on his tiptoes, barely tall enough to peer into the belly of the oven, the warm air tickling his nose like the tail of a cat. The sweet potatoes hung on tiers of wire rings like so many fishes. He pointed to a particularly enticing one: plump, uniformly baked, and oozing with golden syrup. Baba did not have money for an entire potato to himself, so the vendor sliced it diagonally in two. His mittens dangled from the ends of a string as he reached out for a steaming wedge, then sank his small, even rows of teeth into flesh the color of apricots.

Sparrows cried *ji-ji-zha-zha* overhead upon the bare branches of the elm. Baba wondered, Now where are those little birds going to find something to eat? I have a sweet potato, but how will they find food in the snow?

Then, munching as he made his way slowly to school—located in Zhongnanhai, the old Imperial Park, forbidden to commoners during the reign of the emperors—he looked behind him to admire the solitary strand of footprints stamped in the dusting of fresh snow. If there had been early-bird schoolmates, he followed their tracks, which led him in through the park gate. By the time he had sauntered down the long, meandering covered gallery, its beams painted in glorious detail with scenes out of history and literature, every morsel of sweet potato had been transferred from his hands to his stomach, and he had arrived at the door of his classroom.

Baba liked the intimacy of the *hutong* and gardens, but what sent his heart soaring was the panoramic view atop the ancient wall that wrapped itself about the old Imperial City. When his father was in the Miyun mountains north of Beiping, supervising his newly acquired gold mine, Baba was free to range as far away from home as his courage allowed.

It was only a short walk along a wide boulevard to the Xuanwu Gate, whose arched portal led one south to the Outer City. The gate was surmounted by a two-tiered tower whose roof, during the glory days of the last dynasty, had been tiled in shiny green ceramic. Now grass grew in tufts between the broken gray tiles.

Crumbling flights of stairs to either side of the gate, built from the same gray bricks as the wall, led to what Baba thought was the top of the world. The top of the world, he figured, was wide enough for two horse carts to travel, side by side, had horse carts been able to pick their way up the stairs.

Once on top, he dared not venture too far beyond the gate tower, for the grass grew progressively taller between the broken bricks, and unseen creatures rustled there, going about their mysterious business. In autumn he risked the ghostly critters to harvest wild sour jujubes, whose wafer of brown flesh melted away into pure tanginess, leaving a perfectly round pit for him to roll on his tongue.

Facing south, and peering out from a channel in the crenelated rampart, he saw an uncharted ocean of gray roofs, punctuated by a temple tower here and there; he gazed down upon the progress of mule carts, horse carts, a rare automobile, and the hawkers in the marketplace; his bright eyes pried into private courtyards, landscaped with miniature mountains, and saw children jumping rope or playing with black dogs and mop-tailed yellow dogs.

Baba scurried to the northern rampart and leaned out, taking in the hubbub of the Imperial City. There were the four painted ceremonial archways at the Xidan intersection, through which a trolley threaded. *Dang-dang-dang-dang!* The conductor sounded the bell with the lever at his feet, scooting pedicabs and pedestrians out of his way. Prominent were the train station, two white dagobas, the pavilions atop Coal Hill; and within the Forbidden City, where emperors once lived, roofs gleamed like vast sheets of gold: no grass grew there, for the successive warlord governments were careful of upkeep.

When Baba visited this lofty perch in winter, the world bore a fierce, lonely beauty. The roofs were pillowed white, some showing ribs of black where tiles protruded. The streets were mantled white but for a black track in the center where carts made their way. Coal black crows crying *gua! gua! gua!* came to alight on the velvet silhouettes of the bushes and trees. It was a landscape painted in the traditional Chinese manner: ink on paper, enlivened by a tiny bit of vermilion where pillars and gates, lacquered red, blazed away in spite of the cold.

When Baba was brave, his courage was as big as a ripened summer watermelon; when he was timid, it was the size of its seeds. The tower that surmounted the gate—vacant and dilapidated—loomed dark and emitted vapors. Baba feared to enter. Its thick pillars, which decades ago had been painted in vermilion, were now gray, the sun having licked them clean of color; some sections had turned brown, and the paint buckled like the skin of a roasted potato. Overhead, Baba could hear the ruckus of rats and mice, the chatter of sparrows that swooped in and out. Swallows in springtime found propitious nesting places under the eaves.

If alone, Baba ventured into the shadow of the tower with his heart in his throat, and at the sudden *pa!-pa!-pa!-pa!* of a wild pigeon's wings his heart hit the roof of his mouth and shot back into his stomach. If he had come with his little friends, he and the boys threw broken bits of tile to frighten the birds.

When evening sliced into the day, Baba scrambled back down to earth. He loved the thrill of the cold and lonely outpost in the sky, but the company of men in scholarly long gowns, walking in pairs on the streets and chatting amicably, serene and urbane, was preferable in the night.

Nearing the Xidan shopping district, he saw the food vendors lighting their lamps, a few neon signs blinking along Changan Avenue—the Avenue of Eternal Peace—the silhouettes of people gliding past shop windows and doors, steam rising from sugared chestnuts and dumplings.

His short legs churning, he threaded his way through Huaili Hutong, past the residence of wealthy Wan Fulin, whose imposing walls hid the treasures of brass cranes and lions taken from the old Summer Palace; then past Beida Hospital.

Home. It was beginning to snow.

"It is already inky black night! You're very late! Where have you been, may I ask?" Nainai, my grandmother, scolded as she held open the gate.

My father walked past his towering, glowering mother, pretending to wipe his nose: loudly he sniffed twice into his coat sleeves—a gesture that was half defiance, half studied nonchalance.

But who would feed him now, this unwashed refugee? Where would he find a roof to shelter him tonight? There was not one soul in the city who was watching the hands of the clock, anxious for his return.

He felt gutted by anxiety and disappointment: to reach Beiping had been his goal; now that he had arrived, he realized he was only beginning a journey, not coming to the end of one.

By evening he had found shelter at Rongxian Hutong, or Yarn Alley, where Manchurian refugees gathered, at an estate that belonged to a wealthy family who had fled south, taking everything with them except the chandeliers. Here Baba registered and spread two shirts on the brick floor to claim a sleeping space.

But in a few weeks, when the shelter came to be squeezed tight with the host of Manchurian students flooding into the city—driven here by the intensified fighting in the Northeast—Baba, along with many others, removed to Fayuan Temple—Temple of Buddhist Origin. It was one of the largest temples, and the most popular one, located in the southwestern section of the Outer City. Here, the refugee population would soon swell to several hundred.

The abbot at Fayuan Temple wielded great power in the religious and secular worlds. He was able to bend the ears of those in government, and had access to a wealth of funds: the order's vast landholdings brought in much rent. It was said that many of the successive abbots over the years could not resist the lure of gold; they lined their own pockets by secretly selling art objects—antiques from the Tang dynasty down to the Qing—bronzes, porcelain, and priceless ceremonial implements. It was even rumored that the abbots were an amorous lot and kept mistresses on the sly. It was no surprise that the position was highly coveted and contested behind a facade of ascetic tranquillity.

On the day of their arrival at the temple, the students passed through a long series of lush courtyards nesting against one another. In one of them, Baba caught a glimpse of a gracious room, the walls hung with old paintings, steeped to a golden brown by the richness of the years, and an immaculate white canopy spilling down from the ceiling over a bed. "This must be the abbot's chambers," someone whispered.

Finally, walking into an immense court-

yard—the temple walls lined by regiments of pines and cypresses, among whose branches no birds came to trill or play—the students came to rows of long, rectangular buildings whose pitched gray roofs had grown mossy; each building was partitioned into smaller units, each of these units with its own entry and a small latticed window.

Ah, these look decent enough; must be guest houses for visiting monks, Baba thought. But to his great dismay, upon entering, he was struck by the smell of the cold and damp—the smell of desolation. The chill seeped into his bones. As he stood mustering a seed of courage, the darkness slowly gave way to a feeble green light, which revealed a perfectly round mound that came up to his waist. It resembled an oversized *mantou* and had been built from brick and covered over with gray plaster. Before the hump stood a short table set with two candlesticks, an incense urn, and a photograph of the deceased. Yes, the dead, for this was in fact one of the hundreds of grave mounds that lay in the rows of buildings whose interior walls festered with mildew; the refugee students had been offered a bed among ghosts.

Wandering the limit of the grounds, Baba estimated over one hundred chambers of various dimensions—some contained two graves—and he learned that the family of the deceased paid rent to the temple each month; the price varied according to the size of the chamber.

In one of the rooms, instead of a grave mound, Baba found a plain casket, spanning a pair of benches. He recognized the name brushed in ink on a slab of unvarnished wood, placed upright on the offering table. "Wang Yitang," it read.

"Wang Yitang . . . Wang Yitang . . ." Baba murmured to himself. "Of course! The political head of all Huabei during the Japanese occupation. And I saw the man when I was small.

Back then I had no idea of his power. And had I known, it would've meant nothing to a schoolboy serious about having his fun."

His school had been converted from the Hall of Bright Promise, and the schoolyard spilled out into a square shared by the neighboring Hall of Benevolence, where important men of government came to confer with one another. Both sets of buildings sat in the old imperial park. Oftentimes the police tried to shoo the boys away when meetings were taking place, but the children did not budge. You're on our territory; this is our school, they silently argued.

Just outside the Hall of Benevolence stood four fishbowls, the largest in the world; Baba was able to snatch a glimpse into one if he pulled up on its rim and jumped with all his might, or if he stood upon the shoulders of a crouching friend. When he struck the side of a bowl with his fist, it resonated with a *goonng-goonng*, grumbling like the stomach of a gaffer awakened from his eternal nap. Supposedly they had once been gold-plated, but when the last emperor was chased off the grounds, folk came and scraped away the splendor. Now the fish-

bowls loomed black and only mosquito larvae jerked in the sullen rainwater.

Each afternoon, when school was out, Baba and a handful of classmates made a dash to play their mad, passionate games of marbles in the shadow of the fishbowls. (Baba skimped on breakfast to buy his marbles.)

The boys drew a square in the dirt, dubbed "the pot," to which each contributed a plain marble, known as "the stake." Baba knuckled down and shot "the chief," his smoothest, prettiest marble, swirled with blue, green, yellow, and orange; he aimed to knock out one of the stakes in the pot, which he would get to keep if he managed not to leave his chief mired in the pot. Striking someone else's chief killed that particular enemy: the boy whose dead chief it was, was knocked out of the playing, and had to forfeit any stakes he had come to acquire over the course of the game. He was, however, allowed to hold on to his own chief.

On one particular afternoon, only two chiefs remained alive to do battle: Baba's and Fatty Kong's.

Fatty was a self-proclaimed descendant of Confucius, who lived in the sixth century B.C., and his nickname described him well: his doughy thighs poured out of the legs of his summer shorts and pulled the fabric taut. He had uncommonly small nostrils, which made it hard for him to breathe, and this gave him the habit of wrinkling his nose and snorting. But in spite of his portliness, Fatty was the reigning king of the marble shooters, and was famous for his style—known as "dropping-cannonballs-from-on-high." Like a billiards player's, the fingers of his left hand formed a bridge, and he used the back of the forearm to support his shooting hand. He narrowed his long, slim eyes, and with a *"piata!"* struck with deadly accuracy even at great distances, to the dismay and grudging admiration of the others.

On this afternoon, after several games, Fatty's pockets were bulging with all the marbles he had won. Baba's pockets were empty.

"Let's make this more dangerous: if I kill your chief, you lose him to me. If you kill mine, I'll hand mine over to you—my prized marble, my last marble," said Baba. His heart was burning with hope and fear. It was to be a fight to the death.

The air was thrumming with tension, the rest of the boys kneeling all around. Fatty Kong's pocket swelled with their lost marbles and they hated him. They were rooting for Baba, naturally, but the pressure that was brought to bear upon Baba in the role of champion made him nervous and cranky. The opposite was true of Fatty Kong: the greater the pressure, the steadier his hands and heart.

Just at the moment when Baba came to shoot, three black sedans pulled into the square, and out tumbled uniformed police. From the central car, one old man in a long, flowing gown unfolded.

"Hey, that old man there is Wang Yitang! He's a friend of my grandfather," a boy suddenly yelled out, scattering Baba's concentration.

"Shut up, you son-of-a-slave! I don't care if he's the Jade Emperor himself," snapped Baba. "Don't say another word!"

Out of the corner of his eye, cramped in frustration, he caught a glimpse of the old man lifting the skirt of his gown as he wended his way up the steps, to disappear into the Hall of Benevolence.

Well, in a matter of minutes, the game was over. Baba's beautiful chief, with the four swirls of colors, had also fallen victim to the darkness of Fatty Kong's pockets. He was heartbroken.

Fatty gloated over the tribe of boys: he did not smile, he did not say a word, he did not even look at them, but, pretending to take interest in the clouds overhead, he stuck his thick hands deep into his pockets and stirred and stirred the marbles, making opulent clacking noises.

I don't give a darn, Baba groused silently as he removed his schoolbag from a pile by a fishbowl. Descendant of Confucius, indeed! You're no descendant of the sage: Confucius spoke of the grace of yielding to others, you pig.

Baba wanted to tackle Fatty, but he thought better of it: the boy was far too stout for him to wrestle down on his own.

It almost seemed as if Fatty Kong could hear Baba's silent rebukes, for he stirred the marbles in his pockets and made them sing all the more vigorously.

So Wang Yitang was the man escorted by all the police on that day many years ago, Baba thought, staring at the coffin. He was certainly a powerful one. But now he sleeps here in a shabby little box. They all seem to have forgotten that he needed a proper burial.

A sense of dread pricked him, for he knew Wang had not died a pretty death. He had ascended to power with the backing of the Japanese, and soon after their surrender in the summer of 1945, he was arrested by the Nationalist government as a traitor. Wang had not foreseen the total defeat of the Japanese by the Allies or that the Japanese legation would be powerless to harbor him. The winds of Chinese politics being extremely fickle, the foreign legations had been insurance against arrest and imprisonment for the defeated party of a power struggle. The Dutch embassy was a very popular one for fugitive Chinese military and political leaders.

As he was kneeling before the executioner, Wang had pleaded for clemency: "O Great Leader, show me mercy!" But as he repeated, "O Great Leader—" his breath was cut short. A bullet tore into his back and exploded his heart.

For him, too, it had been a fight to the death, but he had been playing against Chiang with his life, not marbles, Baba mused.

"Shot in the back. A violent end. I certainly don't want to sleep with his spirit tonight," Baba said out loud. The other students in the chamber nodded in agreement and scattered.

Where the photographs identified the occupants as lovely young women, the chambers were quickly taken up. A female ghost will be less prone to violence, the young men reasoned.

Baba made his bed in a chamber occupied by an old man and woman, partners in the kingdom of death as they had been in the realm of the quick.

It was bewildering to pillow down next to the dead. Fear lodged in Baba's chest like a stone. He shared his chamber with three students, but he knew no peace on that first night. Dark thoughts could not be chased away by talk.

"This innkeeping for the dead is good business," said Baba, getting a general laugh. "Yah, the dead are less demanding as guests, I'd imagine."

But no matter how they tried to dispel the gloom, their topics always seemed to stray back to the unsavory. One young man, with a sickly hue to his face, was partial to telling stories: "There was this wealthy family in Liaoyang. An unmarried woman in their household had died, and because she was no kin, they did not bury her in the family cemetery. They let her casket rest in an outer room while they waited for her family to come claim her.

"One day, it so happened that a traveling scholar came around at dusk, asking for a place to sleep.

" 'This is good,' the master of the house said to himself. 'We've been hearing strange noises in the darkness. Let this fellow sleep in the room next to the dead and see if he notices anything queer.'

"In the middle of the night, the young man was awakened by a creaking and scraping noise hard by. He peered out from beneath his covers. A heavy breath made the flame of the lamp grow green and diminish to the size of a soybean.

"In the morning, the family found him in a swoon. They saw an open wound on his back, upon which they plastered a piece of chicken skin in remedy.

"In a matter of days, the skin stuck to his flesh as his own, and black stubbles began to sprout. At first he tried plucking them out, but it hurt too much, and he left them to grow into black feathers. . . ."

Similar stories did not help to still the trembling. As Baba imagined he heard the rustle of silk gowns that had been moldering in the graves, wild thoughts of escape stiffened his body as tight as a spring. But it was only someone rising in the middle of the night to use the outhouse.

As the weeks passed, Baba grew accustomed to his extraordinary quarters. If awakened in the early morning hours by the music of the monks, he would walk, guided by the sounds, past the houses of the dead—where the unholy light from candles flickered in the chambers—to the temple hall where the monks were chanting the sutras.

He loved to see the long rows of tall candles, flinging soft halos upon the hairless, smooth faces of the monks, to hear the ringing of the *qing* and the crisp *kok-kok-kok* of the "wooden fish."

Here at the temple the students were given two meals a day, each consisting of a single, coarse *wowotou*—cornmeal roll—and a bowl of gray soup. Sometimes, if they were very lucky, six students hunched over a tin of salmon, leftover American military rations from the Pacific war, doled out to them by relief organizations.

"The abbot certainly eats well. We saw *mantou* of white flour sent to his room, along with big bowls mounding with plump, glistening kernels of rice. Our stomachs are always growling these days. The Nationalist government does little for us, and the city government would soon be rid of us," the students complained in the night. Their hunger grew more acute once they lay down. Baba, curled up on his side, massaged his stomach, vainly trying to dissolve the pain that would not go away.

"Well, we Manchurians have never been popular among folk here," one young man, propped up on his elbow, explained with a sigh. "We inherited their animosity from before our time. Among the handful of warlords who came to rule the Middle Kingdom after the fall of the Qing dynasty was a Manchurian, Zhang Zuolin. He had beginnings as a redbeard. In 1924, after defeating the native warlord, Wu Peifu, he swept here into Beiping. Zhang ruled like a tiger. He chased out the old officials and supplanted them with his own men. Even the old abbot at this temple was replaced with someone loyal to Zhang. Since those warring years, the Manchurians have been known as enemies.

"My father served Warlord Zhang in the mid-twenties here in Beiping, and I used to hear him talk of an incident...." Baba listened carefully to what the fellow had to say.

Zhang Zuolin, having been evicted from Huabei in 1922 after a brief two-year occupation, recaptured the region with new European armaments in 1924. It was at this time that a colonel serving in the Manchurian military came to live in Beiping (then known as Beijing, or

Northern Capital). Wang was his name. He settled on a *hutong* in the western part of town.

Because he was sensitive to the fears of the citizens, Wang took care not to parade around his new neighborhood in his uniform. He wore his civilian clothes, most often a flowing blue gown.

One summer evening, after supper, he took his three-year-old daughter for a stroll. Neighbors had opened their front gates and sat upon the steps, their legs spread wide, cooling themselves with spade-shaped "banana leaf" fans, softly chatting, their bellies full and round. Swarms of enormous gray dragonflies flew low, foretelling rain in the night.

As the two approached the house of a wealthy neighbor, suddenly a barking dog came pelting out of the gate and lunged at them, snapping at their legs. Wang whisked his daughter into his arms.

The dog continued its assault. Wang hurried forward to the pair of servants who were lolling at the gate.

"What's the matter with you people!" he cried. "Why don't you call off your dog?"

The men made no reply; they did not bother to hide their smirks of bored amusement. Since they served in the household of the wealthy, they themselves took on airs too. They looked on in disdain at the dark-skinned man with bulbous eyes. His alien accent marked him as an outsider, a hayseed.

"But the dog didn't bite her," one of the servants said in the characteristically lazy-tongued Beiping drawl.

"It has frightened her terribly."

"But it didn't bite her, did it now?"

"No, but it took a bite out of me!"

"But it didn't do you any damage. And if that were the case, one would simply have to put a few stitches in your gown to set things right." The oily manner and speech of these men were typical of jaded city folk.

Wang carried his daughter home.

The next morning, dressed in full uniform, he proceeded to his headquarters, whence he marched back to his *hutong* with four rifle-bearing soldiers.

They pounded at the gate of the wealthy neighbor until the red door was finally opened a crack by a servant.

Wang looked a different man in his stiff uniform, but upon second glance, the servant recognized him, his expression changing from a scowl to a stupid grin.

"Have your master come before me!" Wang growled.

"He's not home."

"Bring your mistress then!"

After a protracted wait, a youthful woman with oiled hair smoothly pulled back in a bun arrived, yawning; but upon seeing her stern guests, their rifles pointed straight at her, her languorous eyes snapped open. She paled beneath her powder.

"Bring the dog!" Wang ordered.

The woman's ruby lips trembled. The servants fidgeted.

"How's the little miss, your honor? We were certainly worried that she'd taken fright yesterday—"

"Get the dog. Now!"

Hearing the threat of violence in Wang's voice, the neighbors who had gathered just outside the gate to gawk scattered. Some listened with their heads stuck out their front gates; others, through the crack left between the two panels of the doors; the very timid shut their gates entirely, but pricked up their ears to listen from behind their high protective walls.

Gunshots rang out, followed by the command "Let's go!"

The *hutong* fell into a ponderous silence.

"Did somebody get killed?" the quaking neighbors mumbled behind the walls. Eventually, they poked out their heads, one by one, and slinked back out into the *hutong*.

The dog lay dead in a puddle of blood before the gate, which was thrown wide open. Beyond the gate, a screen hid the courtyard from view. There came no sound. Eventually, the household did manage to shake itself out of its stupor, and the servants carried the carcass inside. With basins of water they washed the blood from their steps and then softly closed the door.

From that day forth, whenever Wang—in civilian or military clothes—strode through the *hutong*, every last one of his neighbors slipped inside, afraid to show their faces lest they unwittingly incite the wrath of the terrible Manchurian.

"The citizens of Beiping had great fear of the men from the Northeast," Baba heard his fellow student conclude as they sat within the sallow sphere of candlelight, the grave mound looming over their shoulders. "This and similar incidents only fueled their hatred, furthered the rift. It's been nearly twenty years since warlord Zhang was defeated by Chiang Kai-shek and evicted from this city, but we are still stung by the venom of those years."

In June of 1948, the fighting in Manchuria grew in bitterness and intensity. The universities in the Manchurian provinces that had not already evacuated their faculty and students were now removing them south in a big hurry. Thousands of students had been flown to Beiping by the end of the month, adding to the congestion.

To the citizens of the city, the refugees were an eyesore and a nuisance. "Cut off their food. Starve them out!" they said.

When the city government refused food shipments to the shelters, the students forced themselves on private establishments.

"The rascals are getting out of hand," said the outraged citizens. "They order huge meals in restaurants and then refuse to pay. 'Bill the city! The city is responsible for this,' they have the nerve to say as they pick their teeth. The cooks come after their tough little necks with cleavers; then those rotten eggs return in force and smash windows."

"Since they can't be driven off, these beggars should at least be made useful," others suggested. "If poor relatives come to mooch, they should be given some task like watching the front gate."

The Beiping Municipal Council convened on the first day of July; they made the recommendation that the students be conscripted to defend the city against the encroaching Communists.

The Manchurians' angry response came as no surprise to anyone.

"Assistance comes to us from the Central Government—the Nationalists—not the city of Beiping; it is the Central Government that feeds us, not the folk of this city. The council has no jurisdiction over us. First it tried to starve us out, and now it wants to kill us. The council has no right to force us to bear arms," the students asserted.

Baba listened to the debate swirling like a typhoon in the refugee shelters where the students were congregated. His heart brimmed with a troubled rage. "I have always hated the military, that of the Eighth Route and the government. I've done my best to stay out," he said to the others. "I know life under them both. In the name of saving China, they rob and bully. I know the terror under the Communists, and I know the cruelty of the Nationalists. I trust neither side.

"The Americans sent George Marshall late in 1945, hoping to negotiate a coalition government. He left in failure after a year. The Americans never understood the ways of the Middle Kingdom: as there can only be one sun in the heavens, there can be only one emperor on earth. Mao and Chiang both want to be emperor, so each seeks to murder the other. How could there ever have been cooperation? And it's us—the nameless and unimportant—who are the small animals being trampled underfoot, now that the two bulls have come to fight. No, I won't go willingly into either army.

"But the Beiping Municipal Council has the silent support of the Nationalist military in Huabei. If they want to send us to fight the Communists, what can we really do? We are powerless."

Instead of awaiting conscription, the students organized the Refugee Manchurian Students' League and, with strength in its ever-growing numbers, it took the offensive, demanding a public apology from the council to be published in the city papers. Baba's heart surged with renewed vigor now that the students were on the offensive rather than waiting to be attacked; he no longer felt like prey, limp in the predator's jaws.

The council refused to apologize. The refusal fueled the students' anger; they increased their demand and insisted that Xu Huidong, the speaker himself, personally come forward to apologize.

On the morning of July 5, 1948, Baba joined the massing students in front of the five-storied council building on Western Changan Avenue —Avenue of Eternal Peace—to demand the appearance of Xu. The air was charged with impatience. Baba climbed up the steps and looked all about him to survey the stream of faces, not so much for anyone he knew, but to find out what was contained in all the hearts.

Heaven above! We are more than a thousand strong, our sensibilities, perceptions, and histories spilling into one another's, Baba thought. We are forming a river of will that is gathering force and momentum.

Baba's pulse raced; he recognized the youthful faces as mirrors of his own, understood the anger of their frustrated dreams. He saw the hope that also welled. His sense of aloneness melted away. The more the bodies jostled for room upon the steps, the more his heart clamored in his chest in anticipation of drama. White banners emblazoned with big black characters, which told of the universities represented in the demonstration, were unfurled and waved above the throng. Trolleys came to a halt before the crowd; it would have been futile for them to press on. Pedicabs, being more agile, managed to steer their way slowly through the crowd.

The citizens of Beiping went about their own business, barely cocking an eye at the congregation.

The day drew on. Xu failed to appear. His presence and a few digestible words for the students would have easily soothed their inflamed souls. But the speaker of the Municipal Council hid instead.

It was a furnace of a summer day; the air rubbed against Baba's body, heavy and thick as fur. He was miserable from thirst and hunger. Not even a minor official had ventured out of the building to acknowledge the students' presence. Anger's flame continued to rise.

In the early afternoon, Baba shaded his eyes with his hands and studied two pedicabs approaching from the east. A bare-chested student stood atop each of the seats. As they advanced upon the crowd, they raised their clenched fists high above their heads in a gesture of defiance. Blood trickled from their fists and down their naked arms.

"*Da ta men! Da ta men!* Strike them down! Strike them!" they screamed at the top of their lungs, bared teeth flashing in the sun. Their cries raised the hairs off Baba's neck.

Blood also flowed in rivulets from their faces. Are their wounds real or merely theater makeup to dramatize the plight of the students? Baba wondered.

It was likely the latter, but the mere suggestion of blood ignited passions like stray sparks in a sere autumn field. Suddenly, the young people sitting on the steps of the council building rose in a crescendo of roars that convulsed the very air. They battered down the doors; they stormed into the building, smashing windows with chairs and tables; they cycloned up the staircase, wreaking havoc on the upper floors. In the building were only a handful of secretaries and maintenance workers, sweating fear into their white summer shirts.

"*Da ta men! Da ta men!*" Baba chanted outside the building, and the words banged like gongs in his head. Young men straddling the shoulders of others defaced the sign above the entrance that read "Beiping Municipal Council"; in red they painted over it the words "The Council of the Local Tyrants and Venal Gentry."

Now that damage had been done, the air was spiked with tension—a heady anticipation of confrontation.

"Unity is strength...tougher than iron, stronger than steel...we will fire upon the fascists. Death to those who deny democracy...," the crowd sang.

My father was only nineteen years old, but cynicism had encrusted his soul like a wealth of barnacles after all the interminable wars. He believed only in his own strength and will, and very often his intellect would wander off alone into a fog of doubt against the truth of men. Yet in a moment of song, in a moment of raising his voice up to the sky, his soul was flooded by the prevailing mood: cloudless, hopeful. His face was beaming, flushed with passion for a future that was peaceful and purposeful. He was freed from the cage of alienation. Patriotism, idealism, love—these emotions had been scattered until the united voices of the Manchurians drew them to his heart again.

"Strike down Xu Huidong!"

"Strike down Fu Zuoyi!" roared the crowd, denouncing the military commander who was playing a part in the mischief against the Manchurians.

"The speaker will not show his face," came a grim voice that roused the crowd like the sounding of a horn. The black-browed youth, eyes glinting with bright fire, cut a splendid figure standing atop the steps. "It is mid-afternoon. We can't wait any longer. We know he is hiding at his residence. We will go there and force him out!"

Baba was swept eastward along the Avenue of Eternal Peace in a wave of delirium. With cries of "Down with hunger! Down with oppression!" the students marched in formation behind the banners of their respective schools; Baba fell behind the banner of the Refugee Manchurian Students' League. They stormed past Tiananmen—the Gate of Heavenly Peace, hung with the faintly smiling portrait of Chiang Kai-shek.

Soon they had come to Chongwenmen Avenue. To their right was a large, vacant tract. A gate designed as three archways stood at its southwest corner. It led into the Legation Quarter, where foreigners and wealthy Chinese made their homes. Through the gate, the first residence to the right belonged to Xu Huidong. Baba made his way through the crowd to have a better look.

By four o'clock, thousands of demonstrators had come to assemble in the vacant lot.

"Xu Huidong!—" called a student leader, thrusting his fist high into the air.

"*Chu lai!* Come out!" the crowd joined him to finish the sentence. When signaled, the crowd sat down in silence upon the hard yellow earth as one body.

In front of Xu's residence, jittery guards defended the entrance. Volleys of rocks and bricks were exchanged, Baba ducking to miss a flying brickbat. Several young men were bleeding. Foreigners watching the skirmishes from the upper-story windows of buildings across the way threw down bandages, cotton, and medications.

"Execute Fu Zuoyi!"

"Execute Xu Huidong!" the students cried, their voices turning hoarse, resolve gleaming from their dark eyes.

In the late afternoon, as shadows wrapped about houses and boles of trees, a low rumbling emanated from inside the Legation Quarter. "Something is terribly wrong," Baba said to himself. His heart grew afraid even before his eyes were made aware of the danger. Through the archways he saw the approach of armored personnel carriers.

Helmeted soldiers emerged from the vehicles and set up six light machine guns on stable mounts in a row just beyond the gate; behind their weapons—stomachs flat on the ground—they positioned themselves to fire.

"They're only bluffing; they do not dare shoot!" Baba cried. "Why shoot unarmed youths?" The students held their positions.

As the summer sun began its certain plunge behind the houses and trees, the Beiping police chief, a battalion leader, along with a handful of city officials, came forward through the gate to negotiate with student leaders.

"Speaker Xu is not at home. He will address you tomorrow," they said.

To Baba, standing at a distance, the talk between the two sides appeared cordial. The student leaders came to an agreement and decided to call off the demonstration for the day; nothing further would be accomplished by a vigil except to prolong hunger and fatigue.

"About face!" As the leaders of the respective universities called for retreat, the crowd spontaneously erupted into song: "Unity is strength—"

Baba's heart surged, throbbing with pride, but these three words were all that he was able to sing out before a queer noise erupted. Fear galloped through the crowd like the wind, and hearts went suddenly cold.

The sound was innocent enough—like the abrupt flight of sparrows—the wing beat of many birds. These were not warning shots fired into the sky; the sounds came from guns aimed at flesh.

Baba hugged the ground without a moment of thought. He was just paces away from the guns, but to his good fortune, he had been standing at a wide angle from the gate, behind a row of poplars. Those in the direct line of fire were mostly students from Changbai Normal College in Jilin Province.

There came a huddled silence of amazement, split only by the *ta-ta-ta-ta-ta* of the machine guns, where but moments ago songs of defiance had filled the air.

The taste of dirt was in his mouth. Someone had fallen full upon him. He struggled to breathe. Both his legs were pinned to the ground. The firing seemed to last an eternity, though he later realized that it could not have lasted more than a minute or two. He heard a shrill noise; when he managed to turn over, he saw bits of tree bark skipping over his head against the dusky red of the sky.

When the firing suddenly stopped, cries of pain and panic were heard. A stream of human cries now and again shaped itself in the air, ter-rible and incoherent. The orderly columns had collapsed, and a mad confusion of bodies struggled to break free. Baba scrambled to his feet and ran, his heart beating wildly. A coldness and numbness was in his limbs. He had no other thought beyond an overwhelming desire for life.

But the firing began anew. He stayed on his feet and hurried away in a crouch like a four-legged beast. When the second barrage came to an end, he picked up speed. He could hardly believe he had been spared a bullet in the back.

"Wah! You've been hit!" he shouted, motioning to a young man as they scrambled toward the Avenue of Eternal Peace. The blood was conspicuous across the fellow's white shirt. It looked so unreal, like canvas splashed with red paint in a delirium. When the youth understood Baba's words, he stumbled, then slumped to the ground in a swoon.

Ah, if I hadn't made him aware of his wound, he would surely have stayed on his feet, Baba thought, bending over the body. He dragged the youth to safety.

Looking back toward the darkening square, his eyes found trouble piercing the gloom; he saw staggering shadows. The students had mostly been struck below their waists. He lurched back into the confusion to help.

"You're wounded!" He heard voices that were directed at him. Three young men converged upon him and, grabbing his arms, tried to steer him away toward the street.

"No! No! I'm all right! The blood's someone else's!" he cried.

Along the Avenue of Eternal Peace, the string of wounded stained the asphalt black with blood.

Meanwhile, vendors, shopkeepers, pedicab drivers, and passersby who had witnessed the attack in the fading light cast away their indifference and came to the rescue amid the chaos, the spasms of curses and cries. The pedicab drivers, hale youths and old granddads, pulled the wounded onto their vehicles and pedaled to hospitals at furious speeds.

Darkness had sprung with an unrelenting swiftness. No one dared approach the neighborhood of the gate, where most of the dead lay.

As black night drew down a blind, soldiers stole out through the archways and, hunched low to the ground like scavengers, began dragging away the bodies; they would hide the evidence of murder, cold-blooded murder, for the students had been felled from behind.

Baba did all he could manage to do for the wounded that evening. As the dead could not be recovered, he and the lucky ones returned to the shelters.

Students sat singly or in small groups in the sultriness of the garden, away from the walls that pressed in on them, each thinking his own thoughts, bowed in grief.

The weeping in the night disturbed Baba's reflections and sent them reeling back to Manchuria and the family he could not return to. The cold cornmeal rolls he was gnawing on stuck in his throat.

When weariness wholly came down upon him, he closed his eyes; he dreamed of raising his fist and straining to sing "Unity is strength . . . ," but the storm of gunfire overpowered his voice, and he awoke in the dead hours, chilled to the marrow.

AT MID-MORNING ON January 31, 1949, Baba watched victorious Communist soldiers march into Beiping, threading through Xizhimen, a western gate in the ancient city wall. First came a pair of tubas, at the forefront of the proud, if ragtag, marching band. Though the instruments were dented—the tubas most obviously so—they had been spit-polished to a bold shine. Then came the ponderous show of cannons, Japanese and American made, towed by swaybacked horses, followed by teams of six soldiers in gray quilted uniforms, who worked the big black guns. But cannons brought only glazed looks to the eyes of the Beiping citizenry.

Baba made his way to Xisi, an intersection famous for its four ceremonial archways. There the crowd jostled to hear the young men and women of the drum corps strike up music—*Dong!-Dong!-Dong!-Dong!*—their instruments like red watermelons, slung across their chests, resting against their hips. These were sharp performers, with movements spirited and precise. The din was not unlike the joyous and lucky noise of Spring Festival, which pounded to the beat of one's own heart. Sparrows were scattered from bare branches and sent wheeling into the sky.

Since 1900, when the troops of the Western powers had come to suppress the anti-foreign Boxer uprising, and the Empress Dowager had fled disguised as a crone on a mule cart, the citizens of Beiping had witnessed countless authorities march in and out of their city. In the wars of the ensuing decades, they neither cheered when a new warlord arrived, nor lobbed abuse at the defeated as they fled.

The coming of the Communists was but another spectacle in a long string of ordinary spectacles. The crowd stood silently gaping, no more enthralled by the parade than by the wedding and funeral processions which had occurred regularly in peacetime.

Few had imagined the Communists would devour Manchuria and then threaten territories in Huabei to the south.

But the Nationalists made one fatal mistake after the Japanese surrender: Chiang Kai-shek had refused to induct the generation of excellent professional Manchurian soldiers trained by the Japanese.

Chiang, a man of the South, would not accept their sincere plea to join his army, deeply doubting their loyalty. He was reminded of his old antagonisms against the Manchurian warlords Zhang Zuolin and his son, the Young Marshall Zhang Xueliang.

"Whoever Old Chiang will not take, Old Mao will warmly embrace," the Communists said as they campaigned. Their ranks swelled with the best fighting men to be found anywhere in the Middle Kingdom.

When civil war raged in Manchuria, the diminutive soldiers sent from the hot and humid southern provinces (whom the Manchurians dubbed "monkey soldiers" because of their dark skin and stature) were no match against the natives on the frozen battlefields. Their bodies shivered violently in their baggy uniforms. Needless to say, the Manchurians knew their own terrain; having sprung from that soil, their thick hides were adapted to the fierce winters.

Once the great Northeast fell to the Communists, with their ranks strengthened by the steely Manchurian soldiers, they swept their way south of the Great Wall.

When Tianjin, to the southeast of Beiping, fell to them in the fall of 1948, Fu Zuoyi, the commanding general of Huabei, sat brooding in the ancient capital. He decided to order the retreat of his crack troops from the city of Zhangjiakou, which lay to the northwest of Beiping; but their numbers were decimated as they tried to make their way back. With the loss of both Tianjin and Zhangjiakou, it was as if Fu's pair of wings had been clipped.

Beiping itself soon came under siege. As access to Nanyuan Airport was cut off, Eastern Changan Avenue was plucked of its trees, cleared of trolley cables, and made into a runway. The Nationalists ordered flights from Nanjing to evacuate high-ranking government officials and celebrated scholars.

It did not take long for the people of Beiping to know the biggest demon of the siege: hunger. They, unlike the Manchurians, were not in the habit of storing grain. Each morning they went to market for the necessities of that particular day. Emptiness soon came to grind like a stone in their bellies.

The voices of the food vendors wandering the *hutong*, singing the names of delicacies, went silent and were sorely missed in the night, when the mouths of the mah-jongg players would water upon hearing the cry of *"Taaang-saaann-jiiaaao-di-maaan-tohhh!"*—triangles of steamed pastries filled with hawthorn jam.

Twenty years ago, Fu had tasted the bitterness of the besieged. Over the course of a harsh winter, his soldiers became skeletal and developed signs of beriberi: their bellies protruded and their legs became so swollen they could neither fight nor flee. The women of the city had begged Fu to surrender: "We are eating the husks of rice and sorghum and fermented distiller's grains . . . even rats, the ones that haven't starved to death. Please think of our children!"

Fu did surrender to the enemy, and after he had made his escape on a bicycle, he hired a poor but talented poet to sing of his courage under fire; the poems were printed in the newspapers, and the publicity made him famous throughout the land.

From this cruel ordeal two decades before, Fu Zuoyi understood the madness of resistance in Beiping now. In the throes of battle, the ancient capital—the heart and soul of the Middle Kingdom, raised over seven hundred years ago —would surely have been tumbled by cannon fire, and her true wealth—her talented artists, poets, intellectuals—starved to death or killed in the fighting. Neither the Nationalists nor the Communists wanted to bear the responsibility for her destruction, and so both sides breathed a deep sigh of relief when Fu met the conquerors outside the city wall.

On that last day of January, after watching the performance of the drum corps, Baba made his way back to his latest in a string of shelters, a building near Xidan on Shifuma Street, to collect his twice-a-day bowl of cornmeal mush. His heart was leaden: he was again mired in Communist territory. It was only a year and a half since he had taken flight from Manchuria on foot.

Within a few days of the arrival of the Communists, Baba read a bulletin posted by the new Beiping Military Commission. "All Nationalist military police and spies must immediately surrender themselves and turn in their weapons," the dictate began. The string of words that followed tightened around Baba's soul like a noose: description of punishment to those who would not comply.

There is a particular Chinese horror of *luan*, disorder. Disorder under Heaven provides conditions ripe for revolution. Disorder was a friend to the Communists when power was not theirs, but now that they had come to power, this devil had no place by their hearth.

The finest way to maintain order was to root each man to his own community; members would bind themselves to one another with their prying eyes and eavesdropping ears, reporting any transgressions to authorities. The Communists' system of state-sanctioned backstabbing was cousin to the brainchild of a minister under Qinshihuan, the first emperor of a unified China. The *baojia* system had worked so flawlessly that when the minister himself fell out of favor and tried to flee execution, he could not escape from the web of his own creation. Emperors over the course of nearly two millennia had developed the *baojia* system of social control into high art. It had been enforced to a greater or lesser degree depending upon the mood swings of the successive dynasties. The Communists had inherited the ways of yore, and their mood was black.

Beiping was a nightmare for them to administer. Not only were there Manchurians, but also a vast number of refugees from other cities in Hebei and other provinces. They did not belong to any community and were in constant flux.

In the anxious days that followed, the Communists tightened their grip over the populace, and neighborhood committees, which ac-counted for the movement of each man, woman, and child, mushroomed. One sprang up on Shifuma Street in what was formerly a private home. Baba was handed a notice by a grim committee member which declared, "If you are a citizen of Beiping, bring your residency paper as proof. If you are not a legal citizen of Beiping, you must come and fill out forms to apply for temporary residence status. If you do not comply, you will be imprisoned."

A temporary residence permit was just that. The Communists pressured everyone to return to their native towns and villages. With each passing day, Baba felt more keenly the loss of his freedom of movement.

With anxiety mounting in the city, the refugee student shelter was transformed. The former camaraderie had crumbled and was replaced by stealth. The ways of the new rulers had come to pervade society like a bloom of algae choking off oxygen in a body of water that had been teeming with life. Baba sensed a muffled uneasiness as his fellow students, those with whom he had sang the words "unity is strength," trickled away one by one. Each had quietly packed his belongings and disappeared without saying a word to anyone. Each person, with averted eyes, hugged his thoughts to himself.

Where have they gone? Baba wondered. It was frightening not to know. Perhaps they had gone back home.

But Baba did not have a home to return to.

What are the chances that I would be permitted to remain in Beiping? he wondered. And if allowed, do I really want to stay? Is it time for me to flee southward?

Why are there so many intelligent people who do not wish to take flight—like Eldest Brother? They say they believe in the new government.

His brother had been evacuated from Manchuria along with the majority of the students and faculty of his university in the summer of 1947. He had glided into Beiping by plane roughly a month after Baba had limped in on bleeding feet. The pampered eldest grandson of the fallen, scattered House of Yang continued to receive monetary support from the Patriarch's secret funds. But Baba saw little of him in the ancient city, for his brother had his own circle of fashionable friends among the intellectuals.

Eldest Brother, when we last met, hinted that he had joined the Communists. What mo-

tivates him to do so? He has seen for himself the destruction and bloodshed in Manchuria.

Well, there's that saying, "All crows under Heaven are equally black." The Nationalists aren't any good either, there's no doubt about that, but at least in their chaotic territory I can get lost in the crowd. No one would bother with an insignificant person like me. There would be room to move about, room to breathe....

Baba took solitary walks in the northern section of the Imperial City, through the dilapidated temples, along the banks of frozen lakes marked by black stems and pods of the withered lotuses. He tried to gaze into the future but could see very little that would help him to decide his next move. To stay in Communist territory would not be easy, but it would be far less punishing on him physically than trekking south in the middle of winter, venturing into an unfamiliar landscape where his way would not be illuminated by the bright and steady light of a certain destination.

No one could help him make the decision whether to stay or to go; the burden of the morrow fell to him alone.

It was during this quietly frantic time that Baba came to visit a clansman. He was a young officer of the Liberation Army—as the Communists now referred to their forces—and had marched into the city, triumphant, on that last day of January. The vigorous, handsome youth spoke of the compassion of the Communists. "You must join with us and destroy the parasitic landlords, those who suck the blood of the people," he exhorted.

Baba studied his familiar features. Does he really speak from the heart? he wondered. A woman in her fifties, aged beyond her years and sitting in a corner of the boardinghouse room, coughed. An anger that could not be voiced welled inside Baba's chest. He stared at his companion, but his eyes did not see. The past pricked his soul.

In 1938 Baba was nine years old. His father had moved the family to Beiping. They rented a house near the old Imperial Park, on the same *hutong* where a rich and powerful branch of the Yang clan lived.

Men of this branch had served in the high offices of the Qing dynasty and the ensuing Republican government. The master of the house was an old man Baba addressed as Second Great-Great-Grandfather. He had the look of the Yang men: tall, with bushy eyebrows, large luminous eyes. He lived with his concubine, a woman as beautiful as the full moon in early autumn. As a prelude to chatter, her face always bore a bewitching smile. She was thirty years her husband's junior, and it was her charm and peerless social skills that helped him maintain his popularity and prominence in high society. They had four sons.

The youngest was a comely child whom Baba called by name—Xiao Hao—but only at school. On all other occasions Baba, according to custom and etiquette, respectfully addressed him as Youngest Great-Grandfather. They were both in the fourth grade.

Filial piety, which guides a Chinese in all his relationships, entails respect for one's senior and reciprocal love and affection on the senior's part for the younger. But filial piety flowed only one way from Baba to his immature, but senior, clansman.

Around the time of the Spring Festival, Baba and Xiao Hao played with toy swords and sported brightly painted masks of characters from opera, legends, and literature. Baba was careful not to strike Xiao Hao with his sword, but the other came after him in earnest.

"Suffer this, you devil!" Xiao Hao cried in operatic language. He had taken on the part of a legendary warrior whose weapon of preference was the *biao,* a dartlike weapon. "We are the great Huang Tianba!" he cried, referring to himself in the plural. With these words, he picked up a piece of brickbat and hurled it with all his might at Baba, striking him in the ankle bone.

Baba scrunched down and rubbed the hurt, tears welling in his eyes. He could feel the foot going numb. His face, under the mask, expressed misery; under the mask of the other boy there was glee.

At home, Baba hid his injury from his mother, for it was his parents' policy to scold first and ask questions later. He would not find soothing words to assuage the pain. And besides, even if his parents were to sympathize, they could not possibly complain to Xiao Hao's family, who had seniority in the Yang clan.

But the foot swelled like an eggplant, and his mother saw that he hobbled in the morning. He was taken to a doctor.

For two months Baba limped. His condition was obvious to Xiao Hao, but not once did the boy comment upon it.

Each morning, except Sundays, Baba would stop by the house of his wealthy kinfolk, there to be joined by Xiao Hao for the walk to school. Baba stood between a pair of stone lions that guarded the entrance and tugged the bell cord threaded through a hole in the red door. A girl about his age would come to open the gate. She wore her hair in pigtails and was dressed in the coarse, dark blue cloth of a servant.

Old Cow, his rich relatives called her.

Old Cow had small eyes and a dark, round face; she looked like a long-forgotten pancake that had been put away in the gloom of the pantry. Her movements were wooden, without a hint of grace.

Under what circumstances her family had sold her Baba never knew, but it was certain that they were in dire need of money. Perhaps her father had died, and the little that her mother earned as a caretaker of a cemetery near Baiyunguan, the White Cloud Temple, a lonely quarter outside the city wall where the wind wailed and kicked up yellow sand, was not enough to feed all the children.

A ten-year-old slave girl could be bought for ten yuan; Old Cow was purchased for a sum equivalent to four sacks of flour.

Second Great-Great Grandfather, who comported himself with dignity, never struck Old Cow, but everyone else below him in the household pecking order found her a convenient target for their abuse. Even the other servants, following their mistress's example, struck her or kicked her without provocation; she was a whipping post upon which to vent their own defeats and disappointments.

Baba sometimes asked her, "What's your real name?" or "How many brothers and sisters do you have?" But she never replied. She kept her eyes downcast. Violence was the sole message the world had imparted her. Like a battered, dumb animal, she seemed no longer capable of recognizing human speech except in the form of commands.

"Mother, what will become of her when she grows up? Isn't there anything that can be done for her?" Baba asked Nainai one day. "It's so unfair. Our relatives—they don't like the sound of the brass door knockers—they say the pounding is rude. Visitors tug on the bell instead, but it rings in Old Cow's room behind the kitchen where the kindling is stored. She's disturbed by it night and day. It's as if they've tied that bell directly on her ears. It's simply beastly!"

"Hai," Nainai said and sighed. She wiped her hands on her apron and then felt Baba's face. "I don't know, Number Four. All I know is that when a child bumps his head on a table leg, a mother's heart aches as she nurses the bruise. If someone slaps the child, anger fills her entire heart—she feels more pain than if she'd been the abused one.

"I don't know what can be done to help her . . . the girl was born to eat bitterness. It is her *ming*—her fate mandated by Heaven."

Old Cow was the first to rise in the mornings. She could hear the cook snoring on a nearby cot as she dressed. She swept the courtyard under the winking stars. Standing on tiptoe, she fed the goldfishes in the enormous bronze bowls and then watered and tended the pomegranate tree.

When Baba stopped by on his way to school, Xiao Hao was often still in bed. Old Cow squatted on the floor and helped him pull on his stockings. If the stockings came to be twisted, the boy—eyes still puffed with sleep—screamed "Imbecile!" and landed a kick in the hollow of her chest, knocking her to the floor. Old Cow's face remained immobile, as if numb to pain, but the fat tears that tumbled from her eyes and splotched the floor said otherwise. She silently picked herself up and continued to assist her young master with his clothes.

"Oh, why did I get stuck with this brat," said Baba silently, clenching his teeth. At New Year, he was made to kowtow to Xiao Hao, who sat imperiously on a carved rosewood chair, and accepted Baba's obeisance with obvious glee.

How he hated to walk with the boy in the mornings; but both the boy's mother and his own father forced him to watch over this half-pint great-grandfather of his. Sometimes he would purposely skip out on his duty as escort and wander alone to the Courtyard of the Luo Clan to buy breakfast, savoring the food and the solitude. At least I've saved Old Cow one trip to the gate this morning, he thought as he munched on sesame cakes.

After the boys had gone, Old Cow dusted the rooms filled with precious antiques and teak furniture, and emptied the chamber pots and the spittoons. The eldest son had married, and it also fell to her to wait on the demanding newlyweds.

At midday, the master and mistress finally awoke from their fattening, golden sleep. After Old Cow attended to their hygiene, she helped the cook, a big-bellied, cantankerous woman, in the kitchen.

A stinging slap snapped her head backwards. "You wretch!" cried the cook. "If I catch you nodding off again, I'll pare your hide.

"Hurry this on over to the master and mistress. If I hear them gripe that the soup's gone cold, you won't see a thing for supper," the cook said, shaking a rice bowl. "Now get!"

"Old Cow, run out and fetch the rickshaw boy; I'm going shopping in Wangfujing," her mistress would order after the midday meal.

If the woman chose to rest at home instead, Old Cow prepared the opium paraphernalia for her on a silver platter. She worked the opium tar onto a tiny silver spatula and held it over the flame of a lamp until it softened and bubbled, ready for the pipe. Once it was in the pipe, she held the bowl over the flame. When the tar began to give off smoke, her mistress, reclining against pillows on her bed, put her mouth to the silver stem. The pupils of the woman's large eyes, under coal black brows, constricted to pinpoints as the drug came to enslave her. If the procedures were not attended to with care and the necessary deftness of hand, the mistress's rosebud lips parted to reveal sharp white teeth and to spew out even sharper words. Old Cow was duly kicked by bound feet shod in dainty red slippers of silk.

Not a minute of the day passed without some task to fulfill.

After supper, the master and mistress entertained the wealthy and powerful of Beiping at the mah-jongg table. Old Cow poured tea, lit cigarettes, and continually swept the floor of melon seeds and fruit peel. Her face was drained of blood. She stared at the floor, never gazing about her at the laughing faces, bluish through the haze of the tobacco smoke. She shook her head and widened her eyes to prevent the velvet curtain of sleep from drawing across her mind. Between games, the guests smoked opium and she attended to its preparations. And at midnight, she served them food that the cook had fixed in advance. When the last of the guests had departed, and the gate was finally locked, it was but a few hours to dawn.

If the master and mistress had decided to attend the opera instead of entertaining at home, Old Cow awaited their return, eyeing with envy the two pampered Pekinese dogs curled in slumber. A blow to the head greeted her for being slow to open the gate when the master and mis-

tress returned in the small hours. Old Cow served them their late-night snacks before they retired to bed. When she finally stumbled onto her own cot, hers was the sleep of the dead.

The year Baba and Xiao Hao entered the sixth grade, Old Cow was no longer to be seen. A new girl opened the gate in the mornings.

"Where is Old Cow?" Baba asked.

"Oh, that Old Cow," said Xiao Hao, screwing up his eyes. "She went home." Baba never heard anyone in the boy's house refer to her again.

Some months after the slave girl's disappearance, Baba heard Nainai say, "This morning, a peasant woman walked all the way to our house from the White Cloud Temple."

" 'My daughter told me not to ask her old mistress for help, but to come find you, dear lady,' she said to me. How tired and vague her eyes seemed.

"When I followed her outside the gate, I saw Old Cow in a hired rickshaw. Her head was swollen like a pumpkin. Her eyes were mere slits. When I lifted the filthy quilt that covered her, I saw that her fingers were as thick as sticks of carrots and her arms purple and as big as logs.

"I gave the mother a sack of rice and some silver for a doctor. 'Do not seek the witch doctor but a real doctor,' I said to her. When she took the money, she said to me, 'Merciful Buddha, my girl is too sick to pay you her respects; I'll do it for her instead.'

"*Tian-yah!* Heavens! To my chagrin, she fell at my feet and knocked her head on the ground with such energy, I could hear the *ge-dong, ge-dong, ge-dong* as her forehead struck the floorboards." Nainai slowly shook her head, and wiped away tears with a sleeve, leaving a big wet blotch on the indigo cloth.

A couple of days later, the mother returned. Nainai gave her a few yuan for paper spirit money to burn at the temple. Old Cow was dead.

By the time Baba had finished sixth grade, the Japanese had seized his father's gold mine, and the family moved back to the ancestral plains of Manchuria.

When Baba returned to Beiping as a refugee student in the summer of 1947, nearly a decade later, he found out that Second Great-Great-Grandfather had been dead for many years. His opium-addicted concubine, now in her fifties, had smoked away the family fortune and was living in two rooms in the back of a boarding-house. Her quarters were devoid of all furnishing except for a bed, a table, and two chairs. Her face was as barren of beauty as the room.

She must have smoked away the home and all its costly curios, Baba guessed when he first came to visit.

She kept no more servants. The woman cooked a bowl of noodles with her own two withered hands. Even though she was destitute, she had not relinquished her genteel habits. Tiny porcelain dishes filled with condiments, relishes, and cold pickled salads graced her table.

Out of courtesy, she invited Baba to partake of the meal. Baba was hungry but knew his manners.

"It is only one paltry bowl. How could I possibly ask her to share the little there is? I'd be stealing food from the mouth of a penniless widow," he said to himself.

He had come to pay his respects bearing no gifts to his elder, breaching *li,* the inviolable etiquette of Confucian society that guides daily life like a religion. He was keenly aware of his failure of *li.* He had not even been able to buy her half a pack of the cheap cigarettes to which she had become addicted, once she had no more antiques and paintings to sell. She extracted pleasure even from the butts, using a cigarette holder to draw out every last possible puff.

"Your youngest great-grandfather has joined the Communists and is campaigning in Shijiazhuang, a strategic crossroads southwest of Beiping," the woman told him.

When the Communists entered the city, triumphant, Xiao Hao was among them. He had been made an officer in the Liberation Army.

"Yes, you must join with us—bring justice to those abused by the rich landlords," Xiao Hao repeated, shaking Baba from his memories of Old Cow. "You must join to liberate the oppressed!" The room had no heat and the young man's breath steamed.

Since Xiao Hao's return, Baba had come a handful of times to visit him at the boarding-house. His gray padded jacket proudly bore the insignia of the omnipotent Beiping Military Commission.

"You must learn to love the people!" he exhorted as he handed Baba several pamphlets, one of them titled "On the New Democracy," written by Mao Zedong.

Baba studied the face of the zealot. The cold eyes of the child he had known were now the eyes of a cold man.

What do you know of the people? Do not instruct me to love the people! These angry words were at the tip of his tongue, but he did not unleash them. "In Manchuria, I have not seen 'the people' mistreated; the lies justify murder and the wresting away of home and property," Baba said to himself.

"At the House of Yang, Uncle Zhao, who had beginnings as a redbeard, and Uncle Yu, who was hired to break the ice in winter over the old well—they always ate their meals with the family. They celebrated Spring Festival within the embrace of the family. They were family! When Uncle Zhao decided to strike out on his own, the Patriarch gave him a gift of his favorite dappled mare and a good deal of land.

"No, in Manchuria I have never seen folk torment others as you did Old Cow.

"Certainly this aged society of ours has its disgraceful flaws which allow abuse, but it can't be cured by wholesale murder of those who own land. Cruelty and greed fester in the hearts of men—rich and the poor alike.

"Old Father Heaven has eyes—I do not doubt it for a moment. Justice will be done in the universe. Change is the only thing certain, and change will always come. Those with fortunes will one day lose them; those in want will one day come to know abundance...."

"Those are nice boots you have on," said Xiao Hao suddenly, breaking Baba's train of thought. He pointed to Baba's feet and threw a darting, almost imperceptible, glance over at his mother.

When Xiao Hao left the room, the woman came forward from her bed and mustered a tattered remnant of her old smile. She said, "Yes, you know your youngest great-grandfather has told me how much he admires your boots. Can you give them to him as a gift?"

"But these are my only shoes...Eldest Brother just gave them to me when he saw that I was shivering from the cold," Baba said to himself.

"He could certainly use those fur-lined boots now. How can he get by on those cloth shoes of his?" the mother continued. The coquette was now sallow-skinned, with gray circles under her eyes, but she was still in possession of a honeyed tongue.

"You must know that everything your youngest great-grandfather does, he does for the good of the people." Baba knew it had been her habit to coerce, to cajole, to wheedle gifts from others even while she had been wealthy.

But Baba understood her heart now: she was pleading with him as a mother. Since she could not afford to buy a pair for her precious child, she could certainly ask someone else for them —even if she had to take unfair advantage of another mother's child.

How could he refuse? She was his senior by four generations. When he was a tot living in Tianjin, she had descended upon his family for a visit, wearing a cape of black brocade lined with mink, her hair slicked back in a netted chignon and ornamented with jade flowers. It was as if a great ancestor, a revered family god, had revealed herself unto them in a vision. The family had prepared for days for her call. When she arrived, the children kowtowed at her feet and ran.

"Hadn't she said to me when I fled here to Beiping a year and a half ago, 'Number Four, do not apologize for not bearing gifts. Times have changed. If the world was as before, how could I think to let you sleep among the dead at the temple? I—your great-great-grandmother —am the one to feel my shortcomings.'"

Baba had been deeply touched by her speech. Perhaps she had spoken out of empty *li*—out of courtesy, out of habit—but sincere or no, her words had warmed him, a homeless youth in a city where not a soul cared whether he should live or die.

"I—I have none other to wear than these," Baba finally replied haltingly, staring at his feet.

"I'll give you another pair to wear," the woman said.

In March of 1949, when the cicadas were still burrowed deep in the frozen earth—so painful was the cold, as the Manchurians say, it felt as if cats were chewing on one's fingers and toes—Baba made up his mind to go away. He began his slow trek south, away from the Communist lines, wearing a pair of thin cloth shoes.

BABA SANK DOWN onto the steps leading to Beiping Station. He hugged his bundle to the hollow of his chest, which thumped with a dull pain, an indescribable desolation that made his breathing shallow. Watching the decaying sun enflame the yellow tiles of the tower across the way and the shadows piling up in gray mounds at its base, he felt paper-thin, brittle. The ancient edifice had once defended the Imperial City, raining sheets of arrows down on marauders, but in modern times, its deep windows were boarded up and its interior converted into a cinema. Ten years ago, his family had gone there to sample the newfangled silent movies.

I left Manchuria sure that I would go back, but tonight I am stealing even farther away, Baba thought. All that he had ever known in life threatened to vanish from him forever. In time of peace, a young man with an unusually live and sensitive spirit and an abiding love for learning would have winged into the future like a swallow in spring; now he was pressed down into the dust by the immense weight of the here and now.

There was no need for him to consult fortune-tellers: the morrow could not possibly have held out a kernel of blessing to him. And yet raging deep inside my father's soul was the indomitable spirit of the Monkey King, ready to vault into Heaven and consume the peaches of immortality, one after another, ready to wage war against Heaven itself for the prizes that he felt were due him. This spirit urged him onward.

He arrived in Tianjin just past midnight, the station dark except for a few hand-held kerosene lamps that bobbed along the platform like feeble, straying thoughts at the edge of sleep.

I am immaterial—an insignificant ghost, a dilute spirit that must sneak away under the mantle of darkness without a sound.

Tianjin had been without electricity for many months. Buildings damaged by shelling hunched in the dark and listened to their own wheezing. Woven rush mats covered cavities and fissures in walls and ceilings, and planks made sightless the broken windows.

The Tianjin-Pukou line had been destroyed, but on the morrow Baba would roughly follow the railroad south on foot.

He surmised the Communists had not seized the southern lands, for he had read in the Beiping papers that they were recruiting men to cross the Great Yangtze River more than two thousand *li* away. He, too, had to cross the Yangtze: his freedom lay there.

"There's no turning back now. There's only one direction to go, and that's south," an inner voice urged. "As long as you keep pumping your legs—as long as your heart continues to hum—you will cross the Yellow River, and you will ultimately cross the Yangtze."

It was early March, spring according to the lunar calendar, but the snow had only recently melted away. It was still cold enough to freeze a wayfarer on the road, leaving him as stiff and lifeless as an old washboard. Baba stumbled into the yawning night splashed by stars and curled up in sleep against a wall outside the station.

In the morning, he took a short train ride to Jinghai, the last depot at the southern limit of Tianjin. Walking beyond Jinghai, he saw no mule carts, heard no squeak of horse wagons. Grass that held its breath the entire winter under snow was drained of life, sucked as white as bones, and thrust out in ragged tufts from the sallow earth.

He had grown accustomed to fear—it hounded him like the dry shuffle of his own footsteps—but now it was loneliness that nipped at his ankles. One tiny soul lost under a sullen sky that breathed of its own enormousness in hollow undertones. Old man sun did not risk letting down his golden whiskers.

I am too small. Even less than a grub slinking through the grass. I am an inconsequential speck of dust that will be carried away at the whim of the wind, Baba thought. If the sun momentarily touched a warm finger to his back and unkinked it, the landscape seemed friendlier, and he would say to himself, "A tiny speck has its virtue: easy to slip away." But when he spied a village sprouting out from the folds of hillocks, then the voice inside him cried, "Too big! You are far too conspicuous. If there are soldiers, their eyes will pierce you."

Men ventured beyond the threshold of their homes even more rarely with the arrival of the Communists. Their vistas encompassed only the brim of their hats. To visit kinfolk in another village, one had to have sound reasons before a road pass would be issued by the authorities. All individual movements were strictly overseen.

Before his departure from Beiping, it had been necessary for Baba to wrangle a road pass from the People's Police. It would have been easy for him to come by papers for a return to Manchuria—all refugees were pressed to go home—but for travel to Shanghai in Nationalist territory, well, that was another matter. What sort of business could a Manchurian student possibly have in Shanghai? Each man, woman, and child filled a very specific niche in the vast jigsaw puzzle of the landscape. He was exposing himself to arrest in requesting to go where he did not belong.

I must risk it . . . go to the police station . . . it's crowded there, pressed full of people wanting documents. In the confusion, they just might issue me a road pass to Shanghai, he thought. As they say, "When the water is murky, there are fishes to be had."

At the People's Police he filled out his request form and waited in the lobby full of sharp elbows and knees. He waited the entire afternoon, his body clenched like a stone. When he finally heard his own name called out, he wished it had not been.

But he had nothing to fear; he met with neither questioning nor threat of jail. The administrators were so overwhelmed by paperwork, they impressed a crisp red seal of approval without even glancing at the details of his request.

Now Baba was traveling with a legitimate pass. As he walked away from Tianjin, he sensed a darkness, swiftly deepening, stretching, bending all its will toward the South. It was summoning all men to its power.

And if I make it all the way across the Yangtze, will the South still be free? he wondered.

He hurried along the dusty roads that stretched from one scraggly village to another, but soon located the old Grand Canal, the main north-south waterway of the North China plains. He climbed up and walked along its dirt bank. Only vessels of shallow draft could travel its irregular course. It was now much less important than in ancient times, and over the centuries it had filled up with silt. He knew that it meandered from Tianjin down to the great Yangtze; it would ultimately lead him to the South.

Upon its gray water, Baba saw no sail, no barges pulled by horses or mules. Gusty wind raked up waves. A poplar, warted and black, leaning against the sky like an old broom, grew in isolation on the opposite bank.

If the waterway brought him near a village no larger than a handful of huts—smoke slanting out of chimneys, the faint fragrance of human habitation—he still feared a checkpoint; so he crept along the interior slope of the bank, along the water's edge, fearful of interrogation by soldiers. During the day, unless forced to ask for directions, he evaded the villages, but in the evening, he was pressed into the company of men by the cold and loneliness.

Oftentimes, sensing the rambling course of the old canal would force upon him a longer march than necessary, he descended from the bank to walk the village roads. These were ribbons of yellow unraveling before him, roads of light, fine dust that smoked when fanned by the gentlest breeze. With each step, he sank into the soil, which made his progress slow and strenuous, like paddling upstream. An occasional crow, flying over the fallow fields, ripped a corner out of the silence with one startling *gua!*

If he heard a sound like the grumbling of Grandfather Thunder chasing after him, he leapt to the roadside, for bearing down upon him was sure to be a military truck, dragonlike with its staring, round headlight eyes and leering grill mouth. The beast coiled down the narrow road, its roiling, throbbing yellow body of dust trailing into the distance. If there were other vehicles tailing the first, one could not see them in the maelstrom.

These American-made trucks had been seized from the Nationalists. The captured drivers, trained by the Americans, were no less valued by the Communists: who else would be able to operate the vehicles? And more important, who else had the skill to maintain them? The men of the Liberation Army, who began their careers as guerrillas making surprise raids, certainly had no familiarity with the workings of such beasts.

The drivers were treated like kings. And because the hearts of these mercenaries were for sale, it was an easy matter for them to undergo a chameleonlike transformation and turn Red. They were acutely aware of their esteemed position. They did not brake for anything. As they flew by, their faces became contorted into a scowl, a passionate hatred for the lowly creature creeping along the road on its own two legs. Had it been convenient for them, they would have kicked Baba into a ditch like a flea-bitten cur.

Smothered by the long, dusty tail of the dragon, Baba slotted his eyes and held his breath. He stood motionless, straining his eyes southward, long after the vehicle had become but a beetle on the shelf of the horizon. "If I manage to make it across the Yangtze, will the South still be free?" came the pestering question that soughed in his ears like the wind.

———

While he had traveled the roads of Manchuria, he had come across Communist checkpoints only at the edge of town. But now in Huabei, he was often surprised by soldiers standing sentry over the road of the Communist advance, far from areas of human habitation.

Several days out of Tianjin, as he strained up an incline in the road and rounded a bend, he heard a voice that snapped in the stillness like the one damp firecracker left over from a celebration: "*Zhan zhu!* Halt!"

A lad in the shade of a hillock seemed to have sprung from a hollow in the ground. He was barely taller than his rifle, the butt of which he struck on the ground with great authority. He was a slightly more mature rendition of a bare-bottomed country boy with big ears, hunting for birds with slingshots. He wore an oversized army shirt with big pockets, which may have been from the uniform of a captured Nationalist. His trousers fluttered like pennants.

"*Jian cha, jian cha!* You're to be inspected!" The soldier hopped from one foot to the other in his excitement. His eyes glinted feverishly and the flush in his face rapidly spread to his ears and neck. He had been more startled by the encounter than his captive.

Just like a grasshopper in the furrow of a field, Baba thought, sizing him up. How long had he been standing in this barrenness, waiting to spring on a poor fly like me?

Baba slowly set his bundle down, playing upon the other's eagerness. He peeled back the cloth like a piece of fruit. "Only clothes and books," he explained as he revealed the contents.

Something caught the youth's fancy, for he craned his neck and blinked hard. Reaching down slowly, he picked up a thin little volume printed in Beiping, containing the lyrics of popular songs. He balanced it upon the palm of one hand, and with the other pawed its pages. He must have had a few days of schooling, for in a small wispy voice, he crooned, "When will my love return to me? . . ." He was oblivious to everything but the tune flowering in his head.

"He's got to be a recent recruit to 'liberated district'—Communist-controlled territory. How else could he have learned these new songs from the city?" said Baba to himself, studying the fellow out of the corner of his eye.

He recognized the same uneasy dithering on the part of this soldier as he had seen in all the others who had stopped him: each had coveted what belonged to him, but would not openly ask for the prize. The Communist leadership mandated that the soldiers of the Liberation Army were not to take a single needle, not a strand of thread from the people.

Am I not of the people? One soldier snatched my fountain pen, and that was far more costly than a needle, Baba mused. Greedy soldiers had lightened his load, relieving him of many useful items, such as notebooks and pocketknife.

"Comrade, if you are interested in this songbook," Baba said, touching the youth lightly on the elbow, "take it as a gift." Elongating shadows that warned of a frost-bound night made his heart burn to be on his way.

"We men of the Liberation Army do not sing these songs," replied the lad without lifting his eyes from the book.

"Yes, but I know the soldiers of the Liberation Army serve the people, and in service of the people, you can sing them these songs," Baba said, slipping him a smile of innocent craft.

The little fellow's mind seemed unable to round the corner of the face-saving proposal. He was silent for a moment, the slow wheels turning. The wind kicked up dust devils at his feet. He pursed his downy lips.

"We in the 'liberated district' do not sing these tunes," he declared once again, furrowing his brow and tapping the pages with a brown finger.

"Hai, good music is good music. It can be sung anywhere," said Baba.

The soldier stared without expression at the pages, but Baba knew there was passion there. Then after a moment of teetering silence, the youth snapped closed the songbook and slipped it inside one of his big pockets, all in the wink of an eye: the wheels of his mind had fully negotiated the corner. With the other hand, he brusquely waved Baba away. "Beat it, scram!" His dumb gesture said it all. Now that Communist tenets had been violated, it was best to be quickly rid of the witness.

Baba tied his bundle and hurried on his way. The sun was growing feeble. Only for a brief hour at midday did he feel its warmth. He pulled up the collar of his jacket; the wind cut against his face and hands like blades.

Aside from obtaining a road pass before departing Beiping, he also had to find a way to weight his empty pockets with a few silver pieces. Elder Brother had given him two costly winter garments that he had brought out with him from Manchuria: a foxskin coat and a bunchy sheepskin gown whose whorls of fur were patterned like white chrysanthemums. With the arrival of the Communists, it had become inappropriate for anyone to wear clothing that flaunted wealth. It was now "fashionable" to wear old clothes and look proletarian; hands callused from honest toil were preferable to soft ones, smooth and white from counting money or limply holding a pen. The beautiful garments fetched only five silver yuan at the pawnshop. In good times they would not have been sold for less than four hundred silver pieces.

From a vendor outside Xuanwu Gate who sold used military gear and clothing, Baba purchased a water bottle and a khaki canvas jacket to keep out the prying fingers of winter. The jacket was American made and had been discarded by a Nationalist soldier. He also purchased an assortment of shirts and trousers. Clothes would be more useful to him than money in the countryside. Clothes were difficult for the peasants to come by. The cities, the manufacturing centers, had been held under the Nationalists, and few goods were able to pass out into the Communist-controlled countryside. Conversely, grain from the countryside could not reach the city folk. The country folk went naked; the city folk went hungry. Baba would

be able to exchange a piece of clothing for a warm meal and a roof over his head at night.

The two silver yuan that remained to him, he sewed into the linings of old shirts for safekeeping.

As the afternoon of another day drew toward evening, he instinctively yearned for rest and protection, as when he was a small child. Baba saw the silhouette of a walled city in the distance. Dusk had already gathered within its high ramparts.

As the road swept to the right, he came upon a wayside inn. "Too many days without proper rest . . . I daresay I deserve a hot meal and a night's mend on a kang," he said softly to himself. "I'll spend one of the two silver pieces I've hidden away." The coins were popularly known as *datou*—"big headers," so named for the corpulent profile of Yuan Shikai, the deceased first president of the Chinese Republic, minted on the face.

But as he approached the flat-roofed mud building, an inexplicable chill pricked him. Maybe the inn seems a bit queer because the front entry is set on the west face instead of on the traditional southern, he thought. As a geomancer would say, that's bad *fengshui*—bad flow of wind and water. He hesitated a moment in the gloom and pushed open the door.

Three men whispered together conspiratorially, sitting cross-legged upon the kang. They eyed him doubtfully, with their long-stemmed pipes planted into their mouths.

"Landlord!" Baba called out, for he saw no one that fit the title.

"Oi!" came a gruff reply from deep in the back of the building.

"I need a room for the night!"

From an open door at the far end came grunts of acknowledgment: *"Hao! Hao!"*

"Will you take *datou*?" blurted Baba. He had no paper money issued by the Communists.

Someone must have been cooking bread rolls in the kitchen, for a big cloud of steam, bearing a sweet and yeasty fragrance, suddenly burst into the room from where the voice had come.

"Ooh! This here is an old-time 'liberated district!' It's illegal to carry silver. If you've got any *datou* on you, hand 'em over NOW!" An enormous fleshy head, bronzed like a roasted pig, stretched out of the fog. The eyes were so large and set so far apart, it seemed the man could glimpse his own ears. He resembled the greedy and vile innkeeper in the classic tale *The*

Water Margin, where guests were minced up for dumpling fillings.

"Hey, you Nationalist son of a rabbit!" the man cried after him as Baba turned and fled out the door.

Farther down the road, he came across more inns, but he had lost all inclination to inquire about a bed.

Night was fully upon him and the temperature dropped like a stone. A sickle moon sliced through the rack of clouds. He walked another seven or eight *li* and knocked upon the door of a hut where a needle of light pricked through a window.

"Lao Da Niang! Lao Da Ye! Old Mistress! Old Master!" Baba pleaded outside the door.

"Gan ha de ya? What is it?" a creaky country voice answered.

"I'm a poor student. Can you give me a place to sleep for the night?" The door opened and a woman, nearly doubled over by the weight of her years, stood before him.

"Come in," she said.

The room had no furniture except for the kang, upon which a hollow-bellied old man rested. A few broken crocks sat squatly on the dirt floor. The smell of terra-cotta and dust.

"Grandmother, a small token for your generosity," Baba said. He extracted a piece of clothing from his bundle and offered it to her.

Years sloughed off her face as she broke into a grin. She carefully examined the white cotton shirt by lamplight.

"*Hao. Hao.* Sit. Go ahead, sit on the kang. Put yer feet up," she said with markedly greater enthusiasm for her guest.

"Have you had supper? Ah, we've got some leftovers. I'll warm 'em up for ya." She noiselessly hobbled toward the kitchen. Baba followed and helped to start up the fire.

Posted above the stove, where the Kitchen God and his wife traditionally presided, were two portraits of men with great heavy faces, one of whom wore an army cap. The images were crudely drawn in charcoal upon ragged, yellowing paper, much like the ones he had seen done in pencil or ink, hanging over the stoves of the homes where he had stopped in to ask for water.

"Granny, is that the Kitchen God and his wife?" Baba teased.

"Ah, we in the 'liberated district' are not to have the Kitchen God anymore," said the old woman dryly, no regret in her eyes, which were like raisins.

"Then who are these?"

"One is Mao Zedong. The other is Zhu Dei." She pronounced "De" as a rustic "Dei," and Baba had to keep from laughing.

"Why aren't you allowed to have the Kitchen God? Why do you now pay homage to Mao and Zhu?"

"Those above—they tell us to have these fellows up on our walls instead," she said and pointed to the portraits with a knobby, arthritic finger.

"'Those above'? Who're they?"

"Those above...those above...you know, the officials."

"And what magic do these two venerable beings possess? What do the officials tell you about their powers?"

"They say one represents strength of mind, and the other, skill in war. They say that these two will bring a good life to us."

While Baba slowly chewed the gray pancakes the old woman served, he gazed fixedly at the new gods in the dim light until they disappeared from his vision. Memories filled his heart entirely.

Fourth Uncle, the bachelor uncle, had taken it upon himself to police the children at the House of Yang.

"Hey, you mongrels! Good-for-nothings!" came his familiar growl. "Who's able to take a nap with all this racket!" He was a man with a long nose, slightly hooked at the end, and heavy brows spilling over his eyelids. A willow switch was in his hand.

Baba, Third Brother, and two cousins needed no further explanations. With looks of terror shot across their faces, they turned tail and ran for the gate at the back of the North Garden. They ran for their lives. A mad pattering of small feet.

"I've told you devils to keep quiet!" The men of the Yang clan were tall; one of Uncle's long strides covered more ground than several of their short, strained steps.

They were gasping for breath as they reached the gate; one of the cousins fell across the high threshold that prevented the chickens and ducks from escaping the garden, and the other three piled on top of him, their arms and legs struggling, like pinned insects. "Idiot! Why'd ya have to fall!" the top two cried.

Fourth Uncle lashed Baba ruthlessly with the switch, for it was he who lay on the top of the pathetic pile of bodies. Uncle seized him by the scruff of his neck with his thick, hot hands and pelted him with blows to the head, back, and bottom. He whipped all the boys in turn with the switch.

Oh, how awful it was! Tears of fear. Tears of pain. High-pitched pig sounds just like those at the slaughterhouse. Then the pint-sized prisoners of war, their faces screwed up in the agony of the vanquished, were marched back in single file to the courtyard, there to stand motionlessly with their hands clasped behind their backs within chalk circles that Uncle had drawn on the ground. Perhaps there would be no dinner.

But when the long-awaited twenty-third of Twelfth Month rolled around, suddenly the willow switches disappeared. The broom handles, the big kitchen ladles, the pipe bowls were no longer applied to tender young heads and bottoms in punishment, but were reserved solely for their intended uses.

This day marked the beginning of twelve days of euphoria for Baba. No more spanking. No more scolding. It would not do to mar the celebrations of the Spring Festival—the lunar New Year—with the caterwauling of unhappy children. (Fourth Uncle, however, was still keeping tally of misdemeanors, the punishments to be meted out after the holidays.) The stringent rules and regulations of the House of Yang would be swept away. Luscious lawlessness would prevail, for the grown-ups would be busy in their drinking and gaming.

Every bone in their bodies, down to the tiniest in their toes, immediately sensed the freedom—air swelled their chests, their torsos and limbs felt expansive, their joints loose and limber.

It was on this day that the Kitchen God made his yearly ascent to Heaven, rendering his report on the family's behavior to the number one god in the sky, the Great Jade Emperor.

Throughout the year, from a shelf high above the kitchen stove, in a temple made from the stalk of the sorghum plant, the paper god and his mate watched the goings-on in the home.

The God was the keeper of the kitchen fire and, naturally, the one who keeps the fire also keeps the belly sleek, round, and full; for this

reason, he wielded great power and was indisputably hailed as "the Lord of the Household."

From the morning of the twenty-third, a great slaughter ensued—a flurry of chickens, ducks, and geese came under the cleaver. An unfortunate pig, reclining upon its back with its four legs tied together, was given the coup de grâce by a professional butcher. The blood of the animal was drained into tubs, which later came to be mixed with sesame oil, soy sauce, and "five spices" for sausages.

Baba could not get enough of the fragrance, fleshy and keen, inflating the kitchen. Frying fat. Fresh noodles. He inhaled deeply, tired of the winter diet of cabbage and soybeans. He and the other children were sent to the storage room, there to polish the brass hotpots with ash to gleaming. Their small hands performed the duty with ardor; the children knew of the approaching evenings of feast.

But that night, when Baba, Third Brother, and the three cousins sat down to celebrate at a table of their own, to their horror, Fourth Uncle came to join them with a face like a judge from Hell, capable of turning soy milk into bean curd. The boys considered themselves the most wretched beings on earth and wanted to weep into their bowls.

Second Uncle had made an unexpected return from Shenyang, and Fourth Uncle, the youngest among his siblings, had been bumped from the Patriarch's honored table. Thus demoted, the man was hardly in the best of humor.

Fourth Uncle sported a pair of fashionable wire-rimmed spectacles known as "tea glasses." They were not corrective lenses but circles of crystal, tinted brown (thus the name). They were de rigueur for those with pretensions to refinement and learning.

Baba hated these glasses with a bitterness that curled the hairs on his toes. Because of the tinting, he could not gauge the direction of his uncle's critical gaze.

Uncle was not in the mood to eat. His nose dipped toward his bowl, but his eyes rolled around in his head like searchlights.

Dried shrimps and crabs that gave a taste of the sea to the soup stock swam about in the boiling hotpot. The crustaceans hadn't enough meat on them to get stuck between one's molars, but the children's hands itched to snap them up because of their colors and shapes, their swirling appendages all neatly intact. Fourth Uncle's frosty glare kept their chopsticks at bay.

Twice-cooked pork, striated with fat—a

winter delicacy—also tossed about in the pot. Baba nibbled the lean and left the fat in his dish. When he reached in for another piece, his Uncle's chopstick clamped down onto his with a clack!

"Eat the fat!" the man demanded. "You are not to waste good meat. What do you intend to do with it, leaving it in your dish?"

In Baba's entire eleven-year career as an eater, he had never learned the art of consuming fat. Were he to swallow the slippery white piece of flesh lying cold and iridescent on his plate, it would fling itself out of his gullet like a fish leaping out of water, followed by the bok choy, tofu, and bean vermicelli he had already ingested.

When he looked at his uncle's sullen face, he knew the man was in no mood for disobedience. Spring Festival or no, Uncle seemed perfectly willing to deal him a blow. But before he could lock his jaws, he heard the words "Feed the dog with it" scamper out of his own mouth.

"What!" roared Uncle.

The other boys silently stared into their bowls, shrank into their clothes, fearful of attracting thunderbolts by sitting too tall.

"Eat it!" hissed Uncle. Baba glared at the offending piece of blubber. Nausea rippled in his throat.

But deliverance suddenly came in the form of an aunt, bearing a plate of pickled cabbage for their table. From the opposite end of the table, out of Uncle's reach, Baba hopped off the kang and ran away.

Thus a perfectly good Spring Festival dinner, which he had awaited all year long, came to a sorry end.

After the rich evening meal, family members lumbered into the kitchen behind their stomachs, sucking their teeth. The Kitchen God and his wife were escorted down from the shelf to a table positioned in front of the stove. Nainai lit three sticks of incense, two sticks of red candles. She placed three tiny porcelain cups filled with sorghum wine before the temple, along with oranges, pears, and a large bowl of candy made from wheat. She kowtowed three times to the pair, and then placed their temple on the earthen floor.

During the day, the children had constructed miniature horses from the soft white core of the sorghum stalk to bear the god and his wife up to Heaven. The journey would be great, so they made sure the man and wife had plenty of fresh horses. These sorghum steeds now encircled the temple on the floor.

The womenfolk chanted,

The name of the Kitchen God is Zhang.
He rides a horse and carries a gun.
On the twenty-third of Twelfth Month,
He rides to Heaven to greet the Great
    Jade Emperor.
Speak no evil; speak no ill.
Sing only praises about our clan.

All year the Kitchen God had been witness to squabbling, talebearing, lying, and perhaps even stealing. He would soon have an audience with the Great Jade Emperor and would reveal each of their uncharitable, cramp-hearted deeds. He would tell all. The womenfolk, therefore, daubed the mouth of the god with sticky wheat candy, hoping to seal his tattling lips or, at the very least, sweeten his words. For good measure, they sealed his wife's mouth too.

After the song, the temple and the horses were set afire. In one great whoosh, everything was reduced to smoldering ash, which Nainai, with one deft sweep of the broom, removed to join the writhing red embers in the kitchen stove. The god and his wife would not return until the following week, on the thirtieth—the last day of the lunar year—precisely at noon, when a fancy new temple would be awaiting them on the shelf above the kitchen stove.

During the send-off ceremony, the children had squirmed with impatience for the distribution of the sesame-coated red-and-green-striped candy, which were pulled into luscious, glistening strips or shaped to look like miniature pumpkins. Now they could eat their fill.

Because the treat rapidly melted in his hands, Baba placed the uneaten portion in a small basket and hung it outdoors at the end of a string, under the icicle-encrusted eaves, where dried string beans had dangled in the summer. He made sure to count the pieces in the basket so that he would know if his brothers or cousins had helped themselves to his sweets in the middle of the night. When he went to bed, his tongue, lips, and chin were coated red and green and scabbed with sesame seeds.

Baba shared a kang with Third Brother and two cousins. Sleep was not in them for all the excitement.

"The Kitchen God will most certainly say lots of nasty things about Fourth Uncle," Baba announced, his memory pricked by the day's hurt.

"But we've stoppered his mouth. He won't be able to say a thing," one of the cousins answered.

"You guys don't know, but just before my mother sent them up in flames, I picked off the candy stopping up his wife's mouth," Baba replied.

"What good will that do? He's the one who's supposed to talk," the cousin said.

"Haven't you ever seen her cherry mouth? That's the blabber kinda mouth," said Baba. "You know how our mothers and aunts sit with their heads stuck together, whispering and cooing and breaking out in big laughter. Women-folk will talk. They always do. She'll tell the Great Jade Emperor Fourth Uncle's been cruel to us."

"Well, what if the Great Jade Emperor really wants to help us, what will he do to Fourth Uncle?"

"Oh—he'll put a big stone in his path and make Uncle trip on it and break his stupid glasses," said Baba.

"That's hardly enough!" the cousin argued. "I think the Great Jade Emperor should make him fall on his face, break his stupid glasses, and grow him a bruise the size of an egg right in the middle of his forehead."

There was a moment of silence, imaginations whirling away in the darkness. Third Brother squirmed; he did not like the talk.

"Aiya, but then Uncle will come to look just like a gander with a bump between his eyes!" piped up the younger cousin, surprise in his voice. He had not said a word until this moment.

The portrait of Fourth Uncle as a stupid, waddling goose stirred laughter deep into their bellies. They kicked the wall and pounded the kang with their small fists in delicious malice. Then they quieted down, suddenly afraid that Fourth Uncle, prowling next door like a giant spider on the wall, had overheard them.

Baba pulled the heavy cotton quilt up to his nose and closed his eyes. He saw the god riding the sorghum horse that he himself had crafted —the one that had been lovingly, painstakingly detailed with hooves and a swishing tail.

The god had chosen his horse from among the thousands and thousands of other white horses made by all the children in the city, for it was the prettiest one among all that were borne to Heaven upon sinuous swirls of velvet smoke.

Up, up, up into the great blue liquid expanse and through the emerald-encrusted Heavenly

Gate to where flowers bloomed for tens of thousands of years.

And once inside the dazzling palace hall, far beyond the clouds, kneeling before the Great Jade Emperor, the Kitchen God swallowed the sticky candy plugging up his mouth, cleared his throat, and recited the mountain of wrongs and abuses that the grown-ups had heaped upon Baba's innocent soul.

The vision of the past receded. Looming before his eyes were the gray portraits of Mao and Zhu, mortals who had come to relieve the Kitchen God and his wife of their faithful, age-old watch over the hearth, over men's hearts. These two fellows had come to silence the voices, stopper the mouths of folk with sticky fear. Will they manage to keep the bellies smooth, round, and full? Baba wondered.

That night the old folk shared their kang with Baba. He was shaken awake several times by the *hrrrough* of the husband's roof-rattling cough, which became more insistent with the approach of dawn.

No sooner had the east revealed a tiny wedge of red than the old woman roused Baba from slumber. The old man was already up and anxiously pacing the floor.

"Hurry. Best not to lose time. Best be chasing the road," they said to him nervously. They knew the mortals, newly standing sentry over the kitchen stove, had set a different standard of charity, frowning upon hosting strangers at one's hearth. The old woman shooed him out the door as a housewife would chase a stray rooster from her kitchen.

Baba shouldered his sack and hurried south. Time was pressing, for even as he slept, the forces of Mao and Zhu had not been idle.

爸，的漫画

As THE DAY grew weary over the fields, Baba heard the faint jangling of harness bells, the *dia, dia, dia, dia* of tiny hooves, and the squeak of a cart. Looking over his shoulders, he spied a shaggy donkey, the diminutive, soft-eyed northern breed with long frosty lashes, pulling its load. In the thickening dusk, Baba could make out the creature's white eye rings and the single red tassel that adorned its brow band.

"Ah, how I wish for lodging, however lowly. Even fleas and bedbugs would not disturb my sleep," said Baba to himself. The cart soon caught up with him. The driver sat on the sideboard, one leg crossed on the shaft and one leg left dangling.

The donkey hung its guileless head and flicked its tail, paying Baba no mind; the driver, once even with Baba, cocked an eye at him but did not speak.

He does not look a man of the city, nor wholly the rustic. A tainted version of the latter. Likely someone who runs goods between town and country, Baba thought.

"Brother, what's the city up ahead?" he asked the driver.

"Deizhou," said the man. He pronounced "Dezhou" with the wild lilt of a Shandong Province native. Baba had left Hebei behind a handful of days ago. The farther south he would travel, the stranger the dialects would sound to his ears and the more alien he would feel.

"Are we close? How many *li* to Dezhou?"

"Ai, far. Twenty at least."

"That's still more than three hours' worth of walking," said Baba under his breath. He was sorely disappointed. His calves thrummed with pain. It was suddenly chill, and a crescent moon could be seen faintly like a white scar.

The driver continued to keep pace with him, an obstinate shadow at his side.

Baba understood the desire wrapped in the man's dogged silence, but he had no intention of spending one of his precious *datou* on a ride.

Neither was he willing to exchange a piece of clothing. "I can't very well split a pair of trousers down the middle and give the fellow a leg of it. Better keep walking," he told himself.

After a while, seeing that there was no business to be had, the driver tapped the donkey's rump with his stick and hurried the beast on without a nod of farewell. *Dia, dia, dia, dia*, went the donkey's dainty hooves. *Ga-lang, ga-lang*, went the harness bells, making a sound of evening, a sound of vague yearnings. Baba's heart quivered.

Even as the cart distanced him, he could still make out its silhouette as it emerged from the bends in the empty white road. He drew a deep breath, determined to hasten his own steps so as to keep the cart in sight and see where it would lead him.

A handful of *li* down the road, he saw the unmistakable outline of a walled city rise out of the land, black against a sky festooned with the first stars.

"That must be Dezhou. The fellow lied. It's hardly the distance he said it'd be."

On the thinly settled, prosperous plains of Manchuria, a stranger upon the road would have been offered a ride for free, but Shandong Province—land-scarce, and famine and plague prone—was a place of an altogether different heart.

"Well, no matter. I'll certainly be able to find food and shelter soon." He lost sight of the cart once it sliced deep into the opening darkness.

Shortly, the road came to flow along the base of the city wall, sections of which had crumbled, the bricks lying in black heaps on the ground.

"This place must've suffered some fighting in recent years. And it seems to me the city was heavily fortified in ancient times: its walls rise far taller than those of other cities I've come across since leaving Beiping."

He saw that it would be futile to seek lodging here outside the wall: there was no lamplight beckoning. He could not go farther without food and rest.

"I'll have to take my chances and go inside the city." He searched for an entrance, but instead of finding a gate, he saw that a large section of the wall had been sliced away, leaving an abrupt gap like a missing front tooth. "The cut in the wall itself is perhaps two or three centuries old."

As Baba stood outside the opening and peered in, he saw flickering points of light like holes in the black mantle of the night. When he stepped through the gap and walked forward, the lights multiplied and bobbed like the phosphorescent will-o'-the-wisps he had seen as a child, swirling and tumbling about among grave mounds.

"My eyesight is growing worse; the lights jump about." He did not mind rising early, but he hated walking in the dark: years of malnutrition had resulted in night blindness.

He stopped and squatted, to steady his gaze.

"Ah, that explains it . . . lights reflected on a moving stream or a small lake swept by the wind. But it's a long way off and the ground is uneven—full of potholes—and bricks from the tumbled wall are all over the place. I must take care not to fall into the water."

He picked his way down an incline and felt his way along the curve of the bank toward the lights, drawn rapidly forth by voices and scents that wafted his way with a change in the wind.

In short time he was bathed in the warm glow of a night market, and his heart rejoiced. Oil lamps dangled from peddlers' stalls. All kinds of savories beckoned: noodles; golden fried dumplings; crispy pancakes; fluffy white bread rolls; and honey-colored roast chickens, sweating luscious beads of fat. Merry gatherings hovered like moths around the more popular fare.

Baba walked the limit of the stalls and then backtracked to review the offerings. The sizzling, spitting dumplings prompted pangs of hunger most mercilessly; the sour twisting he felt inside threatened to unravel the seams of his stomach.

"City folk probably won't take clothes as payment. Maybe there's a black market for my silver," he said to himself.

He saw a stall, empty but for the vendor wearing a dark apron and a brown felt cap, who was bent like a sickle over the griddle, spinning pancakes. Baba took courage, approached, and whispered, "Elder Brother, do you take *datou?*"

The man's eyes came immediately alive like a pair of slippery fishes. He dipped his head and scanned left and right; seeing that there was no one within earshot, he murmured in a quick, small voice, "*Xin, xin. Gongdao, gongdao*—yes, yes. I'll be fair to you; I'll give you a fair exchange."

Baba sat down at a table. "Give me two and slice 'em up for me."

As the man stacked the resulting triangular wedges of pancakes, Baba reached into his bag. From the sleeve lining of an old shirt, he squeezed out a large silver coin and handed it to the vendor. The man palmed it and quickly slipped the money through the collar of his jacket, deep inside his shirt.

"Have something hot with that." The vendor ladled Baba a bowl of soup, satisfaction palpable in his caressing voice.

This done, the man pulled out a wad of greasy, tattered bills of varying sizes and denominations from his apron pocket and, under the lamp, began counting. He counted twice with his crusty yellow fingers, nodding and mumbling to himself all the while.

The man came close and whispered, *"Gongdao...si de, gongdao.* It's a fair exchange...yes, a fair exchange. I've already taken out what you owe me for the food." There were onions on his breath.

He said *"gongdao,"* which only means he's shortchanged me, thought Baba. But what can I possibly do? I'm at his mercy. It's illegal in a Communist district to have silver. I can't very well eat the coins in place of pancakes for supper.

Once he had had his fill, he rubbed his happy stomach, wrapped the remainder of his pancakes in a towel, and went in search of lodging.

He came to a large, barnlike building. Upon entering, he saw a man with a bald patch and a face blackened by a three days' growth of beard, who sat behind a table equipped with an abacus, an ink slab, and some brushes. Dull with weariness, the fellow let out a yawn that revealed gaps where his teeth had rotted out.

"Landlord, can I get a bed tonight?" Baba asked.

"Da gan fang," the man replied, smacking his gums, obviously not the garrulous sort. "We don't provide bedding."

"That's fine."

Lamps hanging from beams illuminated the hall. Along the length of two walls, rush mats covered a bunchy layer of hay. Mice rustled beneath. Baba looked for a secure corner, but found them all occupied by recumbent forms.

Once he settled on a spot, he untied his shoes and removed them. The shoes rarely left his feet; he would put them back on before going to sleep for fear of thieves in the night.

As sleep sneaked up on him, he heard the squeaking and crunching of hay as someone walked onto the mat. He pried his eyes open and saw a man dusty from travel, but with a peaceful and benign expression on his square face.

The stranger set his things down, unrolled two blankets, and snapped each in turn vigorously in the air. Then, taking one of them, he folded it in half, lengthwise, scrupulously smoothing out the edges. The other blanket he folded into a square and placed at the foot of his bed. He shaped a pillow from his sack.

Even in such unsettling times, this man pays exquisite attention to the details of his life.

Seems to be an experienced traveler—knows how to take care of himself, Baba thought.

When his nest was finally built to his liking, the man plumped down with a great, juicy sigh, crossed his long legs, and felt for something inside his shirt pocket. He pulled out a cigarette, lit it, and narrowed his eyes as he took a deep drag.

Baba sat up to put his shoes back on his feet. His neighbor watched him with keen interest as he pulled his big toe back, through a hole in his socks.

"Brother, where did you come from?" the man asked him.

"From Beiping."

After falling silent for a moment as if to consider Baba's words, the man suddenly volunteered, "Dezhou roast chicken is certainly delicious."

Baba cocked his head and studied the man's face, dusty except for the area around his mouth, shiny with grease—roast chicken grease, no doubt.

"Yes, roast chicken is good," said Baba, swallowing hard. "Brother, where're you headed?"

"*Hui laojia*—returning to my native village. Home to Manchuria. Going home to my wife and son. Been on the road far too long. My mother and father are getting on in years."

"I'm from Manchuria also—been away almost two years; my home is in Xinmin."

"Me, I'm from further north: Jilin."

Once Baba had his shoes on, he settled down to sleep, pulling his jacket over his shoulders. But his neighbor was in a talkative mood.

"How's travel in the North? What's the situation like? What are the road conditions?"

"The railroad is open between Beiping and Tianjin and also from Tianjin north to Shanhaiguan. North of there, I don't know."

Baba saw that the man was silently calculating the number of days it would take him to reach home. "You only have about two weeks' worth of walking to reach Tianjin; if the trains are running north of Shanhaiguan, you'll be with your folks in no time."

The Manchurian smiled at the good news, blew smoke out of a corner of his mouth, and meditated on the patterns clinging to the air.

"Where're you returning from?" asked Baba.

"Jiangnan—south of the River."

This revelation shook the sleep right out of him. He sat up. The man had come from land south of the Yangtze, the free South! "How's the situation down there?" he asked.

"What place are you aiming for?"

"Shanghai."

The Manchurian drew long and hard on his cigarette before he spoke. "As I see it, you should forget about the South. Go home. Family's important. I've been to Wuhan, Changsha . . . just about every big city in the last three years. Right now, it's all chaos."

The subject animated him; his voice grew loud. "Here, have a cigarette."

"I don't smoke," whispered Baba. "Brother, please lower your voice. Everyone's asleep."

"Oh, oh, yes, yes." The man looked about him wide-eyed. Happy to be headed home, he found it hard to contain the immensity of his joy. He skillfully worked the remaining stub of his cigarette into the tip of a fresh one.

In a hush he continued, "Chiang Kai-shek stepped down in January. Li Zhongren, the vice president, has taken his place." Once again the topic seemed to ignite the man's passion; his voice began to stretch louder and louder.

"Chiang is hiding out but is still manipulating things behind the curtains. Li is pretty much powerless—no soldiers to back him up. You know, the Communists have prepared a million

men to cross the River. They won't be able to hold 'em back."

"Brother, Brother!" Baba hissed. "Don't talk of Chiang and Li here. Don't talk so loud. This isn't the place. You must be careful mentioning those names."

Once again, the man lowered his voice. He hovered close. "Do not go to the South, my young friend. Go home. Believe me, I know the situation well. Believe me, the Nationalists are worse than demons." The man batted his eyes unhappily and flicked away cigarette ash from a sleeve.

"South of the River, each man thinks only to save himself. *Wan le! Wan le!*—The end! Finished!" He made a slicing motion with his hand across his outstretched neck and bared his strong white teeth.

The bad news crashed like cymbals in Baba's ears, and he did not wish to hear more. He lay back down, feeling tired in every bone. He tried to go to sleep, but the man's words *Wan le! Wan le!* continued to buzz in his ears. He could no longer entertain illusions of peace in the South, nor the vague hope of attending school.

Yes, I know they're corrupt, but at least one's able to walk about freely in Nationalist territory. That's better than the chokehold here in the North. The man's far too excited about getting home and doesn't see that he's running from the mouths of tigers into the mouths of wolves. . . .

If the Communists do not cross the River before I do, maybe I'll have a chance to go even farther. An idea suddenly took shape in his mind: "Maybe I'll even leave China. . . ." It was like tossing a pebble of hope to another shore. He had no plans—no thoughts about what land would possibly offer him refuge. With these hopeful musings, he fell asleep.

He was awakened in the early morning hours by a sound like air forced out of bellows —*whoola-whoola-whoola*. It was his neighbor snoring. The lamps had been extinguished in the night. He rubbed his eyes and saw a faint glow of daylight through the papered windows. He could not afford more rest.

The innkeeper, stretched out on his cot behind the table, was also snoring with his mouth sprung open when Baba walked past him and out the door.

In the eastern sky the sun was a red blister. The vendors had dissolved in the night like inhabitants of a ghost city, and fog hung over the water. He walked through the gap in the wall and continued down the road, the breeze riffling the dead grass beaded with dew.

He walked all day. When the crows fell out of the sky, and bats, flitting here and there, replaced them, he came upon lodging in the environs of Pingyuan.

If this is the city written about in the *Romance of the Three Kingdoms* (a fictionalized history filled with intrigue and thick with swords, spears, and arrows) the city is—let's see now— somewhere around seventeen hundred years old he mused.

The innkeeper, gnawing on a chicken bone, measured Baba up with a pair of squinty eyes embedded in a small, sharp face.

"The folk here'll tell you I'm honest in all my dealings—so have your rest for a night under my roof," he said and crushed the bone between his molars, making sucking noises.

Baba was led beyond the kitchen to his room, in which the stained kang gave off the scent of road and sweat.

"Here we don't grudge the bed fee if lodgers call for food from our kitchen," said the innkeeper, his forehead oozing grease. His hands were tucked deep inside opposing sleeves.

"What have you got to eat?"

"Noodles."

Eagerly he awaited the food, but when a large steaming bowl was brought to him, he was disappointed: there was more broth than noodles, and what swam in the bowl were broken pieces. He chased the segments around like a man scooping for eels in a pond. "Well, at least the broth isn't too bad," he groused. He was still hungry and ordered another bowl.

Once he finished this, his stomach sloshing like the sea, he lay down and closed his eyes.

He had no inkling how many hours he had slept when he was jolted out of a beautiful dream: visions of fried dumplings, the oil spitting merrily in a pan.

"*Wei, wei!* Get up!" He felt a jabbing in his ribs.

He opened his eyes to someone shining a lamp into his face. The tip of his intruder's nose was darkened by a birthmark.

"*Suan zhang!* Time to square up!" cried the innkeeper's son, rattling his abacus.

For two paltry bowls of noodles, he doesn't need the help of an abacus, thought Baba as he sat up and rubbed his sore ribs.

"One bowl, three mao; two bowls make six mao; and a night on the kang comes to a total of nine mao! Wei! you owe us here nine!"

"Nine? That can't be. And bed fee? But the man told me I wouldn't have to pay that." Baba blinked hard.

"You devil, what place have you come across that does not charge bed fee? No one stays for free. Nine mao! You hear me? Nine mao!"

Baba reached reluctantly inside his jacket and pulled out a wad of bills, dark and unpleasant smelling, but no matter how many times he counted the money, he came up short.

"It's all I have," he said. This was not the truth, of course; one silver yuan remained to him, sewn into the collar of a shirt, but he could not possibly part with that.

"Anh, so you want to make things unpleasant, do you? I'll turn you over to the authorities if you're thinking to fool with me."

"I don't have any more money, I tell you. Here, take it. You can count it yourself."

"All right, all right, we'll take what you've got. We're decent folk here. Anyone in Pingyuan County will tell you that. Hmh, you look like a rotten beggar, anyway."

The man pocketed the money and went thudding out of the room, leaving his victim simmering with unvented rage.

"Bandit!" Baba muttered in the darkness. "What he took from me was far more than what I owed."

He tossed about fitfully. In the utter silence of the night, anger sawed away in his ears like a field of crickets. The sense of justice was deep in him. Even as a child, he had a keen understanding of fairness in the marrow of his small bones.

When Nainai and the children joined Yeye in Tianjin after Manchuria fell to the Japanese, they lived in a section of the city called Dawangzhuang—Big Village of the Wang Clan—in a spacious house of five rooms, the grounds enclosed by a wall. Across the way was a similar compound, but the rooms were split among three different households, one of which was the Zhang family.

The wife hailed from a poor district south of the city known as Yangliuqing—Willows Greening—famous for the colorful New Year prints which decorated its homes during Spring Festival, and for its beautiful women. Many an impoverished family sold its daughters into prostitution. Mrs. Zhang's husband was only a minor clerk in the Tianjin city government, but she was all too happy to have escaped the poverty of Willows Greening and, of course, to have eluded the brothel.

Mrs. Zhang was as delightful as the first golden burst of forsythia in early spring and, like Nainai, was in her early thirties. Baba was more than a little in love with her, for she had lots of nice smiles and soft words for him.

Because Nainai lacked knowledge of the customs and etiquette of the new city, she relied heavily upon the friendship of Mrs. Zhang to fill in the gap.

Nearing Spring Festival, many a peasant came knocking on the front gate, selling dried stalks of the sesame plant. The burst pods had already released their seeds and looked like pale flowers.

"We have come to bring you *cai*," the peasants announced at the gate. Nainai looked at the small bundles, but hadn't a clue as to their use; they certainly had little worth as kindling.

"As you know, *cai* (kindling) is a homonym of *cai* (wealth)," Mrs. Zhang explained. "The peasants have come to bring you prosperity in the New Year. We in Tianjin arrange the stalks in vases and hang strings of paper coins from them. I'll show you where you can buy those and other sundries for the holidays. For now, give them two coppers. That will be generous enough."

The pair of neighborhood water vendors— wheeling a lidded oblong tub that was fitted

with a spigot—arrived on the last day of the year. Water symbolized the flow of wealth into one's home, and because of the holidays, the vendors expected to be rewarded with cash, rather than paid with the bamboo tokens that each household had purchased from them in advance. On these niceties Mrs. Zhang also instructed Nainai, for back home in Manchuria, wells had provided all the water for the family's needs.

And on matters of fashion, Mrs. Zhang was also quite the authority. Padded jackets of peach red cotton were in vogue the season of Nainai's arrival in Tianjin. The sleeves were rolled up, and the topmost frogs of the mandarin collars left strategically unfastened, revealing the lining of pale pink. At first, Baba had thought the jackets rather gaudy, accustomed as he was to the more sedate colors Manchurian women preferred, but he soon came to appreciate the blush that was reflected upon the women's cheeks by the exuberance of color—or were they glowing from the sheer joy of wearing such jackets?

In due time, Nainai was led to a dry goods shop by Mrs. Zhang, and there she purchased enough peach red fabric to tailor two jackets. Mrs. Zhang's long slim fingers turned out one for Nainai and also one for herself. Her husband's meager earnings could not keep her in fashionable clothes, so her association with Nainai was a happy and fruitful one. She would often come plead her husband's case, hoping that one word from Yeye—who had sway in the Central Government—would bring about a better situation or a raise.

The Zhangs had one child, a daughter who, like Baba, was born in the Year of the Dragon. Her name was Dahe, or Tall Lotus. She was a quiet girl with bright, intelligent eyes framed by inky brows. But Nainai would often wonder out loud, "If that pretty thing was the woman's real child, would she slap her around the way she does and drag her out of our house by the flesh of her cheeks when it's time to go home? I suspect Dahe isn't her own. The child hardly cries; she only purses her lips, as if she's all too used to being treated so. The little thing's not allowed to go to school—has nothing to do all day long—it makes one think the couple intends to raise her and sell her into the brothel."

Whenever Baba followed Nainai over to the Zhangs', he was intrigued and a little frightened by what he found propped up against the wall at one end of their kang: a boy rag doll with a knot of hair in the middle of his forehead, painted eyes that stared eerily, and white tubelike arms and legs sticking out of a little flowered frock—all the handiwork of Dahe's mother. The doll sat behind a miniature table upon which a rice bowl rested. Just before suppertime, the woman always said, "Dahe, it's time to fill up Liuyou's rice bowl."

How unearthly it is, with its blanched skin and blinkless eyes, thought Baba, returning the doll's stare. Likely to come to life in the dead of night and do evil while everyone's sleeping. . . . It's also got such a queer name: Liuyou. I guess it means "To have and to remain." Does this mean that Mrs. Zhang is praying for the birth of a boy child? Is this the reason she's so unkind to Dahe . . . because she's a girl? She's especially nice to us boys. I hope she has a boy real soon; maybe then the cruel horns will fall off her head.

Dahe liked to spend time at the House of Yang. Nainai was gentle with her, and Baba, being the same age, was good company. The child's only toy was a girl rag doll in the style of Liuyou, but with two braids fashioned from black yarn. It had no name—at least Baba never heard Dahe call it by anything—and was dirty and greasy from being dragged around everywhere the child went.

As soon as she came over to visit, Dahe un-ceremoniously tossed aside her doll. Baba had toy automobiles to scoot along the edge of the kang, but she preferred a set of building blocks of assorted geometric shapes, painted red, green, blue, yellow, and white. They came in a neat wooden box made to contain all the pieces snugly. The set of blocks was Baba's favorite toy. He liked to build houses and boats and streetcars.

One afternoon when he came home from school, he looked for the building blocks but could not find them anywhere. He had not touched them for two or three days, but he remembered very clearly he had set the box that contained them flush against his writing desk on the kang.

"How strange. I've turned every drawer inside out. We don't share a courtyard with other families, so how can they be missing? My older brothers don't care for them at all, so they can't be responsible." He missed his toy terribly.

Several days passed. Then one afternoon, when he trailed Nainai over to the Zhangs', he saw Dahe squatting alone on the kang. She was intent on something. She was playing with blocks. She was playing with his set of blocks!

When Dahe saw him, she hid them under

a pile of quilts with the quick movements of a squirrel.

Baba caught his breath in surprise. "Those belong to me!" he said to himself. "She knows I saw them: why else would she turn bright red? She must have filched them while I was away at school and lied to her mother that it was a gift from my mother."

Stealing was repugnant to him, and the act deeply wounded his concept of the world. He was angry, and wished to call her on her dirty deed.

"Yet if I cry foul now, her mother will surely pinch and beat her something awful. I'd hate to see that. Also, if I tell on her, it would wreck the relationship that's flowered between our families.... But on the other hand, if I don't speak up right now, I'll lose them forever."

"Yes, but she really loves them," a voice deeper inside him argued, "and this may mean that she really needs them. This girl has a terrible need for something else to play with besides her dirty old doll. If she was a boy, she would have been given lots of toys. Oh, Dahe! Why did you have to steal?"

In the end, Baba did not breathe a word about the theft. With the passage of the days, he learned to forgive Dahe, but he also learned to watch out for her. He made sure to put away his other toys very carefully before leaving for school.

How long have the innkeeper and his son gotten away with their evil business? Baba sat bolt upright, a worm gnawing inside him. Although the room was cold, he felt his anger like a fever. He could forgive Dahe for her iniquity: his soul's sense of justice, a finely calibrated instrument, had weighed in favor of the girl and her unhappy circumstance. But against the thieves at this roadside inn, the scales tipped in favor of avenging himself; every ounce of him demanded satisfaction.

And yet I cannot raise a stink here, get into an argument or fight with them ... they'd probably turn me over to the local authorities and then I'd be in more trouble.

When he lay back down, an idea offered itself.

Last night, after I had settled into my room and wiped the dust from my face, I noticed the innkeeper enter the kitchen with two empty glass bottles; when the man emerged, the bottles were filled with golden soybean oil.

The oil must be held in the pair of enormous brown vats I saw; they were half my height and probably wider than my embrace.

He slipped off the kang and listened. Not a sound. He crept softly down the corridor and into the kitchen, then felt for the vats like a blind man. Shifting the wooden lid from one, he lifted a corner of the quilt that covered the mouth and dipped his canteen, emptied of water, into the oil.

Gudu, gudu, gudu—the vessel drank its fill, making soft opulent gurgles. Baba wiped its lip clean on the quilt, capped it, and shifted the telltale greasy patch to the back.

"I'm simply taking back what's mine," he said to himself, but the melancholy of having to steal was in his heart.

Oil has become even more precious in wartime. How can a common little roadside inn be in possession of such a vast quantity? If ordinary folk should be found hoarding, surely they'd be punished.

I'm certain these men are secretly selling it at black-market prices. They must be in league with the village authorities . . . explains why they rob me so boldly.

The innkeeper's thin-slotted eyes followed him out the door at daybreak. He marched all day under a sky gray as a gray rat. He left Ping-yuan far behind.

At dusk he arrived at a village and knocked on the door of a peasant's hut. The family was overjoyed to receive the oil in exchange for a meal and a bed.

And what a meal he was given. The daughter-in-law made fresh noodles—long, thick noodles in hearty soup, not broken pieces in watery broth.

He slept soundly that night. What he had always expected from others in their dealings with him was a bit of fairness. But war and poverty have never been fertile ground for such a delicate plant.

"OH, I'D SAY another twenty *li* or so and you'll be at bank of the Huang He—the Yellow River." The old man in the shop, shriveled and dark like a roadside *Tudi Gonggong*, the neighborhood god, handed Baba a dozen *mantou*. Joy filled his furrowed brow as he received a pair of trousers in payment. The garment was worth far more than a dozen *mantou*; the man counted out a handful of dirty, evil-smelling bills to Baba, making up the difference.

Peasants who had come into the shop pawed the shirts in Baba's bundle, and asked if he would sell. Baba shook his head. These folk are so in want of clothes, they can't afford to dress their scarecrows, he thought.

"So you want to cross the Yellow River?" The old man felt his wispy beard and his eyes blazed with tales. "You young ones wouldn't know, but in the old days, before the big steel bridge, it wasn't such an easy affair to get across," he said to Baba. "Summer floods you can understand, but in springtime, just when the ice starts breakin' up, floes as big as houses and rising tall above the water would crash and weigh on each other, putting boats in mighty big danger. If the temperature suddenly dropped, the ice formed around the boats and froze them dead in place. Sometimes a great wind would kick up from the northwest, bringing a storm of yellow sand which covered over the ice entirely.

"You asked about the bridge. Hai, in my seventy years, how many times have I seen it destroyed by the crazy mix of fightin' armies, to be fixed and then wrecked again. One such time, as I walked on narrow planks laid across its tottering carcass, folk got caught in the crossfire. A woman who had a baby slung on her back lost her balance and drowned.

"Right now, as far as I know, the bridge is intact. People still go back and forth on it, but you'd best have your papers in order—it's crawling with soldiers who're afraid Nationalists might come blow it up."

The Jinan Bridge—named for the city on the other side of the river—was crucial to the Communists' southward advance and crucial to Baba's flight.

So far on his journey, he had been able to skirt the major checkpoints—slip away from the nets like the moon floating on water—but if he were to try crossing the Jinan Bridge, a meeting with soldiers seemed inevitable.

"Don't know 'bout the ferries, whether there's likely to be any. That all depends on the weather and the mood of the water. I kinda doubt it, though, seeing how big the wind has been blowin'."

I'm in a real fix now, Baba thought. I've got to get over to the other side without delay. Something is warning me that I can't lose time. But the river is just where I'm afraid to get to. Will the soldiers let me across? Will they honor my road pass? What if they arrest me as a spy? He was drawn forward by necessity, but his heart was resisting, pulling back from the great Yellow River.

The Yellow River, second to the Yangtze in length, but first in the hearts and souls of the people, is the cradle of Chinese civilization. Trickling down from the snow-capped Kunlun Mountains, it gathers strength and streams east through the loess plateaus of the great northwest provinces, there given a heavy burden of yellow silt.

Yellow water, bringing yellow earth to yellow people. The river gives us the color of our skin, folk say. From the river basin were born the sons and daughters of Huangdi—the Yellow Emperor.

But due to the violent changes in its lower course over the centuries—like the lashing of a dragon's tail, bringing disastrous floods—the river also bears another name: China's Sorrow. Enormous bureaucracies had been maintained by successive dynasties to manage the Yellow River dike works. When the southern dikes in Henan Province were blown up by government forces to slow the enemy during the anti-Japanese war, millions of lives were lost to the flood waters.

Water: what gives life also has the power to destroy—a lesson Baba learned in childhood.

He was two years old and had toddled after his second brother to the Western Marsh, where a corps of bullfrogs had bumped and racketed all summer long among the cattails. When Second Brother turned away, Baba wandered into the deep, and suddenly found that he could not touch his toes to anything at all. Everything around him went *hei-bu-long-dong,* murky. Water filled him as if he were an open jar.

Second Brother turned around in time to see Baba's bare bottom and hear *bu-dong! bu-dong! bu-dong!* as his feet kicked the water. He towed Baba back to the bank and pumped his chest and stomach. Out of Baba's mouth came marsh water along with three or four black polliwogs.

This was Baba's earliest encounter with the *hei-bu-long-dong* deep, but his fondness for water only grew.

Fifteen *li* to the northwest of Xinmin soared Gaotai Mountain, which could be seen from a great distance on the plains. Halfway to its slopes, there ran a quiet stream along whose grassy banks grew colonnades of ancient weeping willows, dripping their luxuriant green strands of tears into the water. On their return from outings to Gaotai Mountain, tired, dusty, and hot, Baba and his small friends invariably bathed in the stream in the shade of the trees, joining the tribes of children from miles around who had also discovered the enchantment of the spot.

One summer day, they struck upon smooth gray *ge-le,* clams, some as large as abalones (though the meat contained was but a tiny scrap), buried in the clay river bottom. It was easy for them to feel the clams with their bare feet, especially if the clams had buried themselves on edge in the silt. After working them loose with their toes, they dove headlong and brought up the treasures cradled in both arms.

The shadows grew long as the sun began to set, but the children were reluctant to go home. Suddenly, a voice cried out, "Someone's drowned!"

Every last one of the boys leapt out of the water and scrambled up the embankment. They perched dumbly like little birds who had lost their song. They watched the bubbles rise and break and fan out in rings all along the glassy surface. Could the boy still be alive and be blowing bubbles from down below? they wondered. The water flowed in silence, keeping its secret.

Someone suggested they link hands to fish for the child.

"No, can't do that!" a boy warned. "If you go down there, his spirit will grab your legs and drown you, making you take its place."

They could think of nothing to do, and after all hope had vanished, they wrapped their *ge-le* in their clothes and went home.

That night, Baba was scared and miserable, but he dared not tell the grown-ups about the drowning, lest he be prohibited from going swimming again.

The following day, the news of the accident spread all over Xinmin. "He was the only son

of the House of Luo, from the east side of town," folk said, shaking their heads. "A house with only one son, as the saying goes, is like the grass that sends down only one skimpy root; when the frost comes down, it's the first to die."

A party went out in search of the body. Baba tagged along and the men fished out the bloated, bluish-white corpse, floating facedown, snagged on the root of a willow. It was just a little ways downstream from where only yesterday they had all been making merry.

"No more swimming! No more going after *ge-le!*" the grown-ups scolded Baba in the evening. It was during the latter days of the Japanese occupation, when rationing was in effect. The special treat of clams in the stock had made the cabbage soup so much tastier.

In the following spring, when Baba and his friends walked to Gaotai Mountain to harvest branches of snowy pear blossoms, or when in the fall the trees bore fruit and the boys returned home, bare-bottomed, hauling stolen pears in the knotted legs of their trousers, they would peer down at the water as they passed the stream and think of the *ge-le,* and when they thought of the *ge-le,* they remembered the drowned child. They watched the bubbles come up and break on the surface of the slow-flowing stream, and they shivered, thinking of the spirit that still lurked beneath, wanting one of them to take its place in the *hei-bu-long-dong* deep.

Henceforth, Baba did not go diving for *ge-le,* but he did not stay away from the other rivers, the Liao and the Liu, where he became a strong swimmer.

But strong as he was now at twenty, he would not be able to swim the Yellow River. Countless streams he had been able to ford, but he could not cross this mighty, turbid river of legend and history.

Baba left Sangzidian and pressed south. The sky had swallowed clouds and looked ready to spit rain.

Naked yellow earth. A world of one shade. No trees to either side. Hardly a thing for his eyes to rest on. What tiny shrubs he came across were tenacious and stingy of color. Their branches held close, their roots tucked in the soil as if prepared for the next flood, the next sandstorm. They were prepared to survive, having learned their lessons against excess, against shooting off long stems, luxurious leaves, against putting forth a boon of flowers. Existence was a continuous struggle to simply remain the same size. It is no easy matter being born a man; it is no light burden being born a plant.

Mid-March already, and spring is not willing to show its face. What about in other provinces? What about back home? The petals of the pear blossoms must be falling like snow, thought Baba.

For days he had been walking across the sandy soil of Shandong Province, across uneven, ancient riverbeds, where folk scrabbled a thimbleful of sustenance from the land. The rare hut was invariably a ramshackle, crumbling affair, without even fence posts to mark a meager garden.

In Manchuria, farmers harnessed horses and mules to the plows; even the poorest among them had at least an ox to turn the fields. But here in Shandong, instead of draft animals he saw two or three people, as twisted as scarecrows, yoked to the plow. And once he neared, he saw that the beasts of burden were women and children: the men were lost to the long string of wars. Waves of anguish washed over him.

The Chinese word for "plow," thought Baba, contains the ideograph for "ox." Now it seems we must replace it with the ideograph for "man."

The iron turning plow was invented in China in the sixth century B.C., and not until the seventeenth century did the Europeans import the technology which finally freed them from slavery to inefficiency. Why have we regressed while the West has outdistanced us?

Why do we Chinese eat bitterness in silence? Baba stopped, rubbed his tired legs as he followed the painful progress of the women and children in the fields. The rulers down through the ages have claimed that the people have a voice. We have no voice. We are dumb as oxen. Is this why we have replaced the beasts? Is this punishment we have brought upon ourselves for remaining complacent?

These were no novel questions. He had come to inherit them from the generations of youths who passed into old age and death, those who had dreamed of and struggled for a vigorous new China where children would grow up with full bellies and a future.

He had been closely following the sabotaged railway; the course would unerringly lead him to the bridge.

Some fifteen *li* out of Sangzidian, as evening inked over the land, he saw a large object ahead of him on the tracks, issuing smoke and steam.

"A train? Could it really be a train?" cried Baba. He ran forward a few steps, straining to see.

So it was. A train at a standstill. He had not been able to see the smokestack, for the engine was on the far end. Engaged to the engine were two open cars filled with crushed rocks—ballast to stabilize the ties. The repair of the tracks had evidently just proceeded here to the northern bank from somewhere south of the river. A soldier stood high atop the gravel pile in the second car, waving a baton as he directed laborers on the tracks.

Baba bowed his head, hoping to shuffle past without being stopped.

"*Kuai xie-ah!* Hurry! Hurry! Finish unloading and we'll be heading home!" The soldier's voice boomed like a wagoner calling to his team of mules.

"Ah, this is my day"—Baba's heart raced on hearing the familiar accent—"here's an opportunity," he said to himself.

"*Tongzhi!* Comrade!" he hollered to the tall soldier with the flat, spare face of a northerner. "Your talk is of the Northeast! Are you a *lao xiang*—a brother from Manchuria?"

"*Shi-ah!* Are you also from Manchuria?"

The man smiled broadly, crooked his legs, and leaned dangerously forward to catch Baba's face.

"Yes! Hey, can I hitch a ride with you?"

"Sure, why not. We're just about to go."

Though there was no need to shout, the man continued to cry out. "Go on up ahead. Climb up on the engine. Tell the fellow—the engineer there—I said you could get on." The emphasis was on the word "I," for the man was ostensibly proud of his own authority and seemed to wear a habitual expression of self-satisfaction.

Baba clambered up on the narrow metal platform running along the side of the engine. He was happy to be off his feet, resting his back against the warmth. He set his bundle on his lap and gnawed on a *mantou* in silence.

It was some time before he felt the motion of the train, and once it got under way, he realized it was not going to be an easy ride; the engine bucked like a wild horse. He sat back down and gripped the narrow railing, afraid of being tossed off like a leaf. Big chunks of soot pelted him and lodged painfully in his eyes. Through tears he strained to see into the distance.

The river was close at hand. He could not hear it for the noise of the engine, but he could sense it as surely as the blood coursing through his own body.

"There it is at last. The bridge!" The great dark steel expanse of it loomed and stretched before him. He did not know whether the clamor in his ears was the sound of the train or his own heart storming.

A smoky blur in the distance. His eyes flew to the southern bank, mysterious in the raw gray evening.

"It is as I've been told: the bridge is crawling with armed men at the checkpoint—and as far as I can make out, on both sides of the bridge."

Stiff black figures flashed by like posts; but even under the shroud afforded him by speed and the hurrying night, Baba felt the menace of eyes upon his thin body and hunched motionless lest he be discovered.

But when he heard the great booming concert of the river below—the many voices of the yellow race: proud voices, savage voices in songs of joy, in songs of lament; a crescendo that joined the din of the engine—he smiled to himself.

Had he been able, he would have stood up, thrown his arms high above his head, and waved in joy. He would be immune to searching fingers this evening. He would make it across the great river in magnificent style, at the head of a roaring, unstoppable train. "Tonight . . . tonight . . . ," the voices sang to him, "tonight the Huang He is the river of life."

"AI, LET HIM be. Let the young 'un spend the night." The wife of the shopkeeper shrugged her shoulders, looking cold and weary. "He'll do no harm." Baba had fallen asleep in a noodle shop, slumped across the table, his head resting upon his bundle. He had crossed the Yellow River at dusk and had arrived in Jinan, the capital of Shandong Province; in exhaustion and relief, he slept as if utterly drunk from sorghum whiskey. The wind hissed and fretted the eaves and banged the door.

"How can we? We don't know his story. What if the night patrol finds him here?" the man replied. Baba was pushed back into the night as thick and dark as molasses.

He crawled onto a woodpile wedged between two buildings, seeking shelter like a sick bird flung from the sky. It was a long, tedious night; rain fell and pattered like mung beans.

The following day, he shuffled among the crowds, fearful of drawing unfriendly eyes to himself, a stranger in a strange city. When evening descended, he hovered like a moth near the food stalls, where oil lamps threw a halo of welcome. The night market nested in the side of a raised roadbed and was sheltered from the March winds that threw handfuls of yellow sand. From a vendor he ordered the Shandong speciality, *suilubao,* meat-filled dumplings, fried and steamed in a pan to savory, crackling perfection.

As the chill and hunger were chased away by food in his belly, the night seemed less hostile; the knots in his body loosened a little. "Can you beat that. I made it across the Yellow River. I'm a fish that has slipped past the cormorants," he said with a sigh.

Just as his tongue darted and curled around the last morsel, he heard the marching of many feet on the road above him. He turned to see a column of soldiers on night patrol.

He had already paid for his meal, but with the soldiers nearby, he did not dare stand up. He felt the lamp hanging above him at the food stall suddenly burn too hot, too bright.

Please let them pass. Please let them go away . . . , he silently prayed, shrinking and hunching into his jacket.

But it was as if the very fervency of his wish attracted what he hoped to keep away. The approach of heavy footsteps.

"Get up!" He felt a slap hard across his back.

I must have raised suspicions around town by my questions about the road leading south. Someone must have reported me. Baba's thoughts were met by a soldier's stare, bristling with winter.

The patrons of the night market gawked and suspended their chopsticks in midair, but kept on working their mouths like cattle. *What terrible crime has the young bandit committed?* their narrowed eyes silently asked.

"Show your papers!"

Baba fumbled in his jacket for them.

"This student ID is three years old. It's no longer valid. And your road pass—this was issued in early February. It's nearly the end of March. Where've you been all this time?"

"In Beiping. February was too cold to start out on the road."

"It says here the road pass is for travel to Shanghai—why are you still slinking around here in Jinan?"

"Take him away!"

Two soldiers came forward, removed his bundle. "*Zou!* Get going!" they ordered. Through the streets and alleys they herded him, prodding his back with their rifles. Jinan had seen heavy fighting and was without electricity. Baba lost all sense of direction. Gutted buildings stared with hollow eyes into the night, their walls ringing with the strange voices.

They came at length to a guarded gate and stepped quickly through. Then, twisting and turning along the paths between buildings, they made their way inside the compound. Suddenly Baba was pulled to a halt, sharp and short, and thrust into a room lit by kerosene lamps whose flames burned orange and low. The acrid smoke from the lamps irritated his throat.

"Ah, please take a seat," said a solitary soldier at a desk. His face was clean-shaven and pleasant, and he indicated a stool with a smile like that of a shopkeeper to his customer.

He's too well-mannered for a soldier, thought Baba.

Rummaging through Baba's bundle, the man found the one remaining silver yuan that had been carefully sewn into the collar of an old shirt.

"Have a rest. Not to worry," the man said in the slow drawl of one from Hebei Province.

"Where's your family? Your hometown? What school did you attend?" the man asked in a velvet voice, and in a precise, even hand, he recorded Baba's answers. Baba relaxed a little. "Looks like I won't be mistreated here," he said to himself.

The methodical, patient questioning extended for hours like a sluggish stream that seems to make no progress toward the sea; a fire burned in Baba's eyes and his ears buzzed. It was long past midnight when his questioner finally rose, stretched, and left the room, only to be replaced by another man, in civilian clothes, who entered with a gust of cold air.

Under the man's overhanging eyebrows, one eye rode higher than the other. The right eye was larger and roved; the left focused steadily on Baba. He spoke with the thick accent of Qingdao to the southeast.

"We have investigated your situation fully, and we say you lie." The man slapped the back of his hand into the palm of the other. "Let me tell you, leaving here won't be so easy. Better come clean. It'll save you much trouble later. But we're in no hurry, no hurry at all. You'll tell everything sooner or later...."

There was a rash of footsteps outside the building—the changing of guards or perhaps fresh troops of the night patrol assuming their watch over the city. Then Baba heard a smooth, metallic glide and a sudden crash, cavernous and deep, which raised him off his stool: the closure of a heavy iron door in some part of the building.

"Get up!"—the man's thick fingers dug into Baba's shoulder mercilessly—"You have no right to sit before me.

"You've said it was too cold to begin your journey in February. You also claim you're a student. Lies! We say you are a member of Unit Nineteen!" The man leaned closer, breathing into Baba's face.

"Wha-what?" Baba was stunned by the accusation.

Unit Nineteen was the Nationalist military police that had been active in Beiping. When the Communists erupted into the ancient capital at the beginning of the year, they were in fierce pursuit of its remaining members, routing out the individuals like sewer rats. Unlike common soldiers, the captives of Unit Nineteen were not allowed to join the Communist ranks after "reeducation." What became of these prisoners remained a mystery.

His interrogator was undoubtedly familiar with Beiping and the Nationalist military organization; he was no recently recruited rustic like so many of the stripling Communists who had detained him by the roadside.

"Talk! You're a spy, aren't you? Confess. Ah, so you won't talk...your silence proves your guilt."

When Baba had been detained in the shadows of The Witch Doctor's Portal, to protect himself was to say very little. But in the hands of a seasoned professional interrogator—as this man undoubtedly was, a man who would not hesitate to crush him—burrowing his head in silence did him little good.

"Nineteen had no Manchurians. How can I be a member?" Baba said. And in his bewilderment, he blurted, "The Manchurians are of Unit Seven."

The man drew his eyebrows together, reared up to his full height. "Anh!? Go on. Let's hear it. What more do you know?"

"Unit Seven soldiers were recruited in Shenyang, and when the railroad was still open, they were transferred to Beiping and barracked at the Lama Temple. And—and a year ago, they sailed for Shanghai," Baba stammered.

"You've been sent to us from Shanghai to spy, eh? So your road pass is then a forgery."

Baba trembled and his tongue cleaved to the roof of his mouth; he had played into the man's hands. But before he could sputter out words in self-defense, the man lunged at him with the weight of a granite mountain in his fist; the blow landed on Baba's chest. He was thrown

back, his spine rammed against the wall, and he slid to the floor.

"Stay!" he heard the man say, but it was an unnecessary command: Baba was a helpless human heap, gulping for air, choking as if smoke were filling his lungs. He dared not move for the pain. Every rib felt splintered.

The man stepped outside, soon to return flanked by two soldiers, who wrenched Baba's arms back and handcuffed them.

"Outside!"

Baba's legs had gone soft. He was dragged into the night. The world was murky, as if seen through the bottom of a brown bottle. The yellow glow from a light source behind him revealed a stretch of brick wall inches from his nose. He felt the stab of a gun in his back. His eyes grew dim.

"Talk! Tell the truth! If you talk, we will be lenient. You were sent here by the Nationalists, weren't you!"

Baba understood nothing in his terror. The man's heavy Qingdao accent rattled meaninglessly in his ears. He was only conscious of the racking pain in his lower legs, feeling as if the muscles of his calves were slowly being ripped and wrenched forward, twisted like *mahua*—deep-fried, braided dough.

Kukuang-kukuang-kukuang! The swift, sure sounds of bullets jammed into guns and the bolts slammed forward.

So it is now. Now is the end. My folks will never know how I died . . . where I died. . . .

When he last saw his mother in Shenyang, she had gazed into his face, eyes colorless and numb—had she sensed that he would not be returning? As she brushed away a piece of stray hair, he noticed for the first time that frost had already alighted upon her temples.

Kukuang!

He stood shivering, waiting for the big, all-encompassing roar, the searing, ripping, black explosion at the base of his skull that would sever him from pulse, breath, and heart-beat.

The man's voice broke over him—"Talk! The truth!"—but it sounded far away, chased into the night by a hovering call of someone soft and protective.

"Little one, come look," Nainai said to him.

He had followed his mother—plump and pretty in her thirties—into the big North Garden to harvest chives for dinner. Like fresh snowfall, white cabbage butterflies cloaked the field of lacy white blossoms.

When Nainai bent down and scooped up a bundle of cut chives into the skirt of her apron, a butterfly was swept up inside. She held the hem tightly to her breast.

"Number Four, come look. Mama's caught you a butterfly."

Baba followed her into the house, where she plucked the creature from the chives and held it out to him. He pinched its folded wings between his thumb and forefinger.

When he released the butterfly, it flew to the south window. He clambered onto the kang and watched it flutter against the panes.

He pinched the wings and tossed it into the air. Once again, it flew toward the light.

Baba continued to play with the butterfly, but with each successive capture and release, the creature became less willing to flutter. When it would fly no more, Baba discovered silvery wing dust lost upon his small fingers.

It's dying, he suddenly realized. I don't want it to die . . . how sad it would be for it to die.

He ran back out into the North Garden with the creature cupped in his hands. He heaved it into the air, hoping with all his heart that it would take flight. It plunged, spiraling down like a white petal.

Yet, mere inches from the ground, it

suddenly spread its damaged wings and was scooped up by a draft.

Initially it hovered low, but the farther away it flew, the higher it climbed. Higher and higher—up, up, up—until Baba could no longer identify it, could not tell it apart from the thousands of other cabbage butterflies suspended above the field of flowering chives.

"And I thought I was in the North Garden. Why did I remember the butterfly after all these years?" He had awakened to the feel of the icy floor and realized he was huddled in a corner of a room, drenched in sweat, rills crawling down his back and neck. With each breath, a pain shot through his chest, and he slowly touched a finger there. He was cold and sick, but thoughts of the butterfly lingered like a bright white hope.

How he had made his way back to the room of interrogation he could not remember; certainly not on his own pair of legs. His tormentor was nowhere in sight.

With the first glimmer of a cold, still dawn came a soldier who bore himself as straight as a young pine. He blew out the lamps.

"Stand up," the man said, motioning. His speech was unquestionably Manchurian.

Baba winced. The pain in his calves was like cuts from poisoned blades.

"Please take a seat on the stool," the man said. He laid out the contents of Baba's bundle on the table.

He questioned Baba in detail about his school in Shenyang, the Number One Polytechnic: "What was the color of the building? How many stories? Where was it situated in town? What other buildings stood in the neighborhood?"

The soldier, whose fair, stern face neither threatened nor displayed kindness, often nodded in the affirmative as Baba made his replies.

When he answered, "The building of the police academy was formerly occupied by the Shenyang Legislature," the soldier leaned back in his chair and asked no more.

He must be a native of Shenyang...must have been trained at the former Japanese police academy in the same neighborhood as my school, Baba thought. The man has the physique that the Japanese used to demand of their recruits....

"Understand this now," said the Manchurian, rising and looking keenly down at Baba. "Jinan is a very complicated place." Baba understood the implied meaning of the word "complicated": the city had only recently been captured by the Communists, and the Nationalist underground had yet to be eradicated.

"If you should be taken by another unit, you'll find yourself in trouble again—and they may not deal with you as gently as we have.

"The city is not a place for you to linger; I suggest you leave immediately.

"We're returning everything to you, even your money," the Manchurian continued, patting Baba's cloth sack. In that gesture, and in the gentle inflection of his voice, Baba sensed the man's humanity. "It is illegal for you to have silver, but we see that you have very little else. We don't care what you do once you are in Chiang Kai-shek's territory, but don't spend it here.

"Check your belongings: make sure everything is there."

Baba's heart clattered with joy; he felt no inclination to look through his bundle. A guard walked him in the direction of the gate.

He blinked in the sun. The air was cool and moist, and he welcomed the morning, fragrant with hope, upon his face. He saw that the buildings in the compound were built upon foundations of reddish stone, the color of ripe persimmons. "This must have been a Nationalist detention center; it's now just as useful to the Eighth Route Army," he said to himself.

He did not look back once he walked out the gate. He would fly high. He would fly far.

BABA WALKED INTO the evening. Clouds fingered a full moon that seemed to him like a canine eye, peering down through the opening of a sack. He had been over a fortnight on the road, traveling through nameless hills, where stunted trees knew everything about thirst.

He knocked on the door of a mud hut to ask for shelter. It opened to reveal a small grub of an old woman, her face as weathered as the land. The moonlight slanted into the back of the room, where an old granddad and a girl rested.

When he had eaten the leftover porridge of millet and corn that they offered him, he asked, "How much farther east does 'liberated district' run?"

"Oh . . . only 'bout thirty *li*—to the hamlet of Lancun. That's 'bout the extent of it. Don't know the situation beyond. The door's shut to us." The voice of the gaffer was choked with coughs, like a cat spitting out a fur ball.

"What news!" Baba said to himself. "Only hours to liberty! Lancun! Lancun! I heard rumors that Qingdao City, beyond Lancun and pressed against the Yellow Sea, is still in the hands of the Nationalist government. Liberty is near at hand."

He had not walked south along the Jin-Pu Highway, as he had planned, but had veered southeast, having been told that it was well nigh impossible to cross the Yangtze River by this closely guarded route. The way southeast was little trafficked, and he hoped to slip out the back door while the Communists were attending the main gate. He had grown even more fearful of soldiers after his interrogations in Jinan; once you have been bitten by a snake, even a coil of rope looks venomous.

If I make it across the last checkpoint in Lancun—and I pray that I will—I imagine the folks beyond will be better off. They won't be wanting these clothes in exchange for food and shelter.

"Travel light. Let go of things that are no longer useful. Pass them on to someone who needs them," I once heard Yuan, the Daoist beggar, tell my grandfather. . . . He kept several shirts and a couple of pairs of trousers, then gave the rest to the old woman.

She was in raptures. After admiring each piece of clothing at length, she clambered atop the kang and, with a wondrous sprightliness, reached up to retrieve the basket that hung from the ceiling on a wooden hook tied to the end of a string. The contraption kept mice and other varmints out of the food.

"Here, this is for the road," she said, revealing to him the contents of the basket: two *bobo*—heavy sorghum pancakes—that had turned a terra-cotta red with age and were embellished with a rich patina of mold; long white hairs erupted from splotches of blue.

"Don't mind that," she said, sensing Baba's hesitation. "It's a bit fusty-musty, but it'll do you no evil. A bit of dirt'll do some good." She scrubbed the cakes vigorously with the palms of her dry old hands.

"My young'uns all grew up big and lively on this . . . no problems, no problems at all. Coddling fussy eaters only makes them grow up limp and dull."

Baba laughed but did not refuse her. He felt as if he were on a visit to the house of his *laolao*—his maternal grandmother. She spoke with directness from her fine old country heart.

He felt inside the pockets of his jacket for any remaining Communist currency. "Here, Granny, I won't be needing these, either." He handed her the crumpled bills.

Her happiness brought words bubbling out of her mouth. "I have a son. A soldier. Went to fight the 'small devils' twelve years ago. Don't know when he'll be a-comin' back."

The Japanese surrendered nearly four and a half years ago, thought Baba. He was probably killed. But for his parents' sake, I hope that he's been kept by the Nationalists south of the Yangtze. Short on soldiers, they hold on to their men with an iron grip.

"The boy left us this young'un here." The old woman pointed to her granddaughter, asleep on the kang. "Her ma is away now at her own folks'. She's there most of the time on account of our boy being gone."

"Their son must certainly be in his thirties now," said Baba to himself. "Now it's just these three—the too-weak and the too-tender—under a broken roof. The old folk probably keep alive by taking odd jobs in the hamlet and by gleaning the fields after harvest."

"Hai, maybe it's a good time for the young ones," the old woman said with a sigh, staring at the child, whose unworried slumber breathed tranquillity into the room. "They say the world will be better—even for the girls, they say—but for us old folk, there ain't much left. We're too old to be pricked by hope's needle. We'll just shuffle along as always, changes or no."

She was silent for a moment, and then she looked up at Baba. "I hear they check over travelers real hard in Lancun. Inspection is tough—why, the big fish Nationalists from Jinan—many of 'em tried to run away down that road, but they were nabbed in Lancun and carted back."

A shadow wrapped itself around Baba's heart. "I remember reading 'Fight to Jinan! Capture Wang Yuewu!' painted on the dirt walls just outside of that city," he said to the old woman. "Was Wang one of those taken at Lancun?" Wang was the former Nationalist governor and the military commander of Shandong Province.

"Ah, *dui-le, dui-le!* Yes, yes! The one named Wang! The biggest fish!" said she, clapping her hands together.

Her husband gave her a stiff look and fidgeted with his bedding.

"Old woman, no more talk. No more talk," he squeaked, clearly uncomfortable with the turn of conversation. "Quiet. Quiet. The night is old. The lad needs his rest."

With little warning, the oil lamp was extinguished.

Baba slept fitfully, alternating between excitement and fear. Will they let me through at Lancun? My road pass is perfectly proper. Worries racked his dreams, and when he was awakened in the middle of the night by the creaking of the hut, its bones contracting from the cold, he saw the moonlight striking upon the hanging basket which had held the moldy *bobo.*

Baba had seen just such a basket long ago, at an age when he was not yet big enough to climb onto a kang by himself. Nainai had borne him in the direction of Inner Mongolia to Erlingsuo on a cow wagon, to visit the house of his maternal grandmother, Laolao.

Although his grandmother had died long before he tumbled into the world, Baba referred to the House of Liu as Laolao's house.

Out of a basket, resting on a high shelf just below the ceiling, would come tasty egg biscuits called "baldies," because they looked like the tops of smooth, round, hairless pates. He had his happiest taste of freedom at Laolao's house, deep in the countryside.

When Baba's family returned to Manchuria in 1940, after an absence of many years, Nainai's nephew, who was a year or two older than she, came to see her at the House of Yang. He had headed Laolao's house ever since his father, Nainai's eldest brother, passed away. The aunt and nephew had played together as children and grown up side by side.

This man, whose brows were slightly graying, was Baba's cousin, and whenever he came to the House of Yang for a visit, Baba clamored to go with him on his return to Erlingsuo. The journey, more than one hundred *li* by cow wagon through ice and snow, took an entire day.

The cousin had fathered a son and two daughters. The son had taken a wife, and the older daughter had been married off. The remaining girl was seventeen. She was six years Baba's senior, but addressed him as Youngest Uncle, and he simply called her Er Yatou— Second Girl.

"The countryside's far better than the city!" Baba declared upon sighting chickens, ducks, geese, dogs, horses, and cows on the farm. In the barn lived a pair of hairy donkeys with large, soulful eyes, and these, without a doubt, were his favorite beasts. One of them was used to mill grain, the other for riding on trips to neighboring villages.

In Xinmin, Baba had often seen folk trotting about on donkeys, but he had never had the good fortune of actually stroking one.

His first order of business upon arrival at Laolao's house was to run into the barn, untie one of the donkeys, and lead it out the front gate.

Second Girl was given strict orders to watch over him. She trailed after him to keep him from getting hoofed by the beast. A young woman at seventeen had far more interesting things to occupy her time than baby-sitting an unruly little boy.

"What's so fun about this? . . . What can be so much fun about walking a donkey?" she muttered under her breath.

But Baba soon grew greedy to ride the animal. He eyed the big block of dung that had been collected for fertilizer; dirt had been shoveled over it and ice had come to encrust the top of it. He climbed atop so he could launch himself onto the back of the beast from a higher elevation.

"Why climb on that! If you want a ride, I'll give you a lift up," Second Girl said in exasperation. "Now sit back on its rump and not the skinny part around its waist."

To Baba's delight, the buttock of the beast warmed him up more quickly than a charcoal brazier. Second Girl took the rope and walked the animal in circles, but even after half a dozen spins, Baba showed no signs of tiring.

What a nuisance you are, said Second Girl's eyes, which narrowed in clear disapproval. "Okay, let's go. Let's go." With these words she led the donkey back into the barn. Baba was satisfied—for the moment.

Once inside the house, Second Girl climbed on the kang, crossed her legs, pulled out her long-stemmed pipe, lit the tobacco in the hot coals of the brazier, and proceeded to puff away. Baba, for want of something to do, climbed up on the kang after her.

Second Girl did not look at him, luxuriating in the privacy of her own thoughts, but Baba watched her every expression, every gesture. Her cheeks and the tip of her nose were ruddy from the cold. "She's as pretty as an apple," Baba said to himself.

When her eyes did alight on her half-pint uncle and saw that he had been scrupulously studying her, she tipped her head back with a sniff of annoyance. As she looked away, though, there was laughter in her eyes. Her lips curled

and parted in a slight smile, revealing just a few pearly whites clenched on the mouthpiece of her pipe. "She has pretty teeth," Baba said to himself.

But he did not sit watching for long. He thought of the pigeons roosting in the barn; his heart itched to disturb them. "You'd better not go into the barn; the horses might let their hooves fly and kill ya," Second Girl called after him as he ran outside.

Extracting a willow switch from a pile of kindling in the barn, he poked the rows of baskets that hung from poles. Within these baskets, braided from millet stalks, pigeons lived among the chickens. *Pa!* The birds flew out in an explosion of feathers. The pigeons were mostly gray, with black bands on their wings, and a few were pure white. Like the chickens, they did not like spending time outdoors, since the roofs were covered with snow; they preferred to scratch for grain in the mangers.

Second Girl gritted her teeth as she rounded up the chickens; she scattered sorghum from a willow basket and called *gu-gu-gu-gu-gu*. And she threw Baba angry looks.

While she found him a nuisance, Baba tended to like Second Girl more than dislike her; after all, she was giving him all the attention an eleven-year-old could possibly want. He also respected her because she was very capable.

Just how capable, he learned a few days into his stay at Laolao's house.

"A ewe's 'bout to drop her lamb. I reckon in a few hours," she said to him after she had herded the sheep back into their pen at dusk.

Toward midnight, swinging an oil lamp, she went to check on the animal. Just as she had predicted, there was an additional member to the flock, its wool matted and wet.

"It'll freeze to death in this weather." Second Girl ran for her big apron, rubbed the creature dry, cradled it in her arms, and carried it into the barn. There she set the tiny thing down where she had made a nest with hay. Then she led the ewe to its baby by tugging on an ear. Second Girl did not sleep a wink the entire night, and neither did Baba, who tailed her every step.

In the ensuing days, Second Girl continued to keep an eye on him. Although he could be aggravating, in time she came to find him, on the whole, entertaining. A friendship of sorts developed between the two.

"Second Girl," Baba would say, "how 'bout you tellin' me a story."

Short on stories, she sang him a song instead:

Wagon wheel cabbage, ye-yiii-ye.
Wild Second Sister lives in South Mountain.
In her oiled hair she wears jade flowers.
Niu-da-niu-da, she returns to visit her
*   mother's house.*

"What's 'wagon wheel cabbage'?" Baba asked.

"Don't know . . . but see, Second Sister's a new bride, and she comes home for a visit. She's proud of her new husband's rich house—it's better than her mother's—so she's showin' off —*niu-da-niu-da*, swiveling her hips and shoulders like there's no one better.

"Her folks ask her, 'Will you be coming back often?' and she says, 'When Mama and Baba are around, I'll visit as often as I can.'

" 'But when Baba and Mama die?' they ask her.

" 'When Baba dies, I'll wear white and weep before his coffin. When Mama dies, I'll come burn incense and kowtow before her grave.'

'What about when Brother dies?'

" 'When Brother dies, I won't be coming around, since I don't care much for his wife; but when Sister-in-Law dies, I'll strike up a merry tune on the old wash basin.'"

Second Girl's own sister-in-law didn't much care for this song, and gave her sharp looks from across the room.

After finishing off a bowl of tobacco, Second Girl said to Baba, "You keep running outside. It's terribly cold out there. Will you stay in if I make you a bowl of popped corn? Then you tell me some stories, Little Uncle. You must have lots of stories from living in the big capital. Heard you lived where the Emperor was living."

Going to the south side of the yard, she dug under the snow for sand and carried a shovelful to the kitchen in her apron. Then she poured the sand into the wok and asked Baba to feed dried sorghum stalks into the fire underneath.

Once the sand was sufficiently hot, she threw in a handful of kernels of corn and covered the wok. "Those 'big horse teeth' type of corn don't work. Look big, but explode real small; just the opposite with these," she told Baba as they listened to the delicious crescendo.

When the wok went nearly silent, she dumped its contents, sand and all, into the middle of a big round sieve. After a vigorous shak-

ing, what remained in the sieve was clean, white popcorn.

"What's it like to be the Emperor's wife? Did you ever see an Emperor?" she asked Baba as he munched. She filled the bowl of her pipe with tobacco.

"There isn't an emperor anymore, but I have seen where they used to live. The buildings are roofed with golden tile and filled with lots and lots of things: foreigners' clocks, and small trees whose leaves and flowers are made of green and pink gems."

"Heard it's nice to be the Emperor's concubine," said Second Girl.

"What's so great about that?"

"Eat well, wear nice clothes, ride in a big embroidered sedan...."

"I know there was an emperor's concubine who was shoved into a well and drowned. I've seen that well."

"Why would anyone want to kill her? Who would do such a thing?"

"Oh, probably 'cause the Emperor's sister tattled to the Emperor's mother about her, and the mother ordered her to be killed."

"Hhhaaai." Second Girl released a long sigh. She blinked hard and drew smoke from her pipe.

"Must be nice to be an emperor then," she said.

"Well, there's a hill behind the palace. It's pretty up there. Once when the enemy came, an emperor escaped out the back of the palace and hanged himself from a tree on that hill. I saw that old cypress; it's got a chain around it to keep people from peeling its bark for a keepsake."

"Why would the Emperor hang himself?"

"He got scared."

"What a worthless emperor.... So that's what it's like to live in the big capital, huh?"

"Haven't you ever been someplace nice outside of Erlingsuo?" Baba asked.

"Oh, I've been to my *laolao*'s house once."

"You have a *laolao* too?"

"Of course. My mother's mother."

"What's your *laolao*'s house like? Where is it?"

"Just like this place, with plenty of geese and ducks. Somewhere outside the Old Wall to the west. Nothing much interesting to say 'bout it though."

As long as Baba didn't run outside and she had to chase after him, Second Girl found Youngest Uncle tolerable. In time, she worried a little less and gave in to many of his wishes.

"You don't have to worry. Give me the rope. I'll be all right. I won't fall off," Baba said as he attempted to throw a leg over the back of the donkey.

"Well, just as long as you ride only this one, shod with nails that keep it from slipping on the ice."

Once settled on the animal's back, Baba nudged its belly with his heels, and the little beast began trotting off.

"Hey, not so fast! Come back, you! Come back!" Second Girl yelled as she ran after them, but she could not keep up.

In contrast to life at the House of Yang, here at Laolao's house Baba could do practically anything without threat of punishment. He was a regular little emperor with no enemies at the gate.

The following winter, as soon as he was let out of school for the holidays, he was off to visit Laolao's house. This year, Second Girl did not watch over him as he ran about the farm, scattering birds and pestering the donkeys. There was an air of dreamy distraction about her as she sat upon the kang, surrounded by a covey of women, fingers flying over their sewing and embroidery.

It was not until several days later that Baba came to realize Second Girl was to be married off. Marriage had no meaning for him other than that she would leave Laolao's house.

This knowledge colored the mood of his visit.

Second Girl's father said to him, "Little Cousin, we'll be sending her to her new family soon. You must stay on while we're gone. My son and his wife and kids will still be here, and they'll keep you company."

"Where's she going?"

"Near Xinmin County, just ten or so *li* outside the Eastern Gate. A place called the Hamlet of the Guo Clan. She's marrying into that clan."

"If Second Girl's going away, I don't want to stay here," said Baba to himself. "How many more days till she leaves?" he asked.

"Three. The cabinets—part of her dowry— have all been made ready, and she's working on her trousseau."

"If there's room, let me go with Second Girl. I can make my way back to Xinmin from her new place."

The journey wold be over one hundred *li* to the Hamlet of the Guo Clan, down a road Baba had never before ventured.

The family owned an old-fashioned horse wagon, with steel-rimmed wooden wheels, rather than a newfangled one with rubber tires. They borrowed two additional wagons from fellow villagers.

Before the midnight departure, the travelers ate a big meal.

The first wagon to leave Laolao's house had been piled high with wedding furniture. In the second wagon rode the bride and her chaperones, mostly elderly matrons.

Baba did not want to join the cabinets, and neither did he wish to squeeze in with six or seven graybeards in the third wagon.

"Come, come, Little Uncle. You come sit with me and keep warm under the quilt," Second Girl said, wrapping him up until only his face peeped, like the moon. The floor of the wagon was lined with a thick felt rug.

As he was bounced along into the darkness, he could hear the driver of the first wagon signaling to those behind him by cracking his whip high in the air.

Baba knew the third cart was following close behind when the gaffers struck up flames with their flintstones to light their pipes. The women in his wagon didn't smoke, because, away from the brazier, they had no way to light their tobacco. And their long-stemmed pipes were inconvenient for travel; the men smoked short pipes.

As the deep purple sky lightened to lavender, they came to a hamlet called Second Terrace, where, by prior arrangement, a family that owned a house with a large yard was awaiting them with steaming bowls of porridge. The travelers could rest awhile before moving on.

The sun was at its winter zenith when they finally arrived in the Hamlet of the Guo Clan. Neighbors' homes had been borrowed to accommodate the wedding guests who had come to attend the celebration, which would last for three days. All about the hamlet, there was a mood of happy upheaval. The wedding ceremony would take place early the following morning, but in the meantime, the bride, accompanied by her chaperones, disappeared from the eyes of the merrymakers.

That afternoon a big wagon drawn by a pair of white horses, owned by the groom's family, brought Nainai in from Xinmin City. As she was the bride's great-aunt, and also the oldest living member of the Liu clan, she was treated with the utmost respect.

Seeing her away from the stove for the first time, Baba looked at his mother in a new light. Her oiled hair was pulled back neatly, and she wore a velvet headband with a notch in the back to allow for her bun; upon arrival, someone placed an auspicious red flower there. A big black woolen coat with a beaver collar draped her shoulders. She was magnificent to behold, and Baba's small chest puffed with pride. There's definitely a different air about folks from the city, he mused.

"Why didn't you stay longer in Erlingsuo? Gone all that distance and you come back this way so soon?" Nainai said to him. "Well, you can stay with me tonight."

Long before cockcrow, at two or three in the morning—as far as Baba could tell—all the wedding guests were roused from deep sleep to eat. Baba did not care to fill his belly, but it was custom. Folk bustled about in preparation of the wedding ceremony, which would be enacted before dawn. Baba was much too enamored of sleep to attend; he went back to his dreams directly after the meal.

When he did awaken, by his own volition, the bride and groom had already been recognized before Heaven and Earth as husband and wife. He watched Second Girl—now Mrs. Guo—take out tobacco from a newly embroidered pouch and fill the pipes of her in-laws and those of the guests.

She certainly looks happy. Her eyes are glistening like pools of water—the look that Mother insists comes from her side of the family, thought Baba. The bride looked splendid indeed, the natural blush of her cheeks heightened by rouge. She wore an embroidered pink wedding gown and red velvet flowers in her hair. She was the sunrise itself.

Second Girl's so beautiful, and everyone says the groom is a handsome fellow, but I don't find him nice-looking at all. What a stupid broad face he has. Baba barely favored the man with a glance out of the corner of his eye. He's no match for her, he thought.

The celebration would last two more days, but in the afternoon, Baba and Nainai boarded the wagon for the ride back to Xinmin. Second Girl came to assist her great-aunt, and the groom bowed deeply to his new kinswoman.

The drunken wagoner was jolly, and with a snap of his whip in the air he sent the pair of white horses on their way.

Baba faced the back of the wagon and looked at smiling Second Girl, standing outside the gate. He watched her figure diminish and then disappear altogether once the wagon rounded a bend. After a few more curves in the road, he lost sight of the house entirely.

Deep in his soul, there was a sense that all was not as it should be in the world. "Laolao's house had such a wonderful thing, and they manage to go and give it away," he said to himself. In that moment of melancholy, he didn't think of Second Girl as a person but as a precious object. "Such a good thing, and they gave it away to that trifling hamlet.... I wouldn't have given away such a nice thing just like that." The more he thought of the situation, the more disturbed and uncomfortable he felt. Something just wasn't right inside his chest: it felt smoky and sour and stuffy in there.

Once they left the narrow village road and made their way onto the main highway, he saw no more of the hamlet with its peaked thatched roofs, circled by leafless willows whose branches hung down like catfish whiskers all the way to the ground. Baba finally turned around and faced forward.

He studied the horses' fat rumps, their long tails, and the way their manes shook. He thought of how their pairs of ears were growing out of their heads like new bamboo shoots, and he liked the sudden blasts of vapor that flew into the air out of their noses.

But the hypnotic *chwa-ta-chwa-ta-chwa-ta* of their hooves could not lull his heart. He felt he had lost something. Forever. What it was he had lost, he couldn't quite put a finger to or explain. But he knew it was something beautiful, something fine.

He left the old folks' hut and was back on the road again, in the still, gray hours before dawn. It seemed ages since he had heard the reveille of roosters. If there's still one around, it's too frightened—like me—to sing, Baba thought.

At dawn, out of the horizon, out of that morning's sunrise like a red-hot pan, he saw the silhouette of a strange creature come snaking toward him on the road. It looked like a colossal centipede with its multitude of wriggling legs.

"A column of soldiers," said Baba in alarm, his steps faltering. "Peasants do not march in file." He could not tell how far the column stretched down the road.

He jumped the roadside ditch and dashed over to a tangle of willows, running so fast he seemed to leave his frozen shadow in the middle of the road. Arriving at a stand of willows, he rested his back against an ancient bole and pretended to be asleep.

As he heard the tramping of disorderly foot-steps, he peered through his eyelashes; the figures in the column were reduced to smudges.

"Strange. These soldiers, marching two-by-two, carry no guns." When the first of them was only a stone's throw away, he saw that the column consisted entirely of women with bobbed hair, in olive uniforms. They looked his age. The first few pairs filing past him only craned their necks to stare at the improbability of the scene: a young man—from the looks of him, no peasant—in desolate country, far from human habitation, resting under a tree hung with dew. But the ensuing ones were knavish and naughtier.

"*Wei!* Get up! You lazy little wren! *Tian liang-liu! Tian liang-liu!* It's sunup!" they sang like a flock of waterfowl, in their slip-sliding provincial accent, jarring to Baba's citified ears.

The girls had spied him scurrying off the road, out of their way; he had fooled no one. They clapped their hands in unison and tried to flush him out of the grove, laughing and jawing: "*Tian liang-liu! Tian liang-liu!* It's dawn—dawn of a glorious new age!" They were delighted with their own raucousness and humor. Their leader did nothing to restrain them.

A riotous serenade sung crescendo by a mob

of females was no music to Baba's ears. He shut his eyes tighter. What else could he do in the face of hundreds of women warriors?

At last, their merry chortles and squawks began to recede. In the distance, their formation, once again, came to look like an overgrown centipede. Silence returned to this land of red soil in eastern Shandong.

The weather was fine—warmer now that the days were lengthening and he was farther south. But the grasses were still yellow stubbles, relics of last year's hope. When he was hungry, he dined on a *bobo*, breaking off bite-size pieces as he journeyed on. By early afternoon—when he had finished an entire cake, mold and all—he had come to the edge of Lancun.

So this is it? I didn't think it would be a fortress here, but I thought they would set more guards, he thought.

Lancun was but a barren spot with a scattering of mud huts; one would have been hard pressed to define it even as a hamlet.

In the distance, he saw three armed soldiers pacing the width of the broad dirt road.

"Go on into town. You'll see a couple of comrades standing sentry outside a building. That's the inspection station," they told him.

They stood tall, proudly wearing their Liberation Army uniforms, so correct and fashionable.

Baba reached the compound and walked past the sentries. Laughter and snatches of song, like a shower of petals, greeted him in the yard. He followed the voices inside.

The papered windows were propped open, and a breeze pushed in from the south, rustling the loose sheets of paper on the desks, bringing a taste of the sea, which he knew was not far away.

A handful of men and women in vigorous youth were making merry, teasing one another, going through the droll, twisting motions of the *niuyanger*, a country dance step. He felt misplaced, forlorn, as if he had walked in on festivities uninvited.

"I'm—I'm traveling to Shanghai," he said haltingly.

"Where's your road pass?" said one of the young soldiers, but his attention was held elsewhere. He swiveled his head to lob glances and sweet words at the women.

Baba relinquished his road pass. The soldier unfolded the document, set it down upon the table, turned, and walked away.

Baba stared wistfully at the paper. The

newsprint upon which the form was printed had become brittle; the creases were in danger of splitting from the countless foldings and unfoldings, and the writing had faded to a teary blue. This document, which contained a vague promise of freedom, had lain against his heart, day and night, across two provinces. Often, when he was alone and anxious, he had brought it out, to gaze at his own name written across the top.

While the young soldier was reimmersed in talk with his friends, Baba stood in silent agony, feeling thin and brittle. Why make me wait? What are his intentions? Can I go? Yes or no? His heart labored between hope and despair.

It was some time before the soldier turned his attention to him again.

"Untie your sack."

Baba set his bundle down on the table, but even before his jittery fingers had worked loose the second set of knots, the soldier's arm shot straight out before his own chest, waving in remonstrance.

"Ah, ah. *Xing-le, xing-le.* It's all right. That'll do." He had received an eyeful of the one remaining *bobo*. He motioned with a disdainful flick of his chin for Baba to retie his bundle—to remove the furry, offending entity from sight.

With a quick, crisp motion of his wrist, he affixed a big red seal on the road pass. "We're holding on to this document. The guards just down the road will be signaled to let you through."

"Can it be true? Can it be just this simple? And I've been fearful of this inspection all along—didn't think they'd be so easy with me," Baba said to himself, fearful that joy would yet be crushed.

"But then those 'big fishes' the old woman spoke of, loaded down with all their treasures —I'm sure they met with an entirely different sort of reception. Now if only they had had one of my modest *bobo* instead of all their gold . . ."

As he turned to leave, he heard a blithe young voice: "Look at that one go. He's way behind the times—doesn't know it's the beginning of a fearless new age. The old society will soon be no more. We're going to do away with the old ways like a worn pair of shoes." Laughter ensued, sounding like the twittering of sparrows at the bursting of a red, red sunrise.

These words did not anger Baba, but brought on a smoky sourness to the hollow of his chest. He felt a sudden sense of loss. What it was he had lost was too vast to put a finger on. But he knew it had been something beautiful, something fine.

THE ROAD THREADED down a slope and brought Baba to the brink of a deep fissure in the land. Dry brown reeds taller than a man swallowed up the path below. Baba hesitated a moment, waiting for courage to catch up with him, then climbed down into the gloom, dense with the vapors of decay. The light grew faint. He was suddenly cold.

His joy at passing inspection in Lancun was now diluted by fear, for this was no-man's-land, where Communist and Nationalist scouts scuttled in silence to spy on the others' camp. In fairer times and nearer to home, this landscape would have looked serene and beautiful to him; but the days were uncertain and he was nowhere near home.

He was disturbed by the profound quiet. He trembled all over as he crept through the stillness like a brown rat. He stumbled along the bottom of the gulch for a long time, squishing mud underfoot. But as the road gradually ascended, he saw evidence of human activity: reeds had been cut for kindling, revealing the tender spring growth beneath.

Suddenly, five boulders sprang to life and blocked his way. The men wore the ordinary garb of peasants, but guns were jammed conspicuously into their belts.

"Who are you! What have you seen on the road? Any troops?" they demanded.

"Open up the sack," one man ordered. With his right foot he nudged Baba's bundle as if prodding a dead animal. The *bobo* with its wealth of blue mold made another timely appearance. He was sent on his way.

Hurrying forward, Baba scrambled out of the gulch and climbed out into the open, visited by the rush of wind. He felt the sun's warmth press upon his face. To the east, the massive peaks of Laoshan glowed red against the sky.

By mid-afternoon, he had made his way to the edge of Cangkou. For the first time since surfacing from the silent vigilance of the "liberated districts" he saw the high-flying Nationalist flag, heard it snap in the wind: a blazing white sun against a blue sky, cornered on a field of red.

After a brief exchange with soldiers at the checkpoint, he officially entered Nationalist territory, where travel would not require a road pass. The absence of eyes upon him was palpable, delicious. He had regained his freedom of movement.

For the most part, he had wandered alone; now he met with more and more folk on the road: farmers balancing baskets on shoulder poles, horse carts, mule carts, donkey carts laden with produce and goods—a flurry of activity everywhere. He was finally free to lose himself in the hubbub, noise, and confusion that were characteristic of a freewheeling, exuberant capitalist city.

What immensity of color and noise! He stared hard: his eyes had long been starved by a leaden emptiness, a gray sterility; now they felt fat, sleek, and full.

In the "liberated districts," chickens and ducks were a rarity, but now his ears were greeted by the birds' din in the abundant, prosperous markets, and in the hands of determined wives who had destined them for the kettle.

At last, as the westering sun hung low, he neared the city of Qingdao, the Nationalists' refuge on a nub of the Shandong coast. Suddenly, from behind, a rude and barbed noise sliced right through him. A military truck elbowed past, spilling him into the roadside ditch. He looked up in time to glimpse a flash of bared teeth and the laughing faces of soldiers.

Further up the road, also headed in the direction of Qingdao, a peasant was struggling along, pushing a wheelbarrow with an immense central wheel that protruded out of a wide platform. Upon this, a pair of large rush baskets rested. As Baba looked on, with his heart knotted in his breast, the truck barreled down the center of the road, sideswiped the wheelbarrow, flung it like a rabbit into the air, and landed it upside down in a piteous sprawl by the wayside. Had he wanted to, the truck's driver could easily have steered clear on the wide road. The damage done, the truck disappeared, leaving a cloud of red dust in its wake.

"Ai, at least the poor fellow is unhurt," said Baba as he ran forward, but when he arrived at the scene of the spill, he saw the man squatting amidst a sea of yellow, as if picking dandelions; broken eggs lay everywhere, for this had been the precious cargo. Their chopped straw cushioning was strewn all over, sticky with a shiny, yolky mess.

How long must he have spent plodding through the villages to collect these eggs—five here, half a dozen there—in order to fill two entire baskets? He watched the man's mute, concentrated struggle to rescue those that had cracked but had not spilled their contents. He could not see the man's face—only the slow trickling of sweat down his neck and bent back—for the fellow did not once lift his head; he was oblivious to everything except the sea of damage.

Baba hurried forward to help, but the naked sense of loss and futility he felt left him sick with powerlessness, sick with hatred. There was nothing he could do for the man, no words he could utter to assuage the pain.

Relieved as he was to have fled the Communists, he knew the cruelty of the driver was a symptom of the rot in the very soul of the Nationalists who claimed to govern. "When the master is savage, so are his servants and his dogs!" he said to himself.

"No government exists here. Under Heaven there is only chaos; each man is out for himself, just as the traveler returning to Manchuria described it to me in Dezhou."

He reached Qingdao by nightfall and managed to find shelter in an empty schoolhouse.

On the following day, he was directed to a temple where beggars were fed. Buddha figures, their golden skin glazed by the smoke of incense and candles, radiated age and mystery like a dusky moon. Offerings of flowers and food grew in profusion upon the altars. As always, he felt healed and refreshed among the Buddhists, and for the moment his heart did not

need to speak of the journey ahead. The sun beat down on his thick black hair and warmed him as he awaited his turn among those who had gathered in the courtyard.

A lay brother stood high atop the stove and ladled porridge from a black cauldron into waiting pots, pans, bowls, and basins in upheld hands. Another pair of burping, gurgling cauldrons awaited to the side. Any leftover gruel would be sold to farmers as pig feed.

Baba welcomed his ample share—enough for three people—in an empty, gallon-size tin can; the container burned his hands. The mean service did not matter; the porridge was thick, not watery. The fragrance of the rice overwhelmed him. What luck to have good fare! He could not recall when he had last savored sweet, white rice.

He found a quiet, sunny spot next to potted azaleas, and watched sparrows take their dust baths as he ate with the help of the chopsticks he had fashioned from willow twigs.

He devoured the entire tin of porridge. His stomach was distended, but the rare ache of fullness felt good.

Twoom-twoom-twoom-twoom . . . , he heard over the wall of the compound. The thrumming came from what looked like a huge dragonfly that rose straight up into the sky. *Twoom-twoom.*... Baba rested his chopsticks on his lips as his astonished eyes followed the contraption's vertical ascent and watched it hover. This was his first sighting of a helicopter, testimony to the presence of the American military.

Qingdao was but a patch of land sandwiched between the Communists and the sea. Without the Americans to prop them up, the Nationalists would have been swept into the ocean long before. But this will soon come to pass, with or without the Americans, Baba thought. I've got to get away. I've got to find my way further south.

But there were only two ways to leave Qingdao: by air or by sea, and he had not the money for either.

There's no sign of fear or panic among the folk here, he thought as he continued to slurp his porridge, sweat beading upon his brow.

The rich say they don't care what new dynasty Heaven hurls down on them; they'll do as they've always done, grease the palms of those who come into power to keep them happy and off their backs. The intellectuals, they hope to become heroes of a new age; many in their sincerity and naïveté welcome the Communists. The poor claim they have nothing to lose. But all wish for this chaos to end.

Who doesn't wish for an end to this disorder? But I know of efficiency—an efficiency that enslaves. Yes, it is chaotic under the Nationalists, but in the wide cracks and fissures of their system, freedom is allowed to weave and skitter about. I'll take disorder over watchfulness. I know what it is to live life as a whisper, fearful of the gaze that strives to keep me naked and pinned to the ground.

Baba sought the help of the monks for passage to Shanghai. The Buddhists did not worry their shaven pates about a Communist takeover—their souls were focused on Xitian, the paradise in the Western Sky—but they were generous in their assistance to those who wanted to flee.

"*Emituofo*, Buddha is with you, young man," said a monk, bringing his palms and fingers together at his breast. With these words, he held Baba with the depth of his eyes. There was no hurry in his walk; no worries were folded into his brow. "Few boats are available these days, but there's a freighter run by the Commerce Department, and she sails for Shanghai the day after tomorrow. We can arrange a free passage on deck."

True to his word, the man presented Baba with a ticket the following morning. Baba said a silent prayer in thanks; he felt a deep gratitude toward the disciples of Buddha who had extended him kindness on his journey, fed him when only the wanton wind from the northwest filled his belly.

On the day of departure, he picked his way through a maze of chain-link fence and barbed wire, watched every step of the way by Nationalist soldiers, by military and harbor police. It was no easy matter to reach the ship; his belongings were inspected countless times.

They embarked at noon. The deck was thronging with men and women, young and old.

As the vessel maneuvered past tiny islands in Jiaozhou Bay and headed out to the Yellow Sea, Baba leaned against the railing to sightsee.

The European buildings, the church spires, nestled in the foilage of spring upon the rising slope of the land, told of an earlier story. They spoke of the shame of an enfeebled old China, badgered by the Germans in 1898 to grant a ninety-nine-year lease to the seaport, which was then taken by the Japanese in 1914, after the outbreak of the First World War.

The water was bird soup, the air thick with gulls and terns flying up, down, east, and west.

What a day! The water's just like the Patriarch's glass vase, blue-green flecked with gold, thought Baba. He gulped down salt air and felt his chest expand like the sky. It was little wonder that the majority of Qingdao's citizens were complacent. What could ever distress the surface of the placid bay? Certainly not the April breeze that barely scraped its surface. Lying in this bubble of sun and ease, the people could not imagine distant thunder and far-off rain.

I am penniless today, but I would never force my way into those homes across the bay and take what isn't mine in the name of just redistribution of wealth, Baba mused. If a man wants to better his lot, he must work for his comforts, bit by bit, just as Fourth Grandfather labored all his years.

When Baba went to visit Fourth Grandfather's family in Shantuozi one winter, it was the seventeenth of the lunar month. The moon was late in rising but still reigned bright and round in the eastern sky. Instead of eating with his cousins, he was invited to sup at the elders' table, where Fourth Grandfather presided, sitting cross-legged upon the kang.

into a steaming bowl and clamped down on string bean, pumpkin, gourd, translucent green-bean noodles, all in one greedy foray. He deposited the entire haul into his open mouth. The tip of his tongue, impatient to curl around the savories, poked out from the gaps where he had lost the pairs of upper and lower front teeth.

Never had Baba seen a man enjoy his food more. *Tee-la-too-loo*—Fourth Grandfather slurped the fare with an ardor that made even the fatty twice-cooked pork seem appetizing.

Although the furrows of age were dug deep, and his skin was the color of old bronze, the man was sound, through and through. He loved to laugh—not with huge laughter, but persistent laughter that came hissing out between his teeth. Even as he talked, if one were able to listen to his sentences stripped bare of their meaning, one would unmistakably hear laughter, emerging like ditties sung by his soul.

Fourth Grandfather had three grown sons and an increasing number of grandsons to work the fields. His family gave off an enviable aura of health and strength; even his draft animals seemed more able and powerful than his neighbors'.

When Fourth Grandfather was young, his

The old man heated a small pewter flask, which contained sorghum whiskey, in the fire pan. Picking up his chopsticks, he reached eldest brother had gambled away the family fortune, and as a result, his father had died from anger. What little remained was divided among the four younger siblings. Fourth Grandfather bought land with the money. He worked hard, and with the income from surplus grain in the good years, he acquired more land.

When he reached sixty he retired, handing over the management of the farm to his eldest son, Huaisheng, though de facto power still rested in his own hands. He continued to perform his daily round of chores, for idleness was no pleasure.

"Fourth Granddaddy, have you ever been to the big city?" Baba asked. The old man licked his lips, wet with whiskey.

"I've spent my entire life herding pigs, herding cattle, herding horses, driving the wagons, turning the soil. Xinmin is the biggest city I've ever been to," he replied. "You won't find me traipsing off to Shenyang, pretending to some refinement. Country folk like me—we've got too much soil caked on our heads; as soon as we scratch our scalps, big clods come tumblin'. They'd spot us hayseeds with no trouble.

"Huaisheng, your eldest uncle sittin' here, has been to the big city, and you know the story of what happened to him."

It wasn't so much the clods of dirt that fell from his son's scalp—rather it was the expression the tall fellow wore upon his face that broadcast to everyone his honesty, simplicity, and gullibility.

In the year that Fourth Grandfather retired, Huaisheng drove the sorghum at harvest time to Xinmin in his father's stead. After selling off the grain, he itched to make an excursion to Shenyang. In Huaisheng's concept of the world, a man could not fully claim the reigns of responsibility until he had experienced the city, had allowed its essence of sophistication to seep a bit into his pores. Besides, now as the head of the household, he wished to demonstrate his keen judgment, initiative, and concern for the welfare of all by taking home something nice that could not be had in the country.

"Huaisheng, don't put all your money in one place. Stick some in your socks, lest the pickpockets get at it," Nainai recommended, pointing to her own ankle.

The man smiled a wan little smile as if to say, "How can you think so little of me?"

He returned from Shenyang in the early afternoon.

"Why're you back so soon?" asked Nainai.

"Elder Sister was right. A crook slit the inside pocket of my padded jacket and stole the money."

"Then how'd you manage to get back?"

"Well, I took Elder Sister's advice. I tucked a bit of the money into one sock and wrapped the leggings tight around the ankle. I had just enough put away down there to get back here on." Huaisheng's face betrayed no great sadness or bitterness. He did not further elaborate on his Shenyang experience, but repeatedly turned his jacket inside out and poked his fingers through the slit, demonstrating to one and all where his money had made its exit.

On Huaisheng's following trip to Xinmin, after he had taken care of business, it was in his heart to have another go at the big city: he simply could not accept the idea that he wasn't savvy enough to visit there. This time he made sure to keep all his money inside his socks. He returned to Xinmin late the same afternoon, shouldering a bolt of plain black cloth, beaming proudly like a huntsman who had bagged a boar.

"Elder Sister, I didn't spend too much money, and look what I was able to get," he said to Nainai with a broad smile. "It was a real bargain."

"Hope you didn't get hauled off by the donkey drivers," Nainai responded. "Check to see if you've truly got a bolt there. You should have a hundred meters if you didn't meet up with swindlers."

When the bolt was unfurled and measured, sure enough, Huaisheng owned less than fifty.

"In Shenyang, near the train station," he explained, "there was a ring of folk listening to the street vendor, watching the fellow throw down bolts of cloth on other bolts lying in a big pile. *Guandang! Guandang!* He made a lot of racket.

"'Seventy yuan! Any takers? Fifty yuan! Thirty yuan!' the vendor was crying. At the call of thirty yuan, there was a whole lot of customers, yelling 'I'll buy! I'll buy!' At this time I also jumped into the bargaining. I felt pretty darned good when that vendor chose to sell to me."

"Well, those buyers were his own men," said Nainai.

"Looks like I've been hauled off by the donkey drivers again," Huaisheng said, laughing a cold laugh. "What a fool I am. Go to the big city twice and twice get taken for a jackass!"

"Those big cities—all that noisy mess 'n' stir—what's so good about 'em," declared

Fourth Grandfather, and with a burst of *ts-ts-ts*, laughter escaped from the gaps in his teeth. He tilted his head back and downed hot whiskey contained in a small cup that held no more than three thimblefuls.

"Ahhh." He released a sigh of deep satisfaction. "We're quiet in the countryside, so clean and comfy; who's got it better than us? This place suits me just fine. Yes, the countryside is by far the best."

"Your fourth grandfather's been to the edge of Black Mountain County," said Huaisheng to Baba with a giggle.

"But that's only forty *li* or so. That's not far."

"But it took three whole days."

"How come so long?"

"Why, when I was in my forties," said Fourth Grandfather, picking up the thread of the story, "redbeards came to this village when the sorghum grew real thick and tall, and everywhere you looked, it was like a tent of green gauze—that's why when the redbeards come during summer, it's called 'hunting the green gauze.' They come in small groups on foot so they can run and hide in the sorghum. If the redbeards attack in the winter, when the sorghum has been cut down and snow covers the ground, it's called 'stalking the white pelt.' In the cold season they come in big numbers, riding on horses.

"Well, one summer they came and tied me up, hearing of my wealth and having news that my second brother—your grandfather—was a rich man. They decided to kidnap two more fellows and strung us up together by the elbow in a row, just like ripening cucumbers on the vine. During the day, they stashed us away in the sorghum. When it was dark, they took us into a village, and after shooting off a couple of rounds, they demanded food. They'd cover up our faces with cloth so folk wouldn't recognize us, and while they ate, we sat by ourselves in a room where no one could talk to us.

"Even during the day, with eyes uncovered, it was hard to know where we were, because when the sorghum grows that tall, east, west, south, and north look just 'bout the same.

"On the second night, as we sat blindfolded in a hut, we heard the sound of gunfire and then a long silence. We were afraid to move. Some honest folk finally ran into the room and cut our ropes with swift whacks of a cleaver.

"'Hurry and get! What are you sittin' there for! Go before they return,' they cried. It seemed the men of Warlord Zhang had come into the village, and our kidnappers got scared and ran. We crawled off the kang and escaped into the sorghum with pieces of rope dangling from our elbows, and quickly lost sight of one another.

"I kept hearing rustling all about, footsteps behind me, thinking the redbeards were comin' after me. I hopped around from field to field— had no idea where I was runnin'.

"When the sun was up, I went into a hamlet where I was given food and directions. I made it back here to Shantuozi in just half a day.

"Well, that was the second time I'd ever made it outside my village, and, oh, I can tell you, it's best at home. There's no more going abroad for me at my age."

After supper, glowing with contentment, Fourth Grandfather smoothed his beard and alighted from the kang. He wrapped a black sash along the hem of his short jacket, tightening it around his belly, sealing in the warmth, keeping out the fingers of frost. He pulled the fox fur tongues of his hat down about his ears, forehead, and the back of his neck. Now he was properly outfitted to walk the icy highway, following in the tracks of wagons to collect fertilizer, the road apples dropped by horses and cows. If cattle had been herded down the road by drovers, he was assured of a bumper harvest.

"It's dark and cold out there, aren't you afraid of wolves?" Baba asked, scampering off the kang after the old man.

"Why should I be afraid of a few wild doggies?"

"You've been walking the roads at night for years and years—have you ever come across wolves?"

"Lots. Soon as I wave my arms around and cry *hoorr-haarr* a few times, or if I take my pipe and rap it against my good ol' pitchfork, the doggies take off in a panic."

At the threshold of the front door, Baba asked, "Aren't you afraid of ghosts and demons?"

"I'm honest and loyal. I set my heart at the center nice and proper. I haven't treated anyone ill—why should I be fearful of ghosts? Like they say, 'If you don't do no one wrong, there's no need to fear even if demons come knocking at your very door.'"

Then with a snort, Fourth Grandfather said, "Boy, you are a mighty nuisance with all your questioning." But the rebuke could not hide the look of amusement in his eyes.

In the yard, the old man took up the pitchfork with its five fingerlike prongs and shouldered a big willow basket. From Shantuozi he would walk the ten *li* along the main highway to the hamlet of Heituozi.

Animal droppings froze soon after they hit the ground, so it was neat pickings for his pitchfork, scraping the black patties on the snowy road and swinging them over his shoulder and into his basket in deft, unbroken strokes.

To the old man, this activity was not work or inconvenience on a chill winter night—rather it was meditation on his good fortune and on the bounty of life. He thoroughly enjoyed the quiet hours on the road alone with his thoughts, puffing on his pipe all the way to and back from Heituozi.

As soon as the patriarch had gone, the young folk at home came alive. They said, "On the street out back, a traveling storyteller has come; let's get him to hie over and sing a few tales and tap on his drum" or "I hear at so-and-so's there's a couple of brothers who know how to throw 'donkey hide' puppets. Let's ask 'em to put on a show in the wing where the hired hands are staying. The kang's heated real toasty in there."

The brothers duly arrived, and sitting between a paper screen and a pair of lamps, they manipulated flat puppets cut from heavy, oiled paper against the back of the screen; the figures were controlled by thin, flat sticks of bamboo attached to hooks at the wrists, elbows, knees, and other points of the body. On the other side, the audience saw black silhouettes punctuated by pretty lighted patterns where tiny holes had been made in the puppets.

The players had fine country voices; they told anecdotes and sang operas like "Snow in June," "The Butterfly Lovers," and "Shazibao," a story in which a mother kills her young son to be with her monk lover. These stories exhorted the audience to loyalty, piety, and chastity. When the performers were thirsty, they were served fried sorghum tea in big mugs.

Even though the house was crowded with friends and neighbors, the master was away, and how spacious the house seemed to the youngsters. They knew the old man would be gone for three to four hours, and they were free to laugh out all their laughter from the bottom of their bellies.

It was nearing the midnight hour when Fourth Grandfather, after adding the night's collection of dung to the compost pile, made his way back to the house. Coughing a few times at the threshold to announce his presence, he then muttered, loud enough to be heard, "Ah, why hasn't the goat pen been shut like I said."

Once he had gone and set the goat pen right, he was again heard to grouse at the threshold: "Now, why haven't the cows and horses been fed properly."

After puttering around in the yard, making sure that all animal matters had been fittingly taken care of for the passage into night, he finally came inside to inspect the matters concerning the humans under his roof.

Although he disapproved of the young folk burning up oil for nothing but fun, he would come into the wing where the shadow puppets were being played, shake off the snow from his jacket, tuck the fox fur ear flaps inside his hat, and sit awhile in the back of the audience to take in the show.

At the conclusion of a ditty, he would declare, "Wasting precious oil. Sing one more and let's have an end to all of this." Afraid of seeming to enjoy the show too much, the old man soon shuffled off to bed.

At the end of the song, no one dared ask for more. The neighbors stretched and yawned and trooped out the door. The puppeteers rolled up their paper screen, put away their lamps, and departed into the night.

The youngsters of the household extinguished the lamps and tucked themselves into bed. It was not easy for them to follow the example of their patriarch, a man who had worked hard and saved his entire life, allowing for few personal luxuries—just a small flask of sorghum whiskey, now and then, on a chilly winter night.

A white heron standing on a floating log unkinked its long neck, untucked its other leg, and with a couple of easy flaps winged toward land. Baba stared after the creature as it soared over the Qingdao homes whose pristine facades basked in the warmth and brilliance of the sea, their occupants innocent of the impending storm that would shake down the seeds of their labor.

When the Eighth Routers came, they appealed to men's base nature. They condoned spontaneous land-grabbing. Peasants with poorer land—many must have been neighbors, folk Fourth Grandfather had friendly dealings with—beat Fourth Grandfather up, threw him out of his home, took his horses, mules, cows, and grain in his storage and divided up his land in the name of justice.

The old man would not have understood,

Baba thought, why someone like himself—who had always centered his heart—had come to suffer at the hands of demons.

When evening fell over the sea, those who had paid for a bed in the cargo hold descended. Baba lay down on the open deck. The sky yawned and swayed. The heavens cradled him. He felt himself a winking star among the stars, rocked by the universe, adrift, aloft, lulled by the gentle *ba-taa, ba-taa* of the sea.

Justice is not in the hands of man. Justice is not in the universe. There are only the inevitable, impersonal laws of change and flux.

That which grows full and fat with blessings will grow thin, and that which is thin will grow fat. It is the Dao, the way of nature, the endless cycles of growth and decay, a cosmos spinning with opposing, conflicting forces.

This was the first time Baba had taken his feet off the mainland in all his youthful years. The land, his country, his China, lay slumped somewhere to the west like a dazed leviathan which no human medicine could cure. Across the water, beyond the Yellow River, farther north, beyond the Great Wall, far away, was the ghost of his sundered home and family.

How will Fourth Grandfather make out? Killed like so many others had been?

But to be forced to live his last days as a beggar would be far crueler. In old age, the limbs are brittle . . . the flesh more difficult to keep warm. Who will look after him?

Baba was borne to uneasy slumber in the embrace of the sea and sky.

On the morning of the third day, he thrilled to the sight of land. The glimmering buildings were the towers of cosmopolitan Shanghai. Yellow water fanned out into the green sea; this was the great meeting of the Yangtze, China's longest river, and the East China Sea.

In the near distance, from the water that appeared even more turbid under the scrutiny of the mid-morning sun, a mast protruded. There was no sign of the hull.

"She sank, oh, about a month or two ago," a deckhand told Baba. The man's hair stood on end, whipped by the wind. "Xu Zhen, the former governor of Liaoning Province—say, isn't that your home province?—he and his entire family are still down there, swimming in the deep."

Baba stared down at the troubled water. His knuckles whitened as he gripped the cold metal railing.

"She rammed into rocks in the night. A great many people died, the rich and powerful scurrying from the fighting in the north. Lots of money and jewels sank with them . . . certainly lots of gold." The man wet his lips and plumbed the depth—oh, what sweet torment. He looked as if he would fish the treasures out with his eyes.

Lame-legged Xu—the students named him that because of his bad limp, Baba remembered. He had seen the governor many years ago in Manchuria. The man had graced them with his presence in Shenyang during the food shortage that had followed upon the surrender of the Japanese. Xu had sat down with the students in the dining hall. Touching a bite of the steamed sorghum and soybeans—famine food—to his lips, he had said with a smile, "*Hao, hao*—good, very good." His enthusiasm had convinced no one.

"Yes, that's all that remains of the ship," continued the deckhand, eyes now climbing up from the water to the tip of the mast. "That's what remains of her—the *Taiping*, the Great Peace.

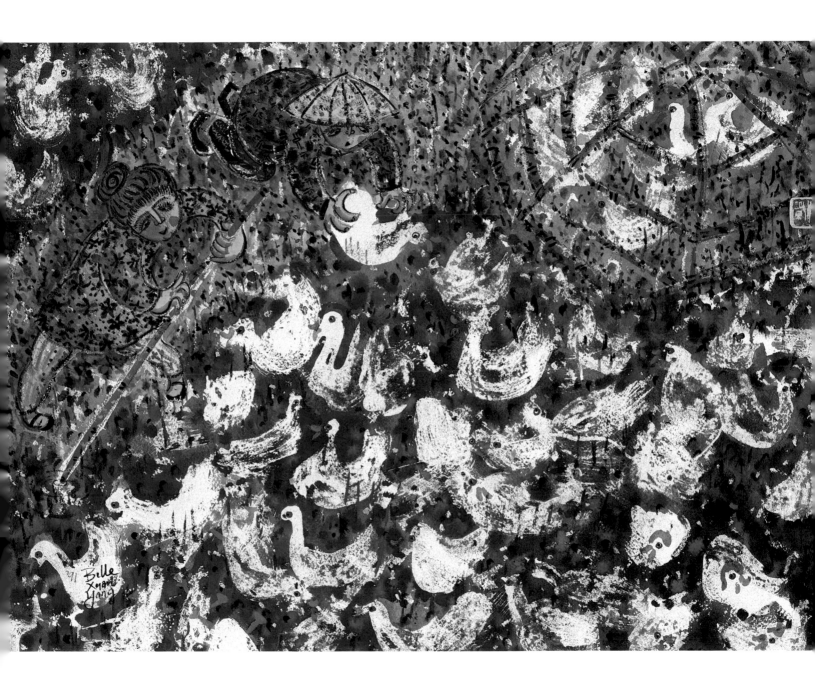

THE CLERK WITH his trim pink fingernails at the Shanghai City Hall tried to back away from the unwashed bodies that stank like fermented fish sauce. He wrinkled his nose. Baba was among those who engulfed him with their odor; he hadn't bathed in over four months, not since Beiping, before the city surrendered to the Communists.

"We're students. Refugees from the North," clamored the ragged flock, gabbling in a motley of provincial accents. "We need a place to sleep." They had met on the boat from Qingdao, and having just disembarked, they stood unsteadily, still feeling the sea's swell and buckle.

The clerk, with his oiled hair parted down the middle as was the vogue, wore a pair of gold-rimmed spectacles that emphasized the elegant curve of his brows; the man slowly adjusted his tie. His clean scent breathed forth and reminded Baba of a luxury he had never fully appreciated.

"*Hao-le, hao-le.* All right, all right," the clerk replied in Mandarin. "We'll see to finding a solution. Please, please, remain outside the building, all of you." He hustled them outside.

They did not have long to wait. A black truck, polished to gleaming, came to an abrupt halt in front of the building.

"Go on, go on. Please get on." The clerk motioned them to board from a distance, remaining upon the top step of the building.

The vehicle drove off with the students pressed together, hunkered down on the open bed like animals being shipped to market.

So this is Shanghai . . . I'm finally here. The place is even more splendid than I had imagined. The buildings are so much taller than in the North, Baba thought as he stared at the edifices that pointed to heaven.

Shanghai, 1949. The empress of the East. Asia's greatest port city. Churning the water: steamers, sampans, cruisers—boats of every size and shape. On the streets: more than thirty nationalities elbowing one another, vying to seize a fortune, a living, or simply a bowl of rice.

"Even the bootblacks and rickshaw boys are better dressed than I am," Baba said to himself. He absorbed the collage of movements—trolleys, pedicabs, motorcars, trucks, and bicycles, the sidewalks bristling with pedestrians—as the truck steered through the hubbub.

Shanghai spread along a tributary of the Yangtze and drew its strength from that mighty river, more than three thousand miles long and miles wide in certain sections. The Yangtze: equator of the Middle Kingdom. It was little wonder that in the minds of Shanghai's citizens the river seemed a formidable redoubt against danger.

Folk here seem as unaware as those in Qingdao had been, thought Baba. Aloof, unconcerned. It's as if the Communists were not swarming on the northern bank—at their very door. As if no blood had soaked the country.

And if they do realize the danger, they're certainly doing a good job of ignoring it.... Maybe the specter of it is far too enormous for people's minds to grasp.

The tall buildings were gradually replaced by less prominent structures as the truck rolled southwest. Eventually they disappeared altogether, replaced by emerald rice paddies and fields, blossoming in purple milk vetch.

"This is odd . . . where are they taking us?" the students, craning their necks left and right, asked one another. Why had they left the rush and noise of the city for this void?

These questions were soon answered. The truck came to a halt before a gate; CAOHEJING POOR CITIZENS' ASYLUM, the sign above it read. The gate opened and the truck was allowed into the compound.

Inside, crowds of men and boys in loose gray pajamas, which flapped about their lean figures, surrounded the truck and stared, slack-jawed, at the newest inmates. Their shaven heads were covered with white crust that flaked like snow when scratched.

"Poor citizens"—the euphemism for beggars, those who had been found loitering in the fashionable sections of the city, who were a nuisance, an eyesore, an embarrassment. They had been grabbed from the streets and dumped here, penned in by the high walls constructed from bamboo.

The beggars, however, seemed content; the schools of children making happy noises as they chased one another around the compound, kicking up dust; the old men meditating on their chess moves and waving away flies with their fans. Here they were fed every day and were doctored for minor ailments. They would not be able to find better accommodations elsewhere.

Many of the students, however, were not so pleased with their new situation. They were not prevented from leaving the compound as the beggars were—but many protested bitterly nonetheless: "We are scholars, members of the most respected social class. We stand above the farmers, workers, and merchants. It's degrading to be placed with the scum of society."

"So what. I am no more than a Shanghai beggar," Baba said with a shrug and a chuckle. A soft breeze with a twist of unidentifiable fragrance stroked his skin; and for the first time in many months, he felt his muscles relax, down to the smallest in his small toe. It was full-blown spring with all its stirrings.

He was taken along with the rest to a vast building constructed entirely of bamboo, with pallets built along the walls. Insects sprung from the caves above and grass invaded from below. Cosmopolitan Shanghai: he had heard about this glamorous metropolis since childhood and visited her in the movies. He had always wished to gaze upon her beauty for himself.

Roughly one hundred refugee students were already in residence. How they had made it south of the Yangtze, Baba did not know.

One morning, a week into his stay, trucks arrived at the compound. Some eighty students were herded on board, driven into the city, and unloaded at the entrance of a public bathhouse. The place was empty; it seemed that it had been reserved for them. Baba had never seen a bathhouse such as this: the pristine white tiles glistened with the chastity of a sanctuary. Two baths, the size of swimming pools, were filled with steaming hot water.

The students were each provided with a towel, a toothbrush, toothpaste, and a bar of fragrant pink soap.

Like dirty brown ducks that had not gone swimming the whole of winter being driven into the spring-thawed pond, they waddled into the baths, dove, splashed, sputtered, bobbed in the water, and made much noise as they dissolved the rich patina of dirt and grease from their bodies. When they emerged, they were lily white again.

Afterwards, the students were processed in the adjoining mirrored hall, where thirty male barbers in white frocks were in attendance behind thirty barber chairs. After the shampoos, their scalps were raked with fine-toothed combs for the tiny white eggs of lice. The barbers, all the while they worked, twittered and nattered away in Shanghainese to one another like a row of sparrows. Their dialect was indecipherable to Baba and the others. They were probably laughing about these "mud turtles"—these bumpkins from the barbaric North.

After their haircuts—after their hair had been made smooth, fragrant, and shiny with pomade—the young men were told to choose clean attire from big boxes piled high with donated clothing. Then each person was handed a white paper bag filled with glorious edibles: bananas—rare to the North and hinting of tropical heaven; chocolates—ambrosia! they rolled their eyes in ecstasy; breads, cakes, and an assortment of foreign sweetmeats that were gobbled up faster than their tongues could curl.

Thereafter, they were divided into groups of six.

"You'll be taken to the theater," they were informed.

How come we're getting such good treatment? Who are these benefactors willing to provide entertainment? wondered Baba. Ah well, I don't care. The prospect of a movie or play warmed his heart. It felt good to drift along in a group, a welcome change from decision making and constant vigilance.

Once through the door of the theater, they were ushered down the aisles, but instead of being seated in the audience, they were led up onto the stage and asked to stand in front of the curtain of red velvet.

Now I begin to see... we are the entertainment.

"We are refugee students from the North." A young man came forward to address the audience in a hesitant voice. His gaze was lost and limp beneath troubled brows. His speech had undoubtedly been rehearsed. "We have seen rivers of blood spilled. Red blood of the rich and the poor.... If the Communists come to power, life will never again be the same for you. Your way of life, like your big buildings, stands seemingly indestructible, but when the storm comes, everything will be swept away...." Behind the speaker, the screen of the students stood as silent witnesses to Communist atrocities.

Initially the near-capacity crowd of well-to-do Shanghainese listened closely to the speech, but as the room grew increasingly hot and stuffy, they began to fidget, cooling themselves with fans, or flapping hats and newspapers.

"If the Nationalists want us to scare the audience into donating money to their cause—why, they should have stuck us up here in our stinking, natural state," whispered Baba to a youth next to him. "This won't work: these men and women won't believe our plight with our nice, clean clothes and hair smelling of flowers."

He felt over one hundred pairs of eyes at an unbridgeable distance upon him.

Then someone in the theater began to hiss, bringing on a crescendo of hostile, unruly clapping. "Get off. Get off the stage. Start the show. We want to see the show. Get the Nationalist flunkies out of here."

It was futile to continue. They left the stage and slinked out the back door and into the street.

"Let's proceed to our next event and give our talk there," said the group leader. "And afterwards, I am told, we will be treated to a banquet."

"Count me out," said Baba to himself. He slipped away in the crowd. He sauntered west along sumptuous Avenue Joffre, staying his persistent hunger with the remainder of the cakes and sweets.

There was a time when, sparked by idealism, he would have served innocently as someone's propaganda tool; but in the years of strife his soul had become encrusted with cynicism like a rock by barnacles—now it was wary of passion. He found his way back to the asylum, happier to beg a bowl of gruel than to be feasted.

The days that followed were leisurely. He allowed his body and spirit to mend. He did not try to peer into the future. He did not try to anticipate the great tide of events. But neither did he blind himself to circumstances, as the people of Shanghai did.

He made excursions into the city under a splendid sky graced by an occasional tuft of white cloud. Along the banks of the waterways, willows put forth showers of shrill green leaves; *wheet, wheet, wheet,* sang orioles, brilliantly, ardently, foolishly, too much in love to search for insects in the trees. He strolled the waterfront and main street—known as the Bund—with hands thrust deep into empty pockets. He ambled along Nanjing Road with its dazzling department stores; one even boasted an escalator. He toured the Suzhou-style garden of Huang Jinrong, the kingpin of the Shanghai underworld.

But his sightseeing was cut short.

The meager fare he received at the asylum, consisting of rice porridge, steamed bread, and cabbage soup, was not enough for a still-sprouting young man. He had been small in childhood, but at age twenty, his body was undergoing a sudden spurt of growth; he had come to tower over his peers.

Lately his hunger had become relentless.

To supplement his diet, he snatched freshwater crabs the size of silver dollars from the nearby rice paddies. He carried them back to the compound in enamel washbasins, to cook in a tin can over a small fire. The crustaceans hadn't enough meat to catch between his teeth, but at least having a taste of something in his mouth fooled his belly for brief periods of contentment.

But crabs and shrimp and assorted foods from the sea and stream were known to the Chinese to aggravate infections. And sure enough, a sore on his upper thigh took a turn for the worse, ballooning as large and red as a pomegranate. Medical attention was available at the asylum clinic, but Baba was too impatient to line up in the morning behind the dozens of children waiting for mercurochrome to be dabbed upon their scabby shaven heads.

When the sore gave hints of ripeness, he took a segment of sharpened bamboo and plunged the point into the pustule. When the pus and blood had been drained, the flesh cupped in. He washed the wound with the dingy water of the rice paddy.

Miraculously, within the week the wound closed, and he felt no more pain, only the reassuring itch of healing. He continued to scrabble for crabs.

During this period, a belligerent faction of students who had insisted on finding housing suitable for their status as scholars moved away to an empty classroom at a nearby high school. Once they were established there, they defended their territory jealously and would not allow others to join them.

"Why all the fuss?" said Baba. "Why do they set themselves apart? Wherever we make our beds, we still have to beg for our daily rice from others."

Baba had plenty of time to reflect on his state of dependency, shed of all pretenses during his period of rest and convalescence. Often, his memory came to light upon the family of Grampy Wang, his particular aversion for the man now diffused by a new understanding.

One fine winter day in the year Baba turned thirteen, a wagon drawn by two little donkeys entered the South Gate. It brought unannounced to the House of Yang an old man, his son, his daughter-in-law, and all their worldly possessions, pots, pans, and ladles rattling and banging.

When the wagon pulled to a groaning stop in the yard, the threesome hopped off and began studiously removing their belongings, piling

everything against a wall along the eastern wing.

The man, whom Baba addressed as Grampy Wang, had fallen upon hard times. He came not to claim mere monetary assistance or a few *dou* of grain from kinfolk—Baba's fourth uncle had married Grampy's daughter—but to place his entire family under the care of the Patriarch. There was no doubt in anyone's mind that the Wangs meant to stay.

The threesome hailed from a village known as Yang's Ridge, some forty *li* to the north of Xinmin, where the old man had a mud cottage and a few dozen *mu* of thin land. Had there been pairs of strong hands in the family, the Wangs might have been able to scrape by even on poor soil, but there was only Grampy, who was too brittle, and Grampy's son, as pale and tender as a bean sprout. Their dire situation was aggravated further by the death of Grampy's wife. It was then that the old man had thrown his hands up toward Heaven in a gesture of surrender.

In the confusion of their arrival, it was decided to put the Wangs up in the building next to the mill.

The kitchen of this building was used in the winter to warm up the frozen feed before serv-ing it to the pigs, and for boiling the bristle off the poor creatures after they had met the cleaver. The wok used was so large Baba had to scramble up on a stool to peer down into it.

In the adjoining room was a nice, dry kang which extended down the length of the southern wall. This room was unoccupied and served as storage for the several vats of pressed cabbage that over the winter turned into *suancai,* tasty in firepots and soup.

But a few weeks after the Wangs had settled into this building, Grampy departed with his bedding rolled up under his arms to join Baba, Baba's third brother, and his two cousins in the boys' quarters. It was a room which most grown-ups did not relish visiting, for the children were raucous and disorderly, living like a troop of tumbling puppies.

But Grampy Wang had no choice: he didn't get on with his daughter-in-law; their relation-ship soured like *suancai.*

The boys' room was built with a pair of long kangs, but the northern stretch was never heated, since the stove connected to it, which would have piped hot air into the tunnel of bricks underneath, was not used for cooking. Grampy Wang shared the southern stretch, the side that received the morning sun, taking for himself the coveted warm spot against the kitchen wall.

The boys did not care for their new roommate; though they were disorderly, at least they were conscientious about their hygiene. The same could not be said of the old man.

Grampy Wang had thin, wavy hair that sprouted atop a moon face. His red eyes were as small and round as those of a fish. On his forehead was an obstinate dark patch—sunburnt, dirty, and scabbed—which flaked in a flurry of skin whenever he scratched it with his hangnailed fingers. This forehead of his and the neighboring geography of his face never met with a good scrubbing.

When Grampy spoke, or rather mumbled, his words emanated from beneath his long mustache, which curtained his mouth entirely. His voice, choked with phlegm, made it even more difficult for the boys to decipher his country dialect.

His daily garb was a loose-fitting wadded jacket that fell all the way down to his knees, the top two brass frogs of which he never bothered to fasten. The jacket had once been dark blue but was now scuffed and faded to a dusty gray.

The boys would not allow him to join his bedding with theirs in the closet during the day, fearful of the swarms of lice that likely grazed on his body. The old man had no choice but to keep his bedding rolled up in his corner, adding to the general untidiness of the room; he dozed, slumped against it, during the day.

Beyond his slovenly attitude, the man had no knack for talk with children, and this further diminished the boys' interest in him.

"All the emperors under Heaven are named Zhao," the old man said one day. But Baba, who had had a few years of Chinese history at school, knew that not all Chinese emperors were named Zhao.

"Why do you say so?" he asked the man.

"Now, if you had read for yourself the list of all the surnames, you'd see that Zhao is at the top of that list," Grampy replied, tugging his chin whiskers with a faraway look in his eyes.

"But the man who established the Han dynasty and was its first emperor was named Liu, not Zhao," Baba argued.

"Oh! Even he was named Zhao before he was a Liu!" said Grampy Wang without blinking.

On winter mornings, when the shutters had been removed and the light flooded into their room, Grampy Wang squatted on his bedroll with his eyes shut tight. From beneath his quivering mustache came a strange droning. This spooked the boys, for it was like keeping company with a witch doctor who had become possessed by a demon.

When the days had warmed up a bit, Grampy was to be found outside in the mornings, kneeling at the base of the southern wall, facing the sun. And as always, he was mumbling under his mustache. His recitals were conducted religiously: once in the morning, once at high noon, and once at sunset.

"Grampy Wang, what are you mumbling there?" Baba once asked.

"I'm recitin' the 'Solar Sutra.'"

Baba had never heard of such a sutra among all the Buddhist scriptures. "What's the benefit of the 'Solar Sutra'?"

"To keep the home safe and peaceful."

"Can you say the sutra out loud so we can hear it too?"

But the old man refused. "If I make it so as you can hear it, it won't work no more, and besides that, Granddaddy Buddha there up in the sky'll be angry, and he'll throw down bolts of lightning and give us thunder to teach us a lesson."

The boys laughed at his idiosyncrasies, which were mostly harmless. But what they did find offensive and unbearable was the old man's bad cough, which transformed their nights into nightmares.

It began with a low purring like a cat's, which then transmitted itself into a lengthy, high-pitched *Ahhhaahaa*. This was followed by a terrible *Ker-Ker-Ker* that ended with a *Piang* as the man's spittle landed on the floorboards. This last gesture was a longtime habit of Grampy's, for his home in the country had dirt floors.

A spittoon was provided for him, but he was forgetful, and when he remembered to use it, he only managed to hit the rim.

Quite understandably, none of the boys wanted to clean up after him. None relished the idea of even coming near the spittoon; they were ready to burn their room, purify it with fire. In the end, Grampy Wang's daughter-in-law was coerced into cleaning up after him in the mornings, for she preferred even this chore to having the old man share a room with her and her husband.

Grampy Wang's coughing was not the only offense to keep the boys awake. The old man also talked in his sleep; he farted; and he ground his teeth. None of them wanted the space on the kang directly next to such a lively old man. They bunched together at the far end, though it was decidedly colder there.

On one particular night, the boys were awakened by the sound of the old man's cries.

"Long-worm! Long-worm!" he sounded the alarm in the wee hours. "We've got a long-worm in here." "Long-worm" was dialect for "snake."

"Oi! Get up. Quickly. Get up. The lamp, the lamp. Put a flame to the lamp, someone."

When the electric light was switched on, it revealed no snake. A calico cat leapt off the kang, landing lightly on the floorboards.

Now, the boys' room was residence to any number of cats, which came and went through a tiny opening in the wall, made especially for their feline convenience. They loved to curl up on the heated kang on winter nights.

"A cat's tail! You felt a cat's tail," Baba said morosely to the old man. "See, Grampy, you felt her tail, which must have been cold to your touch, since she's just come in from the outside."

But no amount of explanation would convince the old man otherwise. He attacked his bedding vigorously and came after the boys' quilts for a thorough shaking out.

"Long-worm! Long-worm! I know a long-worm when I feel one. It slithered right by my ear. I felt it. I felt its cold skin with these hands of mine."

The grown-ups would not listen to the boys' complaints. "He's your elder, and you must be respectful. There's nothing wrong with having him sleeping among you," they scolded. "As you well know, we're tight on space. Where do you propose we put him, if not in your room?"

The boys remained silent to this question, for they knew exactly where the old man should go: back in the building next to the mill with his son, daughter-in-law, and the vats of *suancai*.

Since protest was ineffective, they decided to make a nuisance of themselves to drive him away. In the middle of the night, they shot Grampy with barrages of laughter; they chattered and warbled songs; they banged on the walls and flopped about on the kang.

But their energy was wasted. The old man was not the least ruffled by the racket; he slept right through their performance, and did not honor them with a single objection.

Now, Grampy Wang's son was a fifteen-year-old lad. As was common for country folk with their youngest boy, he was given the nickname "Gada," which was dialect for "Nubbin."

Little Gada Wang had a round face after his father's; a pointy tuft of hair lent his head the shape of a peach. He wasn't much of a talker, but when accosted, he smiled a splendid shy smile, revealing a front tooth stained yellow.

Gada's marriage had been arranged by his and his wife's respective families long before either had come into the world. She was twenty-one, six years his senior, and far broader and taller than he.

Tanned, as peasant girls were, she was also muscular and robust. Her ruddy cheeks, the color of ripe sorghum, puffed out slightly around her mute, pursed lips. Baba never saw a smile grace her face. She had spent all her days deep in the countryside, and she was intimidated by life in Xinmin, living among well-to-do folk with newfangled, modern amenities such as electric lights. She hid herself away in her sister-in-law's room and passed the days sewing and stitching shoes, appearing only at dinnertime.

One day that winter, Baba heard that little Gada Wang had caught a cold and was troubled by terrible stomach pains. He was fed hot porridge to sweat out the illness, but the pain wouldn't allow itself to be sweated away.

A traveling herbalist, shaking his doughnut-shaped rattle, was waved down on the street and brought in to see Gada. Medicine was prescribed, but the stomach pains only grew worse.

When Baba paid Gada a visit, he found him rolling from side to side on the kang, curled up like a prawn and whimpering, *"hei-ya, hei-ya"* in his nameless agony.

Grampy Wang stood nearby, browbeating his daughter-in-law. "You good-for-nothing wife," he said, glaring at her with his round, bloodshot eyes. "You demon. You're sucking away my son's life. You've been nothin' but trouble and bad luck. If he dies, it'll be all your doin', and then we'll see how you like your days as a widow."

His barbs grew more pointed as his excitement mounted: "See the bad way your nose grows. And see how your cheeks swell. And just take a look at the way your neck bunches down into those shoulders. Just from an eyeful of you, a fella knows to expect no good."

And the daughter-in-law stared down hard at her little husband as she knelt on one knee behind his pillowed head like a runner at the starting line. She said nothing, but from the big beads of sweat forming at her temples, Baba knew that her heart was afire with worry and fear.

"Why are you hurting? How does it pain you? What's making you so ill, little husband?" she must have been saying to herself. "Is it a demon that's got a hold of you?"

Baba felt intense sympathy for her. She seemed all alone in the world, friendless, burdened by her own unspoken anguish.

After venting the last drop of venom, Grampy Wang took leave of the miserable pair.

As it seemed that nothing more could be done for little Gada Wang, it became a foregone conclusion that with a few more sighs of *"hei-ya, hei-ya,"* he would expire from his stomach pains. Folk got sick; folk died. Folk died every day. It was just that simple.

But after a month of torment, little Gada Wang suddenly got well on his own. His wife was seen knocking her head on the floor and lighting incense before the altar to Buddha in gratitude.

Now it so happened that one day, several months after Gada's bout of illness had passed, Baba's fourth uncle ran across a friend on the street who specialized in tailoring Western suits, and to this fellow he said, "I've got a young

brother-in-law; how about if I send him around and have him work under you?"

And so little Gada Wang began his three-year apprenticeship with the tailor, during which time he would be given room and board but no money. Gada ironed, swept the floor of scraps, ran errands, and was given all manner of odd jobs. Only after the tailor had wrung out of him a couple of years of menial labor would he be allowed to sew a button or stitch up a hem.

In short time, Gada's wife was permitted to live with her husband, for the tailor figured he was getting another pair of hands to help out for the price of one.

When the building next to the mill had been vacated, the boys clamored to have Grampy removed there, but the old fellow had found his nest with the boys quite to his liking; he seemed thoroughly to enjoy their company. He complained to his daughter that the children were trying to get rid of him, and when Fourth Uncle got wind of the situation, the man descended upon them for a tongue-lashing.

"He's a fine old fellow. Why are you trying to get rid of him?" Fourth Uncle said. "Besides, it'll be a great waste if we have to light the stove in the building just for him alone. And should the old man get it into his head to start up a fire himself, he'd probably burn the whole building down. Leave him alone. No, he'll stay right here with you in this room."

Since Fourth Uncle, the severe police of the children, was prone to rapping them on the skull with a stick, they argued no more and braced for the prolonged pleasure of Grampy's company. "All things come to those who wait," they said, trying to comfort one another.

At the end of three years, little Gada Wang's apprenticeship with the tailor came to an end. He had picked up the craft with surprising quickness. He continued to work for the tailor, but in addition to room and board, he was now earning money.

It was also at this time that the tailor offered him another room fitted with a kang, where his father was invited to stay.

In this manner, the Wang family came to live under one roof again. An arrangement satisfactory to both the old man and his daughter-in-law. An arrangement quite satisfactory to the boys.

It was easy for us children to laugh at Grampy Wang behind his back, thought Baba,

watching a column of ants parade along the edge of his pallet at Caohejing Poor Citizens' Asylum.

In retrospect, it seemed to him that the man had possessed a certain grace of character: he bore his fate patiently.

His "Solar Sutra" may not have been so odd after all. It was his soul's silent yearning for better days, just as a plant yearns for the sunlight. It was prayer for peace between himself and his daughter-in-law. It was prayer for the well-being of his cherished son, who would one day be his sole support. When it seemed that his boy might die and leave him at the mercy of others, only then did his frustration vent itself on his daughter-in-law.

How little did we children guess of the violent winds that would come to shake our lives. How could I have imagined that one day I would be begging food and shelter from strangers?

Yes, he was no different from Grampy now. He also longed for a roof of his own that did not leak. Food in his belly and something extra in the larder.

But did Grampy have desires beyond these tangibles? Had he in his youth yearned for a tranquil place, an expansive place, a fertile place where every fiber of his talents and abilities would be allowed to grow, to leaf, to flower, and to bear fruit?

At the moment Baba was stretching every fiber of himself simply to live another day.

The students at the asylum paid close attention to the newspapers every day; they scoured the pages for reports on the standoff along the Yangtze.

Baba knew from rumors that the Communists, under Generals Chen Yi and Lin Biao, were coiled to spring with a million men from the northern bank along the section between Shanghai and Nanjing, the capital. Another million were prepared for the second wave of attack. But little information about them was given in the Nationalist-backed papers. The only stories were about the victories, one after another, the heavy blows dealt to the enemy by the courageous government troops.

Baba had long since learned to interpret propaganda: "Victory after glorious victory" only meant "Defeat followed by humiliating defeat."

On the morning of April 22, it was reported that on the preceding day, government troops at the Jiangyin sector, a city west of Shanghai, had "fulfilled their duty and been transferred elsewhere."

Had "fulfilled their duty"? Baba chewed on the words like pieces of gristle. That can only mean that they were routed. Jiangyin is on the southern bank—the Communists have crossed the river! The newspaper was snatched out of his hands by the students pressed all around him.

The troops that had taken Jiangyin then maneuvered south to swallow the cities of Wuxi and Changzhou, both situated west of Shanghai along the railway to Nanjing. Now Shanghai was cut off from the seat of the Nationalist government.

On the very day that the students learned of the crossing, Zhenjiang, a city to the west of Jiangyin, fell, and this advancing host threatened the capital itself.

"Shanghai is declared under martial law by order of General Tang Enbo, the supreme commander of the Nanjing-Shanghai sector!" the students heard announced over the radio on the following afternoon.

"Have the Communists entered Shanghai

also?" they asked in alarm. Rumors were rife. Glued to the radio, they awaited further news. No one could stomach food that day.

"I've got to get going. Farther south. But not on foot as before," said Baba to himself. Strength and stubbornness were in his body. "Are the trains still running?" Like an ant on a hot griddle, he spent his last nerve-wracked night at the asylum. The silent shadow from which he had so recently emerged was growing and deepening. He faced the specter of an engulfment by this darkness for a third time.

At the first hint of daylight, he began the long trek to Shanghai North Station; he was practically running in his panic and managed to arrive shortly before noon. The depot was a seething, surging sea of black-haired masses, like one faceless animal with a gigantic body and thousands of pairs of legs. The city's inhabitants had finally opened their eyes to the war, and terror was now a tidal wave. Anarchy reigned. No one bought tickets; no one tried to sell tickets. A torrent of people rushed the platform for the southbound train to Hangzhou. Baba fought his way into a compartment, squeezing his way on board through a window.

Wedged in a slot by the door, he stared out as the train rolled south. Luxuriant jade paddies alternated with fields of flowering mustard. He saw peasants working the fields with hoes, and some seemed to be singing as they bore produce to market in baskets dancing at the ends of shoulder poles; in this land of plenty, they worried little about the rise and fall of rulers and their respective dynasties.

In the early afternoon, the train pulled into the station at Jiaxing.

"Extra! Extra!" the newspaper boy screamed above the din. "Nanjing is lost! The capital has fallen!"

THE TRAIN LURCHED as it approached the Hangzhou station; refugees riding atop the boxcars tumbled off their perches to their deaths. The train soon pulled to a stop at the crowded depot.

"Let us get off! Don't push! This train won't go on!" yelled Baba.

Mountain pressing against mountain: neither those on board struggling to get off nor those on the platform pressing to board managed to shift the equilibrium. The dark-haired multitude stormed the station, stirred to a frenzy.

In time, the crowd eased away from the entrances, allowing the passengers to step off.

This was lovely, legendary Hangzhou; as every soul in the Middle Kingdom knew, there was Heaven above and Hangzhou to rival its beauty below.

Baba roamed the now lonely banks of Xihu—the Western Lake—where willows growing atop the dikes dipped their long strands of viridian into the still, still water. Cars were scattered along the lakeside streets, abandoned by their south-fleeing owners when their fuel tanks ran empty.

At the Zhejiang Art Academy, on the edge of the lake, he looked on with envy as a student sketched the pavilions on the far hills—not everyone had forsaken beauty in time of uncertainty.

"I'd give anything to remain here and study painting," said Baba, daydreaming.

After resting two days in Hangzhou, Baba was ready to fight his way back onto a train.

He fed himself into the tide of humanity that surged inexorably toward the station, thousands and thousands of trudging feet. He slipped away from the mob at the entrance, circumvented the platforms, and entered the marshaling yard where cars were sorted for forwarding to their destinations.

The long assembly of passenger cars and freight cars at the terminal was packed, nearly bursting at the metal seams.

When the train pulled away from the platform, the engine backed the assembly into the yard and disengaged, leaving a knot of humanity bound for nowhere.

The quick and limber extricated themselves and bolted for the string of cars that had been newly engaged to the engine. The old and the infirm were left behind, wailing piteously. Countless were injured in the melee.

For endless hours, the engineer was busy sorting and assembling flatcars, open cars, boxcars, and passenger cars. Many boxcars were locked and likely contained military equipment.

When the sun melted into a red puddle to the west, the engine backed a long train into the terminal.

An insane, roaring crowd, galvanized by hope and fear, grappled, punched, clawed, and kicked to get on board. Chests melted into backs, backs pressed against fierce elbows and knees. Groans, shrill cries of anger and pain arose. How many met with death, their heads trammeled by countless feet, ribcages crushed in the fray, no one knew or cared. A blind, mindless force had taken possession of the horde, and no mortal—no, not even divine will—could dispel it now.

Baba managed to gain a foothold on the steps of a passenger car, but no matter how hard he shoved, he could not advance inside. A slight outward pressure from the moiling, heaving masses within would have launched him straight onto the tracks below. A resourceful neighbor, who shared the steps with him, tied a length of rope to the handholds to either side of the door and corraled them both into safety.

The train lumbered out of the station as the sky turned the color of amber and smoke.

Once the train had proceeded across the Qiantang River Bridge, south of the city, the tracks veered sharply east. As the train wrapped around a wide bend, Baba was able to see it in its entirety from his position just back of center. It stretched longer than any that he had ever encountered; human bodies encrusted it, wriggling out of windows and doors like ants feasting on a snake.

The wind was cool and welcome against his face. The roadbed with its jagged gravel hurried by in a gray blur.

Shortly after dark, the train came to stop where the awaiting hordes at the Shoushan station were poised for their assault to get on board.

Baba was shoved up the steps and into the compartment, all the way into the corner of the L-shaped corridor. Another dozen or so folk managed to force their way on. Now the danger was not falling off, but suffocating. He worked his back against a wall and dozed as he stood, awakened only when the train squealed to another stop; each time he would feel the crush of the mobs as they pressed their way on board. He was immobilized where he stood.

Shortly after midnight, the train pulled into Jinhua.

"This train will not go any farther! We've got to board another!" came the sharp cries. The refugees now struggled to extricate themselves from the cars.

In the small hours, rumors of departure inflamed the crowd on the platform. Baba clambered aboard one of the grimy open cars with collapsible sides used for hauling coal.

But the train did not stir for hours. Not until the approach of dawn did he hear a loud *kuannng!* and feel the impact of the engine as it engaged the string of cars.

It was as if the noise had been a signal to Heaven, calling upon it to add to the misery of the human beings below: big drops of rain began splattering. Baba raised his jacket over his head like a tarp to ward off the blows.

Many people bolted out of the open cars and tried to force their way into the boxcars, already stuffed with bodies, but Baba remained: he preferred the wet and the cold to suffocation.

He crouched in a corner, but when departure was rumored, he was forced back onto his feet: a crush of bodies spilled in from all sides,

piling against him with dead weight. Like a toothpick in a container, he stood bolt upright, wedged between his neighbors.

When dawn seeped into the sky, and the chill had seeped down into his joints, the whistle blew and the train slipped forward, wading through the crowd that was still scrambling to board in the pouring rain.

Stop and go. Stop and go. The stopping was part of the going.

At one of these standstills in the middle of nowhere, the younger of two brothers who stood next to him climbed off to urinate in the narrow space between the cars. When the train began slowly rolling forward again, the man was still fumbling with the ties of his cloth belt.

Baba had been watching the man through a fog of misery that had virtually turned all his perceptions inward, but a sense of danger shook him into awareness when the train began slipping forward.

Hurry up and climb back on, he silently urged the fellow. What's taking you so long?

The young man reached up and groped for a handhold. Perhaps because of the rain, or maybe weakness from hunger, his hand slipped off. His eyes flickered with a supplication for a fraction of an instant, and then dimmed. He vanished beneath the following car. For an interminable, astonished moment, everyone strained to see his body. The car was electric with terror.

"Ah, he's all right," folk shouted when one leg appeared between the moving wheels. But then as the body flopped out from beneath the car, they saw blood coursing from the other leg: the foot had been mangled, now a red knot of flesh. The victim tumbled down the embankment and into the long grass studded with rain.

"*Aiya! Aiya!*" came the frenzied wail of the elder brother, the muscles of his neck taut like cables. He tried to leap off, but the train had gathered speed and folk held him back, releasing him only after they had come to a halt once again.

They watched his forlorn figure, fading behind the sheets of slanting rain as he stumbled back up the line. Of course he would find his brother, but would he find his heart beating or find it stilled?

The train lurched on. Numbness returned, and Baba did not look back up the tracks.

They had been traveling southwest across Zhejiang Province and entered Jiangxi Province in the night. The rain continued to smash down from the heavens. So unchanging, steady, relentless, it was futile to think of anything else but the misery and the rain. He had long ago given up saying prayers asking for the rain to cease.

In the day, Baba saw the red soil of Jiangxi, heavy with its liquid burden, unable to absorb a drop more, running rivers of russet tears.

The roadbed had softened, had been nibbled away, gouged away by the water. This was the cause for the train's frequent stops; it was necessary to investigate road conditions before proceeding.

Baba hung his head as he stood in the foul dampness of the car, hoping to see the landscape inch back, to feel himself inch forward. Destination no longer mattered; only the going mattered.

Rarely did anyone speak, each locked in his own prison of pain, hunger, and fear, face ashen like a ghost's, evil to behold for the utter misery reflected there.

Baba fell in and out of wakefulness. Familiar faces skimmed his memory and bobbed before his eyes. Eldest Brother came before him as he had last seen him in Beiping at the beginning of the year, in the initial days of the Communist takeover.

When I told him I would be fleeing south, Eldest Brother replied, "You go first, but we shall see you in the South very soon. Yes, very soon." At first I didn't understand; I thought he had meant that he would be running too.

There was a definite change in him; he must have come under the sway of his leftist friends. He didn't come straight out and say it, but I'm now certain he had joined the Communists. "But we shall see you in the South very soon" was his hint that the Communists would soon take over the whole of China. That explains his patronizing smile....

I've always known the Communists were not strangers, but now I see they are blood. It is my own brother coming after me, bearing arms against me.

Eldest Brother, humorlessly dignified as he always was, could never look upon Baba without narrowing his eyes in disapproval. In his opinion, the eleven-year-old played too much and spent too little time at his studies. Once he wrote a hortatory poem and posted it in Baba's room.

After staring at it for days without understanding, Baba asked, "What does the couplet mean, Eldest Brother?"

"The first line says a boy should be studying under the lamplight past midnight. The second line says that by cock's crow, he should be up and have opened his books again, for in his youth, he must be of resolve."

"But what am I to be resolved about?" Baba asked.

"Resolved to acquire knowledge and grow up to become an official, an important man in the government" was the reply. In traditional society, men of scholarship aspired to lofty seats in government, whence would come fortune and renown. Although Baba heard and understood Eldest Brother's words, he did not grasp their relevancy to his own tiny life; he decided not to pursue the subject with his sibling, seven years his senior, a young man whose face rarely relinquished its self-satisfied grimness.

Yet Baba was silently wondering, what's so great about becoming an important man? If everyone acquired such great knowledge, and everyone grew up to hold high office, who would remain to be ordinary? Who would make toys like the wooden *gar,* and send it spinning into the sky with a bat? Who would hollow out a willow twig, drill holes along the length of it, and blow nice little tunes? Who would be left to do all these happy things?

Why should everyone stay up all hours and not sleep? Why should everyone become so smart, competing to be the bigger official? He did not understand Eldest Brother's philosophy of life at all.

Now if everyone flew kites, everyone would be so happy—even the grown-ups. Then they wouldn't need to fight with each other, dashing teacups to the floor and hurling furniture. And they wouldn't need to take it out on us children when they get nowhere with each other....

Yes, he would be resolved. He resolved one day to buy the biggest, longest centipede kite with its segmented body, its fluttering feathers at the ends of its claws, and eyes that gyrated in the wind. Such a magnificent kite would require at least a half dozen boys to launch it, with a rope instead of with string.

For now, Baba had his eyes on the more modest kites: butterflies, swallows, and goldfishes, all of a simple design.

During the twelfth month of the lunar calendar, country folk made kites out of paper glued to strips of bamboo, and painted them in festive colors—predominantly brilliant reds and greens. These kites were sold at market or hawked on city streets; with the extra earnings,

the peasants could expect to fill their bellies with something special during the Spring Festival.

But Baba knew not to ask his father for a kite. Yeye was the eldest son of the Patriarch, and was required to set an example to the rest of the family. At the House of Yang, whose innumerable children tumbled about under one roof, if a child of his were to ask for and receive a coveted knickknack, then all the other children in the household would have to have one too. For this reason, Baba did not bother to plead for a kite; he already heard an unequivocal "No!" ringing in his ears.

And because he received no spending money, he would have to acquire a kite by some other means. Fortunately, he had been born with clever hands that knew their way around paper, bamboo, and paint.

But the grown-ups frowned upon Baba's making his own kite.

By the time children were old enough to be splendidly and endlessly clever in play, capable of entertaining themselves in ten thousand different ways, grown-ups began to make heavy demands on their hours, taking advantage of their keen ability to memorize and recite.

By age ten, they were excellent as messengers; although their little legs weren't long, they carried news quickly to their destination. Baba, with his uncanny memory and eloquence, was highly employable. The time needed to make his kite would be hard to come by.

Aside from the opinion that toymaking distracted the children from their tasks, the creative process smelled of destruction to the elders.

The bamboo strips for the kite frame would be extracted from summer blinds, now rolled up and put in storage for the winter. If these could not be had, a length from a bamboo pole used for hanging out the wash would be hacked off and then thin strips whittled from it; bamboo was not grown commercially in the North and was thus very dear. Candles would be removed from the altar to Buddha, with a muttered supplication for His tolerance, since a flame was needed to flex the strips of bamboo. Sheets of paper used for papering the windows would be slipped out from the reams which also lay in storage. Flour would be pinched from the pantry, and mixed with water to make glue. Tools would be surreptitiously borrowed: the kitchen cleaver for whittling bamboo and Mother's scissors for cutting paper—these the grown-ups guarded jealously, for they would be dulled.

Once Baba had gathered the assorted tools and materials, he set to work in his room, plumping down on the kang, his lower lip drawn over the upper in concentration.

An earlier creation of his had been a simple square affair, the frame constructed from three strips of bamboo. It had a long tail and wiggled in the sky unsteadily, like a tadpole struggling upstream. With experience in his pocket, he was ready to tackle a more complex design.

"I can take the general design of the swallow kite and turn it into a Monkey King. It'll require six strips of bamboo. The swallow's wings will become Monkey's arms, and the forked tail his legs," said Baba. The Monkey King was his hero, always keen to upset the authority of mortals, gods, and demons. The project would require many days of diligent labor; since the sun went down early in winter, he had to make the most of his hours.

But it seemed to him that each day, no sooner had he set up to work than it was lunch or supper time—time to clean up and put away his tools and materials, for his kang had been chosen as the dining area for its proximity to the kitchen.

After he had finished constructing the

framework and had pasted down the paper, he began to paint Monkey King's white face, with its triangle of red where the eyes, nose, and mouth came together, his flaring nostrils, his golden tiger robe, his black boots pulled over crimson trousers; paints were no problem to obtain, for he had a set of watercolors for use at school.

Just as he was applying the finishing touches, his sister ran in bearing a message: "Father wants to see you in his room right away!"

Totally absorbed in his kite, Baba mumbled acknowledgment. He was reluctant to drop his brush and allow his paints to dry and cake. He hurried to complete the detailing, urged on by the knowledge of his father's impatience and monstrous temper. But the longer he kept at his work, the more engrossed he became, and very soon he had sealed his attention airtight from the noise of the world—and even himself.

Suddenly, he found an ashen, contorted face looming before him, eyebrows winging in wrath. His father's big claws wrenched away his kite, and with a snap! snap! snap! splintered it into many pieces, a tatter of colors, which the man then fed to the stove. Baba's face erupted in crimson, the faint expression of contentment

gone, the anticipation of pleasure dead on the floor of the oven. Flames would lick his kite clean of existence, leaving the smell of smoke to sting his memory.

Then his father yanked him off the kang, boxed him across both ears, and kicked him in the leg. "I've called you, and you don't come. You're still messing around here," the man said.

"Now, listen!" His father grabbed his arms and shook him hard. "The Patriarch says on the sixth day of the New Year, he wants to invite Grandfather Lu and Grandmother Lu on Big East Street to a midday meal. A carriage will go for them. Take them the message. Go! And come back with their reply without dawdling."

Dazed, his ears ringing from the abuse, Baba sped away to do his father's bidding, forgetting his fur cap, running all the way to the House of Lu, his warm breath issuing from his mouth like smoke from a little steam engine. The hot vapors of exertion poured out the collar of his jacket.

Upon arrival at the House of Lu, he remembered the rules of etiquette that had been drilled into him by his elders. He walked sedately—no running was allowed indoors. When presented, he bowed deeply before Grandfather and Grandmother Lu and then straightened up like a pole.

"My grandfather, the Patriarch at the House of Yang, requests your presence at a midday feast on the sixth," he announced with difficulty, his lips bitten numb by winter. "A carriage will come to your gate at noon for your convenience." Once he had conveyed his message, he was not to interrupt the talk of the grown-ups with childish prattle.

Grandmother Lu saw that his ears were red from want of a fur cap. "Why don't you sit for a bit and warm your hands?" she proposed. But Baba knew he must not accept the invitation. Should she offer him candy from the cabinet on the kang, as she had done on previous occasions, he was not to reach for a piece. Should she offer him a cup of tea, it was to be politely declined.

"What a comely lad! Look how well-mannered Yang Laojun's grandson is. Just like a big person."

He bowed and made his exit.

"It was hard to make Monkey, and now he's been fed to the oven. But I'm not going to give up," he said to himself as he retraced his steps.

"For stealing the peaches and pills of immortality, Monkey was condemned to death in the furnace of Lao Jun, the Daoist sorcerer in Heaven. But at the end of forty-nine days, he burst the lid and jumped out. The whites of his eyes were tempered fiery red while the pupils were pure gold. He came out with even greater powers to make trouble in Heaven."

Like his hero, Baba was never one to languish in defeat; his soul was busily, silently, stubbornly plotting to succeed. He figured he still had enough materials for another go at a kite. He certainly had enough enthusiasm.

"And I won't make it in my room this time. They won't be able to find me if I work on Uncle Zhao's and Uncle Yu's kang," he said to himself.

Upon his return, he noiselessly removed his tools and materials to the building next to the mill where the hired hands lived.

The lighting in their room was poor. It had but a small pane of glass on the lower tier of the latticework window, through which the winter sun pressed hard to come in. The top tier had been papered over, as was the fashion in Manchurian homes. The kang, however, was toasty warm, for the connected stove was in constant use for making bean curd, the entire building now fragrant with holiday cooking.

Uncle Zhao, the ex-bandit, and Uncle Yu, the man charged with breaking the ice that formed over the well in the winter—these two were a holy, protective presence, sympathetic to his need for unhampered space. The two bachelors left him alone to his endeavors, and did not complain of his creative mess; they drew smoke from their pipes, went about mending their padded winter *wula* shoes, clothing, and tools.

Every now and then, Baba set down his work, emerged from this haven, and wandered about to make his presence felt in the other parts of the House of Yang, for he did not want to raise suspicions by his absence and bring the grown-ups sniffing to his hideout.

In a handful of days, he had finished his kite, down to the last detail of painting tiger fur on Monkey's robe. Baba was euphoric: the reincarnation was beautiful and strong.

But there was one more piece of material to be secured. Where would he manage to obtain the precious string to fly his kite?

In the armoire of his parents' bedroom, which smelled of mothballs and cool mystery, his mother kept her sewing notions in a satchel. The glossy silk embroidery threads were far too extravagant for his use. He would go after a skein of undyed cotton sewing thread spun by country girls.

But its removal would not be easy, especially at this time of the year, when there was little outdoor work and folk studiously evaded the cold. One or both of his parents occupied the room most of the day; his father, in the habit of meditating, reciting Buddhist sutras, or simply brooding, rarely left to go anywhere at all.

He knew he must wait, bide his time until company should arrive at the house, at which hour his father would leave the room to greet them in the ancestral hall; his mother would certainly be occupied in the kitchen, preparing savories to honor the holiday guests. This was the moment for him to snatch the treasure.

And very soon, Heaven provided him with the opportunity. When company came calling, Baba wasted no time. He skittered like a mouse straight to the armoire. Cold vapors seeped out as the doors swung open on squeaky hinges. He scrabbled inside. Once he had extracted a skein of white sewing thread from the satchel, he made sure to put everything back in order.

Should his mother notice his theft, she would surely come after him with the short-handled sorghum broom used for sweeping the kang. But the risk was worth taking; and besides, he could outrun her, and she would let the matter drop by the end of the day.

Now his kite, his pride and joy, would fly. He was fevered with anticipation.

Monkey vaulted into the sky from the grounds of the big South Garden, now cleared of the vegetables that grew in summer. The ice crunched under Baba's feet. The crispness of morning settled in his nose.

But his pleasure was short-lived.

"Grandfather wants you to run over and find his friend Old Hu, the poet, and invite him over for supper," a cousin came to say. Once Baba had returned from this errand, it was the same miserable story—someone wanted him for one thing or another. Each time, he was forced to yank Monkey back down and oblige the wishes of the grown-ups.

As long as he lingered in the South Garden, he remained victim to their interruptions. From the house, they could see the pernicious reason for his truancy, juggling in the sky, and they would scold, and would know that attached to the kite at the other end of the stolen string was Number Four.

It was clear to him that he must go elsewhere. He would run as far as he possibly could, head southeast and hide in the dunes, the sand deposited by the River Liao. There in a big trough of sand—the shadowy north slope piled with snow—he wouldn't have to lean his body into the biting wind blowing in from Mongolia.

There he would finally be able to satisfy his cravings for play, unfettered by demands and obligations. A couple of cakes filled with sweet beans would hush his hunger, should he even feel his hunger in all his fun. Freedom and sunshine would be enough to fill his belly.

His kite settled as a tiny bright spot in the sky of cerulean, scoured of clouds. Laughter and the barking of dogs drifted on the wind, for other children had also discovered the dunes, and they came to fly their kites too. Baba proclaimed Monkey superior to them all.

He had been reading a "books for little folk" comic-book version of the picaresque *Journey to the West*, and he knew by heart all the adventures of the knavish Monkey, chosen by Guanyin to accompany the monk Tangseng on his pilgrimage to fetch Buddha's teachings from the Western Paradise.

"Monkey dove into the ocean, fought the Dragon King in his underwater palace, and took away one of the pillars that had held up the Eastern Sea. That's why the water today is full of big, rough waves where once it was all flat and smooth.

"The stolen pillar was golden. It grew long when Monkey breathed on it. It could shrink down to the size of a needle and let Monkey carry it, tucked away in his ear. The pillar was his magic weapon.

"Monkey could ride the clouds, too. In one single somersault, he traveled one hundred and eight thousand *li.*"

But how far is one hundred and eight thousand *li?* he wondered. He knew Laolao's house was roughly one hundred *li* from his hometown. By horse wagon, it took most of the day; by cow wagon, it took even longer.

Now one hundred *li* was a great distance, but one hundred and eight thousand *li?* That plumb fell off the rim of his experience. "One vault takes him too far for me to even imagine," he said to himself.

The longest object to his knowledge was the Great Wall, known officially as the Great Wall of Ten Thousand Li. Where it started, where it ended, he did not know, but he figured Monkey could go more than ten times the distance of this unthinkably, impossibly long structure.

My very own Monkey also somersaults when the wind blows hard, turning around and around, but never falling, never failing. No one, nothing will ever defeat him, thought Baba as he stared up at his kite and felt its fierce pull.

"Wah! Monkey is splendid. The grandest creature of all.... I am Monkey King! I'll vault

away—far, far away from this big, noisy family. I won't go home. I don't care if they punish me. I'll go one hundred and eight thousand *li* and more. They'll never be able to catch me...go far away...I'll go where no one will ever make me do things I don't want to do. Someplace where they'll leave me alone...."

Days merged into nights as the train minced on bound feet westward. A violent wind whipped against Baba's sodden clothes, which adhered to him like cold reptilian skin. The wind threatened to extinguish the spark of life in his body.

"There's no way I can steer a path that would meet all the demands of others and fulfill my own needs as well," Baba said to himself.

Years ago, Eldest Brother bowed to family pressures for an arranged marriage...yes, he was called home from Beiping, and not only was he forced to abandon his sweetheart, a fellow student at the university, he was also made to drop his law studies. His Western-style education was corrupting him, the elders said.

But why didn't he act: walk the path of protest that he seemed to have set out on? Why after all the fuss, the quarreling, a year of willful silence on his part while under virtual house arrest, why did he suddenly go limp? It seemed ironic to Baba that a personality so steely, so contentious would not act to fulfill himself.

And it seems Eldest Brother has again bowed to the will of others. How can he turn to the Communists—those who destroyed our home, destroyed his position as the eldest grandson who stood to inherit status and wealth?

Maybe he feels that by joining, he is overthrowing the Confucian proprieties that had cramped his youth. Hasn't he simply chained himself to another authority? Perhaps his desire to become an official, a man of importance, rules his life, and it doesn't matter to him what sort of government he joins.

It came to Baba suddenly that a rift of inclinations had sundered him from his brother, had always kept them apart.

On the following day at dusk, the train pulled into Nanchang, the capital of Jiangxi Province. It would go no further.

Baba hauled himself off slowly, throwing each leg, which felt as heavy as a sandbag, over the side of the car. He had sensed the purple swelling crawl from his toes into his ankles, calves, and thighs; now he could see the damage for himself. The metal eyelets of his shoes were embedded in the flesh of his feet like nails set into the bark of a growing tree; the exposed part of his feet had puffed out of his shoes like risen dough—he was surprised the swelling hadn't burst his shoelaces.

He was frantic with hunger, but the vendors had skittered home with their baskets of cooked rice, fearful of the crazed swarms that descended upon them at the train station.

On the following morning, fresh rumors were set off across the platform like a string of exploding firecrackers: "The Communists are almost here! They are headed our way from Jiujiang!" A chill more awful than the rain descended.

Leaning on a stick of bamboo for support, Baba hobbled and bobbed, fighting the surging, pitching mob for a space on one of the departing trains. It seemed an eternity before the engine finally began to strain westward.

But only hours out of Nanchang, at a bend in the road, the train groaned to a full stop. A final rest. The subgrade had caved in; the tracks had collapsed. "The bridge up ahead is out!" he heard someone yelling.

Train or no train, Baba had to put food into his stomach. He extricated himself from the car and staggered away from the railroad, entering a countryside oppressive with heavy, wet foliage and layered with strange undergrowth. Birds warbled unfamiliar riffs. Like a marionette's, his weak arms and legs moved disjointedly.

When he came to a small village, he begged for rice. A peasant, dark, gaunt, and bony, with suspicion shot through his eyes, gave him a chipped, battered pan to cook it in. Under the narrow eaves of the man's hut, as rain cascaded like a white veil, Baba managed to start a meek fire from the grass and twigs that he had scavenged. It gave off mostly smoke that burned his eyes. The half-cooked rice tasted of misery and want, leaving a bitterness in his mouth and a sting in his throat: he had been given old, moldering rice that pigs would have found distasteful. But he was lucky to have even this.

He ate until his stomach was knotted and hard. Then he retraced his steps, fearful of straying from the tracks, for without facility in the Jiangxi dialect, he could neither ask for nor receive directions.

The railroad led him westward to the village of Zhangshu, Camphor Tree, where back in the late twenties, the Nationalists and the Communists had engaged in their first skirmishes. A dozen *li* beyond Zhangshu, he came to the bank of the River Gan, Jiangxi's east-west divide, running north into the Yangtze. Sections of the steel bridge had washed out. Many of the refugees from the train had also walked here, and now they knew there was no possibility of crossing by rail.

And the rain redoubled after a lull. There was not a dry patch of ground anywhere, no train station to shelter Baba. He sought a place to rest in a grove of towering bamboo.

He managed to wrap a pliant young plant under his arms and across his chest and back. This setup allowed him to doze upright with his feet planted in the mud. When the wind blew, he was rocked by the swaying bamboo.

The rain dribbled down his back, plopped down from the leaves onto his head, and rolled into his eyes. One minute he was wrapped in a watery dream, the next, awakened to a liquid delirium.

In contrast to the trains, where the bodies plastered against him kept him warm, he was now alone, and only his own spare body burned away in the night.

Although it was already May, the hours before dawn were wintry cold. His teeth chattered uncontrollably, wildly, like a woodpecker knocking against a worm-eaten tree.

But a friendly voice from childhood, of an old man whose hut had sheltered him during a summer squall, came to him. Baba listened as he shivered and convulsed.

"Ai, before your time, there was a doctor Zheng who owned many hundred *mu* of fat, black soil on the far bank of the Liao," the voice told him.

"One day, the doctor sent a crew of eight across the water to work the land. As so often happens in the summer, the wind quickly swept in big mountains of black clouds, and just as quickly, the rain came pourin' down. The laborers hailed a ferry for the return to the other side, but the river had swelled and couldn't be worked with poles. The craft twirled and whirled downstream like a leaf. The ferrymen—they were strong swimmers— they jumped into the water, abandoning their passengers.

"The boat ran aground on an island far downstream. Hai, during the night, seven of the eight died from the cold.

"Doctor Zheng had to pay huge sums to the seven families in reparation. Seven coffins were paraded down the main street of Xinmin to the music of a big flock of trumpets. What a magnificent sight. A funeral to be envied.

"And you know what that one survivor told me? The one man who had made it home said that each of the seven men let out a crazy 'ha-ha!' just before he died. Imagine that. A sudden 'ha-ha!' "

Baba was awakened by the creaking of the bamboos as their stems rubbed against each other in the wind; it was a tortured sound, like keening for the dead.

"I guess I'm not about to die—haven't heard myself let out any crazy laughter just yet," he said. The memory had forced a smile and cheered him a little.

When the dawn arrived across a low, leaden sky, he released himself from his bamboo cradle and tottered forth on his cane. Walking warmed him and brought some feeling back to his numb legs.

He returned to the bank of the Gan, there to join the thickening crowd of refugees waiting for the water to subside. As the day wore on, more and more people arrived, hobbling and leaning on bamboo staffs. They stared with lusterless eyes into the river. A mass of humanity uprooted from their homes, carrying the barest personal belongings. They thought not of the future but of the present—the dull ache in their stomachs, the soreness in their legs, their blistered feet—and they wondered how they would manage to cross the Gan.

On the following day, Baba saw men carrying rafts to the edge of the water. They were haphazard affairs, logs loosely lashed together with ropes. Shrewd and industrious peasants saw that there was profit to be made from the plight of the refugees.

It was foolhardy to cross on such flimsy crafts, but many were driven to do so by terrifying new rumors that the governor of Hunan, the province to the west, would capitulate and cross over to the Communist camp.

In the afternoon, the clouds parted, and sunshine, as if from another century, beamed down. Wisps of fog curled in the bosom of the receding hills. The distant stands of bamboo, laden with water, bent and curled like green feather boas. Even the river had curbed its temper a little.

Now is the time to go, Baba thought.

He removed his clothes, bundled them into his sack, and secured the sack upon his back. Wrapping his arms around a log, he pushed off from the bank and into the water. As he entered the middle section of the river—where the water ran swift and turbulent—he realized that no matter how hard he kicked, he would not be able to propel himself to the other bank if he continued to hold on to the log. At the risk of drowning, he let go.

He kicked and he kicked to escape the pull of the deep. His lungs felt as if they would burst; his hamstrings were cramping. When at long last he had struggled across to the far bank, he had been carried many *li* downstream. He crawled onto the sand, collapsed on his stomach, heaving and choking.

There on the western bank of the Gan, a woman with tears rolling out of her vacant eyes offered two silver yuan to anyone who would find the body of her beloved. The two of them had been classmates at Changchun University in Manchuria, thousands of *li* to the north; they had traveled the great, bitter distance together. To save money, he said he would swim. She had waited hours on shore for him after she had crossed on a raft.

A scrap of driftwood was planted in the mud. She had not even the means to scrawl his name upon this hasty memorial.

MY FATHER HAD walked a handful of days westward after swimming the River Gan and had crossed into eastern Hunan Province. Thousands of refugees were now converging from all directions upon Zhuzhou, hoping to find passage on the Yue-Han line south to Guangdong Province. Communist forces were expected to sweep into this city soon, bringing with them stillness and silence, but what invariably preceded them was a wave of humanity, lunatic and shrill.

On the platform at the Zhuzhou station, two armed soldiers stood to either side of an entrance of a passenger car, a sure sign that there were military bigwigs on board. The pair fingered their rifles, but the threat of arms did not deter the students who rushed forward.

"The trick," Baba told himself, "is to keep pace with the crowd at all cost. Move, move, keep moving forward. Stay upright. Lose my footing, and I'll be sucked down to my death." Like teeming blackbirds, should one be felled from the sky by cold, disease, or prey, the rest would swarm on without a thought, without a memory, without a break in their wing beats.

Inside the car, the crush of bodies sought room to flow and spread, thrusting through every crack and crevice. There were people on top of and beneath tables. Some perched with toes curled along the edges of the seat backs like giant featherless birds, and others stretched out, recumbent on the narrow luggage racks that hung just below the ceiling.

Baba could hardly draw breath; but seated quite comfortably—three to each side of the table—in the first booth from the entrance was a fat general, his comely young wife, and four of his officers.

But the youths surging on board sensed the inequity of the situation, and they sought to avenge themselves upon the party and their sense of privilege.

Baba pressed against one of the officers. He tried to squeeze in next to one for a seat, but was lashed by curses.

Why do you have it so good when we're flattened against one another like salted fish, said Baba silently to himself. The guards you've posted are useless to protect you. They've been shoved down the aisle and haven't enough room to lift their guns.

A female student, her long hair braided in two thick plaits, gave a sharp cry: two young men with mischief on their minds had thrown their body weight against her. She lost her footing, fell backwards, and landed seated atop the general's table. Her face and throat reddened furiously; she could not extricate herself from her awkward position.

"You students are bandits!" wheezed the general, his back now pressed against the window. "The country is in chaos because of you!" He jabbed a finger, impressively cushioned with fat, at the crowd. "Bandits! All of you!"

"You sons of turtles!" came the peppery Sichuanese from the lips of his wife. A pair of eyebrows penciled as fine as slivers of the new moon arched in anger. "When we get to Hengyang, we'll have you all arrested!"

"Don't puff yourselves up with your stinking ranks and positions!" a young man shouted from a few feet away. "We're all in the same boat. We're all trying to save our own necks.

"You suck the blood of the soldier. Why aren't you out there at the front, fighting the Communists? Dogs! Where're you running off to with the loot, eh?"

It was evident from their parcels, overhead and underfoot, that the six were fleeing with as much as they could carry.

Obedient country folk, all their lives silent before those who manipulated their lives like puppets, found their voices, encouraged by the fierce irreverence of the students.

"Clobber 'em! Clobber 'em dead! Beat 'em up! Throw the bastards out the window!" they cried in a cacophony of dialects from the far end of the car. The farther away, the louder the expletives, the greater the bravado. In a crowd, a man may heave to levels of fury he could never have had the courage for alone.

Barbed words were tossed into the air like fighting cocks.

All the while, the officers tried to slide the young female student off the table, but her inertia prevailed; to their dismay, a young man wearing an insolent smile on his face hopped on to join her on the table.

"Toss the fat one out the window. Go ahead, throw all the bastards in uniform out the window!" The country folk continued to shout their recommendations.

Confidence had gradually drained out of the general's face; cold sweat beaded and glistened above his thick purple lips.

But in due time, energy began to flag, tempers cooled, fire withered to ember and smoke. From the open windows, the freshness of a day after the rain—the fragrance of the damp earth, agreeably astringent—burst in upon them. The passengers shifted their attention to the passing scenery of Hunan Province, gazing on the swollen green waters of the River Xiang under moist hills, the white sails of the gliding sampans under the sky now slowly cloaked in quiet lavender. Evening was descending.

Clickity-clack-clickity-clack, the rain rolled on at its own temperate pace.

They threatened to throw us into the Hengyang jail . . . we're almost in the city now, thought Baba. I'd like to see what they'll do.

At every stop more people had forced themselves into the car. The general and his entourage were no longer bloated with self-importance, no longer deities unbound by the rules of men; they looked downright ordinary and frightened. Will the students allow us to step off? How will we manage to get all our belongings off? their eyes said, flickering with fear. The six writhed and fidgeted as the train neared Hengyang Station.

The wife was the first to break the silence: "Where're you students from? Your journey must have been very difficult." These soft words suited her shapely mouth far better than her curses, and she sang them beautifully, like lines from the Beijing opera.

Her conciliatory tune was picked up by her husband: "In times like these, we must overlook minor differences, work together for the good of the country." He scanned the faces of those standing in the aisle, an obsequious smile congealed on his face.

"My dear young friends, we will give you these seats if you'll make room for us," said the officer next to Baba. The faces of those who had been standing were ashen, drained of blood from hours of standing. The man began to squeeze down the aisle.

"Crawl out the window! Tell the turtle eggs to crawl out the window!" came a sullen voice from the far end of the car.

When the train pulled into Hengyang, the general stood up with difficulty; students shot over the seat back like hares to get at the space he had vacated.

As the crowd had been somewhat softened by conciliatory words, he and his people were grudgingly allowed to make their way toward the exit. The wife wiggled out like an otter. Her husband likely popped many a button as he was jostled and shoved by the vindictive, childish, impulsive, anonymous crowd.

One officer, pearls of sweat rolling down his brow, remained on the train to pass the odd assortment of boxes and suitcases out the window

—an unenviable job, as he was forced to worm his way out the narrow opening behind the last piece of luggage.

Beyond Hengyang the train entered mountain country, passing through countless tunnels; from each tunnel the passengers emerged a shade darker, from the smuts flying in through the windows. Shortly after dark, they arrived at Leiyang Station. The train would not be allowed to go farther in the night for fear of Communist sabotage.

Baba lingered on the platform. As he pondered where to find food, a lanky figure, swinging a kerosene lamp along the darkened platform, approached.

"Stationmaster, will there be a train tomorrow morning?" Baba asked. Beneath the dark cap decorated with gold braiding was a longish face which emitted a halo of benevolence.

"Hai, you sound like you're from Manchuria; so am I," the man answered. Excitement was quivering in his voice.

"How long have you been on the road? When did you leave home? Can you tell me something of the Northeast? Ah, ah, but you must not have had anything to eat if you're just off the train. *Lai, lai, lai*. Come along with me. We will put some food in you.

"I can't tell you for sure if the tracks will be safe enough to run on tomorrow morning, but it's certain you won't be going anywhere tonight. Lots of trouble up ahead. Chenxian's been blown apart."

Baba followed the man out of the station and through the slumbering streets, ghostly silent, for they were in a valley cradled by high mountains. Although it was shown as a good-sized town on the map, Leiyang had the feel of a village. The rare streetlight, winking in the night, revealed houses of bamboo plastered with mud, flimsy-looking to the eyes of a Northerner familiar with houses of brick and tile. It's nothing more than a sheepfold, thought Baba as he was invited into the home of the stationmaster.

Inside, a naked bulb dangled from the ceiling like an eggplant. There was little furniture: a couple of low bamboo beds, a table, a scattering of stools, and a wooden bench. The look of a household that has not set deep roots.

"The name is Liu. I am a native of Sipingjie," the man said, removing his cap. His eyebrows tilted down toward his ears, lending his face a wistful look. His hair was streaked with gray, but his body was still broad and muscular. He stashed his long legs under the table.

"When the Japanese began their occupation of Manchuria, I was college age. I fled to Tangshan in Hebei Province. Enrolled at the university there to study railroad engineering. Later on, during the anti-Japanese war, I went even farther south, running all the way to Yunnan Province. That's where I met my wife."

His wife, diminutive, with a silent, spare smile, brought out a wooden pail containing leftover rice and a plate of salted vegetables.

But the stationmaster soon realized just how hungry his young guest was. In no time, Baba had cleaned the pail of every grain of rice, and sat sheepishly staring into his empty bowl, falling silent.

This is curious...how do they cook rice here in Hunan? Baba wondered. This pail looks big, but the rice paddle quickly scrapes the bottom. The base reaches halfway up the side. It's too bad it holds so little.

Liu smiled at him, aware of his intense disappointment. "More!" he called brightly to his wife. The woman bustled in, retrieved the empty pail, and set to the arduous work of stoking the kitchen fire, smoky and cantankerous.

"I've been away from Manchuria nearly eighteen years now," said Liu, raking the stubble on his jaw. "I haven't had a bit of news of home in all this time. After the Japanese surrendered, there was complete chaos—even the Big Noses—the Russians—came scavenging; there was no way to send word to my family. They've probably all scattered. And work has kept me hostage—what with the many transfers and all—so I haven't had the time to go look for them myself. I hoped the government would send me back north, but no, they've kept me here south of the Yangtze.

"I have three sisters, all older. But I am the only son. It's my duty to look after my parents. You know, I feel bad every year near the time of Qingming Festival, because I cannot sweep the graves to honor the spirits of my ancestors.

"I tell you, news of Manchuria is what I crave most of all, but at the same time I'm afraid of the news travelers may bring."

Some time later, the wife brought in a steaming pail of rice, and Baba helped himself to it without prompting.

His host ate nothing, feasting on the harvest of tidings from Manchuria. He questioned Baba ceaselessly. No, nothing Baba told him was hopeful, not at all like the memories that had comforted him over the years: the rich black soil planted to the horizon with sorghum, ripening to a burnished red in the autumn; lying curled up on a hot kang on a winter night, enveloped by the silencelike sound, soundlike silence of snow descending on the roof; whiskers that grew icicles; onion pancakes and puffs of golden fried dough soaked in hot soy milk; the whine of horns and the crash of cymbals announcing weddings before dawn.

"You know, in Hengyang, just to the north of us, there are seventy-two mountain peaks," said Liu. "The highest peak is called the Peak from Which Wild Geese Return. According to legend, the ancients believed that when geese flew south in the fall, they never crossed beyond that point, but splashed down on the waters of the River Xiang to pass the winter. When spring came, off they flew again to return to the North.

"It is told that a woman of Hengyang, separated from her husband, captured a wild goose in spring and secured a letter to its leg. The bird carried her words of love to him who lived in the North.

"Here in Leiyang, unfortunately, I'm too far south even for the geese to reach. If the legend were true, I wouldn't even be able to manage a letter home by the flight of the birds."

Baba was lost in his own reveries, inhaling fragrant spurts of memories. He thought about Manchuria in early spring when the ice broke into shards and the rivers flowed free; tens of thousands of migrating geese, crying *gwur-gwa-gwur-gwa-gwur-gwa*, pumped their vast, powerful wings, their flight formations like black calligraphy. Their passage was clearly visible on moonlit nights, and clearly heard, like the mewling of newborn babes. He guessed some of the hardiest ones journeyed all the way north to Siberia.

He and the other children had been crazed by the beauty, watching the endless flocks that swept over Xinmin, day after day, night after night. They stood with their heads thrown back, silent and reverential, mouths agape, hearts thumping in their throats, watching the enormous beating wings that bore the splendid creatures, as if in slow motion, directly over their heads.

It was the same sight in autumn, though the migration proceeded in the opposite direction. *Winter's coming! Winter will soon be here!* the birds seemed to announce. And to Baba's ears, their cries were touched with a lovely melancholy.

"Generations ago, when our ancestors first moved northeast to settle in Manchuria, what was then considered the savage North, the flight of the wild geese in autumn must have made them homesick for the land south," Baba reflected out loud. Liu nodded, a pensive smile hanging on his face.

When the sky whispered of dawn—Liu's exhausted wife had long since retired—the lively talk had been hushed to a gray sobriety. Baba tried to comfort the stationmaster. "You'll have the chance to go home. We'll both be able to return one day—when the war ends," he said.

Liu nodded, but fear was in his eyes. The sad looks they exchanged revealed their doubts: What kind of homes would they be returning to? The absence of war is not synonymous with peace. To long for one's home from far away is sorrow moderated by sweet, lively remembrances; but to return and find a desert may wither even the most cherished memories.

"You know, if I'd been in your shoes two years ago, I wouldn't have gone away from Manchuria," said Liu. "In all my years serving under the Nationalists, I've only met with disappointments. I'm tired of the endless running around. Why bother fleeing farther south? The Communists will take it all. The only way you can escape is to leave China altogether. But then where in the world would you go? Who'd want you? Where on this Earth would you find a place to rest your weary bones?"

These were no longer strange questions to Baba. Soon he would find himself at the southern tip of the Middle Kingdom with no more room to run. He would have to take to the sea. And if departing from one's native town, leaving behind one's parents and ancestral graves, was considered unfilial, then the act of quitting one's homeland was the ultimate betrayal.

"No, I would not have left Manchuria," mused Liu. "But seeing as you are already here . . . I'm sorry my advice is of no use to you; it is like reading last year's almanac to forecast this year's weather . . . words of a weary, old fellow. . . .

"But I can tell you one thing, though: do not neglect your education. Grab whatever chance for schooling you can get. Only an education offers you a future. If not, your flight will have been quite without purpose."

Baba nodded. He was young. At twenty, he had not learned to be afraid of many things; his ignorance kept his heart and feet from faltering. He would walk boldly into the future not so much because he had nothing to lose, but because for someone as empty-handed as he was, there was so much to gain.

"And another very important thing, do not join the military, whatever you do—hunger drives one to do stupid, desperate things. Soldiering will only lead you to a bad end or rot you as a man. As they say; 'Good iron is not used to make nails; good men are not used to make soldiers.'"

At dawn, Baba took leave of the stationmaster, his spirit renewed by the kindness of a stranger.

The Leiyang station crawled with the stranded passengers of the previous evening; many had spent a fruitless night in search of food in the surrounding countryside.

As a train pulled in hours later, Baba saw that one car was occupied entirely by men in uniform. Must be at least a couple hundred of them, Baba guessed. But how very odd... they file out in quiet, orderly lines from the two exits, each soldier with an arm straddling the shoulder

of the man in front. The men... the men... all of them are blind! he suddenly realized.

"Brothers, what happened to your eyes?" he asked as the last of the soldiers shuffled past him.

"Ah, fighting the 'small devils' years ago. They attacked us with poison gas," one man replied, swiveling his head in the direction of Baba's voice.

It surprised him that the man's pupils looked perfectly normal, not as he had expected, fogged like the cataracted eyes of an old man.

"Make way! Make way!" their sighted leader shouted. "These men gave their eyes for the Motherland. Make way! Make way!"

The crowd parted in silence, allowing the old soldiers to slowly grope their way out of the war.

In the late afternoon of the following day, as the train descended from mountain country into lush land of jade paddies dotted with water buffaloes, the temperature climbed. Baba was entering the Lingnan of yore, territory which consisted of the modern provinces of Guangdong and Guangxi.

In the chauvinistic view of the folk from the

Yellow River heartland, this was the unenlightened hinterland, lying beyond cultured China proper, the place where disgraced government officials had historically been banished. It was a far-flung outpost of the Tang dynasty empire more than a thousand years ago. Intellectuals exiled here wrote poetry to mark their sorrow and to ease their hearts. These poems, evocative of home, have remained popular, especially among the generations of emigrants and outcasts.

At midnight, the refugees arrived in Guangzhou, the capital of Guangdong province. This was about as far south as Baba could run; any farther and he would fall into the South China Sea. To the west was Guangxi, and south of that province lay Vietnam.

Refugee students who had kinfolk and friends in the city sought them out. Baba waded out of the station, through the mass of grunting, recumbent forms lying on the floor.

This city does not shut down. Even at this late hour, a great many food stalls are doing brisk business, he thought.

He walked by one of them and was surprised to see a handgun jammed into the waist of the vendor's trousers.

He doesn't mean to hide it at all—rather, wants to flaunt it.

In Manchuria it was rare to see guns, because the Japanese had banned firearms. After they surrendered, country folk obtained rifles to protect themselves against bandits; but city folk had no need of guns.

Here in the South, though, guns were common even in the cities. The inhabitants of the southern provinces were notorious for the fight in their blood. In the countryside, feuding townsfolk and villagers squinted out at each other behind towering, fortresslike walls, ready to do battle at the slightest incursion.

In contrast to Manchuria, where men were few and land was plentiful, here there was a scarcity of land for the great proliferation of human beings. Men and women of these southern coastal provinces elbowed one another for space, and when the pressure was uncontainable, they sailed for foreign shores.

Historically, the southerners were far less obedient than their northern brothers; they held a spirited contempt for the meddling of authorities. Here secret societies abounded which fostered antigovernment activities.

"It's going to be difficult for me to muddle

along here," said Baba to himself. "In the North, where everyone speaks Mandarin, I had little trouble communicating, but here there are so many dialects and subdialects even folks divided by a river wag their tongues in a different way."

Baba could not comprehend a word of the fast-flying patter of Cantonese on the street. A common language unites and brings comfort, while alien tongues divide and sow suspicion. He knew he would be shunned.

Among the quick-witted, fast-talking, fast-moving Cantonese, he felt ungainly, transparent, and dull. I am even more the stranger now than when I first crossed the Great Wall, he thought.

Since he had no money, he did his stomach little good by merely staring at the array of food offered on the street.

As he stood pondering the eternal question of how to fill his stomach, he heard someone behind him ask in awkward Mandarin, "You are from the North, I think?"

He turned to see a spindly young man, roughly his own age, whose skin under the light of the vendors' lanterns was as dark as tea eggs. The youth's summer shirt and shorts, by contrast, seemed inordinately white.

"Yes, I've come from the North," Baba answered.

"Where from?" the young man asked. His eyes, alert and inquisitive, were as black and glossy as those of a small nocturnal animal.

"I've come recently from Shanghai," said Baba.

"You Shanghainese then?"

"No, I'm a native of Manchuria."

"Ah, then you are from even farther north," said the young man, obviously impressed.

"Where're you from, my friend?" Baba asked.

"I'm an overseas Chinese. I come from Indonesia."

To a native of the tropics, Manchuria, a land of long, ice-bound winters where the very air froze and fell in flakes of white, was a place that existed only in storybooks. It was little wonder that Baba held the interest of this dark little stranger.

"I came to Guangzhou a month ago to see relatives," the young man continued, standing with his hands clasped behind his back. "They say to me, 'Welcome back. Welcome home,' even though this is my first time ever in China." He cocked his head and looked up at the northern specimen in front of him, a full head taller than himself.

"Please. Tell me about the happenings now."

"Don't you read the papers?" asked Baba.

"No, I only know a few characters... enough to write my name. Not know enough to read. I do not talk Chinese well, but I listen better."

"Well, the Communists have crossed the Yangtze and are still pressing south. In places not yet under their control, they have established fierce undergrounds—like in Chenxian, just north of the border, in Hunan Province. There they blew up the Nationalists' munitions storage. All the buildings are gone. Only a few charred trees stand. The land is scarred with craters and deep gashes... like after a fire or an earthquake. The nearby train station is also destroyed. I saw all this as I passed by on the train yesterday. I heard Hunan will fall to the Communists very soon."

"I did not know the Communists crossed the Yangtze until I came here to China," said the young man.

"The situation is dangerous, even though the Nationalist Central Government is still relatively strong here. It is not a good idea for you to stay in China."

"Oh, I'll be all right. I think it is very exciting for me to be here. My father has said to me since I was a child, 'You are born in Indonesia, but your ancestors are from China. They are Chinese. You are Chinese. Never forget. Always be proud.'"

Though the overseas Chinese lived in different communities, separated by the chauvinisms of their home provinces, they were united by their pride in origin and heritage, and overwhelming passion for their homeland. Their sense of patriotism was perhaps keener than the patriotism of those who remained in China, for few had left the Middle Kingdom by choice, but had been pressured to leave by famine and war. The longing for China was especially acute for those stung by discrimination and persecution in their adopted countries. Many saw their stay abroad as only temporary, fully expecting to return home as prosperous men and women.

"Many in Indonesia have given money to China. Lots of money to the Nationalists and Communists," continued the young man. "Others, they have come home to China. They want to give their life to China." The young man's eyes were brimming with emotion.

"That's a very noble sentiment, but too many have already given their lives... too many honorable people are killing and being killed for the good of China."

"To love one's country"—that phrase had little meaning for Baba. It was not his country to love. Did the country belong to him? No. The land belonged to those with the biggest guns, the warlords, the Japanese, the Russians, now the Communists and the Nationalists....

"Do you want to hear how it really is to give one's life to China?" Baba said. "Let me tell you. In the winter of 1945, the winter before I left home, a handful of southern soldiers were encamped on our property. All of them had been wounded. The blood was dried and clotted on their padded trousers and coats in ugly black patches. See, all of them had been hit by Communist fire above the knees, for they had been out fighting in the deep snow. They lay in the dark rooms moaning and crying, 'Aiya, aiya,' muttering deliriously in their Guangxi dialect, which I couldn't understand. No one came to attend to their wounds. No one. No military doctors or nurses. Only a few of their own men, whose milder injuries still allowed them to get around, rustled up cups of rice from I don't know where. You see, we ourselves, a few remaining members of our once large household, we had no food at all; not a single grain even in the silos, which were overflowing in good years.

"Those Guangxi soldiers spent their entire days scrounging for rice and cooking it. They pulled out the latticework from our windows and used it to light fires.

"Many of them died . . . far away from their family. They gave their life to China. Like the people you speak of, they loved China, but did China love them?"

After a meditative silence, the young man, having followed Baba's covetous gaze to a food stall, said, "I think you are thinking of eating something."

Baba smiled to himself: the young man's bad Mandarin was not disagreeable at all.

"*Lai, lai.* Come, come." Baba was invited to sit at a vendor's table, whereupon the overseas Chinese ordered two bowls of noodles with wontons.

In a matter of minutes, Baba had slurped down the entire bowl, whereas his host had only begun to stir the broth in his own.

"You would like to eat some more, I think," the young man said. It was a statement rather than a question.

The second bowl Baba also devoured, and with much noise.

"You would still like to eat some more, I think." The Indonesian ordered yet another bowl and paid for their meal in *gangbi*; the vendor bobbed his head and gurgled with happiness at receiving Hong Kong currency.

"It is long past midnight. Why don't you go home and rest?" said Baba when his host finally pushed aside his unfinished bowl.

"I sleep a lot in the day. Too hot. Little to do. Night time, I like to walk around and look. The trains have not been running. Then I hear about the train full of refugees come from the North. I come here . . . good to be in China, you know. A lot to see, a lot to learn."

"You have been very kind to me," said Baba.

The face of his benefactor suddenly broke into a toothy grin, a big guileless smile. The young man seemed at a loss as to how best express his feelings for his homeland, and upon finding one of her needy native sons—and a rare Manchurian at that—he lavished his affections on him. He had shown no inclination to express approval or disapproval of either the Communists or the Nationalists: that they were Chinese seemed to give him great satisfaction.

They had stopped alongside another stall.

"You would like to eat some of these, I think," the young man said, pointing to grayish slices of meat sizzling in a pan.

"What is it?" Baba asked.

He was told that this particular vendor was serving chives wrapped in soft, thin squares of dog skin.

"Oh, no thank you!" Baba replied, and quickly moved on.

"So then, I am sure you would like to eat some of these." The young man pointed at yet another offering. He walked up to the stall and, upon returning, handed Baba a bundle of peeled sugarcane, sticky with juice. This ubiquitous southern treat Baba found to his liking, for in Manchuria, cane was not grown and sweets were a rare delicacy. The pair ambled along, crushed and tore the cane with their teeth, spitting out the yellowish-white pulp once the juice had been extracted.

Still the young man lingered, did not want to go home.

"The Communists will soon be here. Did you want to take a look at them before leaving China?" Baba asked with a smile.

"You are running away from them. I think the Communists will probably not be good for me either, no?" replied the young man in utmost seriousness. "If they get here and do not let me go, where would I be? . . . I think my mother and father would be very worried about me. No, no. I will go very soon. Go home to

Indonesia through Hong Kong. I must go home and attend university. Maybe afterwards, when I am much smarter, I will come to help China...."

They wandered back to the train station in silence.

"You'd better get some rest. It's the start of another day," said Baba.

"Ah yes, another day." His companion looked distractedly toward the east and said with reluctance in his voice, "Well... good-bye. Good-bye. Very good to meet you and talk with you."

From the steps of the railway station, Baba watched the young man walk way in his unhurried gait, swiveling his head left and right as he took in the sights. His figure glowed unsullied white in the haze of dawn, and to Baba, he seemed to float weightlessly above the fray of the traffic.

THE GUANGZHOU CITY government thought the congregation of refugee students a nuisance and potentially dangerous. From the train station, the roughly one hundred of them were driven out like sheep, across the Pearl River to Five Phoenix Village in the hinterlands. They were given shelter on the grounds of a clan temple, its southern-style roof winging into the sky, its pillars and beams coiled with gilded dragons and profuse with brash colors.

Upon arrival, Baba fell sick. There was no medicine. No one bothered with him. He slept on a wooden bench in the arched tunnel of the main gate. The years of flight, the years of physical punishment had crystallized into one big ache that sat upon his body like an unshakable granite monkey. He had rarely made concessions to doubt and despair; now illness came as a voice that whispered, "Was it right for you to have taken to the road? Don't imagine for a moment that the Communists will be lenient with you. If you are captured here, they will brand you as enemy."

He simmered in a fever. Is this the end? They will abandon me, the others... who would bother to carry along the sick?

Yeye came and glowered down at him in silence. Father, why won't Father give me tuition money? The amount means nothing to him. Classes start in two days, and I still don't have my uniform...all my friends have got them.

His nights were tortured by steely-framed, full-bodied black mosquitoes that knocked againt his head and the temple walls. They lapped up his blood like soup.

What am I running from? I am tired, so tired, cannot get up, lift my legs. Give me water, Third Brother...but why is Third Brother sobbing, his shoulders shaking...why won't he look at me?...I am so tired...What is it that I must urgently do? Ah, I must leave. But I have already left, haven't I. Haven't I already come a great, long distance?

Baba, knowing this was delirium, tried to open his eyes but could not, and at once he was trudging the dusty, interminable road again. Oh, but my legs are so heavy.

In the afternoons, he weaved and tumbled through the paddies to soak in one of the many tame streams that fingered through the land, finally to converge upon the Pearl River estuary. His body burned so hot he shivered in the embrace of the water, but it helped to quench the heat that blazed inside him and offered respite from the July heat that clogged his pores.

Even the healthy ones soon came to lose heart, here in the mosquito-infested backwaters, blinded, day after searing day, by the shimmering paddies. "What are we waiting for?" they wondered out loud, scratching the mosquito bites on their legs. "Are we just going to sit and do nothing until the Communists swallow us up?" They squatted in the shade of the courtyard and drew circles in the dirt. The shrill cries of cicadas resting on the boles of trees magnified the dreariness.

Small bands quit Five Phoenix Village for distant Chongqing in Sichuan Province, heading north again to embed themselves in the turbid heart of China, where a pocket of straggling Nationalist government forces still held. Others crept down a ways to Hong Kong, where the Pearl River spilled into the South China Sea.

Those who had gone to Chongqing—lured by the promise of attending university there—did not return, but the ones who had gone to Hong Kong came back in droves.

"Because we could not speak Cantonese, no one in the city would give us work," a returnee said with a vacant smile, poking the holes in the canvas of his shoes. "It was impossible there—no place to rest. The miserable thing was we weren't kept from entering Hong Kong, we simply couldn't pause for a moment, we were forced to be constantly on our feet. As soon as we'd sit down on the steps of some building or try to shelter ourselves in an alley from the rain, the British police would swoop down on us, threatening beating and arrest. I've never been so tired...walking, walking, walking for an eternity."

In time Baba was able to dislodge that granite monkey from his chest. His fever subsided and he regained his appetite, able to stomach the servings of boiled eggplant and cabbage offered at the temple. Except for weakness in his legs, he felt splendid.

The whispers of doubt were no more. He listened to a bird that cried with delightful mystery from the paddies. "There is room for me in the world, just as there is a place for this nameless ghost of a bird. As long as I stay out of their hands, I'll run, I'll keep going." He was inexplicably happy. He felt himself more than a jumble of bones, nerves, and intestines—an unbridled force.

He sat soaking in a sluggish stream, now a

pleasurable habit in the afternoons at high tide. Only his head protruded above water, like a black stone. Suddenly, a figure appeared along the bank. It was as if a small cloud had skittered across the sun's face. A palpable pall was cast over his heart, but was gone before he had time to understand it.

The youth, whom he recognized from his days in Beiping, was named Pengyue. He was tall, reedy, and his head seemed small in contrast to his exceedingly thick neck.

Two years before, in the immediate days following the massacre of the students outside the old Legation Quarter, the survivors had united to form the Blood Alliance; as long as they remained united, visible, and loud, the government could not swat them dead like so many gnats. But in time, internal rivalries and jealousies began to tear away at the fabric of their unity; the various factions fought for control and worked to undermine one another.

Pengyue had joined the Blood Alliance and had gathered troublemakers around himself, a group of young men always looking to start up a fight. One day they converged on the shelter where Baba had found a sleeping space, but the students there were forewarned. To the surprise of Pengyue and his cronies, they were attacked with ladles, pots, and pans. What Pengyue's excuse for confrontation had been, Baba could not remember.

What the man's purpose for stirring up trouble was, Baba never knew; at the time he thought he was an agent of the Communists. What's he doing here now? Baba wondered and sat up in the water to follow the man's movement among the students lolling on the bank.

A handful of days later, Pengyue called the students at Five Phoenix Village to assemble. Because he was slightly older than most, he had taken it upon himself to assume the role of elder brother.

"Zhejiang, Hunan, Jiangxi, and other provinces to the north are lost," he cried, waving his long arms, his eyes crackling with fire and outrage. His prophetic tone was a blend of inspiration, threat, and resolve. "The enemy hosts will soon be falling upon us. Closer to Guangdong they come, day by day. We have nowhere else to go. The truest course for us is to enter the military—dedicate our lives to the defense of the Motherland." This became his rallying cry: Join the military, uphold China.

Has he switched allegiance? Pengyue now seems to be speaking for the Nationalists. Baba squinted and listened with apprehension.

"You ask where we will go? I tell you where we have been invited. We will sail to the island of Taiwan. Enter the academy there and train to become officers. Yes, you heard right. Officers. The elite." His eyes gleamed with a sense of limitless power and confidence.

"Why not. Sure, why not," the students murmured, their blood stirred by the offering. "We have nowhere else to go. Taiwan is difficult to get to, and entry is restricted. But we won't be training to be common soldiers but officers."

On the following day, Pengyue led the multitude to the famous Huanghuagang, a garden in Guangzhou where seventy-two martyrs were memorialized, young men who had rallied around Sun Yat-sen, the father of the Chinese revolution, against the ruling Manchus early in the century. There, in a festive, holiday atmosphere, drunk with patriotism and swayed by Pengyue's oratory, the students raised their hands en masse to swear allegiance to China. Loyalty, sacrifice, love of country—these ideas had been emptied of their meaning for most of them, but the words still possessed the power to

ignite irrational passions: they sparked sentimental attachment to inherited values.

No names were taken. No forms filled out. No questions asked. "All of us are wanted," they were told by Pengyue in his spotless sincerity. "How fortunate we are to qualify for training. Filial sons of China, we have a shining future as leaders." He was breathtaking, dazzling in his certitude as he raised his fist into the sky.

I have no other choice now, reasoned Baba. There seems to be no possibility for a stay in Hong Kong. Portuguese Macao will likely be just as unwelcoming. I've never wanted to join the military, but there's just no better way to go to Taiwan. I'll manage a free passage off the Mainland a step ahead of the Communists, in any case. And maybe he tells the truth . . . probably no harm. Maybe we will be treated decently, given training as officers; after all, we are not illiterate peasants. . . .

The corps of students was herded the twenty *li* to the wharf at Huangpu. The students slept at night on the pier, avoiding the airless warehouse provided. When the mosquitoes grew too thick and insistent, they jumped into the water to shake them off.

One day, an enormous cargo vessel arrived. *Haixiang* was her name. Three tall officers in immaculte khaki uniforms descended upon the students. Made of some superhuman stuff, they seemed not in the least distressed by the sweltering heat. It was obvious that they had fashioned themselves after the American general Douglas MacArthur: their uniforms were replete with big hats decorated with gold braiding and sunglasses. The only thing they lacked was corncob pipes; but they more than made up for this lack by the belts adorned with gleaming silver bullets and the handguns bulging in their holsters.

When you join the military, you will grow as handsome as we are, their pretty uniforms advertised to the crowd. When you enter the academy, you will find assurance, you will find security from the precariousness of your futures.

As Pengyue consulted with the trio of officers on the pier, an uneasiness reared inside Baba's chest. We've been told only part of the truth.... And again a pall descended upon his heart, sending a long tremor flowing through his body. In the desperate mood of the moment, however, Baba's hopes and wishes would not allow him to ponder whether or not Pengyue's

promises were genuine. He tossed doubt from his mind like a rock. It was not his decision to join the military; it was that the decision had taken him.

On the following morning, the students boarded the freighter and waited for the afternoon high tide, at which time the *Haixiang* was able to slip her mooring and head downriver.

At the mouth of the Pearl, mansions built upon the distant hills were flushed pink by the lowering sun, as luscious as the yolk of a salted egg, soon to slide down into a blanket of dark clouds. They steered due east and saw a rash of lights like fireflies over the land: Kowloon and Victoria. When glimmering British Hong Kong faded and was finally extinguished, the ship was swallowed up by the darkness on the open sea, and all that could be heard was the monotonous lapping of the water, insistent against the hull.

On the morning of the third day, Baba sighted a hump of land that arose like a big green sea tortoise lifting itself out of the water.

"That's Taiwan. We will be entering the southwestern port of Gaoxiong," they were told.

Historically, Taiwan, an island off the coast of Fujian Province, had been a lair for the disaffected. It is shaped like a sweet potato, some

240 miles long and some 80 miles wide. When the Manchus overran China in the early 1600s, the Ming dynasty loyalists crossed the strait, and the island came to be the base for their resistance; fearful that overseas communities would breed rebellion, the Manchus declared that those who clandestinely took to the sea were subject to beheading. Now with the Communists overrunning the middle Kingdom, the defeated were again fleeing to this haven. In the ensuing decades, from this base in the subtropics, the Nationalists would nourish their dream of toppling the Communists and returning home to the Mainland.

In Gaoxiong harbor, as the students waited to disembark, waves of tiny rowboats loaded with bunches of plump bananas, freckled with sugar, swarmed around the ship like aphids clustered around a ladybird. Barefooted, smiling

women called out merrily, *"Ginjio, ginjio"*—"banana" in Taiwanese. They flung coils of ropes up to the students, who tied pieces of clothing onto the ends and lowered them down in exchange for the fruit.

How fragrant. Bigger and sweeter than the ones in Guangzhou. Many students swapped all their extra clothing for bananas. "We'll be getting nice new uniforms soon; won't be any use for these rags," they said, happy to be eating bananas like monkeys and flinging the peels overboard the entire day. Was this fair, full-bellied day promise of even better days to come?

At dusk, a passenger train pulled to a stop on the landing pier. The students boarded the small-gauge train and rode northward a short distance to the city of Tainan. There they were swept through dark streets and into a walled compound. "Number Four Officers' Training Camp," Baba read, catching a glimpse of the sign on the gatepost.

In the compound they were fed under the eaves, eight squatting men per basin of tofu and cabbage that crunched with sand. Afterwards, a dirt training field was indicated as their place to bed down for the night.

When a lone bugle sounded the reveille the following morning, the students on the field sat up to watch soldiers hustle out of the barracks for roll call. These men had only three scant items with which to cover themselves: trunks of an uncompromising purple, black canvas shoes with rubber soles, and a *douli*—a peasant hat shaped like a lamp shade.

After roll call, the soldiers ran laps and did calisthenics.

During a brief recess, a couple of them dashed over to the congregation of students.

"Anyone here from Henan?" one of them asked breathlessly, stooping over them, fear concentrated on his brow as he whispered. "We are from Henan University. We made it all the way down to Shanghai, where the men of Commander Sun told us some pretty lies; they fooled us into joining up and shipped us here.

"They said we'd be trained to become officers, but look at us—stripped down by those sons of bitches and made soldiers. Just the rank and file, to be sacrificed to bullets."

But before the students could question them, the near-naked men had retreated.

Word spread quickly.

"Where is Pengyue? Where's that turtle egg?" they asked. They searched everywhere but could not find him. Baba loitered by the guarded gate, and sure enough, he saw the fellow emerge in a clean white shirt from the officers' quarters, swinging a brown leather case from his long arm. After handing a slip of paper to the guards at the entrance, he sauntered out as if he had not a care in the world.

Hearing news of his departure, the students grabbed their belongings and rushed also to leave, but their path was blocked by guards who declared, "No exit without a pass." The road, unequivocally, belonged to those with the guns.

Pengyue's treachery had now met the full light of day.

"We've been sold!" the students wailed. "No, we will not accept training. Where's that bastard Pengyue? May he and his ancestors roll into the eighteenth Hell."

At midmorning of the following day, armed troops arrived and rounded the students up, forcing them to assemble before a wooden podium set high on a platform. A colonel, his rank indicated by the plum blossom insignia on the shoulders of his uniform, stood before the unwilling recruits. He raised his revolver high above his head and declared, "If any man refuses orders, he will be immediately shot."

After they were divided into squads and assigned barracks, they were ordered to strip. In exchange for their own clothes, they were given what they had already previewed: a pair of purple trunks, a pair of black canvas shoes, and a *douli*. In addition, each man was given a rifle but no bullets.

After they had relinquished all their own clothes, which were then locked away, they were led to be shorn.

"I am now marked as a soldier, with this shaved head of mine," Baba said to himself. "A week in the sun with only the purple trunks and the *douli* and I will be as black as tar. If I escape from this compound, the purple trunks will give me away as a runaway in an instant... but I can't very well run off without the trunks... and even if I did run off naked, my tan and white markings would betray me as easily as the tattoos General Zhu Quanzhong of the Tang dynasty marked on the faces of his soldiers. To brand us is exactly what they intend with this awful getup."

At five the next morning, their new careers as soldiers began. Exercises, breakfast (as a rule, the last to arrive would be beaten; inevitably, one among them would always be beaten, made to swallow bitterness as a prelude to swallowing his food), drills, lunch, half-an-hour nap, more exercises until evening, dinner, night class—propaganda and songs. Only at nine at night were they given an unscheduled twenty minutes to wash and to wander the compound unsupervised. At 9:20 a whistle signaled roll call. At 9:30, taps, and lights out.

Those twenty minutes after class are crucial for my escape—the only free time available to me.

I must leave at the very first opportunity. The longer I stay, the more deeply I'll be mired. The less likely to escape. Go before I lose my courage to run. But I've got to wait for a chance to get back my clothes....

His opportunity came two days later.

It was a Sunday morning. The young men were ordered to retrieve their belongings from storage and spread their clothing on the ground like merchandise displayed at market. The main gate was opened and a horde of old men, matrons, and young girls wearing flip-flopping wooden clogs raced into the compound as if attending a temple fair.

Where did they rustle up all the country folk? Baba wondered.

The Taiwanese were eager to buy the students' clothing, made of good, strong cotton from the Mainland. The Japanese had occupied the island for fifty years and hoarded all the cotton for their military during the Pacific war.

What was left to the people of the island was synthetic materials that shredded when washed and even dissolved when soaked with sweat.

During the tumult of market, Baba approached a member of his squad, also a Manchurian. The lad, a lanky, shy fellow whose slow smile curled like a spoon, had been the last one to arrive at supper on the previous evening and had been beaten till his nose bled. He had stood in silence with arms tensed at his sides, quivering with fear and pain. Baba watched, burning with anger for the injustice, swallowing the cry in his throat.

The young man's name was Chen. Asked what his father did for a living, he had replied, "My father sells small fishes." Baba had been surprised by the touching modesty of this answer. Why not simply say "fish" or "My father is a fishmonger"?

"Sell our clothes and we will be completely at their mercy. You mustn't do it," said Baba to Chen in a small voice. "Stuff your things under the building—into one of the tiny openings in the foundation of our barracks. Go now in all this noise and confusion, while no one's watching.

"Last night I looked over the compound. The wall to the west is too far. The northern gate is heavily guarded. No need to consider the south; that, of course, takes us into the city.

"Our only chance of escape is in the east. There's a hut standing against the wall—the kitchen.

"'You students have been scooped up like little fishes in one big net,' the old Shandongnese cook there said to me. 'Commander Sun, who runs this place, has snatched you up to build up his own private army—an army not for China, not for the Nationalists, not for anybody but himself.

"'Don't listen to their pretty titles: 'general,' 'marshal,' 'governor,' 'reformers'—hai, they're all ugly warlords, wolves and tigers. In their humble beginnings, they were probably called bandits, but after they've killed enough, stolen plenty, grown fat enough to throw their weight around, they're hailed as men of vision, leaders, statesmen.

"'I was a young man with some book learning—had some ambition back then— when I was commandeered into the army. Trussed up like a pig, then roped together with other poor devils by the wrists. We were marched from one province to another over endless roads. Look at me now. Almost sixty years old and still humping it.

"'Why didn't I run away, you ask? Many reasons. I was too tired. I was taken far away from home and couldn't speak the language of the new region; I didn't know how I'd manage to survive if I did take off. Sooner or later, I'd have been picked up by a contending army, anyway. And besides, those who were caught were beat up so bad, I was too afraid to run. Over the years, I just got used to life in the army.

"'I didn't try to return to my village because there probably wasn't anything left of it. During one winter, it changed hands among bandit armies more times than I have fingers to count on. Each time after an army came through, they took everything—like Genghis Khan's hordes. Pigs, corn, potatoes, rice.

"'In the army at least I could eat. I could rob, and not be robbed. . . . Anyway, it's too late for me to think of deserting now. The army is my home. I can't survive without it.

"'But you're still young. Get out before they send you off to die.

"'Beyond the wall are cane fields. A squad circles the compound, but they come around only every half hour or so.

"'Go, go. But be quick about it. Don't waver and—let me say the obvious—don't get caught. If you're nabbed, they'll bring you back in here and beat you with a flat strip of bamboo until your flesh begins to shred off your bones. Then they'll put you in a dark hole for an eternity.'

"These were the things the old cook told me, my friend," said Baba. Chen swallowed hard and nodded.

"Tomorrow night, as soon as class is over, run and fetch your things from under the building and meet me by the back of the kitchen. Don't have the nerve? Don't bother coming. I'll wait only three minutes for you. That's all. If three minutes pass and you don't show, I'll go it alone."

The hours of the following day crawled as they waited for the moment of escape. To make matters worse, "the Supreme Commander," as Sun's men referred to him, showed up that day.

The Supreme Commander stood before the amassed sea of soldiers—both old and new recruits—looking even more beautiful than MacArthur; he wore a pair of polished black riding boots, replete with silver spurs.

Instead of mounting the three steps provided at the back of the platform, the man vaulted up the side like a gymnast.

With his legs spread far apart, arms akimbo, he stood as if Heaven and Earth belonged to him and him alone. The young men standing below sweated in their purple trunks, their flesh blistered by the poisonous rays of the sun. A dull, breathless rage spread through Baba's breast like nausea. He despised the man's smooth face, his strong body, and his voice. He heard little of the man's speech: fear and loathing deafened him.

During evening class, the sergeant said, "Our Supreme Commander, not only is he of high intellect—graduate of Qinghua University and trained in the United States of America—he is also physically superior to most men. Did you all not see? Did you not see how he sprang effortlessly onto the platform in his heavy boots?"

Our Supreme Commander this, our Supreme Commander that. The steps are there for climbing; he should use them, thought Baba, hardly able to contain his anger. Shouldn't have made such a show. Don't tell me about his vault onto the platform; had he the power to hop up onto the rooftop, I still wouldn't follow him.

The hour of escape had finally come. As soon as class was dismissed, Baba made a dash for his clothes. Then he ran for the eastern wall, his impatient legs racing forward, his body self-consciously pulling back, fearful of attracting eyes.

At the base of the wall, he crouched and

counted: sixty counts for each minute. Before the end of the second minute, Chen had come, groping for him in the residual light.

"Remember, no more talk once we are over the wall. Straight into the cane," Baba whispered. "Now go for it."

He tossed his bundle over, stretched, grabbed the top of the brick wall, and pulled himself over. Landing in a crouch, he heard a thud behind him that nearly froze his heart: but it was only Chen's bundle.

The owner soon followed. Together the two of them scurried across the dirt road and into the tall cane.

Five minutes down the straight, wide furrows, scurrying like rodents in ditches, they stopped to listen. No sound of the patrol. The air was still. Not even the rustle of the cane.

Only the sound of their own breathing and the blood rushing in their ears.

The leaves scratched and cut their naked limbs. Baba pulled his trousers over the hated purple trunks. Immediately, he felt human. He was once again an individual with an uncertain future, but uncertainty was a far lighter load than slavery.

"Chen! Where are your things?"

"Ah-ah, I don't know." Once over the wall, the young man had dived headlong into the cane, forgetting about his scant belongings in his palsy of panic.

"Here, I've got extras. Put this on," said Baba, pulling out another pair of trousers.

Just at that moment, from the direction of the camp, they heard the distant shrill of a whistle, tearing off a corner of the night.

HAD THERE BEEN demons and ghosts in the night, they would have crushed them underfoot, they were running so fast. Baba and Chen were already a good distance from the camp, but they kept to the furrows of the cane fields, staying off the dirt roads. But they did not know that they had little to fear from the country police, tilting back in their fraying rattan chairs, bare feet up on their desks, dozing to the strains of the frogs and crickets. No, these men were not in the business of looking for soldiers gone AWOL.

Now that they had made their escape, they needed a place to go, a practical matter they had not considered when they were on the other side of the wall.

"There's probably a refugee shelter in Taipei," said Baba. "Let's try our luck there in the capital." Chen wagged his great wide head in the darkness.

Taipei—just a word on their tongues, but it was like a lodestone to the two homeless souls.

As they seized upon their musty schoolboy knowledge of astronomy, their eyes swept the rash of stars; it is doubtful whether they had actually located the Pole Star to guide them, but they staggered in the direction they thought was north.

They heard the whistle of a train. It was not the crystalline syllable piercing the sparkling emptiness of the Manchurian plains, but a sluggish gargle through humid air. A station was close at hand.

But they were too tired to go on.

With their chins resting upon their drawn-up knees, they slept back to back, bunched together like the tender opposing leaves of seedlings at the intersection of the bunds—the narrow earthen embankments that enclosed each small paddy field.

In the dingy pre-dawn, Baba woke to a shadowy figure standing stock-still a step and a pounce away. A tiny glow of red hovered and plummeted. Baba nudged his friend and hissed, "Someone's watching."

They slinked away, little guessing that the hapless farmer was more frightened than they, dropping his lighted cigarette as his lips parted on the verge of a startled squeak.

At dawn they arrived at the edge of a village, greeted by the not-quite-fresh aroma of human habitation, molding straw, pickled eggs and mustard root, pig feed, and poultry. They felt conspicuous with their soldiers' shaven heads, which were as smooth as pebbles in a river. But hunger drove them to show themselves.

"Douhui. Douhui," sang a street vendor, hawking his fare. "Hahhh. *Manshu ka!*—you're from Manchuria!" he said, switching from Taiwanese to Japanese. As both Taiwan and Manchuria had been under the Japanese thumb—the Taiwanese rebelled against their Japanese overlords countless times without success—this was their common language, though not one of them spoke it fluently.

The peddler ladled them two bowls of hot *douhui*—soft bean curd in light syrup, which slid down their parched throats as slippery as minnows.

"Here, have some more." The man served another bowlful to each, though it was not hard for him to guess that the young men had no money.

Baba brought out a shirt from his bundle and offered it to the man.

"Say, but this is worth much more than what you've eaten." The Taiwanese would not accept payment. He walked them part of the way to Yongkang Station.

Surely no one from the military camp would be searching for them here, two stops north of Tainan, the city from which they had made their escape; but stray glances their way shot needles into Baba's heart. His palms were sticky from fear.

Upon the steps before the entrance to the station, he neatly displayed his few remaining garments. *"Kirei! Kirei!* Pretty! Pretty!" the two young Manchurians cried out in their best Japanese as they shook the mildewed merchandise before a gathered crowd.

Every item was snapped up for purchase, including the square of cloth that had been used to carry Baba's belongings.

From the proceeds of the sale, they were able to buy tickets and wide-brimmed straw hats to hide their shaven heads. With the remainder of the money, they gorged themselves with noodles, star fruit, and mangoes.

The ubiquitous *ga-ta, ga-ta, ga-ta* of the wooden clogs worn by the Taiwanese sounded like a symphony of castanets on the platform. Farmers boarded the train carrying live chickens and ducks in bamboo cages, swinging from the ends of shoulder poles.

The train seemed extravagantly empty. Here on the island—as it had been on the Mainland during time of peace—few traveled from their homes, other than farmers venturing two or three stops beyond their villages to attend market.

The going was leisurely. They were often sidetracked to allow the rumbling passage of a southbound train or a northbound express. They made lengthy stops at each and every station.

Baba was hypnotized by the slowly passing landscape—so green and vibrant, it was painful for his eyes to look upon. Every square inch of workable land under cultivation. Receding mountains, silken in the humid air. Red-tiled roofs tucked in a nest of palms. Buffaloes lumbering in the shallow waters, closely followed by strutting, long-legged white egrets, looking for appetizers in the wake.

A woman with a child strapped to her back tended her garden. She seemed to emerge from the soil as naturally as her climbing beans, one day to return to the embrace of the very same soil. Farther along, with chickens scratching all about, a man stretched out in the shade of a tree, and a woman and a little girl brought the noonday meal in a basket. Baba imagined joining them in a family meal.

Steeped in this all-pervasive liquid tranquillity, a nervousness, nonetheless, rattled the young men's hearts. Two helmeted military po-licemen entered their compartment. Baba and Chen felt conspicuous in their dark Northerners' clothing: most folk on the island were dressed in white or dun. The grime on their faces and the mud that scabbed their legs marked them as culprits even in their own eyes. Fortunately, the MPs strolled past them without a glance in their direction.

"Why should I be made to feel like a criminal? It is others who have lied. Why should I be made to cringe when I haven't done a thing wrong?" Baba said to himself.

Splat! Red spittle landed near his feet. Is that blood? he wondered as he looked anxiously upon the farmers across from him. He had never seen men chewing the mildly narcotic *bin-lang,* a betel nut mixture whose juice stained one's teeth a livid red.

Some passengers were gathered in groups of two or three, their voices soft and low in amicable chatter. As soon as these men entered the compartment, they made themselves comfortable, slipping off their clogs to squat on the wooden benches like roosting chickens, the heels of their feet cracked and callused. They puffed away on cigarettes; some even chewed betel nuts at the same time. Baba guessed they were talking the talk of farmers: about curing a sick pig, dealing with a bad-tempered daughter-in-law, the cane harvest.

The natives knew little about the battles raging across the strait on the Mainland. There were no newspapers, and most of the folk—though they may have spoken the Hakka or the Taiwanese dialect—were literate only in Japanese, the official language that had been taught in the schools. If they had news about the civil war across the water, they did not lose sleep over the matter, for they were, in effect, inhabitants of an overseas island.

Baba leaned forward and rested his elbows on the edge of the window. He watched the black silhouette of birds against the sky at sunset. They seem to be in an extra hurry, he thought. It's as if their wings are beating frantically faster for their return to one specific branch upon one certain tree. They're not wandering aimlessly. They know where they belong.

The heady breeze, pouring through the open windows, induced the tired young men into a drunken sleep. They were awakened in the early evening when the train arrived in Taipei. The hush of the wide avenues was occasionally disturbed by the creak of a pedicab.

———

There was no more room for them at the shelter. The three-storied building on Guiyang Street, in the heart of Taipei, was spilling over with refugee students from the Mainland, each claiming his few square feet on the cold concrete floors. They looked for a place to sleep on the rooftop, but it offered no protection from the rain. The portico was no good either, for it was bordered by open sewers, rank and teeming with plump, thirsty mosquitoes.

Baba and Chen returned to the waiting room of the train station with its neat rows of wooden benches, buffed to a high sheen over the decades by waves of derrieres. Plenty of beds for the homeless. After the departure of the 12:05, they had the place entirely to themselves.

In the following weeks, more refugees arrived, seeking shelter at the station. The authorities got wind of the situation and sent a swarm of railway police to eject the squatters. They bolted the three doors; the entrances would remain locked until five, a half hour before the arrival of the first morning train.

Banished from the station, Baba and Chen found rest at a bus stop set on an asphalt island in the middle of the street. They stretched out upon the long wooden bench under the corru-

gated tin roof, but here they were prey to the whims of the wind, which assailed them with dust. Passing military trucks splattered them with mud.

At Xingongyuan—New Park—they found the protected back steps of the native history museum more accommodating. The concrete was cold but dry. If they tired of the steps, they could relocate to the amphitheater, also on park grounds. The covered stage offered fair protection to the growing number of refugees on nights of heavy rain.

"I remember the endless gray days of autumn back home," Chen said to Baba. "The west wind blowing, the temperature turning suddenly cold, and everyone finding an excuse to sit inside.

"The willow leaves knocked down by the rain—they made little gold crescents on the ground.... When I was small, my brother and I would watch the rain from the windows. A bedraggled rooster or two would strut out from under the eaves, peck through the hay for seeds, look for someone to feed them. But most of the time they just sat under the eaves with necks retracted, looking like sad and bored old men. Well, it's just about that time of year now." Chen twisted his neck to look up into the rain.

The two of them, unable to obtain room at the refugee shelter, scavenged for leftovers in the shelter's dining hall and begged *guoba,* the burnt rice sticking to the bottom of the pan, from the cooks. They had to compete for the food with the scolding charwoman, a large young woman with eyes as big as a buffalo's, glinting gold molars, and wide feet. Her splayed toes looked like a row of unshelled peanuts sticking out of her wooden clogs. She snatched away the bowls right out from under them— even as they ate—for the leftovers she collected in a bucket and sold to farmers as pig feed.

One night in October, as the two friends slept in back of the history museum, they were awakened by the pounding of rapid and frantic footsteps. Blinding spotlights, like a thousand angry moons, surrounded them and swept erratically across the park grounds. They saw myriad shadows of men, running hither and thither like mayflies caught in headlights. This was no dream; something was terribly wrong.

The two bolted from the steps in different directions. Baba shot up the rainspout of a public restroom as quickly as a squirrel. The fronds of the surrounding palm trees and the winged roof of the structure hid him from the unseen predators. His heart thumped against the rooftop as he lay flat on his stomach. Two nameless, terrified souls had also joined him, and they lay cowering beside him, hardly daring to breathe.

Below in the murk, the sounds of batons and boot leather against soft flesh. Muffled groans, the scuffle of feet. Moans of pain. Cries of "Grab 'em! Over here! Get 'em!" Then the noise of engines cut into Baba's chest like a dull knife: trucks were bearing away the captives. The hideous sounds finally died down in the small hours, the secret of the night seeping into the earth.

What remained was a chilly calm, thick with the nauseating smell of diesel. The sweat grew cold on Baba. After a leaden wait in the quiet to make sure that no hunters were still lurking below, the three slithered down from the rooftop, each going his own way in stunned silence. Baba looked for Chen but could not find him anywhere.

The calm he had witnessed on the faces of the Taiwan natives were not in the hearts of the Nationalist leaders who had come from the war-ravaged Mainland. The Nationalists had been forced to retreat in ignominy to this island. There was nowhere else for them to go.

To ensure that they would not be undermined in their last refuge, the Nationalists adopted a desperate policy: Men without jobs or a network of families and friends to vouchsafe them were arrested in broad sweeps of the city. Anyone caught harboring such persons was punished. Thousands of souls would perish for Chiang Kai-shek's growing paranoia.

But Chiang was wrong about these homeless young men. Had they been Communist agents, they would certainly not have been left without places to stay. In fact, these men were so strongly anti-Communist they had left behind their families on the Mainland for uncertain days as sojourners on strange shores.

The captives from the roundups were shipped off to the island of Quemoy or the Pescadores in the Formosa Strait, to labor as coolies building rock fortifications. The lucky ones who managed to return to Taiwan years later seemed to have fear seeping out from every pore. Chen was among them. When Baba was accosted by him on the street years later, he would hardly be able to recognize the stooped figure. The slow smile was no more.

Although he had not fallen victim to the roundups, Baba felt a sense of imprisonment. For a youth who had been able to extend his long legs on the continent, the island encircled by a warm sea was a pea pod, and he was a dry pea rattling around inside. Where could he possibly run to now?

In November, the students at the refugee shelter on Guiyang Street were moved to a two-storied edifice known as the Seven Seas Building. The warehouselike structure had been confiscated by the government because the owner's politics had become suspect. Baba was fortunate to have a place to sleep at this new shelter, for now he was less likely to be arrested as a saboteur, less likely to be pulled off the street and shot.

In a handful of months it would be winter. Though Taiwan is in the subtropics, when the notorious freezing current, the *hanliu,* strikes, fingers and toes turn purple and swell with pain. But Baba was offered a space no one else would take: on the first level, just to the right of the entrance, an area drafty and heavily trafficked.

The majority of the students had bedrolls and personal effects, for they had the luxury of an orderly evacuation from Shanghai by boat, organized by their respective universities. But for Baba, a chunk of steel served as a pillow, and the unsold newspapers that he had been unsuccessfully hawking on the streets were his

mattress and blanket. Many a night, he lay awake watching the rills of rain on the windowpanes, illuminated by the jaundiced light of the street lamps, and he rubbed the top of his head for the reassuring feel of his increasingly thick and wavy hair. In the mornings he would awaken with yesterday's news, the characters imprinted in reverse upon his face and neck.

It was during these tedious days of homelessness that he was told of an old Manchurian warrior named Geng, living on North Yanping Road.

This has to be Commander Geng. The thought of a native from Xinmin, like a patch of sunlight striking slap on his heart, warmed him. *I'll go seek him out. If anyone would be in the position to help me . . .* A character frozen from another page in his life had suddenly reappeared in the narrative, and the old stories coursed in his head like the flow of a great, wide river.

A man with a gun walked up the steps, aimed, and pulled the trigger. The blast rattled the pawn brokerage. Like the snow falling outside, bits of ceiling alighted on the stilled abacuses. The trembling clerks and accountants, blinking hard behind their spectacles, looked up at the hole in the ceiling, their faces alternately flushing red and paling.

"Go. Quickly. See if anyone can identify the villain." The deep voice of the Patriarch at the House of Yang disturbed the hush. No one was particularly eager to comply.

"I couldn't make him out. His sheepskin hat and collar masked his face," said the clerk who sat facing the door. "From where the bullet struck, it doesn't look like he was aiming for my worthless head or anyone else's for that matter."

"He trotted off on a dappled horse, Master. All we could see was the back of him," a man reported back, breathing hard. From that day forth, the Patriarch was never without armed escorts when he went about town to inspect his other businesses.

On the following morning, an envelope addressed to Yang Laojun was discovered slotted between the double doors of the gate. The note inside read, "Deliver ten thousand silver yuan at cockcrow on the fifteenth day of Twelfth Month. We will be waiting for you behind the temple of the King of Hell." A pawnbroker was a natural target of extortionists, for his business served in the capacity of a bank in mid-sized cities like Xinmin.

"That will be in just ten days," said the Patriarch. "I must seek Geng in this matter."

When he told the bandit boss of his troubles, the man said, "Rest assured, Elder Brother, I'll dig out the culprits."

When they later met, Geng told him, "Well, my own boys say their hands are clean. It was another league—with more than three hundred horsemen. They call themselves the Good Brotherhood. I talked to the leader. I told him you're my friend. He has assured me his men will leave you and your family in peace."

The Patriarch showered Geng with expensive gifts: the unspoken price of protection—or perhaps payment to the real extortionist.

The bandit boss wished to be addressed as Commander Geng, and invariably, everyone complied, for he was the indisputable leader of several thousand mounted redbeards.

In his youth, he had blazed across the Manchurian plains on his fast steeds and had enlisted ambitious young men into his bandit army, those who had tired of the honest but tedious labor of tilling the soil. Unlike farming, plundering was immediately gratifying. Geng's men fed off the villages and hamlets, gorging themselves upon the fruits of other men's labor like a plague of locusts.

But the myth of grandeur that consumed Geng destined him to be more than a common bandit. Once he had come to control a vast territory, it was no longer necessary for him to pillage: instead he collected "taxes" from the people. At this time, to further his emergence from the shadow of illegitimacy, he adopted a new name for his men: the Army of the Righteous and the Brave, fashioning them as a patriotic front against the Japanese. The pretty name attracted a different breed into his fold: idealistic students and intellectuals. As a result, the Army of the Righteous and the Brave achieved a great measure of respectability. Its shady origin was all but forgotten.

As the Japanese military, outfitted with the best and the most advanced weapons of war, pushed south from Shenyang in 1931, Geng and his men followed the retreating de facto Chinese army south of the Great Wall, where they were welcomed with fanfare like victors. The people rallied behind the Manchurians as the defenders of the Motherland. The newspapers wrote glowing accounts of Commander Geng and his patriots.

After 1931, however, those in Manchuria received no more news of the once-thunderous, larger-than-life figure of Commander Geng. His legend fed upon the silence.

It was the winter of 1945. The Japanese had surrendered in the summer. The Patriarch paced his study, anxiety detectable in his knitted brows.

"Number Four, an old friend will be visiting today," he said to Baba, who had just turned sixteen. "I need you to tend the fire and serve tea." The Patriarch was lost in thought, slowly stroking his long beard. The snow outside, which was already waist deep, gave no indication of letting up.

It is unfortunate that no one in the family has inherited his good looks, thought Baba. He had outgrown many things, but not his admiration for his grandfather, loving him with a fierce reverence.

At noon, a jeep bounced in through the South Gate and shuddered to a stop in the courtyard. A stocky, short man tumbled out, flanked by two bodyguards. He had a ruddy, unlined face and sported a mustache that cupped the corners of his mouth like parentheses. His movements were vigorous and precise; he had the emphatic ease of someone used to getting his way. An almost imperceptible, metallic light would flare up in his eyes as his voice grew agitated.

So that's what people mean when they say a man has three knives concealed in his soul, Baba thought as he stood behind the Patriarch and studied the face of the guest.

"Elder Brother, we have parted for almost fourteen years. The days have sped by like a weaver's shuttle." A smile played upon Geng's lips. "How you've aged!" he added, paying the Patriarch a high compliment.

"You, my dear friend, have also grown old," said the Patriarch, repaying the tribute. "And I see you are as spirited as ever, Geng."

The two men settled cross-legged on the kang, a small tea table placed between them.

"Hai," Geng sighed. He rubbed and slapped his muscular thigh. "Elder Brother, you know as well as I do that in this world the big fishes eat the little fishes—these in turn eat the shrimps; and the shrimps eat the invisible creatures in the mud." An ironic smile revealed the bitterness in his heart.

"Look at this," he said, tapping the star on the left shoulder of his uniform. "This is all I have to remember the ten thousand men and horses I once had under me. This lone star is all that the big fishes have given me in exchange for them.

"My ambition to expand my power beyond the Great Wall was a dream. I was decorated by the government, given a high rank, but my army was divided up between other military commands."

"But it seems to me you aren't faring badly at all. Looks like you still have many men under you."

"No. I am officially 'the Lieutenant Commander in Charge of Maintaining Order, West of the River Liao,' but I am a leader without followers." Geng's eyes rolled in the direction of the door where his men stood guard outside, and then he continued in a lowered voice: "The driver and the two bodyguards are the only ones serving under me, and even they are provided courtesy of the government. They owe me no allegiance."

He looked askance at Baba, who stood quietly in attendance in a corner of the room, and spoke in an even greater hush: "You know, Elder Brother, I cannot even obtain our friend Fang's audience now. . . . These pretty little stars on my shoulders will not stave off hunger. I need you to speak to that traitor on my behalf. I need you to talk to that no-good schemer—get back what he owes me...."

The two men's faces had darkened and gravitated toward each other. The hushed tête-à-tête lasted well into the evening.

After the Commander had gone, the Patriarch paced the room, his shadow sweeping back and forth, back and forth across the papered windows.

In his career as a redbeard, long years before Baba's arrival into the world, Commander Geng had accumulated a wondrous horde of treasures. It was rumored that much of it came from the fallen imperial house itself: gold tripods, platinum ceremonial vessels, ancient porcelain. He had asked the Patriarch to have some ten cases of these articles locked away in the vault at the brokerage, a fortified building patrolled by armed guards and fierce dogs.

In the year the Japanese attacked, however, there was little doubt in anyone's mind the first place to be ransacked would be the golden belly of the brokerage. The Commander consulted with the Patriarch and removed his treasures quietly, burying them in the backyard of an im-poverished friend named Fang, who lived on East Street. No one knew about the location of the cache—no one except Geng, the Patriarch, and the fellow named Fang.

Soon the Commander and his Army of the Righteous and the Brave retreated south of the Great Wall.

Just a few short years later, a grain brokerage was suddenly established on East Street. Following upon a few years of good harvest, its wealth came to rival the other grain brokerage in town, that of the Patriarch at the House of Yang. The proprietor of the new business was none other than Fang.

"Where did that pauper get his start-up money?" folk wanted to know. Another version of the lore about a three-legged frog was rumored: the mysterious creature had hopped about on Fang's property and had led him to dig in his backyard, whereupon riches were unearthed.

The Patriarch knew the true source of the man's wealth, of course—not a three-legged frog, but a two-legged bandit—but he did not see the point of divulging Fang's secret: the Commander had disappeared altogether and was perhaps no longer among the living.

———

With the Commander's sudden reappearance, the Patriarch knew there would be trouble. He reluctantly accepted the job of speaking to old Fang about the return of the cache. Baba heard his grandfather sigh deeply as he paced and meditated on a solution, for the negotiations were expected to be difficult. He was not wrong.

"I am an honest man," Fang said emphatically when they met. "I've never taken anything that did not belong to me."

Following upon several weeks of impasse, Commander Geng roared in on his jeep to see the Patriarch, flanked by his ever-present bodyguards.

"The governor of the province said he will provide me with five hundred men, that many horses, and all the arms I need," he said, excitement mounting in his voice. His eyes flashed. "I will regain the power I once had, and then let's see who'll be scraping to see who."

The Patriarch relayed the news to the ears of the person for whom the message had been intended: "If what he tells me is the truth, my dear Fang, the old bandit will stand strong once more. And at that time, he'll not only come for those ten cases of treasures, he'll be coming after your tough old hide, my friend."

"But I've long ago sold everything," cried Fang, "and I've put all that money into my business. What am I to do? Help me, Yang. What must I do to appease him?"

In the end, Commander Geng settled for a large, undisclosed sum—enough for him to start dreaming, once again, of galloping across the great Manchurian plains, leading ten thousand mounted warriors.

It was one of that rash of days known as "the autumn tigers," when the sun spread like an umbrella of fire over the island. Streets were desolate; even the flies meditated motionlessly on cool rocks in the shade. On occasion, a person could be spotted making a mad dash across the street, praying against losing a wooden clog in the near-liquid asphalt, then to disappear into the shadows under the eaves.

Baba found the building on North Yanping Road in Taipei.

No proper Chinese would pay a visit without a canister of tea or a packet of cigarettes in hand. But in these unsettled times, no one had much to speak of. "We are so poor we rattle like empty tin cans," people were heard to jest. Baba knew he would be forgiven for bearing no gifts.

In a large second-floor dormitory, he found

a handful of old men lounging on bamboo beds. White mosquito nets were splotched red and black—evidence of small victories in the war against the insects.

Several men were dozing, their cavernous mouths agape, their chins slouching down to their throats. One snoring gaffer held a still-burning stub of cigarette in his raised hand. Others lazily waved fans made from braided palm leaves to shoo away the heat.

"Commander Geng, how are you?" Baba said. "I don't know if you remember me. I am the grandson of Yang Laojun from Xinmin."

The mustachioed, shirtless old man was roused from his reveries. His face was no longer full and smooth, and all his ribs could be counted.

"Ah, Yang Laojun. Yes, certainly. My dear old friend, Yang Laojun.

"Everyone, this is the grandson of a wealthy friend from my home country," the old man announced, for no one else in the room could boast of a visitor.

The sleeping ones continued to snore softly; the half-wakeful ones gave Baba a barely discernible nod.

An immense sadness washed over Baba. These were men who had lived the entirety of their lives in the thick of the Chinese maelstrom, and now they had finally arrived at a peaceful, restful place, an abode where ambition would no longer come to pay its respects.

Commander Geng pointed to the foot of his bed with his fan, motioning for Baba to take a seat. But the narrow bed squeaked and convulsed so violently with his added weight, he was forced to pull up a stool instead.

Disappointment, stony and sharp, was in his heart. He had come here with great hopes for assistance, but the life force that had once coursed through the old redbeard's body would now barely nourish a mosquito.

Baba knew he must continue looking to himself for strength. His pockets were empty, but he had a great abundance of will.

Baba gulped a mouthful of chill autumn air and shivered from its sweetness. Arriving in the middle of the night, he had not guessed the beauty of his new home. Nor the danger. The earth opened up into a ravine just a skip away from the threshold of his hut. The hiss of water on rocks was the only sign of a bottom to the abyss. Along the edge, a twisted old pine grew like a Daoist monk, happy to reign over the stillness.

What can all those folk be up to on that mountainside? Baba stared across the chasm to a green peak brightened with dew. Ah, but those aren't people . . . those are monkeys.

He hurled a rock. The animals were keen to danger; as the projectile drifted away harmlessly, disappearing into the misty blue depth below, they scattered, bouncing from limb to limb, tree to tree. In time, he would learn to recognize the rapid *swa-swa-swa-swa-swa* of foliage, the sound of the monkeys shooting through the forest.

It had taken him three days from Taipei, on the northern tip of the island, to reach this mountain abode, Taoyuan, deep in the Jade Mountain Range. The mountain regions were areas of restricted entry, requiring special per-

mits; even at these high altitudes and rough terrain, the government of Chiang Kai-shek was afraid of Communist infiltration.

Now in the morning light, Baba saw that Taoyuan was situated on a plateau, wedged between peaks that resembled pagodas of malachite. The hamlet consisted of a schoolhouse, a police station, a health clinic, an administration building, a cluster of huts, and an old, vacant pigsty.

During his stay at the Seven Seas shelter, Baba had read in the newspapers about a call for teachers of Mandarin Chinese. More than two hundred people had taken the exam to obtain a teaching certificate, and he was among the thirteen who had passed. He had no contacts in the cities, so he settled for a post in the highlands, where few were willing to venture.

Mountain life marked a new beginning for him. It was autumn, 1950. He had been years on the road. "Primitive as the conditions may be," he said to himself, "—a thatched roof, no electricity, a door supported by four broken chairs to be used as a bed, no newspapers, no radio—I have what I have long hoped for: a job and a place to call home."

His students were no ordinary Chinese: they

were the Bunun, one of nine aborigine tribes. The Bunun lived even farther up the mountain, beyond the plateau of Taoyuan, where colorful birds sang amidst the tangle of ferns, bamboo, wild peaches, cypresses, pomelos, and pines.

The aborigines had sailed to Taiwan from the Malay Archipelago, long before the Chinese, the Japanese, the Portuguese, the Dutch, the Spanish, and the French had come to make their successive claims on the beautiful island. They had not always inhabited the highlands: they were pushed farther and farther up the mountain as the Chinese from Fujian Province crossed the Formosa Strait in the eighteenth and nineteenth centuries and wrested the remarkably fertile coastal flatlands from them.

They had naturally grown wary of the Chinese, sure that every last one of them was a thief and a bandit. Baba, in time, would learn to greet them in their own language: *"Oka dang hai yo shee bos"*—"Do not worry; I have not stolen your peanuts."

Over the course of the centuries, in steady contact with the dominant Chinese culture, their customs and habits slowly eroded away, but in the more inaccessible regions many tribes still clung to their old ways. Bunun women wore short blue jackets embroidered with flowers and dark blue sarongs; the men wore longer jackets and sarongs.

Theirs was a matrilineal society: the woman held property. It was the woman who selected a husband to suit her tastes, someone strong and healthy to till the ground and make himself useful in her mother's house. Should he fail to satisfy her, she was free to divorce him and marry anew.

In neighboring Hongye—Red Leaf—there lived three sisters of royal lineage, three barefoot princesses as wild and beautiful as the azaleas that grew in the mountains. *"Watashi Sabi"*—"I am Sabi," the eldest would say in Japanese, smiling and pointing to herself as she passed Baba on her way down the mountain to market, bearing a basket upon her back which contained a heavy load of deer antlers for medicine, camphor, and hides. Some said she was part Dutch. Tall, with skin light as ivory, high cheekbones, large expressive eyes, she gathered her glossy jet black hair under a blue turban. At thirty, she was still looking for a suitable husband to join her under her mother's roof.

The tattooing of the face was another custom that persisted among the people above

Taoyuan, though increasingly rejected by the younger generation. Men wore black bars down the center of their foreheads and chins. The women wore two black marks beginning from the corners of their mouths, extending upward and tapering across their cheeks—perpetual smiles etched upon their faces.

After many days at Taoyuan, Baba spied a Chinese progressing up the mountain road toward the schoolhouse with a lazy stride, wearing no shoes. This fellow moves slower than a cow wagon, thought Baba. It turned out to be Mr. Cai, the principal, to whom Baba had been patiently waiting to report. Round eyes rolled in the principal's round red face, as if some nonsense would spring from his tongue at any moment.

Cai lived in the flatlands and, as Baba would soon find out, was much more attentive to his lucrative peanut crop than his crop of students at the Central Elementary. In the months to come, Baba would have the run of the place, for Mr. Cai was happy to unload his responsibilities on the newest *sensei,* a Japanese honorific meaning "teacher" or "master." He knew Baba was the best educated of the six teachers, and a Mainlander who spoke Mandarin flawlessly; the

rest of the lot had begun to learn Mandarin only after the surrender of the Japanese.

In the newly constructed schoolhouse, complete with gray tile roof and windows made of glass panes instead of wooden slats, Baba met his students. The aborigine children arrived in loose rags, squishing mud between the splayed toes of their thick, wide feet. Some came with only a piece of black cloth wrapped about their midriffs.

Although water was plentiful—Taoyuan's rainfall exceeded two hundred inches annually —the Bunun neither bathed nor did laundry. They wore their clothes until the fabrics, whatever their original hues had been, acquired the color of the soil. Their appearance was less of a problem than the stench, which became even more intense and overbearing with each rise in heat and humidity.

"Can we put some new clothes on the children?" Baba asked Mr. Cai on one of the man's infrequent visits. "Can we get uniforms made for them so they'll look like proper students?" Baba remembered that he had always worn a uniform as a schoolboy.

"Well, it is a good idea," replied Mr. Cai. He picked his teeth, wearing an expression at once dreamy and wily. "The school doesn't have the money, but if you can arrange it by some other means, you are most welcome to put the little devils in uniforms." He would, of course, lend no hand in the endeavor.

With the help of Zhang, a colleague who had connections with a tailor in the flatlands, Baba was able to find out the price of the khaki uniforms, each set consisting of a cap, a shirt, a pair of trousers or a skirt.

But how were the Bunun to pay for the outfits? They had no money. "Peanuts," Zhang said.

"M'yes... I'll try to get the parents to pay for the clothes in kind. It's spring now. I've seen them planting crops on the hillsides.

"Teacher Zhang, next time you go down the mountain, ask the tailor how many *jin* of peanuts he would need per outfit," Baba instructed.

"Fifty and not one *jin* less," came the reply.

"Fifty is too much.... Ask him how many *jin* it'll come to if we leave out the cap."

But the figure Zhang returned with was still too high.

"What if we changed the design of the shirts from long to short sleeves?"

And still it was too costly.

"Tell you what: let's shorten the trousers, take off some buttons, and get rid of a few shirt pockets," said Baba.

The uniforms could not be pared down any further and still be considered decent: the long sleeves became short sleeves, the long trousers shorts, the skirts were hiked up to knee length, the four shirt pockets reduced to one, the shirt buttons from five to three. The number of *jin* of peanuts per outfit had been shaved down to thirty.

Then came the difficult job of convincing the parents to come up with the goods.

Every Saturday afternoon, after a morning of teaching, Baba trekked higher up the mountain to visit the families of his students, taking an interpreter with him. On his next visit he broached the subject of the uniforms.

The Bunun homes were constructed entirely from bamboo: the leaves of the plant were used for thatching; and the lath work of the walls was bamboo plastered over with mud. The clay floors of the small, square huts were well below ground level. Clearing the low entrances, visitors needed to squat down. Once their eyes adjusted to the darkness, they would make out human forms a few feet away—an entire family on their haunches, sitting around a cooking pot, and all of them—young and old, male and female—smoking bamboo pipes.

The Bunun watched their visitors stumble in the dark, but did not let out a peep, no words or gestures of welcome. They continued to observe in silence, as if idly watching stray chickens wander into their yard. This was the reception Baba received in every home.

Although the measure of thirty *jin* of fresh peanuts—shell and all, straight from the moist ground—was not an unreasonable burden for them, the families were reluctant to pay for the uniforms. They had never been thrilled with the government mandate that forced them to send their children to school, where their heads were filled with all sorts of useless nonsense, when they were needed in the fields. Now they were also asked to pay for uniforms.

Nevertheless, after much strenuous tongue-wagging on Baba's part, they acquiesced and brought down the peanuts by the bag, to be weighed and stored at the school.

Baba lost sleep. Now that he had hundreds of *jin* of peanuts on hand, he was afraid of thieves. He secured the empty classroom that served as storeroom as best he could and hoped for the quick arrival of the tailor. I'm certainly not going to allow the peanuts to go down the mountain without the uniforms, he thought. The Bunun on the whole are mild folk—I've never seen one of them slap or scold a child—but they do carry around short swords. I wouldn't want one used on my thin neck if they get it into their heads that I've cheated them.

After a few short weeks the uniforms arrived. But before he would allow the students to change into the new clothes, he herded them to the nearby Deer Cry Creek, there for a thorough bathing, as if performing a mass baptism. He sermonized on cleanliness as the first commandment of civilization. When the Japanese had governed the island, their police would roust the Bunun in the middle of the night to see whether they had washed their feet. Anyone who did not pass inspection received a sound thrashing.

It was all for naught. Very quickly the clothes turned gray-brown and began to stink. This was not hard to understand: the children worked the fields wearing them and slept in them. Soon buttons were lost and shirt fronts came to be fastened with strings.

Once again Baba herded the students down

to the creek, to wash and to do laundry. The girls were told to go around the bend to wash, while the boys squatted in the stream up to their chins as they waited for their uniforms to dry on the sun-baked boulders.

Now, dealing with uniforms and hygiene was the easy part of his job. The teaching was a long, protracted struggle.

The children were slow learners. What they were taught in the classroom had little bearing on their daily lives. It was difficult for Baba to explain a car, a train, or an airplane when they had no experience with great speed or distances. Once he sighted a rare airplane and pointed out the tiny, silver bird, to the excited warbles of the children.

Their attention spans also tended to be on the short side. On most days, the children would drive their water buffaloes to school and leave them to graze, leashed to trees; but when the bulls grew combative, their young masters leapt out the open windows to break up the skirmishes, trailed by a string of their noisy classmates.

As the school term progressed, Baba discovered that the textbooks and notebooks were missing a page here, a page there, and in some cases, entire chapters.

"Why are these damaged?" he asked.

"Ma and Pa are smoking the books" was the reply. Their parents were using the pages to roll the tobacco they grew next to their huts.

Initially, he requested that the books be left at school, but then the children were unable to do homework and, as a result, they advanced even more slowly.

"Please do not smoke the rest of the chapters," he pleaded with the mothers and fathers, aunts and uncles on his Saturday afternoon visits. "They are crucial to the children's education. Do not smoke the textbooks even after they have finished with them, for they are useful as reference."

Only after months of education did the elders finally leave what remained of the books alone.

One morning in spring, Principal Cai announced that the superintendent of schools would observe the staff and report on the quality of the teaching. It was a yearly inspection, but the man had stayed away for three years: plodding up the mountain to a backward Bunun district held little charm for him.

Baba was charged with hosting the man during his stay, but all he could provide for food was his own daily fare: a meager helping of rice topped with steamed, unripe wild papaya that oozed bitter milk. "This is not going to earn us good marks," Baba said to the other teachers. They decided to obtain a chicken for a welcoming dinner.

A Bunun named Wawan said his girl child needed new clothes, and he was willing to trade one of his chickens for a skirt. The six teachers pooled their money and bought several yards of a flower print. Teacher Zhang's girlfriend was apprenticed to the tailor who had filled the order for school uniforms, and he volunteered her labor; the woman was happy to practice on somebody else's precious cloth.

While the flower print skirt was being made, Baba escorted a skinny chicken from the higher reaches of the mountain down to the school. "Can't very well let the animal grow even thinner while waiting for the superintendent," he said, and diligently fed the poor creature, which he kept tied to a post.

On the appointed day, the bird was slaughtered and tossed into a boiling pot of water. The fat that floated to the surface was so fragrant it sent Baba reeling. It was excruciating to know that very little of the bird would find its way into his own stomach.

At the meal the visiting superintendent licked his lips with every morsel of chicken, his face lighting up with benevolence. Wine also helped to soften him up. When only the cage of bones remained, the man breathed in deeply through his pair of enormous dark nostrils and belched in a manner that revealed his satisfaction. After a brief inspection on the following day, the man returned to the flatlands to write reports filled with superlatives.

Well, the chicken had been eaten, so it was time for Baba to deliver the goods. When the skirt was presented to Wawan, the man wagged his dark head and stood obdurate on his long, thin legs like a heron. He said, "No, no. The skirt is not for this four-year-old child. It is for this one." He pointed energetically to a girl of thirteen or fourteen who stood like a sapling in the shadows.

Baba laughed, but from the man's dreary stare, he understood it was no joke. "Can this be true? I was certain you meant the smaller child," he said. He felt very awkward. In the end, he gave the skirt to the four-year-old as a gift, promising to return with another that would fit the older girl.

He did not ask for further donations from the other teachers but paid for several yards more of the flower print out of his own pocket. Teacher Zhang's girlfriend was happy to receive additional material to practice on.

When it was finished, Baba took the second skirt to Wawan.

"No. No. This skirt will not fit my daughter." The man again shook his dark head. His face was stony as he led a grown woman out of an obscure corner of the hut.

"Now I am certain I have been played the fool; but a *sensei* must not be accused of stealing another man's chicken." He swallowed his rage, gave away the second skirt to Wawan's teenage daughter, paid for more material, and asked Zhang's girlfriend to make an even larger skirt.

At the end of the ordeal, he had spent his entire month's salary for a scrawny chicken, and Teacher Zhang's girlfriend had become quite proficient at tailoring skirts in small, medium, and large.

A year had passed since his arrival in Taoyuan. One night when winter threatened the highlands, he was hurled out of his dreams by a violent, earth-rattling *hrrmmmmmm* more terrible than the passage of one hundred trains. He sprang out the open window and wrapped his arms around the bole of the old pine that grew along the edge of the ravine. The tree seemed to come alive, the trunk wriggling and the branches flailing like arms. The awful vibration threatened to fling him right into the abyss. He closed his eyes and held his breath. The sound of running water at the bottom could no longer be heard, shouted down by the tumult of cascading boulders released from the cliff walls, each rock splintering and setting off many more.

Baba moved away from the edge on his wobbly legs—legs gone weak from fright, convinced that whatever was shaking the world would kill him.

"*Jishin! Jishin!*" he heard his neighbors crying in Japanese. "Earthquake! And I was sure it was the end of the world. Will this commotion never end?"

"*Hrrmmmmmm,*" the earth answered him.

At last when the sound died away and the ground was stilled, he heard the shouts of people groping around in the night for one another. As they regained their composure, one by one they lighted their acetylene lamps.

But aftershock followed aftershock in the night, and each one stopped Baba's heart cold. The great rolling *hrrmmmmmm* sounded in the east, long before the earth actually shook.

The following morning, the citizens of

Taoyuan were able to see the extent of the damage. "It was a good one, all right," they muttered. The buildings still stood—even the rickety pigsty—but the grounds had been rent with deep, wide gashes, as if cut by the ax of a giant. The peak across the ravine seemed to be spewing steam. "The volcano! The volcano has come to life!" they cried in their panic, but it was only dirt, straws, leaves, and feathers let loose in a dark column into the sky.

The most disheartening damage of all was to the road connecting Taoyuan to the flatlands: large sections had fallen. The cow wagons bringing each schoolteacher his monthly ration of twenty-six *jin* of rice would not be able to find their way up the mountain.

The battery-run telephone at the police station was useless, for the line had been severed. They were already isolated; after the earthquake, they could not have been further removed from civilization.

More misery followed. That afternoon, the rains came down in sheets and did not let up. Most folk decided to sleep in damp shelters, hastily constructed from sticks and hay, rather than running the risk of being flattened under the roofs of their homes. All night long, there was the tapping of the rain on the foliage, and the *gua-gua-gua* of the frogs that had yet to hibernate, the only creatures to rejoice.

Throughout the winter, the Bunun labored to repair the road, and by spring of the following year, at last, the highlands were reconnected to civilization. Baba's lifeline was reestablished.

Living in the mountains had its difficulties, but the many pleasures and delights did much to make up for them. The unsullied beauty of the mountains. The clear, sweet water, like nothing Baba had ever tasted before. Bathing in the hot springs that bubbled up from the ground when one dug a few feet into the sandy soil at the bottom of the ravines. The celebrations of the harvest festival, or *matsuri,* when the students skipped school, in spite of admonishments from their teachers.

On *matsuri* evenings, under an autumn moon, the children came down the mountain to beckon Baba to their homes. Each family toasted him with bamboo bowls of strong millet wine, milky white and sour. The old and infirm squatted and smoked their pipes while the young, after the rounds of drinks, urged Baba to dance with them around the bonfire, with a wild boar roasting on a spit. Their arms wrapped around the shoulders of their neighbors, their legs swinging to the hauntingly beautiful songs, they cavorted. The blazing logs cast a red glow upon the faces, the foliage of the palms and bamboo.

Life was generous to the Bunun. Papayas and other wild fruits grew in abundance; deer and wild pigs were plentiful, frogs were to be had in the night; birds could be felled from the trees; even rats were tasty, and they captured them in simple yet ingenious bamboo traps.

In a certain way it must be wonderful to be without a written language, without the burden of history . . . the burden of time, thought Baba. And yet, he was burdened by a past and the hope for a future. He did not simply want to live, he wanted some form of knowledge and beauty.

By the end of his second year in the mountains, Baba was tired—tired of the poisonous snakes that shared his bed, the venomous half-foot-long centipedes that lived in the toes of his shoes, the fevers that plagued him like the aftershocks of the earthquake: he had malaria, but did not know it, the successive bouts of fever coming on him after periods of seemingly good health.

But the assault on the spirit was more difficult to bear. Over time, the fractiousness of the different peoples that constituted the mountain "community" was revealed to him: the Hakka Chinese, the Fujian Chinese, and the Bunun constantly spied and reported on one another to the government. Baba had also become target to their prying and tattling. He grew wise and learned not to venture into the mountains alone; he made it a habit to ask a colleague to accompany him so he would always have a witness to his proper conduct.

Recurrent dreams, verging on nightmares, of his mother and Third Brother began playing in the night. He saw them trudging up the hillocks to the west of Xinmin, beating their way through the scrubby willows. What were they seeking, aside from the kindling whose burden bowed their backs? "It's me. Number Four. I'm here. I've come back," he shouted to them, but they did not pause in their travail. It was late spring—almost summer; the long plumes of pampas grasses shed their fleecy seeds, which flowed in thick streams about his mother's feet. He would awaken in the night, his face damp with tears.

And he had also tired of the loneliness that

wrapped around his soul like an airless sack. I feel as if I have grown mute. I have no real friend. Although the others' Mandarin is poor, it isn't the language that separates—that's just the most obvious aspect—it's the gap between our interests, our experiences. There is no one to speak to from the heart. Sure, there are plenty of people to laugh and jest with, but nothing more. I feel just as empty as chattering with the monkeys in the trees.

What's happening in the outside world now? he wondered, hearing the cry of deer in the night. He sat up in bed and watched the moonlight frost the needles of the solitary pine. What's happening on the Mainland? Month-old newspapers come, already turning yellow. I'm thirsty for some real news. Did I make this long journey just to die in the mountains? . . . Another year gone . . . I am nearly twenty-three now.

He consoled himself by reading poetry from the Tang and Song dynasties over and over again, favorites that he had copied into a tattered notebook. He wrote his own, too, and discovered a friend in the blank page.

But his feelings of isolation continued to grow. Most of the other teachers had families.

"Why don't you marry the beautiful Princess Sabi—marry into the family. You can quit this job and help carry hemp and deer antlers to market. We hear her mother is easy to get along with," the others would tease him. He would only shake his head, hating their stupid laughter.

"I don't want to stay here forever," he said to himself. He felt like a winged seed that had landed on unsuitable soil, ardently wanting to grow tall and beautiful.

Under mounting international pressure, Taiwan was forced to conduct its first islandwide elections. They were to be held only at the county level; nevertheless, they were seen as a crucial first step to democracy.

The two men running for the office of Magistrate of Taidong County came up the mountain on separate occasions to campaign. The first to arrive was Chen Zhenzhong in his ox cart, groaning under the weight of his many noisy supporters. Chen's only audience that day was the few schoolteachers, the nurses at the health clinic, the police, and the handful of Taoyuan administrators. No Bunun showed up; even had they been able to understand Mandarin, they certainly would not have ventured down from the mountain just to watch a man babble incomprehensibly, not even singing or dancing.

Chen was a portly man, dark and squat with a big puffy face.

"We want new roads!" the citizens of Taoyuan clamored.

"*Hao, hao.* Of course, of course," said Chen, thrusting out his large stomach.

"We want electricity!"

"*Hao, hao.* Yes, certainly."

"We want new houses!"

"*Hao, hao.* Yes, yes!"

Everything that was asked for, Chen Zhenzhong agreed to provide.

What a vulgar, greasy face this man has, thought Baba. He agrees to everything much too easily. Beautiful words are not always believable.

The second candidate to arrive was Wu Jinyu, also a heavyset man, but taller, his face gentle and mild. He spoke evenly and did not make outrageous promises. He took copious notes, slowly extracting strips of paper from his shirt pocket, scribbling down his thoughts and observations in meticulous handwriting (even his ten children had been born in a precise order, alternating girl, boy, girl, boy). The same requests were put to him regarding new roads,

electricity, better housing. To these demands he replied, "We are poor in this county. The only tax we collect comes from a few small candy factories. At the present time, we depend almost entirely on the government in Taipei for our rice and the money in our pockets. I'm afraid these big projects you name are far beyond my power and ability. If I am elected, however, I will try to bring these matters up to the people who are in position to effect changes."

"Words to believe in are not beautiful to the ears. This fellow seems the more reliable of the two," said Baba to himself.

After the speech and the ensuing discussion, Wu Jinyu approached Baba. "Teacher Yang, I know you've been living here for some time now. Can you tell me some of your reflections?"

Baba threw back his head and laughed; his big white teeth looked like piano keys.

"Let's say that if the culture of the Bunun has not changed in more than seven thousand years, I've brought them along a millennium. But I myself—I've gone back a thousand years."

"How's that?" asked Wu.

"Since coming here, I've begun to wear shorts instead of proper trousers. I run around in wooden clogs instead of shoes, and my hair has grown shaggy like a demon's. Now I even speak in the language of the Bunun."

Wu Jinyu nodded and smiled.

Then the candidate turned the conversation to a request for help: would Baba canvass for him among the mountain people?

"If you should have any personal difficulties to address, Teacher Yang, please do not hesitate," he added.

The door of opportunity had been flung open for Baba.

"I know it's quite improper for me to be asking you for assistance at this time," he said, "but I have no connections—I know no one in the flatlands who can speak for me. If you become Magistrate, I would like to be transferred to a school in the city of Taidong. I've been here two years now and I feel I've accomplished all I possibly can for the people of this mountain."

Wu Jinyu nodded at this modest request. It was agreed that Baba would campaign for the man.

He worked hard. At every opportunity, he spoke to the Bunun: "Wu seems the more sincere of the two candidates and is likely to accomplish something for us. Indeed, if we vote for him, he's sure to bring us lots of matches."

Yes, matches: they were no small entice-ment. The Bunun had no reason to ask for better housing: they were perfectly pleased with their huts, which they raised in a matter of hours by community effort. And what would they do with electricity? What was electricity? But matches! Magical matches. Now that was a priceless commodity. With matches they did not need to keep constant watch over their fire. If the fire did die, presto! flames would leap again in a mere moment.

As the election day drew near, he diagrammed the ballot and explained, "There will be empty spaces to the left of the two candidates' names, room set side for additional names if there were other men running for office.

"Wu Jinyu's name will be the one on the right. Make sure to mark the box directly above it with a bamboo stamp. Imprint the ballot with a small red circle." Over and over he drew the ballot and demonstrated the proper placement of the red circle. His audience seemed to understand.

On the day of voting, representatives from both sides arrived to ensure a fair election. Deep in the mountains, Baba was still stumping for Wu, urging the Bunun to vote.

But even with the many lessons, a good number of the cast ballots had to be thrown out:

some folk had marked all the boxes at the top of the form with a row of small red circles, seeming to have greatly enjoyed their own artistry; others had marked the boxes above both Wu and Chen; some had placed the red circle exactly in between the two candidates' names.

But all in all, at the end of that historic day, there were more votes cast for Wu than for Chen. Wu Jinyu became the first democratically elected Magistrate of Taidong County on the island of Taiwan.

On the day of his inauguration, a fortune-teller was hired to participate, to ensure good luck and to ward off evil. Men and women born in the years of the snake and cow were told by the man not to show their inauspicious faces. Two *jin* of pork were presented as an offering to the gods when the seal of office was handed down, by the outgoing magistrate, to Wu.

Whether the election improved the lives of the Bunun, my father did not know. But in the spring, he was posted to Xinsheng Elementary in the flatlands, where he would meet my mother. He would not marry Sabi, the barefoot princess, or remain in the mountains, after all.

WHEN THE OLD custodian at Xinsheng Elementary poured hot water for Baba, only half of it went into the teacup; his hoary hand shook like the bobbing needle of a sewing machine.

The man's name was Ren Kuiwu —Ren the Stalwart. He had thick lips and a nose like a bulb of garlic, but the first thing Baba noticed about him was that he had no neck. His big bald head, shaped like a bullet, rested squarely on meaty shoulders. He had to pivot his entire body in order to look sideways or over his shoulder. When he walked, his massive arms, welded to his shoulders by age, did not swing, and his feet shuffled forward inch by slow inch.

He rarely spoke, for, being hard of hearing, he had turned inward, retracting into a private world of soliloquies. Whenever someone cried out, "Ren Lao Gonggong!—Grandfather Ren!" the old man's eyes stared as round as autumn mooncakes, and the furrow between them grew deep; he would stop dead in his tracks, as if standing in a dense grove of bamboo, listening to a bird whose mysterious call had pierced the foliage.

The man had come to Xinsheng Elementary a year and a half after Baba. There were already two custodians—both young and agile—to boil water for tea, to sweep the offices, and to maintain the school grounds. A third custodian was unnecessary, especially one who was barely mobile.

But the Nationalist government did not know what to do with old veterans like Ren. The military was in the business of sending out young men to die quick and simple deaths; it was not set up to care for them in their old age. So these Mainland soldiers, after a lifetime of service, were farmed out to the various schools on the island as custodians.

"This is highly improper. This will not do at all," the teachers said one morning as they gathered in the office before class. "The man is simply too old to be bending his back, pouring tea for us younger folks. The government has foisted him on us, but surely we can lighten his load, give him something easier to do."

And so it was decided that Old Man Ren would be responsible for ringing the big bronze bell that hung at one end of the school corridor. There, under the eaves, they sat him in a generous rattan chair before a table with a wind-up clock that bore numerals large enough for his dimming eyes to read.

Dang-dang-dang! The man yanked on the bell cord three times when classes were set to begin, and twice when classes were to be let out.

"Lao gonggong, ji dian zhong?" the mobs of noisy children stamping past him would sing—"Old grandfather, what's the hour?"

Now that bell ringing was Ren's one and only duty, the Confucian souls of the teachers were set at ease.

As time went on, Baba noticed that Ren would often stand in the office with his massive arms hanging limply down his sides, watching one of the young teachers, Laning, as she attended to the school's accounting, clacking away on the abacus long after most of the other teachers had gone home. He stood facing her, as expressionless as ever. Baba had seen the man smile only once, and it was a paltry shrug of a smile, to brush off the antics of a younger custodian who dogged him with his clowning.

After maintaining his silent stance for an unduly long time, Old Man Ren would respectfully say in his richly inflected Shandongnese accent, "Teacher Lin, *lai yi wan mien ba?*—how about a bowl of noodles?"

The young woman would not hear of Ren spending his meager earnings on her, but after countless such invitations, she finally did accept his offer one afternoon.

The man was ecstatic—showing as much ecstasy as his wooden face could muster. He shuffled across the street to the Heavenly Fragrance Restaurant, and after a prolonged absence, returned with a big bowl of noodles in a wooden case that was fitted with handles and a sliding lid. When Laning was presented the fare, the noodles had already grown cold, but under the loving guidance of the old man's hands, not one drop of broth had skipped out.

He stood nearby and watched with great satisfaction as the young lady slurped down the treat.

Baba was astonished to see the tears arrested in the corners of the old man's eyes—salty pearls poised to fall, but never quite falling. Something weighty's got to be pressing on his heart, Baba thought.

On a Sunday, he dropped by the school, knowing that the man would be sunning himself in the courtyard. He pulled up a chair and sat directly facing Ren, so that the man would not need to twist his body around in order to talk.

"Grandfather, how old will you be this coming New Year?"

"Sixty-eight."

Baba calculated on his fingers. "Ah, so you were born in . . . 1886. A man born in the previous century!

"And your home? Where's that?"

The man opened his eyes wide, as if this would ease his deafness. Both forearms rested prodigiously on the arms of the rattan chair. An occasional fly would alight on his thick, pendulous earlobes—a mark of longevity, many pointed out—but he sat as motionlessly as a bronze Buddha.

"I was born in southern Hebei near the border with Shandong," he replied. "I was the only son. My family had a tiny bit of land. Life wasn't easy.

"When I turned twenty, my parents found me a wife; but just a month after I was married, I was nabbed as I worked in the fields, tied up by the press gang, and made a soldier."

"Whose army were you forced into?" Baba asked. The old man did not know. All he knew was that he had fought under men who upheld the doddering Qing dynasty.

"After I had been in the army for six or seven years, one day we were told to cut off our pigtails. They told us the dynasty had fallen and we were now an army of the Republic. We were told to throw off our Manchu tunics, which came down almost to our knees, with the huge character 'valor' written across the chest. Then we were given modern uniforms called *erchiban,* or two and a half feet, for the now shorter shirts were of this length. Because of this new uniform, we soldiers came to be called 'the two-and-a-half-feeters.'"

"But then at this point did you finally know who you were fighting under?"

"All I knew was that there was a big man at the very top named Yuan . . . Yuan Shikai, I recall."

"What did you do in the army?"

"Well, I always liked to play the *laba* back in my village, so I quickly picked up on the bugle; I sounded the attack—sent the men on with their bayonets."

"Did you fight?"

"Very little. No need for the bugle player to die too. I usually lay low in a ditch, resting flat on my back, pointing the instrument into the sky. Sometimes a bullet would pierce the darned thing even as I played."

"What battles did you fight in?"

"Who knows. Most of the time, we didn't have a clue who we were actually fighting. When ordered to shoot, we shot. When ordered to blow the bugle, I blew my damnedest. Today we fight East; tomorrow we fight West. One battle after another—they were all the same. A string of rotten wars, that's all I remember.

"But I do recall one particular battle very clearly. Around five years after we changed into modern uniforms, we entered Beijing. The enemy leader was called the Pigtailed General, because he kept his queue as a symbol of his loyalty to the fallen dynasty. He made all his men wear the old pigtail too. This was long after everyone else had cut off theirs, you know.

"This general said the people of the Middle Kingdom were faring badly because we had no emperor. He wanted to restore the Son of Heaven. His army flew the old Manchu yellow banner with the big dragon stretched across it."

"Ah, so Old Man Ren fought against that reactionary Zhang Xun in . . . 1917," Baba said to himself.

"Yes, I was in Beijing before they changed it to Beiping—well, it's back again to the name of Beijing with the Communists there now, isn't that right, Teacher Yang?" said the old man, blinking hard. "The Communists call it the People's Republic of China now, don't they, Teacher Yang?

"Anyway, that was my first and only time to the great capital. There we chased the pigtailed soldiers. In their panic, they chopped off their hair. You should have seen the streets! Littered with pigtails. Pigtails everywhere." The old man lifted his brows, staring at Baba with eyes that were utterly round.

"So you were on the winning side," Baba said. "Did you get better treatment from your leaders after victory?"

"No. Winning is the same as defeat, Teacher Yang. If your army wins, you wave the same banner and fight on. If your army loses, you run under a different banner and do some more fighting. It's all the same.

"After many more battles and fighting under different warlords, my army was finally swallowed up by Chiang Kai-shek's. Then I was told it was a great privilege to be a soldier of the Central Government."

And here the man was silent for a moment, staring straight ahead.

"In all those years, I never had the chance to go home. When I was over forty, we came very near to my village, and there I talked to a man who had just been grabbed by the press gang, tied up like a hog as I had been years ago. The fellow had news about my family.

"He said that soon after I disappeared, my wife gave birth to a child—a pretty little girl child. When my parents died, my wife brought her up all by herself.

"But there was nothing that could be done about getting home, you see. Soldiering was my destiny. The 'small devils' were still to come. Well, when the Japanese did attack, I was too old for fighting. I helped move supplies instead. Cooked for the men also. Did odd jobs."

"But your wife must have been still waiting for you," Baba said.

"No. That young conscript told me she left the village after the daughter was grown and gone. Who knows where. It's been too long; can't say that I remember what her face was like.

"So anyway, I retreated with the National-ists to this island.

"They say we will fight to win back the Mainland from the Communists . . . yes, I'd like to return to the Mainland someday—to the home village even though there's probably no one there for me. Like they say: Old leaves must return to the root of the tree . . . yes, everyone's got to go home . . . not get blown all over a strange landscape."

The old man fanned himself, staring over Baba's head, and then continued as if to him-self: "Hope my daughter has found a good husband, a man who treats her proper. My girl would have been just about twenty the year I came so close to the village . . . just about the age of Teacher Lin—yes, a good girl who works so hard long after everyone's gone home. . . ."

Baba had also been watching Laning. Even before he had come down the mountains, he had heard people talk about her as if she were a sage princess. When he finally set his eyes upon her, the force of her spirit surprised him. Beneath the splendor of her serenity, he felt her will, cool and solid as jade.

She is truly as lovely to look at as my old colleague Zhang told me, Baba thought. "If you don't care for a Bunun girlfriend, I can intro-duce you to an old classmate of mine who grad-uated first in her class at the Teacher's Academy," Zhang had said. The rascal offered to play matchmaker, but I am certain he was only boasting; the men, I have noticed, are afraid to approach her. But then I've also seen her stealing looks at me and then blushing fu-riously when our eyes meet.

Unlike Little Plum, the other schoolmistress, with her permanent wave and latest fashions,

must be leftovers from her school days. She's always neat and tidy, but with a distinction, one might even say flair. The clarity of her style and manners lends her an intense beauty; talking to her is like finding a brook after drinking from brackish ponds.... They tell me she wants to go to college in Taipei.

When Baba had arrived at school on the first day, Laning had dipped her head to keep from laughing out loud: a giant ducking to pass through the front door of the office. The young man from the Mainland, with his smiling sensuous lips and his confidence shining like obsidian in his eyes, had worn a new suit cut from the cheapest khaki; his old maroon leather shoes were polished, and his thick, wavy hair had been smoothed back with oil.

Over the months, Laning had maintained a polite coolness toward him. One afternoon, as she distributed the monthly salary, Baba ventured an invitation.

"Will you accompany me for some steamed dumplings in town, Teacher Lin? I'm rich today."

"I am very busy, Mr. Yang." Laning's face colored to her ears as she retracted her hands from his touch. But Baba was not discouraged. He felt bold enough to telephone her and tease

Baba mused, Laning wears her hair blunt cut, and is clean of rouge or lipstick; she still wears the white cotton blouse and black skirt that her from the Grand Luck Restaurant: "Mmm-nh! The dumplings are indeed as good as they say, Teacher Lin."

Now Laning's father also taught at Xinsheng Elementary, and it was Baba's good fortune that Old Man Lin had taken a liking to him. In the second spring of his arrival, he was invited to the family home in the neighboring village of Malan, or Horse Orchid, for Sunday supper.

Baba, in his best and only suit, looked over the hedge of croton encircling the House of Lin, the leaves streaked in a rainbow of colors. The afternoon fingers of light parted the fronds of the coconut palms that grew along the perimeter of the garden, and the patter of bare feet could be heard.

"*Zhuuu-zhu-zhu-zhu-zhu!*" Mother Lin called as she poured feed, a mixture of fried bran and sweet potato leaves, into the trough. Turkeys, geese, and red-faced "fire ducks," crying *ha-ha-ha-ha,* came waddling out of the pen. The chickens roosting in the trees alighted. Mother Lin waded through a sea of feathers and beaks.

When Baba pushed open the gate of the garden, the hinges cried *quok-quaark.* The noise warned Laning's younger sisters, four wild creatures, who shinnied up into the trees and yelled down, "Chibi! Chibi! *Ga! Ga!*" *Chibi* was "tiny" in Japanese, and *ga* was the word for "bite" in Taiwanese.

Ga, Chibi the mutt certainly did, flying to the attack, with a swishing swirl of his tail, electric in his fury.

Another creature in the garden that did not take to strangers was an enormous white gander. With his vicious beak he terrorized unsuspecting neighbors who came to wash their clothes in the stream that ran through the garden—peals of laughter suddenly changed to frenzied screams.

"*Zhuuu-zhu-zhu-zhu-zhu!*" Mother Lin called again. Every chicken, goose, duck, and turkey came running to her, thinking of a meal, and, fortunately for Baba, so did Chibi.

In the middle of a fruit and vegetable garden stood a cottage of bamboo and thatch, spare and clean, divided into three cool rooms. Old Man Lin invited Baba to sit in the largest room, at a semicircular table pushed up against a window whose shutter, swinging up and out from the bottom, was propped open with a stick. A little blackboard hung to the right of it, and written in a firm hand were the words "Shan

Cun Ye Ren—Wild Man of the Mountain Hamlet."

"What does this mean?" Baba asked.

"A wild man is a wild man," came the reply wrapped in an enigmatic smile. Old Man Lin's hair was cropped close, and his skin was as waxy smooth as ripened mango. Baba understood the poetic allusion. Lin had fashioned himself after the Tang dynasty poets, such as Li Bai and Du Fu, who cherished their independence and solitude, far removed from the dust of the contending multitudes. Du Fu had adopted for himself the nom de plume Old Man of the Wilds. Baba appreciated Lin's wit and what he had proclaimed of his sensibilities.

It is perfectly peaceful here, thought Baba. Can life ever be so tranquil for me? Perhaps I can create a garden, too, and live—just as I had wished as a child—like Old Lady Lu and her husband, who kept an eye on the South Garden...where Third Brother frightened away crows and watched the clouds go by.

Baba and his host washed down salty boiled peanuts with wine. Then came stir-fried vegetables, fresh from Mother Lin's garden. When he finished his rice, the bowl was quickly filled again, but digging in, he found a few strips of yam that he knew had been accidentally served to him. He slowed down his greedy chopsticks, for he realized that the rest of the family, who had yet to eat, would be left mostly with yams, cooked on top of the rice in the same pot. The tuber, being cheaper, augmented the diet of a family with eight mouths to feed.

"Each mouthful should be chewed a minimum of thirty times, and swallowed when one is able to taste the sweetness," Old Man Lin advised. "This is good for the body, especially good for the digestion. Try it."

Baba counted as he chewed, but his tongue had a will of its own and pressed the food down his throat long before the thirtieth count.

Old Man Lin was well read and spiced his talk with poetry. He had grown up during the Japanese occupation of Taiwan, and his soul had been nourished on Japanese culture; since their defeat, he had become a voracious reader of Chinese history and literature.

Laning, in her own home, was neither defiant nor shy. Old Man Lin could not help but notice the smiles she exchanged with the handsome young guest when she drifted out of the kitchen bringing out the food, for a second invitation to dinner was soon extended to Baba.

In the ensuing visit, Old Man Lin quoted a line from Du Fu's poetry: "Capture the king and you'll have captured the knave." Baba understood the hint: If you are interested in the daughter, you must win over the father. Old Man Lin smiled at him, his small eyes curling into a pair of crescent moons.

"Do you know Zheng Banqiao's paintings?" the man asked.

"Yes. Back home in Manchuria, my grandfather had in his collection a pair of scrolls. He would unroll them when the mood was right, most often in autumn when hundreds of rare and potted chrysanthemums bloomed in his study." Baba could not help boasting a little about the once-prosperous House of Yang.

Zheng Banqiao was among the Eight Eccentrics of Yangzhou, scholar-painters who displayed idiosyncrasies of behavior and technique. Zheng was a man of high principle, but he often brought disasters upon himself with his quick tongue. He gave up his enviable position as a magistrate to make a living as an artist.

"I am like Zheng Banqiao, who married off his daughter in the moonlight," said Old Man Lin. Yes, Zheng Banqiao was admirable, Baba

thought. The gentleman escorted his daughter to the house of the groom dressed in the beauty of moonlight, unadorned by all the traditional fuss—the gongs and trumpets, the costly red bridal dress. The man made no room in his life for conventions. Laning's father seems to be a kindred spirit.

Just outside the window, hanging from the branches of the *yulan* tree, was a profusion of baskets, spilling, tumbling with orchids. Old Man Lin was a passionate collector of orchids. Enticed by the excruciatingly sweet fragrance of flowers hidden in the forest, he entered the steep mountains, to return only days later with orchid plants in his knapsack and more in his cap; he had named Laning, his eldest, after his favorite flower. He carefully checked the buds and leaves with his flashlight in the wee hours, plucking off snails and slugs and smashing the hapless creatures between his fingers. It was as if he had found the mollusks nibbling on the innocent, slumbering faces of his own children.

"I know you spend a lot of hours at the library in your spare time. Why not come visit us here in the garden instead? There are lots of guavas ripening now."

Baba did not refuse the invitation: he had

set his heart upon that lovliest of lovelies in the garden at the House of Lin. In time, Chibi and the gander ceased to take any interest in him, but the four sisters continued to spy from high in the trees.

On Sundays, Laning would peer out at him from behind the hedge of flowering *fusang* as she waited for him to come sauntering along the bund of the neighboring paddies. Reaching up to pluck the guava she had been allowing to ripen on the tree, she sliced it in two and offered one of the halves to him upon his arrival.

Leaning against the trunk of the banana plant, the two of them spooned out the seed pearls at the heart of the fruit and dropped them into the pond for the fishes to chase. The guava was crisp, cool, and sweet.

"You must know, my father had thought Japan would win the war," Laning explained one day. " 'The Emperor will be victorious. He'll rule the Pacific,' he said. Well, we were immersed in propaganda during the war; how could we not believe what we were told, day in and day out?

"Mother was doubtful: 'What? One tiny speck of a country all puffed up to fight mighty nations?' she said. 'No, victory is only an empty dream.' Well, Mother, though she has far less knowledge of the world, has more wisdom. When the Japanese surrendered, our family was stuck in Guangzhou, where my father had been posted to teach.

"That fall, we lost everything to inflation: sacks of money could not buy a handful of rice, and we lost all our belongings to the sea, during a typhoon, on our return . . . even the shoes on our feet.

"Once we came back to this island, Mother refused to follow Father up and down the mountains to his different posts like a mule. She was so sick of the moves, packing the braided willow trunks again and again. And for the first time, Father listened. He saved money and bought this piece of land.

"The war changed him a lot. Many people call him ornery and cynical, but I remember that other man—the man who had many friends, who had big plans. He used to talk about sending me and my brother to medical school. He'd say he would take the opportunity to go to college, too, and fulfill his life's dream. All his hopes were disappointed.

"Well anyway, when the grass had been cleared from the new property, to Mother's delight, she discovered tidy rows of knee-high guava plants. The saplings grew very quickly and this is why the garden has come to be known in this region as the Bala Garden—the Guava Garden. Because the trees are of a special variety, of a wonderful fragrance and sweetness, it brings folk here from all around."

Baba saw that the land was profuse with other fruit-bearing trees: mango, loquat, papaya, pomelo, banana, red bell-shaped *lianwu,* and Buddha's Head, which looked like the nubby head of the Gautama himself.

Aside from the rice, which Old Man Lin brought home as part of his pay, Mother Lin was able to provide for the needs of the entire family by what the garden produced. At the table she served her family onion, chayote, string bean, eggplant, turnip, and pumpkin. She traded *bala* for meat, fish, oil, cloth, and even soap; and on festival days, vendors came to the garden itself and paid cash for the fruit, which they in turn sold at the temple fairs.

Baba rested his eyes on the stream that coursed through the heart of the garden, dividing it in half; sometimes it ran sparkling, and at other times, murky, depending on the clarity of the water in the rice paddy from which it fed.

A small footbridge joined the northern half of the garden, where the cottage stood, to the southern half, where the fish pond was stocked with Wuguo fish, so called because a certain Mr. Wu and a Mr. Guo, early in the century, introduced this hardy breed from Southeast Asia to Taiwan. The fish needed no attention, feeding on mosquito larvae, algae, and practically anything tossed to them. They multiplied at a furious rate.

On occasion, Laning did laundry as she perched on a slab of rock at the edge of the pond while Baba kept her company. *Flup, flup, flup,* she beat the clothes with a flat wooden bat. The pond boiled with soap suds, which the surfacing schools of Wuguo greedily ate. A thousand pairs of silver eyes stared up at them; a thousand tiny mouths opened and shut, opened and shut.

At times when they were alone together, they were keen to the mysterious bond that charged the very air they breathed. No, they did not need to examine their feelings, holding them up to the daylight; they were in love.

To Baba, the Sundays in the Bala Garden passed all too quickly. They talked. And the sun was at its zenith. They talked some more. And the chickens came flying home from the neighboring paddies to roost. Except for the crickets and the burping frogs, all the creatures in the garden had settled down for the evening.

Sometimes a pitiful *bwaak, bwaa-bwak* was heard from a hen, crying in its sleep.

One day, several months into the bloom of love, Old Man Lin invited Baba down the street to the new cement house which he had recently purchased. Here they could be alone, for the family had yet to move into their new home.

"It seems you and Laning are getting along quite handsomely." The man's face assumed a smile, but his eyes betrayed the seriousness of his mood. "The proper thing now is an engagement. It'll put an end to the gossip that's flying around town. Folk are saying, 'Why is Laning, that beautiful flower, planting herself in that cow's dung from the Mainland?' I've caught quite a few snoopers too. In fact, just yesterday, I saw the doctor's daughter, Little Plum—the one who has been so obvious about chasing you—standing on tiptoe, balanced on the pedals of her bicycle, sneaking a look into the garden. That girl's shameless, with her face painted as red as a monkey's rear!"

But Baba was a stranger to the customs and etiquette of Taiwan. "How does one go about becoming engaged?" he asked.

"Very simple. You arrange for a banquet, and have a restaurant cater the food. We can hold the party here at this new house. You invite about two dozen people, and if you can manage it, you buy a pair of gold rings, one with your name inscribed on the inside, another with Laning's. That's all you need to worry about."

A few days later, Old Man Lin came to Baba again. "I've been thinking, you mustn't forget to bring the House of Lin a gift of cakes. It's a Taiwanese custom; let's make sure everything is done properly. And I must ask you to borrow Magistrate Wu's car. You helped him win the election, I'm sure the man won't mind lending you a hand on this one. It'll look more dignified to have the car parked out in front of the new house. Oh, not to forget one very important thing, you and Laning need a citizen of this community, a person of high standing, to be the official matchmaker."

Baba thought over the last matter, and made his request to Mrs. Tao, the wife of the Taidong County comptroller. She was a tall, fair-skinned woman in her forties who was known all around for her grace, wit, and sophistication, and Baba had had many friendly dealings with her husband regarding school funding.

"With pleasure! I heard matchmaking promotes longevity in the practitioner," the woman said with a broad, mischievous smile. "I'll take care of the gift of cakes for your future in-laws. You can't expect a Manchurian to know how to arrange these things.

"And I'll talk to Magistrate Wu about the loan of the car. I'm certain it will be no problem. Just don't forget to hand the driver some *hong-bao* (a cash gift in a red envelope) to make the ride more comfortable, if you get my meaning; and make sure to seat the man at the banquet table as an honored guest."

In the entire county of Taidong, the sole car to grace its streets was the one that chauffeured the Magistrate and his VIPs. It was an American-built black sedan, purchased secondhand but always kept polished to shine like a mirror. The driver was treated with the respect one would reserve for a scientific genius.

As he ticked off the dates on the calendar, the day of the engagement banquet finally arrived for Baba. He cycled the bumpy, unpaved road between the cement house and the Grand Luck Restaurant innumerable times, tipping the appropriate people generously to ensure that the borrowed tables and chairs would be transported, and, most important, that the caterers would make their deliveries on time. In his excellent calligraphy, he wrote a traditional line of poetry on red paper to grace the front door of the cement house: "Bonded to each other by the string of fate, one thousand *li* long."

As the hour of the party approached, he changed into his suit. He carefully smoothed back his hair with oil, and studied his own face in the mirror, which stared back at him, beaming with joy and exertion. At the appointed hour, he joined Mrs. Tao at her house, where the car was waiting. From here to the House of Lin it was only five minutes by bicycle; by car, it was all of two minutes. No sooner would the driver's foot press the accelerator than it would come down to apply the brakes. The car squealed to a sudden halt in a swirl of dust before the gate of the new cement house.

Without missing a beat, Mrs. Tao stepped out and took charge, made introductions, conducted the symphony of chatter and laughter, keeping the talk lively and moving from theme to theme. As promised, she had prepared a bamboo basket filled with cakes for the House of Lin. All the guests were in high spirits, congratulations flowing in a bright stream from their lips.

"Did you bring the beer?" hissed Old Man Lin, pulling Baba aside by the elbow. "What about cigarettes?"

He had forgotten the cigarettes.

"Quick. Go out and buy some. We can't do without cigarettes for the guests."

Mother Lin's face was infused with a blush deeper than her eldest daughter's. Wearing a cotton dress with a high mandarin collar, she smoothed the fabric across her lap and wrung the handkerchief balled up in her hand. It had been years since there had been an occasion to put on that special dress, stored away in her chest of camphor wood, and it was rare, indeed, that she had no need to stoke a sooty, uncooperative fire to cook dinner for her big family. During the meal, Baba used his own chopsticks to bring her choice morsels, making sure she would enjoy her day of liberty to the fullest. The woman cast him silent, grateful looks.

Laning wore a dress of deep blue which she had sewn especially for this day, and her hair was pulled behind her ears into two pigtails, tied with wide ribbons that matched the color of her dress. It was the first time she and Baba had sat down next to each other, shoulder to shoulder, for a formal meal. Her gaze was sublime; her eyes looked, but they did not see. She and Baba spoke little to each other or to the company, but silently, and with smiles, lifted their cups to accept the toasts. The pair held hands under the table.

The guests were self-preoccupied, each in his turn taking the opportunity to boast of his own importance to the community. "Well, he has just told me in privacy that his oldest one will be going to Japan to study economics," someone said, hinting of an intimacy with Magistrate Wu. They were all small-fry people, trying to see which of them could fling himself highest above the surface of a small pond.

Later, Baba and Laning exchanged rings before the approving eyes that encircled them, amid cheers and toasts of "Prosperity! Health and happiness to the eternal pair of mandarin ducks!"

Old Man Lin, seeing his new house graced by the presence of such honorable personages, couldn't keep from grinning, his slim eyes nearly sealed shut in joy.

When the last of the beer was emptied and the dishes lay in sumptuous disarray, the matchmaker thanked the host and hostess, signaling that the celebration had come to an end.

Outside, neighbors had gathered to gawk. Aborigine children jumped about like fleas, loving the commotion, cheering the roar of the car, running after it as it sped away.

"Your future mother-in-law is a gentle woman, a fine woman," said Mrs. Tao to Baba once they were in the car. "I don't think there's a soul in the village of Malan who will contest that. It's a good sign. It'll certainly mean happiness: find a good mother-in-law, and you will have found yourself a good wife."

"Yes, Mother Lin, she is wholly without pretense, utterly sincere. A kind woman," said Baba with a chuckle. "She feels great sympathy for her animals. Whenever a bird is to be slaughtered for the table, she prays for its soul in her own inimitable fashion: 'I hereby end your life as a humble beast, and I appeal to Lord Buddha that He will soon return you to this world as a son or daughter of a kind and reputable family. *Amituofo, amituofo*—'"

"But one thing, I must tell you," said Mrs. Tao, interrupting. "When the gift of cakes is presented to the woman's family, the basket must be returned with something for the future son-in-law inside. When I retrieved the basket, I lifted the lid and said, 'Eh, now that's very strange, there is nothing in here.'"

"Well, that's excusable. The house has been in an uproar. They must have forgotten."

"No, when they take the cakes out, they must put a return gift inside the basket. Every Taiwanese knows this. Just a little something . . .

even a necktie. Lin should've seen to it. That's only proper."

"Oh, but I have no use for a piece of cloth around my neck, anyway."

As Baba escorted Mrs. Tao to her door, the woman said in a voice dark with misgivings, "I think Old Man Lin will be a difficult fellow to deal with. There may be other problems besides forgetting a gift. Perhaps I'm wrong, perhaps I'm seeing phantoms, but I truly fear you'll have lots of difficulties to bear. . . ."

"Well, the old man has indeed been a bit overbearing in the last few weeks," said Baba to himself as he walked home alone, but Mrs. Tao's warnings floated away from his heart on the evening breeze. He was engaged to Laning and that was all that mattered; happiness was a balm that soothed the many small abrasions. How could problems possibly arise? I know Old Man Lin is fond of me, he thought.

Once engaged, the sweethearts could spend time together without raising small-town eyebrows, and they came to live in their private world of quiet talks and walks in the Bala Garden or out about in Malan. Baba did not miss a murmur, a sigh, the freckles on Laning's face, the nape of her neck, the back of her ears that betrayed her smile when she was turned away from him, the light that snapped in her eyes when she argued a point. Even the tiny beads of perspiration that formed on her temples as she slurped rice noodles Baba found perfectly enchanting, and he would look at her out of the corner of his eye as she ate. When Laning laughed and her alto voice broke out in childhood songs that he did not know, he fell silent; love quivered in his throat.

And again it was the feeling of clarity that overwhelmed his soul, the feeling that he had been touched by a force immeasurably good. The perversions of the world were deflected from him, cast away from him because of the bright protective power which Laning inspired.

They talked about books they had read: the biographies of Gandhi, Helen Keller. They made plans for college. Baba had been given a small scholarship, set up by the government for refugee students from the Mainland. He would be leaving for the capital at the end of the school year. Laning had applied to Normal University, also in Taipei. They were full of hopes for the unexplored territory that was their future, and passionate was their yearning to know it together.

In that year, the movie *Gone With the Wind* had come to Taiwan, and all the young folk were bursting with talk of love amidst the ruins of a civil war. One Sunday, Baba asked Old Man Lin's permission to take Laning to the movie theater—a rare evening date outside the embrace of the Bala Garden. Old Man Lin did not say he approved, neither did he say he disapproved, but with his face averted, he continued to water his orchids.

"Am I imagining this? But he's been a bit remote lately," Baba said to himself, but he shrugged off the small dark cloud.

The pair rode their bicycles into Taidong. Little did they realize that the film would run three and a half hours; when they returned, it was nearly midnight.

Quok-quaark, cried the hinges as Laning pushed opened the gate. Baba stood outside the garden, his protective gaze upon her form as she picked her way up the path, wading through myriad fragrances. It had rained, and the breaths of the *yulan* flowers burst the lid of the night. Suddenly, a man's impatient footsteps. Then the white sound of a slap—the unmistakable idiom of wrath. Reproaches flashed in the darkness: the voice of Old Man Lin. Laning let out no complaint, no cry, no sound at all as she disappeared into the cottage.

Baba stood frozen at the gate. It wasn't Laning whom the father wanted to punish; the act of violence was meant for him. The father's blow could not have been placed more squarely on his face, but it was a vulnerable place inside, heretofore unknown, that was stinging. There was nothing he could say or do to assuage the anguish of the bruised night. If he crossed into the garden to take Laning's part, he knew he would only be bringing her more trouble. Crickets sawed in his ears. A bird in the neighboring paddy gave a croak. He remained immobile long after the sound of footsteps had been soaked up by the damp earth, petals, and leaves. As he rode his bicycle home, the perspiration suddenly felt cold on his chest.

"What was that all about? Why has he made a one-hundred-eighty-degree turn in his feelings for me?"

In the hours of their boundless joy, Old Man Lin had been forgotten, banished to an indistinct horizon. Neither he nor Laning had seen the tension mounting inside the man's chest; Baba had been blind to the curt replies, the iron-clad smiles.

"I know he wasn't angry because of the lateness of our return. No, that's just on the surface of things. His anger lies deeper. Why the violence? . . . That's the answer, isn't it? Power. The man is jealous of losing control over me. Now that I have what I want—the 'knave,' as he put it—'the king' feels he's lost control over me . . . control over both of us."

For weeks the tension grew like ivy, thick and clinging and airless. Very few words were exchanged between the two men at school, and Laning gave Baba long looks, brows lightly knitted, that pleaded for his patience. Anger hammered dully in Baba's veins. Then one day, Old Man Lin approached him.

"Please meet me this afternoon at the cement house," he said.

When Baba arrived, he found the man waiting for him alone in the garden, seated on a stone stool.

"What are you thinking about in terms of marriage?" the man said to him. "You must know our custom here in Taiwan: if the fellow does not marry the girl after six months, her family is free to break the engagement."

The words took Baba utterly by surprise. No, he and Laning had not spoken of marriage.

Their love had no need of plans; marriage, it was assumed, would be delivered of its own, like sunlight and wind, like birdsong. Perhaps it would come after both had graduated from university.

He realized Laning's father would not be satisfied with such an answer.

"Well, I remember a colleague of mine up in the highlands. She set up her wedding banquet at school. I think we can work out something like that. The fifth and sixth grade classrooms are spacious; we can open up the wall that divides them and invite the administration and staff for a feast. The principal can officiate the ceremony."

Old Man Lin's pupils narrowed to pins. "Have you thought of the bride-price? How much will you pay me?" he said slowly.

Baba felt his back suddenly tense. "No, I haven't," he replied.

"The trouble with you is you're a penniless devil without family and still you act big, and talk even bigger."

Baba held his peace.

"A matchmaker has come several times during the past month to speak for a well-respected gentleman."

"Who, who is the hopeful groom?" stammered Baba. He felt as if a brutal hand had squeezed all the air out of his lungs.

"A Mr. Cha. He is the minister of education in neighboring Hualian. The man is willing to put up two hundred thousand yuan for the bride-price."

Two hundred thousand! He made less than two hundred yuan a month as a schoolteacher. It would take him nearly one hundred years to earn that sum. Why is Old Man Lin telling me this? How can he ask a struggling fellow like me to provide two hundred thousand yuan? If he'd asked for only two thousand, I still would not be able to manage it. He must be joking. A house costs only five thousand yuan.

"You know I can't come up with that kind of money," he said out loud. "What do you really want from me?"

Old Man Lin shifted in his seat and glanced away; he would not meet Baba's eyes. *Ruzhui!* Marry into my family! Change your last name to Lin. *Ruzhui!*"

For Baba the words came like an upheaval. Every detail of the moment—the angle of the sun, the heat, the plunge of a deaf leaf—was seared into his memory. The act of *ruzhui* was asked of a poor and desperate man, who would marry into the bride's house, going to live with her parents and siblings. He would be forced to adopt the bride's family name. Even a Chinese woman did not relinquish her family name when she married—there was no such thing as a maiden name.

Ruzhui? How can I possibly cast away my own family name? A name is not just a name. It is one's identity. *Ruzhui?* It is to admit to the world that I'm a failure. It is to sell the possibilities of my future for food and shelter. It is to say I cannot find my way in the world. I may be poor, but I am not spiritually impoverished. I'm young and have my own destiny to fulfill. He is a man; is he not embarrassed to demand of another man something he would not wish upon himself? He has a son; it isn't as if he hadn't anyone to carry on the Lin name.

The blood roared inside Baba's head. Old Man Lin seemed afraid to intrude upon the moment; his silence was edged with discomfort as he stared beyond the fence at the fickle flight of a butterfly. So great a silence had grown between the two men in that moment, any word would have been a trespass. They sat as still as stone gods, the sun shifting their shadows across the oleander. Finally, Baba stood up.

"Do not talk to me of this subject again," he said. His voice was steady, quiet.

Old Man Lin remained seated as Baba mounted his bicycle and rode away without a backward glance.

Happiness, which only a short month ago pried his mouth open into a perpetual smile, had turned to bitterness. Sleep would not come that night as he lay under the mosquito tent.

I did not walk this long road for my freedom to be played like a puppet on the fingers of a father-in-law.

Who is Old Man Lin? Hasn't he told me he conducted his life in the manner of Zheng Banqiao? Hasn't he said he would marry his daughter in the moonlight like the eccentric of Yangzhou? The artist did not ask for brideprice, betrothal money, and gifts from the groom; he did not wish to sell off his daughter like merchandise. I thought I knew Laning's father. He is no ascetic, happy in his garden.

What is his motivation? If I joined him under his roof, I would be contributing my earnings to the family coffer, just as Laning does now. Perhaps the burden of a large family frightens him. He is just as my own father was, a man with weak and narrow shoulders who looked to others to share his burdens. He will never approve of our wish to leave for the capital, to have a future apart from his.

I want to look upon him as a father; I want to become part of his family . . . but not under the conditions he has set.

He seeks to control. The greatest evil is to impose one's will on another; it is hideous to force one's self on another. For all his intelligence, he is a stupid man; he knows nothing of human beings. Anyone who thinks I would offer up an ounce of my freedom knows nothing about me.

Baba understood all at once that the violations, the manipulations that play out on the vast scales of empires were the very same as the power play between ordinary human beings.

Ruzhui? I know Laning would never have asked this of me. I'm sure the old man has not breathed a word of this to her.

Now everything is in her hands. She must decide what she wants to do: whether she wants to be with me or not. Her father may have given her life, but he cannot give her his thoughts.

That winter of 1953, as Baba shifted in and out of memories, sleep, and reflections aboard a bus bound for the capital, he recalled Laning's words: "I know your scholarship will cover very little beyond food and tuition, but don't worry about money. I'll be sending you my salary." It

wasn't so much the texture of her voice that he savored, but the hard edge of her will. Her father had forbid her to see him off, but there she was at the depot. "We are not on speaking terms, Father and I," she had told him.

It must be miserable for her to be under the same roof with him. Even Mother Lin must be suffering, for she has taken my part against her husband: "Let the young people decide their lives for themselves; they are not of our generation."

But Laning and I—our meeting must have been willed by Old Man Moon. Though I know destiny does not impose itself—it must be seized—it's hard not to believe in the legend: Old Man Moon ties the souls of a man and a woman together with the red string of fate, thousands of li long, so that one day they are certain to be united. How else can I explain my journey down the length of China, across the sea to the Bala Garden in the village of Malan?

Now he would be separated from her by the mountains, the interminable mountains running along the spine of the island. He conjured her face in the window glass. He relived the moment of their first kiss at dusk: he had caught her in his arms as she descended from a *bala* tree with a piece of plucked fruit. "I was born in the Year of the Monkey, that's why I'm so terribly good at climbing" were her words.

In Taipei, her letters came to him with pressed blossoms of the *yulan* between their pages, the fragrance as certain as her thoughts and redolent of the rain in Malan.

Twice each week at Xinsheng Elementary in Taidong, Laning received a letter from Taipei.

Though he didn't let on about it, Old Man Ren, the custodian, knew just how much the letters from the capital meant to the young woman. He also knew Little Plum had no compunction about intercepting the letters, for one day he had caught her putting the envelope up to the light, hoping it would divulge its secrets. Each day, he stood loyally at the school entrance, waiting for the mailman; and as soon as the envelope with the familiar handwriting arrived, he carried it to her as rapidly as his shambling old legs would allow.

"How is Teacher Yang?" he would always inquire, his slow voice betraying the concern his face was too immobile to express.

"Grandfather, I have bad news," Laning replied one day. "He tells me he is sick. He also says he has read my name in the roster of applicants who have qualified for scholarship at the normal university. I should like to join him immediately."

"Do you need money for a train ticket, Teacher Lin?"

"Thank you, Grandfather, but I think I can manage it. If I find I don't have enough, you can be sure I'll go to no one but yourself."

Her mother and sisters chirped as noisily as the cicadas in the trees as they accompanied her on their bicycles to the train station the following morning. She carried only one small suitcase of wicker. Her father had sat in his study, immobile and silent. A muffled "Enh!" had been his only response to her quiet "Father, I'm leaving."

When the train with Laning on board neared the stretch of rice paddy just south of her home, she turned heavyhearted in that direction, wondering when she would return and under what circumstances. And there in the foreground, she saw a lone figure, standing amidst the rice, the stalks bowed with ripened grain. An immeasurable sorrow rose in her throat: lapped by the waves of undulating gold was the stooping, motionless figure of her father, his face dumbly lifted to watch the train go by.

The Bala Garden was not hers and Baba's, it had not been the creation of their joined destinies; it could not keep them had they wanted to remain. A garden is a progression. It is not like a painting, which is given form and remains forever fixed. A garden is temporal, a fleeting thing, and even those that do last for a while change personalities beyond the dream of the original gardeners.

As the landscape of her girlhood drifted away, Laning could only vaguely guess of the changes that would come. The Lin family would move out of the thatched cottage into the big cement house, which could withstand typhoons. In the fall, the Bunun who came down the mountains to harvest betel nuts would allow their cattle in through the gate; where previously Mother Lin's hands tended the earth, strangers and clumsy animals would trample. In time, the grass would grow tall again, hiding the stumps of the *bala* which had been mysteriously chopped down. Then very suddenly, one year, Old Man Lin would sell the land.

But as the train bore Laning away from home, away from all that was familiar, the future was feeding her thoughts, suffusing her lungs and her heart.

———

Perhaps Baba was truly—as is commonly said—lovesick, for upon Laning's unexpected arrival, his fever subsided, and though his legs may have felt weak, he held himself as straight as ever. "Times have changed. We are free to marry under the new law, now that you are twenty-one," he told her. After the year of separation, with the dark will of an old man swinging above their heads like a hatchet, they were now unwilling to wait even a week.

At the courthouse, they paid a twenty-seven-yuan fee. In the sea of nicely dressed brides and grooms, awaiting the mass wedding ceremony, they seemed misplaced and were objects of intense scrutiny. Baba wore a frayed but clean shirt and one hungry, gaping shoe on his right foot, the upper coming apart from the sole. Laning wore her usual white blouse and pleated blue skirt.

When the time came, the men and women, en masse, bowed once to the presiding justice. Then turning a quarter of a turn, en masse, each bowed deeply to his beloved. It wasn't nearly as poetic as the legendary marriage in the moonlight, but it was certainly equal in sincerity.

Many years later, after both had graduated from university, they returned together to Xinsheng Elementary for a visit.

"Old Man Ren's not here anymore," they were told. "He got so old he couldn't tell a one-yuan bill from a ten. You know how the kids used to ask him for candy money . . . well, sometimes he ended up giving more than half his monthly salary away just like that.

"He needed better looking-after. We decided to take him to that new place set up by the government."

On their way to visit the rest home for old soldiers in the countryside, Laning said, "I think Grandfather Ren can make better use of this gift we're bringing today. That shirt I made for him years ago, I never saw him wear even once."

"Thought it was too precious."

"Or much too large." Laning gave a soft laugh. "The neck probably slipped off his shoulders."

"Yes, well, you always did think he was gigantic. He was certainly stout . . . a huge, living monument to time past."

When they came to the rest home, the gatekeeper would not allow them into the courtyard and would give no reason why.

"Can't see him now. No, not a good time to see him. Leave your gift here." The man eyed the package held in Laning's hands, his nostrils quivering with anticipation. "I'll take good care of that."

The gatekeeper at the Home for Honored Citizens knew that Old Man Ren couldn't possibly have use for a roast chicken. He had died the previous summer. Ren's dream of making his way back to the village of his birth was buried with him. The old leaf would not be returning to the root of the tree.

ON A CLOUDLESS day, if a man stood on tiptoe and looked westward across the Formosa Strait, he could imagine seeing the bluish hazy hint of the mainland of China, where his daughter, his wife, or his mother lived out her days without him, without news of him. Of course, it was impossible for him to see the Mainland, which lay beyond the horizon, but a Chinese could always sense the looming weight of his native soil. The soul of a Chinese could easily leap across the rift created by politics and go home, a rift as prohibitive to a physical crossing as passage to the farthest star.

The U.S. Seventh Fleet, called by President Truman to the straits in 1950, prevented Communist forces from invading the shores of Taiwan. Even so, rumors of an attack by the "Communist bandits," as the Nationalist propaganda dubbed the enemy, filled the ears, night and day, like the relentless crashing of the waves; and young men like my father who did not blend easily into the landscape of mediocrity lived in fear of imprisonment for speaking words too keen, too bright.

Nevertheless, my father's soul was lighter. He was no longer a *gu hun ye gui*—a solitary ghost, a savage spirit. He was no longer alone on the road but with Laning, my mother, laboring to create a garden of their own. They would bring from the past traditions that would nourish and sustain them, discarding what would poison and restrain. In their garden, they would not blindly bow to their elders' will, they would not kowtow to the tyranny of authority, least of all would they allow their souls to be brutalized by the wars that followed upon interminable wars.

The recurrent dreams of returning to the Manchurian plains, to Old Granddaddy Hill crowned by cypresses, to the South Garden, the dreams of his mother and Third Brother, came rarely for Baba. Yet they did not go away.

When winter rains fell, sounding like the steady spill of dried mung beans upon the roof, and he pulled the layers of bed covers over his head—loving the luxuriant weight—and tucked his knees behind my mother's knees, the old dreams would steal into his thoughts. They would remind him that his journey was not at an end, that his soul would never find rest until the day the war would end and he would make his return.

Mama and Baba, 1953